"Gear writes superbly rolling prose with flair, confidence, wit, an ear for sounds, and an eye for details...And he has another gift: the ability to teach his readers as he entertains them."

"This is a wonderful book...Well-researched fur trade setting, cultures in interaction and sometimes conflict. [Gear has] a special understanding of American Indian mysticism which provides the stamp of reality."

A PANTHER'S SCREAM

SAGA OF THE MOUNTAIN SAGE
BOOK 3

W. MICHAEL GEAR

WOLFPACK
PUBLISHING
— EST 2013 —

To
Harriet McDougal

With special appreciation for all of her hard work over the years. Harriet has always challenged Kathy and me to excel and explore new directions in fiction. You're the best, Harriet. Thank you for everything.

A NOTE TO THE READER

A Panther's Scream is an historical novel set in 1825 on the Missouri River and depicts historically accurate language, beliefs, and cultural practices that might disturb modern readers.

A PANTHER'S SCREAM

CHAPTER ONE

 Predawn mist, like curling wraiths, rose off the smooth surface of the Missouri River. It drifted across the murky swirls of current, over the muddy bank, and into the trees. The eastern sky glowed with the promise of a new day. Against it, cottonwoods, willows, and an occasional ash created a lacery of black silhouettes. Birds trilled and warbled as the night creatures retired and those of day stirred. Dew beaded on leaves and grass, and silvered the stems and branches.

In the distant uplands beyond the river, the slopes were mantled by hip-high grass and isolated spears of juniper, while the dark veins of drainages were clotted with stands of bur oak. There coyotes yipped in final salute to the night as four riders pushed a small herd of horses westward. They quirted their mounts across the dawn-still grass as if in pursuit of the retreating night.

One by one, they would snap a quick look over their shoulders—back toward the river and the camp of sleeping White men. Long black hair whipped in the wind of their passing; fringes jerked and flicked to the movement of their horses. As they rode, they flashed smiles at each other, dark eyes glinting. It had been a perfect raid.

Stealing from White men was easy. And, unlike raids on the Blackfeet or Sioux, no stalwart warriors would come riding in pursuit. No, these White men would stay with their big, ugly canoe. Let them sleep late into the morning, for the *Apsaroke* had shown the Whites how brave and clever true warriors were.

———

Beside the west bank of the river, the keelboat *Maria* floated, her wood sun-bleached and pale in the faint morning light. She lay snugged close to the high bank, tied off by a painter line to a massive gray cottonwood trunk. Dew-shrouded and furled, the baggy sail hung from the spar. Oars and poles had been stowed on the big square cargo box. A trick of the lazy current toyed with the rudder, and the long tiller slipped soundlessly back and forth, as though managed by a ghostly hand.

The crew had camped in the tall grass beyond the boat. Blankets, stretched over lines strung between the cotton-woods, created crude shelters in case of rain. Fingers of hazy blue smoke rose from the ashes of last night's fires.

Men lay scattered like ten-pins, rolled in blankets, their snoring a burr on the still air. Occasionally, one would shift to peer through a slitted eye at the lightening sky, only to surrender himself again to shredding filaments of dream.

Heals Like A Willow had already risen and rolled her blankets. On silent feet she walked into the ghost-gray trees, her back bent with packs. Her people were the *Dukurika* band—the Shoshoni Sheepeaters of the high western mountains.

As the dew-wet grass spattered her moccasins, Willow cocked her head, listening to the lilting cry of the distant coyotes.

Among her people, Coyote was the Trickster—and just after the Creation of the world he became the source of all trouble and misfortune. Not that Coyote was evil like the White man's devil; rather, his insatiable desires led him to impulsive acts. Famine, disease, death, war, incest, and all manner of ills had resulted as the compromise between impulsive Coyote, and his counterpart, the wise and logical Wolf.

Recently, too much of Willow's life had been orchestrated by Coyote. Last winter, after the death of her husband and son, she had left the *Ku'chendikani* band to travel home to her *Dukurika*. During that journey, the Pawnee warrior, Packrat, had captured her and brought her East as a slave—a gift for Packrat's father, Half Man. She'd waged a war of wills with Packrat, broken his

Power, and finally won. A twist of fate had placed her with the White men, who, she had discovered, had a great deal more in common with Coyote than they did with Wolf.

She listened to the last of the coyote's morning song echoing down from the uplands. This time, she promised herself, Coyote wasn't mocking her. She was going home —back to her people, to their distant western mountains.

So silent...too silent.

Heals Like A Willow cocked her head and listened. In the twilight of dawn, she stood like a statue, the packs dead weight on her shoulders. Not even the stamping of a horse's hoof intruded on the morning birdsong.

Placing each foot with care, she approached the camp's picket.

The horses were gone. Willow carefully shrugged out of her packs and laid them quietly on the ground. She sniffed, taking in the old smells of manure and urine. The rope was still tied around one of the trees. Her fingers slid over the smooth end. Only a steel knife cut so cleanly.

There should have been a guard, but she could see no sign of the man. After a night of pacing, the grass would have been trampled. Had a guard even been posted? Trudeau would have been responsible for appointing one of the *engagés* to stand guard. But the day before he and Richard had fought, and Trudeau would have been in no shape to attend to his duties.

She bent down, feeling the manure: cold clear through. Brushing her hands clean on the grass, she looked up at the reddening sky and sighed. Today, with a horse, she would have started home for the *Dukurika* mountains.

What a fool you are, Willow. Coyote was indeed singing for you.

She picked up her packs and warily retraced her way to the camp.

Lowering the packs by one of the smoldering fires, she crouched down beside a blanket-wrapped man. Despite her stealth, he was watching her through narrowed blue eyes. The dim light revealed a patchwork of cruel scars that crisscrossed his ruined face: the sign of the great white bear. His rumpled hair and beard were shot through with gray. He was wrapped in a dirty striped blanket that had once been red, white, and yellow. A heavy Hawken rifle lay within easy reach.

She shrugged and said, "The horses have been stolen. The rope was cut with a steel knife. The shit is cold, Trawis. They have been gone a long time."

He hadn't moved. "Injuns?"

"Are White men that good at stealing horses? I didn't hear a single sound. Not the rattle of a hoof, not a snort or wicker."

"Injuns," Travis growled. "And the guard?"

"I don't think there was one. Trudeau..."

"Hell! My fault. As bad as Dick whupped him last night in that caterwauling, I shoulda seen to it." A calculating look filled his eyes. "I'm betting on the thieving Crows. How about ye?"

"*A'ni,*" she agreed. "Crows. They are this good. But very far away, no?"

"Their country ain't that far." Travis sat up in his blankets. "Five days' hard ride west...maybe six."

"I am sorry they did this. I was going home today." She sighed wearily. "I would have warned you, but I did not know they raided here."

"Shoulda known meself," he growled. "And no, a body

don't usually find Crow this far west. They don't savvy the Rees, nor the Sioux, or Cheyenne." He paused. "If it's Crow."

"You can get more horses among the Mandans?"

The soft dawn light left his eyes like pits, but she could read disgust in the look he gave her. "Hell, gal, them's *my* hosses!" A pause. "And yers."

He kicked a leg out of the blankets to prod at Richard's blanket-bundled form off to the left. "C'mon, Dick. Injuns has stoled the hosses. *Leve!* Let's get at 'em."

Richard muttered sleepily, threw back his blanket. Sat up, but gasped and winced from pain. Even in the half-light, Willow could see his bruised face and swollen nose. Long brown hair hung in disarray, and a wispy beard covered his cheeks. He stretched now, and grunted as he discovered new sore muscles and aches.

She started to reach out, to touch those hurts with tender fingers, but balled her fist instead and asked Travis, "What are you going to do?"

"Go after the damned hosses," Travis growled. "Ain't no cussed Crows a gonna get away with this." He gave her a cautious study. "And, without a hoss, ye cain't run off ter them Snake lands ye been a-pining on."

She said nothing, watching him warily.

"So, Dick and me better get yer hoss back, Willow, or it'll be a tarnal long walk fer ye."

"We're doing what?" Richard asked as he stood up gingerly. He grunted and made a face as he tried to stretch. "Dear God, I hurt."

"That was a hell of a scrape ye had with old Trudeau yesterday," Travis reminded. "Tarnation! Ye damned near chewed the coon's ear off. Last I seen, Toussaint and Baptiste was hauling him down ter the river fer a dunking. He's hurt enough he fergot ter set guard on the hosses."

Richard's expression softened, and he glanced away, refusing to meet their eyes. "I never thought I'd become a common brawler, Travis."

The grizzled hunter stood, back crackling as he arched it. "Yep, wal, life's full of little surprises, ain't it?"

Willow glanced surreptitiously at Richard. He was young, lanky, and possessed a wiry strength belied by his slim body. He wore a fringed hunting shirt, and a knife and possible sack hung from the belt that secured his buckskin pants. Heavy Crow moccasins covered his feet.

She knew his story. Richard came from a place far to the east, a White-man town called Boston. Richard's father had sent him west to carry money to a man in St. Louis, but on the way, Richard had been robbed. To save his life, he'd indentured himself to Dave Green's *Maria*— and Travis had been his guard.

In Boston, Richard had studied something called philosophy, which Willow had decided was a kind of special medicine knowledge. But since he had come to the river he had become more than a seeker after Power. He'd become a warrior and a hunter.

Richard had saved her life when Packrat would have killed her. He had looked into her eyes and seen her soul, as she'd seen his. Unlike the men of her people, he hadn't been horrified at the idea of a woman using *puha* or Power. It had been at that moment, when their souls touched, that she first had begun to love him.

Fool that you are, Willow. He is going back to his Boston, and his Laura. What you wish will never be.

Coyote had tricked her again.

"Willow, I want ye ter keep to Baptiste and Green,"

Travis said as he headed for the boat. "Give Dick and me time ter get back. Then ye can run off. Promise?"

She slapped futile hands to her sides. "Yes. Promise."

Anyone would feel safe around Baptiste, the strapping soot-black warrior. He'd been a slave once, and, like Willow, had killed his owner. She took one last look at Richard's swollen eye and puffed-up nose.

Richard was stumbling after Hartman, groaning as he prodded bruises from last night's fight with Trudeau.

Trudeau had tried to force Willow—and Richard had taken him down for it. But then, bad blood had run between Trudeau and Richard since the first days on the river.

She whispered softly, "Good luck, Ritshard. Be very careful...and come back safe."

Why? a voice asked in her soul. *When he comes back, you will just leave. Either way, your time with him is running out... like water trickling from a snowbank in late spring.*

———

A square-walled tent stood in the middle of the camp. The white canvas had grayed from months of weather and grimy hands. Inside, David Green, the booshway, or expedition leader, was blinking himself awake and stretching.

He called softly, "Henri? You awake?"

The man who slept before the flap grunted, yawned, and rubbed his face. He sat up in his blankets to stare owlishly around at the sleeping camp. "*Oui, bourgeois.* I am awake."

Henri stood, flexing his muscles against cramps and aching joints. As patroon, he was master of the *Maria,* the man who steered the keelboat. Now he bent over the gray ash in the firepit, flicking the remaining coals into a pile, carefully placing twigs atop, and blowing the coals to life. As the flames crackled up, he added fuel and dug out the cook pot.

As Henri fixed breakfast, Green ducked through the flap, and walked down to check the boat. After he'd assured himself she was snug, he made his way through the waking *engagés* and seated himself by Henri's fire.

The patroon had filled Dave Green's tin plate with steaming catfish and grouse meat. Holding the hot plate by the rim, Dave had just lifted his first forkful of breakfast and was chewing methodically when Travis strode purposefully across the camp. The hunter carried his Hawken in his right hand, his left resting on his possibles, powder horn, and the bullet pouch tied to his belt. His graying hair flowed out over his collar from under a battered black felt hat. Travis wore a hunter's leather clothing, some of the long fringe missing. The only new apparel was the Sioux moccasins on his feet.

"*Malchance aujourd'hui,*" Henri said as he glanced up from spooning his own breakfast onto a tin plate. Coffee boiled in a soot-blackened pot, the aroma rising in the cool morning air.

"I reckon Trudeau was too stove up to detail a hoss guard last night," Travis said as he laid his rifle against the trunk of a cottonwood and hunkered down on his haunches. "And I don't know if'n it'd done any good anyhow. I just come from the picket. Injuns stole the hosses last night."

Green stopped in mid-chew. "All of them?"

"Yep. Reckon Dick and me'll go get 'em back." From his possibles, he extracted a tin cup, and pulled his sleeve down over his hand to grab the hot coffee pot. After pouring a cup, he glanced up at Green with cold blue eyes. "Don't call us dead fer at least a month."

"A month?" Green rubbed the back of his neck and frowned. "I don't like it, Travis. A week, you hear? That's all I want you gone."

Travis sipped the hot coffee and made a sour expression. The act pulled all the scars tight across his ruined face. "No telling how far them coons—"

"That's my point, Travis." Green straddled a log and lowered himself to sit. He pulled at his blond hair and shook his head. "I know you, Travis Hartman...and I understand. Some Crow snuck in and lifted *your* horses. You think it's a matter of honor now to get them back— come hell or high water. But I'm serious. I can't afford to let you chase off all over the plains looking for horse thieves. Good Lord, by a month from now, we should be two weeks past the Mandan. I need you here, Travis."

"Now, Dave..."

"Travis, before you go off half-cocked, think about it. We're almost to the Mandan. We need a license to trade with Indians, remember? A license we don't have., which means we don't have a legal right to be here. And Atkinson and O'Fallon—along with half the American army—are somewhere upriver from us. Now, if they catch us, they'll take the boat, lock me in chains, and haul our arses right back down to—"

"Ye don't gotta *remind* me!" Travis gave him a hostile squint. "Dave, I'll be back when I'm back. Ye can't go a-letting these pesky Crow up and steal your hosses!"

Dave lifted an eyebrow, reading Travis's stony expression. "Please?"

With one hand, Henri twisted the ends of his thick black mustache. With the other, he absently poked a long-tined fork into the cooking pone. "The Rees, I think some of them are up ahead. It would not be good, Travis, if you are gone when we meet them."

"Reckon not," Travis relented. "But, hell, ye got Baptiste fer palavering with the Rees. That coon's worth more when it comes ter Rees than this child."

At a nod from Henri, Green handed a tin plate to the patroon. Henri heaped it with breakfast and handed it in turn to Travis. Beyond them, the *engagés* ate by their fires, glancing curiously at the booshway's tent and muttering among themselves. Word traveled fast. Even hardened boatmen got a mite owly knowing that Indians had sneaked through their camp and stolen horses.

"A week," Travis promised reluctantly as he piled into the food. Between chews, he added, "Dick and me, we'll be back afore ye reaches the Mandan."

"You sure you want to take that pilgrim?" Henri asked. "He will be useless! A burden to you out in the prairie."

"You're wasting your breath," Green growled around a mouthful. "Travis still figures he can make a man outa the Doodle."

"Ye'd a never figgered he'd a whupped up on old Trudeau," Travis reminded Green, a twinkle in his blue eyes.

Green stabbed out with a blunt finger. "And we'd a still had the hosses if he and Trudeau hadn't tangled.

Trudeau checks the horse guards each night, and sets the watches."

"Maybe." Travis cocked his head and spat into the fire. "'Course, if these is Crow, they mighta lifted the hosses no matter what. Ain't no better hoss thieves in the world than Crow."

Travis wolfed his breakfast and stood. He tossed off the last of the steaming coffee and dropped his cup into his possibles. "We'd best be hightailing after them thievin' bastards. I told Willow ter stick close ter ye and Baptiste."

"I'll see that she's safe. God knows, she's worth her weight in furs to us." He paused, "Oh, and Travis, be careful. Watch your hair out there."

"Watch yourn," Travis responded, turning and walking away with a hunter's quick step.

"What do you think?" Green propped his blocky jaw on the palm of his hand.

"I think I will not sleep until he return, booshway," Henri answered. "Baptiste, he ees good man, but none scouts like Travis Hartman."

"Nope. I reckon not. I just hope no one gets killed because of this foolishness." And God help them all if the army caught them clear up here without a permit.

———

The sun had barely crested the irregular horizon; nevertheless, Richard's muscles complained it was time to rest. Looking back, he could see the line of trees carpeting the bottom land on either side of the muddy brown Missouri.

Chest heaving, he trotted to the top of the rise and broke out onto the rolling flats with their waving stands of tall bluestem grass and hidden patches of prickly pear.

Each deep breath made him wonder if his ribs were splintered. Scabs cracked when he flexed his battered knuckles. Ugly bruises mottled the flesh on his arms and hips. His face hurt; one eye had swollen almost closed. He reached up with his free hand, prodding at the tender flesh. A year ago, back in the warm safety of Boston, the idea of brawling would have sickened him.

How far have I come from that day in my father's office? Who am I now?

He'd won that fight with burly Trudeau. A strange spark of pride burned brightly within him. That old rational Richard would have despised him for it.

I beat a man bloody. Was that really me who tried to claw his eyes out?

Richard could still remember the rubbery feel of Trudeau's ear clamped in his teeth. He could still taste the man's salty blood.

I was a gentleman once. A scholar, a student of philosophy.

So much of him had died since that cold day in January when his father sent him west.

And what a mess I've made of it since then.

He'd been robbed of a fortune, sold upriver by a murderous boatman named François. He'd worked like a common ox, become the animal he'd once accused

François of being. He'd killed the young Pawnee, Packrat, to save Willow. And, for her sake, he'd beaten Trudeau in a fair fight. Travis had taught him how to brawl like that. Travis had taught him so many things. But to run down stolen horses? That defied even his wildest imagination.

His lungs had begun to burn, his legs to tremble.

"Rest!" Richard called at Travis's retreating back.

The hunter slowed, shooting a glance over his shoulder. "C'mon, Dick. Them coons got nigh ter five hours head start on us. Hell, we's just started. Ye ain't a gonna let an old man like me outrun ye?"

Richard stared down at the heavy Hawken rifle hanging from his right hand. "Old man? My arse!" And forced his weary legs into a trot.

Sweat dampened his collar and waist; his lungs were pulling deeply as he fell into the dogtrot adopted by Travis. The grass made shishing sounds as his moccasins beat through it.

Step by step, Richard closed the gap until he was running beside Travis. "This is crazy."

"How so?"

"We're gonna...run down horses...on foot?"

"Yep."

"But, Travis!"

"They's our hosses, ain't they?"

"A man on foot...can't any more run down...horses than—"

"If'n ye'd shut up, ye'd have a sight more puff fer running." And at that Travis lengthened his stride, outpacing Richard.

He's crazy!

But Richard continued to force his legs into the rhythm of the endless trot.

Puffy white clouds littered the western horizon, gradually vanishing into a bright blue straight overhead. Meadowlarks hung from sunflower stalks and other tall weeds. The sun burned white and hot into Richard's back, hinting of the baking midday to come.

His mouth had gone dry, his throat raw. Still he plodded along, his feet pounding in the cadence set by Travis. Well, the hunter would tire soon, and they'd take a rest. No one could maintain a pace like this for long.

His arm grew tired, and Richard shifted his rifle from one hand to the other. The aches and bruises from the blows Trudeau had given him still hurt, and running didn't help. If he had any consolation, it was that Trudeau didn't feel any better this morning.

A slow smile built. Hadn't Trudeau been a sight? His nose black-and-blue and bent, his bitten fingers swollen— and that shredded ear had looked like something dog-chewed.

Not that I look any better, with one eye swelled closed and a lip puffed up like a dead fish.

With his tongue, Richard prodded the loose tooth in the side of his mouth, and hoped it would firm up the way Travis had assured him it would.

The bottom of Richard's throat had begun to burn. Pants had turned into gasps. A pain stitched agony through his side.

"Travis?"

The hunter continued to trot onward, following the faint sign left by the horses.

Richard shifted the gun again, and pressed at his side as he slowed to a walk and bent double.

After what seemed an eternity, Travis threw a glance over his shoulder and stopped his headlong charge. Richard hobbled forward, gasping and wheezing as he rubbed the stitch in his side.

"Got a cramp?" Travis scowled, his full chest rising and falling.

"Yes... Hurts."

"Hyar, now." Hartman laid his gun down, squinted, and grasped Richard's side. He squeezed hard, fingers digging deep.

Richard groaned at the way it hurt. "Damn! Easy there!"

"Thar ye be, coon. Mountain medicine. She'll run fer a ways again."

"Rest. We gotta rest."

"A while longer yet, lad." Travis scooped up his rifle and started off in that maddening trot.

Richard cursed under his breath, willing himself to follow. Surprisingly, the cramp was gone from his side.

Morning stretched into midday. Richard and Travis alternately walked and trotted, ever westward toward the endless line of the horizon. Eagles soared overhead, turning lazy circles in the sky. The shaggy gray buffalo wolves gave them a wide berth, keen yellow eyes wary as they panted from the heat. From time to time, jackrabbits shot out from underfoot to sail away in long leaps.

Had Boston really existed, or was it just a dream? He could remember his father's hard gray eyes that long-ago day, his remorseless words: "You will not be returning to the university."

If he said that to me today, I'd beat him the same way I did Trudeau!

But that had been a different Richard Hamilton who had stood quaking before his tyrannical father.

Richard frowned as sweat trickled down his hot face. Had the old man been so wrong about him?

Was I really such a silly fool, locked away in my books and philosophy?

What an arrogant boor he'd been, cloaked in lofty superiority. On that long trip to Saint Louis, Charles Eckhart, the Virginia planter, had tried to befriend him. Theyd' travled aboard the *Virgil* as the steamboat chugged down the Ohio and up the Mississippi to Saint Louis.

And I insulted him in return.

Nor had Eckhart been the only one. At Fort Massac, that filthy collection of hovels just above the mouth of the Ohio, Richard had called that human jackal, François, an animal. And for that, François had more than gotten even.

Richard stumbled and recovered. One foot ahead of the other. That's it. Just keep the stride. Step after step, foot after foot.

"C'mon, coon." Travis called. 'Top o' the next rise!"

Richard struggled up the long slope.

"C'mon, coon! We're most of the way there!"

And Richard gazed up wearily to see the next rise beckoning from the distant horizon.

But no matter how long he ran and stumbled and trotted, and walked, and ran again, the goal retreated— like the terrible curse of Tantalus.

No water, no spit in his dry mouth, his tongue half gagging him when he tried to swallow. His raw throat burned from the air he sucked in and blew out with each breath.

One foot ahead of the other. One, two, one, two, one, two...An endless litany.

The feeling was gone from his trembling legs. He had to use a staggering trot, or they'd go rubbery and limp under him.

One foot ahead of the other. One, two, one, two, one, two...

Richard slammed hard into the ground. For long moments he lay there, breath sawing in and out of his lungs. A ladybug climbed along the grass blade in front of his eyes.

Travis asked, "Hurt yerself?"

"Travis?"

"What happened?'

"Fell."

Travis turned his sweat-slick face up toward the sun, squinting in a manner that tightened the pattern of scars. "Reckon we'll catch our wind some, Dick."

Richard coughed, a rasp like splintered wood in his windpipe, then dropped his head face-first into the grass. As he lay panting, he slipped his fingers down to the fetish Travis had given him. The silky long black hair was supposed to bring luck, or so Travis had claimed. From a kind of skunk, Travis had told him. A sign of status.

I feel weak as a kitten. He'd give anything—even his fetish—for a drink of water.

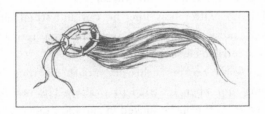

"They's Crows all right," Travis said as his breathing recovered. "Saw a moccasin sign back by that anthill. One of them cussed coons stopped ter pee."

"Is it worth it?" Richard wondered.

"Wal, if'n a feller don't pee, he'll plumb leak all over hisself. So, I'd say—"

"The *horses*, damn it! Are they worth all this?"

"Whose hosses is they? Ours! Yers and mine, coon.

Can't just up and let no thieving Crows steal yer hosses. Hell, them's a year's wages gone up in dust. Doodle."

I lost thirty thousand just as quick, and never thought twice about the money, only my life.

"I'll buy you more horses."

"With what, coon? Lessen ye wants ter steal 'em from the Rees or Hidatsas up by Heart River. Trouble is, where'd ye hide 'em? Stealing Ree hosses, now, that's a coup feather fer yer hair fer sure, but the Hidatsas and Mandans, they's friends. That'd be poor bull, stealing from friends."

"How about Crow? We'll steal from them."

Travis had pulled a grass stem apart. "Now yer talking sense, lad. And, seeing as how we got us a bunch of Crows up ahead—with our hosses, to boot, by God— we'll just go a-stealing 'em back!"

"Oh, my God."

"C'mon, Dick. Since yer so keen on this, ye can lead the way." Travis gripped Richard's hand and tugged him up.

"Water, Travis. I swear to God...I've got to drink something. My throat..."

"Just up ahead, coon. Cain't drink till we gets thar, I'm thinking. Unless ye can suck water outa a grass stem."

"Up...ahead..." Richard squinted at the endless grass. He locked his legs to keep from falling.

"Yep, just up yonder," Travis said seriously. "C'mon, coon. Let's go. We'll walk a mite ter limber up yer legs. Gotta be fast, or them red varmints is gonna get plumb away."

"This is crazy!"

"That's what we're counting on. That them sneaking Crows think the same thing. If'n they don't, we ain't never gonna get them hosses back."

Richard balanced his rifle over his shoulder, plodding in Travis's tracks. Some of the sap had returned to his bones by the time Travis broke into that infuriating dogtrot, and he managed to pick up the rhythm again. One, two, one, two, one, two...

He fingered the fetish, stroking the long black hair as if it were a source of energy.

The afternoon sunlight slanted down out of the clear sky. Richard fell quite often now, each time staring stupidly at the grass.

"C'mon, coon," Travis's calm voice would call down from beyond the haze. Hands would help Richard to his feet, and he'd stagger on in misery.

Everything had a milky glaze to it, like a kind of dream. Voices echoed hollowly inside his head. At times, he was back in philosophy class at Harvard while Professor Ames lectured. Then, he'd hear Will Templeton, his best friend, tell a joke. Laura's gentle voice told him over and over again, "I'll be waiting for you, Richard."

Gone...all gone.

Phillip Hamilton's hawkish gray eyes burned in Richard's rubbery recall. He could see his father's office clearly, hear the *tick-tock* of the ship's clock as he stood before his father's ornate desk. It might have been yesterday instead of last winter. The fire in the hearth crackled and popped, warm against the bone-chilling cold outside the Beacon Street house.

Phillip had sat in his overstuffed French chair, papers in his hands as he looked over his spectacles at Richard. He had asked, *"To what earthly use will you put this 'philosophy' of yours?"*

The question now festered and burned like cactus thorns in flesh.

The greatest blow had fallen later, at supper that evening. In the elegant dining room, Phillip had been devouring a turkey dinner, spearing the steaming meat with a silver fork and chewing mechanically. He raised his eyes and said, *"I've given thought to our earlier conversation. It has become startlingly clear to me that you have no understanding of the world. Therefore, travel is to be recommended."*

How Richard's heart had soared with notions of European cities, learned aristocrats, and cultured conversation.

"...Your universe has been limited to this house, this city and the university. A wide continent stretches out to the west of us. That untamed land is your future..."

Dear God, if the old man could only have seen what would come of that statement.

A cough racked Richard's throat. Memories, like darting fish, slipped through the fingers of his mind.

Father...you've condemned me to Hell.

What had he become in this Western inferno? A murderer, a beast of burden...a dockside brawler. His dry tongue mocked him with the salty taste of Trudeau's warm blood. They'd fought like dogs, gouged, stomped, and bit, until Richard had clamped a hand on Trudeau's throat. To keep the *engagé* from breaking loose, he'd sunk his teeth into Trudeau's ear, arching his back, heedless of the blood as he tried to rip it from the Frenchman's head.

Philosopher? Was that you, Richard John Charles Hamilton? Or the demonic actions of the animal you've become?

He'd fought for Willow, to protect her from Trudeau's rapacious lust.

And I won. She's...safe.

Precious Willow with her soft skin and encompassing brown eyes—an infinity reposed there, reflected in her soul.

"Mirrors," he croaked. "Eyes...like mirrors."

"Ye talking about Willow again?" Travis asked gently. "Hole hyar. Watch yer step, coon. That's it."

One, two, one, two, one, two...one foot ahead of the other. Run...run...run...

CHAPTER TWO

The criminal action, whereby the abstract individuality of the person posited for itself is at last realized, is null in and of itself. But in it the acting entity determines itself as rational, yet formally and only by itself, as a recognized law, has subsumed itself through the criminal action, and been at the same time subsumed under it. The manifested nullity of this action and the elaboration of this formal law through a subjective will, is revenge, which, because it derives from the interest of the immediate, subjective personality, is at the same time only a new injury—and so on to infinity. This progress suspends itself equally in a third judgment which is disinterested: punishment.

—Georg Friedrich Wilhelm Hegel, *Encyclopedia of
the Philosophical Sciences in Outline*

 Boston was baking under the hot August sun. Had Phillip Hamilton cared to glance over his shoulder through the bay window, he would have noticed that even the trees in the Commons looked wilted. But

Phillip's attention was centered on his big ledger book. There he tallied row after row of figures. His concentration was so complete that he didn't hear the knock. Jeffry, his black manservant, opened the office door and cleared his throat, asking, "Master Phillip?"

Phillip leaned back in his overstuffed French chair and made a face as he pulled his spectacles from his nose. He propped his quill in the ink bottle and sighed. "Beastly hot today. And beyond that, I swear, my eyes are getting worse. What on earth will I do when the numbers become too foggy to see any more?"

"Hire a secretary to read them for you, sir." Jeffry strode across the crimson carpet to stand before the ornately carved cherrywood desk. His dark fingers offered a dog-eared envelope, the paper smudged. "This just arrived, sir. A messenger brought it fresh from the harbor."

Jeffry laid the letter on the desk beside the big Bible and the English officer's button—Phillip's trophy from the fighting at Breed's Hill. His leg had been maimed that day, shot out from under him by an English ball.

Phillip picked up the envelope, squinting for a moment until he remembered his glasses and pinched them on his nose again.

In the light spilling through the bay window, he read: "Messr. Phillip Hamilton, Hamilton House, Beacon Street, Boston City, Mass." Phillip broke the seal and unfolded the paper, peering intently at the scrawled words. As he read, he whispered, "March 19, 1825, Saint Louis."

Dear Sir:

I wished to communicate to you that as of this

date, I have received no word from your son, Messr. Richard Hamilton. Your agent, Messr. Charles Eckhart, has contacted me several times with information that Mr. Hamilton did indeed arrive safely in Saint Louis on the fifteenth of March on the steamboat Virgil, and did leave the vessel. His luggage was faithfully delivered to the Le Barras Hotel, along with several satchels of books. It is my unfortunate duty to inform you, sir, that neither your son, nor the banknotes which we agreed would be delivered to me at this address, have appeared as of the time of this writing. I have taken the liberty of waiting for several days before setting myself to pen this letter in hopes that some explanation might be found. Mr. Eckhart has been indefatigable in his efforts on your part, but, after consulting with the authorities, and given the paucity of news, we must conclude foul play in some manner.

It is with great distaste that I discharge this duty of informing you of your son's disappearance. Please rest assured that I shall endeavor with all of my resources to discover your son's situation and recover your monetary interests.

Your Most Obdt. Servant,
William Blackman.

Phillip stared at the letter, reading and rereading the terrible words.

"Dear Sweet Jesus. Did he run off with the money?" Phillip handed the letter to Jeffry and rapped his fingers on the desk, making the brass button dance.

Jeffry read the missive, then folded the paper. A pensive frown deepened on his face. "No, sir. Not Master Richard."

Defeat, like a barrel band, tightened in Phillip's chest until it ached with each beat of his heart. "Thirty thousand dollars, Jeffry. He could do a great many things with such wealth."

"The books, sir," Jeffry said. "Master Richard would never leave his books behind. Even, sir, if he could buy new ones."

Phillip closed his eyes, his right hand groping for his wife's Bible. He dragged it close—carelessly knocking the ledger to the floor—and clutched it to the pain in his chest. "Dear God in Heaven. Tell me he's run off...taken the money. Please, God, tell me that's the way it is."

Yes, run off. Say it's so, Richard. Write me a taunting letter. Tell me how you're spending my money.

He tried to swallow down a fist-tight throat.

"Master Phillip? Are you all right, sir?"

All he could do was grip the Bible. "My God, Jeffry, what have I done?"

———

A hand steadied Richard's shoulder as the world started to spin.

"Easy," Travis soothed him. "Just a little farther, coon. Night's coming. Water with it. Just hang on, Dick. Ye can make it"

"My name's...name's...Richard."

"Yep. If n ye keeps 'er up, coon, I'll call ye Richard, Dick."

"*Richard*..." He staggered. The terrible sun burned his soul. And he was bulling forward, straight into it, until it burned him. The roaring wind would blow his ashes back to the cool, wonderful river, where they would slip between Willow's fingers into the delightful water.

One foot ahead of the other. Run. Charge right into the sun. It would burn away the pain, sear the agony like acid.

"C'mon, coon. That's it. Yer making her, Dick. Ye can do her. That's it. Just a little further. Water's just up ahead." Travis's voice carried him onward, like a flame drawing a moth to its deadly tongues.

"The sun, going to burn..." He wobbled on his feet, propped up by Travis's quick hand.

"Easy, coon. One step ahead of t'other. That's it. Yer some, ye is, Dick. Ye've a lot of guts, and ye can do her."

"The sun..." How odd. It had gone flat on the bottom. He blinked, and it burned into the back of his eyelids.

"One, two, one, two..." Travis trotted alongside Richard, steadying him.

Richard coughed, panting, baffled. The sun grew ever more flat, mashing against the world, being sucked up by the distant black line of the horizon.

"C'mon, coon. Water's just up ahead. She'll drown yer fire, sure. Shining water, Dick. Cold, clear, bubbling wet and cool down yer gullet. All ye can drink."

"The sun's dying," he mumbled, stumbling to a walk. "Look—dying..."

"Yep. Sunset, she is," Travis answered. "C'mon, now. Let's hustle."

Richard pitched face-first into the dark grass. He just lay there, panting.

Tired...so tired...sleep now.

His body felt feathery, light, as if it floated in a warm current...

...And Richard's soul slipped away...

I stand alone, naked, up to my knees in river water. On the bank above me, the trees sway and thrash as a violent wind tears through the branches. My hair is blown and tangled, my beard matted with filth. I look down at my arms, all smudged and dirty. My hands are bloody, my fingers tacky with it as it dries.

I seek Truth. It's all I've ever wanted.

But here I stand, naked and alone, my hands dripping with a young Pawnee warrior's blood. So much has changed that I no longer know myself. Overhead, clouds scud across the sky. Thunder rumbles.

Yes...the river tugs at me. Its soul ebbs and flows past my calves, the current eating the sand out from under my heels in an attempt to topple me. But I have already fallen. Blood drips from my fingers, the crimson droplets vanishing in the water as if they'd never been.

I wanted Truth because my mother died giving me life.

Once I was a student of philosophy. Now, in the murky water, I study my wavering reflection. I don't know this man who stares back at me.

I traveled aboard the steamboat Virgil from Pittsburgh to Saint Louis with thirty thousand dollars of banknotes, my philosophy books, and the knowledge of my own moral, spiritual, and intellectual superiority over the loutish frontiersmen.

The money was my father's, to be invested in the growing Sante Fe trade.

At Fort Massac, on the Ohio River, I encountered a man named François—a known cutthroat. He was more than just a thief and murderer. He had a sense of humor. He gave me the choice of signing a letter of indenture, bonding myself for two years of hard labor, or having my throat cut and my body dumped into the river.

I signed.

He sold the contract to Dave Green, who owns the keelboat Maria. Now, I am an animal, and François is a rich man.

I wanted Truth because my mother was dead, and my father blamed himself for her death.

I flex my fingers, still so shiny with blood. I was with

Travis Hartman the day Packrat rode into camp. I'd stitched up a slice in Travis's side after he'd fought and killed Packrat's father, a Pawnee named Half Man. The hatred in Packrat's eyes sticks with me as surely as his blood on my fingers. He'd taken a slave, a Shoshoni woman called Heals Like A Willow—and she laughed at him just before he would have killed Travis and me.

Packrat turned to beat her, would have killed her before my eyes. That's when I shot him through the chest. So much blood. It pumped out of his body...and here it is warm, wet, and sticky on my hands.

Not long ago, a Sioux wechashawakan—a holy man—asked me, "What are you?"

I bend down and drag my bloody fingers through the water. Streaks of crimson mark their path. The river has become my universe. When I thirst, I drink from the river until the blood beating in my veins is river water I walk its banks with the cordelle over my shoulder, or pole the Maria upstream, my back bent as my feet grip the cleats on the passe avant. River sounds fill my ears: the crystalline drips, and waves slapping the hull. Part of my soul belongs to the river.

I try to wash the blood from my hands, but it remains bright red, warm and wet. Does it stain my hands with murder—or salvation?

I saved Willow's life that day. Once, in a camp by the river, her face inches from mine, she looked into my eyes—into my very soul. I began to love her then, though I am promised to Laura Templeton.

I am a philosopher. I belong in Boston. One day I will marry Laura. I am saving myself for creamy white skin and golden blond tresses. I can't love a dark-skinned savage, an Indian woman of uncertain moral values. Willow had a husband once, bore him a child. So what if they're dead now?

From the corner of my eye, I catch movement in the shadows

under the wind-lashed trees. A coyote stares out at me with pricked ears.

I look around, suddenly afraid. On the far bank, a wolf is watching me with knowing eyes.

I wanted Truth, because it could give me what my parents could not.

Coyote and Wolf frighten me. They have since the night Maria landed at the Sioux village of Wah-Menitu. We traded with the Sioux, and later, they gave us a feast. It shames me that I joined their dancing warriors, leaped and whooped like a savage. It was later that the hideous wechashawakan, Lightning Raven, caught me alone. According to the story, he once fought a monster that pierced his eye with poison. Lightning Raven plucked out his own eye and fed it to the monster, killing it with its own venom. However he lost his eye, only a scarred socket remains. But he'd seen inside me, talked inside my head like some living ghost.

"Will you be coyote or wolf?" The wechashawakan's voice echoes in the corners of my mind. Coyote, or Wolf? And now they are both watching me. Coyote is to the east, in the direction of Boston, of my future as a professor of philosophy. My home is there, and so is Laura, with her golden hair and blue eyes.

And to the west lies the wilderness—and wolf.

I drop to my knees, and warm water rushes around my waist. The river pulls against me. An eagle soars overhead, sunlight flashing from its wings.

I throw my head back and search the blue eternity of sky. Dear God, what do I do?

I close my eyes, and the words of Jean-Jacques Rousseau, Thomas Hobbes, and Immanuel Kant float past my ears. I have traveled into the wilderness, but I have not found Rousseau's man in nature to be pure. Kant's infallibility of pure reason is a lie. Nor do I believe Hegel's phenomenology any more. There is

*no evolution of intellectual life to a higher order—not in a
natural system.*

I wanted Truth because it promised me safety.

*The flaw I have discovered in philosophical systems is that
reality is always lurking in the shadows and slipping through the
brush. Reality has never read philosophy.*

*Now I kneel in the river, looking back and forth between
Wolf and Coyote.*

*Everything I once believed is washed away. I have looked
through philosophical Truth—and seen its horrible other side. I
discovered it to be ephemeral.*

My soul cries for an answer, but I have none.

The wechashawakan *told me that the answers lie in the
West, with Wolf. But in his vision, he saw me freezing in the
snow. He did not know if I survived.*

Truth was only illusion.

That night the wechashawakan *told me that if I returned
to the East, to Boston, and Laura, I would die empty. He said I
would find my answers in the West, in the snow and cold.*

*Now, I hang my head and sink down into the water, terribly
alone as the river swirls around my navel.*

*I wanted Truth. But with each step I take into the wilder-
ness, I lose more and more of myself—of what I believed.*

If I keep going, there will be nothing left.

*I must cling to something. Or was my old life nothing more
than a sham, a trick I played on myself? If all those things I
believed in were false—who, or what, am I?*

*Looking down, I see that the water has washed away my
flesh. Only my bones are left resting on the sandy bottom.*

*I open my mouth, but a skeleton cannot scream. The river
hears only silence...*

"Dick?"

"Gone," Richard sighed as the voice penetrated the
veils of fatigue.

"Got water, coon. Hyar now, open yer mouth."

Wetness trickled on the side of Richard's face.

"Aw, don't you up and give up the ghost on this child. Hyar! C'mon, coon." Arms wrapped around Richard's shoulders, lifting him. "Hell, yer heavier than I figgered. Help me, coon. Stagger along."

Richard sagged limply in Travis's arms, content to be dragged along like a sack of flour. When he fell again, it was to splat face-first into cold water.

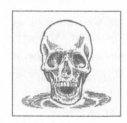

It rushed into his nose and mouth, brought him to. He kicked and floundered, coughing and splashing so weakly he almost drowned before he could crawl back to shore. Lying there, half in and out of the water, he sucked the muddy stuff into his mouth, gulping.

"Enough," Travis ordered, twisting a fist in the collar of Richard's jacket and jerking him back. "Listen, Dick. Don't drink too much, too fast. It'll make ye plumb sick with the collywobbles, hear me?"

"Sick, yes." He bent down and drank some more, pulling back when his aching lungs demanded air.

"All right." Travis straightened, a dark blot against the starry sky. "Take yer time, Dick. I got ter go back and fetch up the rifles. Hear me? Don't you go chugging on that water!"

"I won't."

Richard drew deep breaths, then bent down, sucking

the wondrous water into his mouth. The pungent, smoky taste of mud and humus barely slowed him as he swallowed another mouthful. He tried to spit out the grit, gave it up as hopeless, and crawled out into deeper water to drink more.

He was sitting on the bank, shivering, more asleep than awake, when Travis jabbed a relentless toe into his side. "How're ye doing, coon?"

The whining sound around his ears came from a cloud of mosquitoes that were swarming around him. For once, he didn't care. "I want to die, Travis."

"Yep, a feller always feels better with his belly full of water."

Travis settled beside him and laid out the rifles. "If'n I'd a know'd I'd have ter carry yer gun as well as mine, I'd had ye leave her ahind." He rummaged in his possible sack. "Hyar's jerky, coon. We'd best eat all we can hold, then suck a heap more of this water."

"Where are we?"

"I'd say nigh to thirty miles west of the river. We made good time today. Do her again tomorrow, and we'll have her licked, I'd say."

"Tomorrow? Travis, I can't."

"Got to, Dick. Ain't no other way out hyar. Lessen ye wants ter head back on yer own."

Richard took a slab of the jerky, ripping it apart with his teeth, savoring the juices. He chewed for a while. "You really think we'll get the horses back?"

"Yep. I done this a time or two afore. Injuns, ye see, they don't figger a white man'll follow 'em out. I'll bet prime plews to poor, that these Crow is gonna slow down come sunset tomorrow, and we'll just sneak in and lift our hosses right back."

"And then?"

"We burn a shuck fer the river, coon. Then she boils down ter a race. We gotta hope our hosses can get us ter the *Maria* afore the Crows can run us down. Now, I'm figgering these Crows is pretty nigh fizzled after running all the way ter the river, then beating hide hell-fer-leather back west. I figger we can push the hosses faster than they can foller."

"And if it don't...doesn't work?"

Travis chewed his jerky and shrugged. "Reckon it'll be Katy bar the door."

———

Heals Like A Willow stood at the edge of camp, gazing off into the western twilight. She leaned on the ax, a half-cut cottonwood log before her. Long white chips littered the grass at her feet. The warm wind rattled the cotton-wood leaves and carried the scent of the dry plains beyond the river's uplands.

She closed her eyes and sent her soul flying out into that lavender sky. Where were they? How far away?

She let herself float, seeking, reaching out to touch Richard. If only he'd allowed her more intimacy so that her souls could know his. She'd been able to sense her husband in this manner. He'd never really believed her, just smiled with that warm indulgence when she told him.

Would Richard believe? Did it even matter?

She exhaled wearily, unable to sense him, unable to feel anything beyond an assurance that he was alive.

I'd know if he died.

She nodded soberly to reassure herself.

Just as I knew the moment my husband's soul slipped from his body.

What kind of a gift was that, to sense death? How much better it would be to sense and understand life.

"What say, Willow?" Baptiste asked from behind her.

She started, whirling, the ax swinging up into her hands with a familiar ease. Baptiste de Bourgmont was the strongest man she had ever known, with broad shoulders and arms bulged like pine roots. He wore a white canvas shirt, fine buckskin pants, and tall moccasins. A wide-brimmed black felt hat covered his buffalo-wool hair, and shaded his obsidian eyes. At his belt hung a big knife, a possible sack, bullet pouch, and pistol. His rifle filled his right hand.

The first time she'd met Baptiste, she'd tried to rub the rich black stain from his skin. Though stories circulated among the *Dukurika*, Baptiste was the first black man Willow had ever seen. She still caught herself studying with fascination his broad nose, the set of his lips, and the angle of his jaw.

Willow lowered her ax. "Baptiste, I didn't hear you."

He suppressed a smile at her reaction. "I'd say it be a right good thing you likes me. If'n I's Trudeau, you'd a split my head wide open with that thing."

"Trudeau might do better with a split head. Each half could argue with the other."

Baptiste chuckled again, the sound rich and deep. He scanned the western horizon with thoughtful eyes. "They ain't gonna be back fo' a while, child. Not with Crows to foller. I reckon we gonna be nigh to the Heart River afore they catches up. Don't pay to worry none, Travis'll bring him back. Worn thin, foah sure, but in one piece."

"What would it be like, to go to Boston?" She fingered the handle of the ax absently.

He made a face, stretching his broad lips. "Gal, don't go a thinking on it. You ain't white."

"You've been to Boston?"

"Nope. New Orleans, Natchez, Memphis, Saint Louis...they's enough. Boston wouldn't be no different. White folks marry white folks. Yor nothing but a nigger Injun to 'em, Willow." He paused, studying her from the corner of his eye. "Why? Dick done gone and asked you to go with him?"

"No." She shrugged. "I was just wondering."

He heard the sadness in her voice and reached out, placing an arm around her shoulders. 'Trust old Baptiste, gal. You don't wants to go back there. Dick, I figger he's a hickory down deep. That means a good, solid man. But them other white folk back in the settlements, they cain't see past yor skin, Willow. Dick knows." He paused again. "He ain't been filling you with no stories, now, has he?"

She shook her head. "It's me, Baptiste. I just keep trying to find a way."

"Wal, maybe so he'll come ta his senses and see that the only shining place fo' a coon is out heah, away from them pious damn Christians back in the States." He cocked his head. "And, if'n he don't want you, I could sure take up living in a Snake lodge. Especially if'n someone like you was in it with me."

"You would hate me, Baptiste. Every time you saw the faraway look in my eyes, you would know I was with Richard. It would prick at you like a cactus thorn, and over time it would fester and sicken your soul."

"Aw, I knows that. Willow. I's just trying to ease your mind's all."

She patted the bulging muscles on his right arm. "You are a good man, Baptiste. You will be my friend forever."

He hugged her up under the hollow of his arm. "And yor mine. And ain't no damn white man can tell us different. That's why you gots to believe me when I say you

don't never want to go back there. They'll kill yor soul,
Willow. That's what them whites do to anybody what
ain't white."

"I think I already knew that."

He waved his other arm. "And fo' now, hell, Travis,
he'll take good care of Dick. You'll see."

CHAPTER THREE

And therefore philosophers, who tie themselves to natural reason, suppose that a body can neither be generated nor destroyed, but only that it may appear otherwise than it did to us, that is, under different species, and consequently be called by other names; so that that which is now called man, may at another time have the name of not-man; but that which was once called body, can never be called not-body. But it is manifest that all other accidents besides magnitude or extension may be generated or destroyed; as when a white thing is made black, the whiteness that was in it perisheth, and the blackness that was not in it is now generated.

—Thomas Hobbes, *Elements of Philosophy*

 Richard's head snapped sideways. His ears rang, and his skin prickled.

"What...what?"

"C'mon, ye damned yellerlivered Doodle! I said, *get up!*"

Richard cried out as Travis twisted a handful of his hair and pulled his head back.

From the corner of his blurry eye, Richard saw the hand coming again, flinched just before it hit, and rocked under the stinging impact. The crack might have been the discharge of a rifle. The world turned silver as his eyes teared. Unforgiving hands pulled Richard to his feet.

"Leave me," he croaked from dry lips.

"Ter what?" Travis asked. "I ain't even sure the buzzards want ye."

"What happened?" Richard sagged against Travis and dragged a filthy sleeve across his blurry eyes. Damn, he ought to be drinking those tears instead of wiping them away.

"Passed out, coon. Yer water's gone dry's all. Happens. A feller dries out and plumb falls flat."

"And what if there isn't somebody to slap me awake?"

"Aw, ye'd a come to after dark. If'n ye had the sense God gave a grouse... Naw, ain't nothing dumber than a grouse. If'n ye had *any* sense, ye'd foller the drainage to water. Drainages always take ye to water. Leastways, they do in this country. Them basins way out west, I hear tell ye can foller one out inta the middle of a desert and die."

They were walking again, Richard hobbling on his painful feet, his legs shaking with each step. The sun hovered no more than two hands over the western horizon.

Dear Lord God, how can I keep this up? "Travis, I feel like I'm going to die."

"Good. Reckon so long as yer miserable, yer hanging on. It's when the whole shitaree gets blurry, warm, and fuzzy that yer arse is nigh to being wolf meat."

"I could stand a little of that now. And maybe about three weeks of sleep in a big feather bed, with lots of cool fruit juice in a big, ice-filled pitcher. And Willow...Willow to pour it for me."

"Cain't take her to Boston, coon."

"And I can't go live like a Shoshoni, Travis. What's left?"

"Saint Loowee until it fills up with farmers. Then maybe the Platte. Hell, I don't know. Some fur post like Michilimackinac. They got folks what reads books and got Injun wives to boot."

"My God, what kind of life is that?" Richard sucked at his tongue, trying to get enough spit to swallow—and gave it up as a poor hope. "Fur post? I want to be a professor of philosophy. Maybe...maybe in Europe."

"Take Willow to Europe?" Travis shook his head. "It'd kill her, coon. She's free out hyar. Her people's hyar. Yer asking her to cut her soul in half. And what? So ye goes to England. They'd treat her like a chained bear."

Blink as he might, he couldn't clear the haze from his vision. "What am I saying? I'm going to marry Laura. Laura Templeton. Will's sister—blonde, blue eyes like a morning sky. A lady...delicate...pretty."

"Take my advice"—Travis pulled his hat off, wiped the sweat from his forehead, and crammed the hat back down until the brim shaded his eyes from the sinking sun —"and come with us ter the mouth of the Big Horn. Hole up with Willow fer the winter. Hell, come spring thaw ye might both be so sick of each other ye'll pack yer possibles and light out like Hell's a-fire just ter be shed of one another."

Richard shook his head to clear the sudden blurring, all of his defenses laid bare. "You mean just live with her? Like...like a man does with a wife? Travis, I can't. What would I ever tell Laura? That she wasn't the first? Travis, what sort of cad do you think I am?"

The hunter squinted at him. "Ye ain't never laid with a woman?"

"No! I told you." He squinted hard, struggling to keep his vision clear. "Pure...don't you see? I promised myself. Laura will be the first. We'll be able to learn from each other in an intimate sharing of chastity and virtue. A special...bond between us..."

"Painter crap," Travis said thickly. "I'd spit if'n I had any." He resettled the guns on his shoulders. "Willow's had a husband. Birthed a kid."

"I know. That's another reason I can't..." Richard frowned. "She's not, well, mine. Alone. Do you see?"

"I see a hellacious damn fool."

"What do you mean?" The thoughts were losing themselves in the hazy softness that rose around him. If he just concentrated, the thought would...

———

Travis plodded along for another couple of steps after Dick collapsed like a limp bale of cotton, then stopped, holding a rifle balanced on each shoulder.

He made a face, sighed in the hot air, and turned back.

Richard lay on his side, glassy eyes half-open ,but vacant, one arm flopped into a patch of prickly pear.

"Wal, thank Hob it warn't a rattlesnake." Travis lowered the rifles and grabbed a handful of hair, twisting it painfully. A good hard slap brought Dick back. He blinked away the tears again and groaned.

"Coon, I reckon yer about on yer last legs fer today." Travis licked rough lips with a dry tongue, and scanned the endless grasslands. The horse tracks they followed led up to the ridgetop and disappeared over the other side. Probably to disappear over yet another ridgetop, and another, and so on clear to the Little Missouri.

Damnation, and I promised Dave I'd be gone no longer than a week.

What if the Crow had outrun them? Could he really just turn back empty-handed?

"Travis?" Richard whispered. "I'll be all right. One step, then...then..."

"Another."

"Yeah." Richard groaned and lifted his arm. "Damn. Hurts."

"Ye fell inta the cactus, Dick."

Can't even hold his eyes still. Cuss it all, the kid's given about all he can. Hell. Getting right close, too.

"Tell ye what. They's a ridgetop up yonder. Let's coon our way up there, take a look around. I'll figger where the Crows is, sneak down and lift the hosses, and come back and fetch ye."

Richard nodded, his cracked and swollen lips parted. "Help me up."

Travis hoisted him, then bent for the rifles. Cuss old Jake Hawken for making such a heavy piece of iron, but, by the Lord, it was as good a shooter as could be had, and tough enough that a feller could whack Old Ephraim across the snout and still shoot straight afterwards.

"C'mon, Dick," Travis whispered.

"You know," Richard croaked, "I'm sick to death of hearing you say that."

Not half as sick as I am of saying it.

Just how far had they come, anyway? Step by step, they hobbled onward, any chance of trotting gone.

"Yer a game lad, Dick Hamilton, I'll say that fer ye."

Richard's forehead lined deeply as he puzzled on something. "I had thirty thousand dollars. I'd give it all up for another stream of water." A pause. "And rest."

"By Hob, I'd let ye, too," Travis agreed, balancing Richard on one side, the rifles on the other.

"Sorry, Travis," Richard whispered dryly. "I gave it all I had. Just ran out of..." He wavered, his head wobbly, and frowned again, searching for the thought.

"Don't make no apologies, Dick. I'm just about tuck-ered myself, and I been a-humping up and down these plains fer years now. Ye made a sprite try, yessiree."

"Dear Lord God, I'm tired."

"Me, too, Dick. Reckon we'll sleep on them hosses."

"Water'd set me right."

"Me, too, coon." Travis peered out into the yellow light of the sunset as they crested the hilltop. A mound of stone—an Injun cairn—marked the spot. The ones used as eagle traps had hollow centers where a warrior hid under a bait and grabbed a live eagle out of the air to pluck its feathers. Other piles of stone supported poles with spirit helper standards and prayers tied to the ends. Some were for seeking visions; a young man went there to fast, pray, and sing for four days. This one, old and fallen, covered by lichen and grown up in grass, might have been new when God made the world.

Richard sagged onto the rock pile while Travis took his bearings off the blood-red sun hanging bloated over the western horizon. Shading his eyes, Travis made out the black dots of buffalo grazing in the long draws leading westward. Down there, in the bottom, bur oak, buffaloberry, and plum bushes filled the draws. What caught and held his attention was the snaking line of cottonwoods in the valley bottom. And there, right down where the drainages all came together, a line of black dots moved into the trees.

Over such a distance, he couldn't be sure, but...the animals moved purposefully; and something about the silhouette was just different enough. Men on horses? Or antlered elk?

"Yer a damn fool child, Travis," he mumbled to himself. "Ain't no antlers on elk, not this time of year. All they got is velvet as long's a man's forearms."

A slow smile curled his cracked lips. "Dick? We got 'em, coon. And thar's water down thar, too. Enough to fill our bellies so full we'll piss fer hours."

———

The cool darkness instilled a faint throb of life into Richard's numb body. He followed Hartman, grass whipping around his feet. Overhead, a million, million stars glittered and sparkled against the velvet blackness.

Once, just off to his right, a rattlesnake's *shiiiiish* of warning brought a start to his jumpy heart

"Step wide of the cuss," Travis rasped. "Don't need ter set him off and rustle up the Crows. Just watch yer step. Whar ye gots one buzzworm, they's four or six more."

Richard squinted down at the tall grass, dark under the starlight

Just watch your step? Oh, right enough!

He picked his way in what he hoped were steps inoffensive to anything with a rattlesnake nature.

Downhill was much easier than up, but still he teetered on the brink of falling—the floaty sensation of being cast adrift hovered with dreamlike certainty just at the edge of his conscious thoughts.

"How ye doing?" Travis asked.

"Stumbling along. Half asleep. Ready to fall on my face."

"Wal, at least I ain't having ter carry ye any more. Reckon that's a hair of improvement."

Richard rubbed his gritty eyes. The shakes were eating at his bones. His belly growled. "Travis?"

"What?"

"What do we do when we get down there?"

"Find a drink. Then we scout the Crow camp and fill our bellies. Cain't fight or think when a feller's this dry and hungry. Then we takes our hosses back and rides hell bent fer the river."

Richard stumbled on until they passed into the protection of the bur oaks. Travis wound through the dark trees, skirting patches of brush, and crossed the thickly grassed bottoms to a small, rush-filled stream. There, he dropped to his knees and flopped head-first into the narrow channel. Richard crawled up alongside and lowered his head to the cool flow, sucking down great gulps before coughing.

"Shhh! Ye want the whole valley wide awake?" Travis smacked him with a balled fist. "Drink slow, coon. Ain't ye larned nothing?"

Richard forced himself to suck up a mouthful of water at a time and hold it in his mouth before he swallowed it down. Travis finally pulled him back.

"Best fill our bellies. Hyar's the last of the jerky. Eat up, and we'll drink again."

They sat, backs to a cottonwood, alternately chewing on dried meat and then slipping off to drink.

Richard sighed as he felt life restore itself to his depleted body. "If Trudeau showed up now, he could kill me with one finger."

"Wal, he ain't hyar. And further, he'd a run off long past. Hell, he'd a barely made it up outa the river."

But I did.

Richard chewed thoughtfully. What had he done over the last two days? For almost forty-eight hours, he'd run and trotted and walked and run some more. He'd pushed himself to the end of his endurance, and then found an extra bit to keep going.

"Swaller down, hoss," Travis said, standing. "Go suck up yer fill, and let's be getting on."

Richard got his drink, and reached for his rifle. "Thanks. You've carried it more than you should have."

Travis patted him on the shoulder, then turned and ghosted southward through the trees.

They nearly walked into the Crow camp. Only the white mare gave it away, looking straight at them. Richard's heart hammered, sudden fear tickling in his guts as he realized the dark forms in the grass at his feet were blanket-rolled Crow warriors.

Travis backed away slowly, Richard following until the scrubby oaks hid them again. The hunter leaned his mouth to Richard's ear. "I got this figgered. Wind's from the west. Foller me."

Step by step, they circled until the camp lay upwind. Travis whispered, "I'm going in fer the hosses. I want ye ter take cover ahint a tree. If'n anything happens, I'll holler out that they's surrounded, understand?"

"Yes, but what—"

"When I calls out, ye shout back. Now, peel yer ears, coon. The second ye calls, ye scoot over yonder about another fifteen or twenty paces. If I call again, ye changes yer voice and scoots again. Ye got ter go fast, and ye got ter go quiet 'cause we're making them think they're surrounded. Understand the plan?"

"I understand."

"Ye don't shoot! Not unless they've kilt me and are closing. Ye can always bluff with a loaded rifle."

"But, Travis—"

"Let's go." And he slipped away into the darkness.

Richard took a deep breath, wished he'd checked the priming on his rifle, and followed.

All it takes is one misstep, a snapped twig, and we'll be killed.

If anything, the night had turned blacker as Travis walked out into the center of the Crow camp.

Richard settled behind the rough stump of a bur oak; fear tightened like a band in his chest. Swallowing hard, he lifted his rifle and propped it on the stump.

Travis looked like a black blot against the night-shadowed grass. An owl hooted, the call lonely. Richard's nerves pulled tighter than a cat-gut rope.

The horses shifted at Travis's approach, and Richard's thumb caressed the curved cock with its leather-clamped flint.

Travis bent, his knife flashing as he cut the picket on one side. Then, as if it was the morning ritual, he cut the second side.

"Come on," Richard whispered as his fingers turned sweat-slick on the rifle.

Travis took a step and stopped. He seemed to wait forever. He took another step and stopped.

At this rate, it would be hours before they were far enough way to vault onto the animals' backs and flee.

Richard's lungs had gone tight, his bowels loose. He had to gulp to get enough air into his chest.

And then the Crow warrior sleeping to Richard's

right grunted and stirred in his bedroll. The man growled to himself, unrolled from his blankets, and walked to the edge of the camp.

If my heart beats any harder, it'll split my ribs. How can Travis stand this?

Richard had frozen like stone. Travis had crouched, no more than a black shadow among the animals.

The Crow warrior calmly unlaced his breechclout and yawned as he urinated into the grass. He barely gave the horses a glance as he found his blankets again, and resettled himself to sleep.

Richard's jaws ached, strained from clenching his teeth. His breathing—gone shallow for so long—slowly returned to normal.

Surrounded by Crow, Travis still hadn't moved. *Come on, man, we don't have all night!* Richard thumped his fist on his knotted thigh muscles. Travis Hartman must have nerves of steel to stand there so quietly.

The Crow warrior had evidently fallen back to sleep, because Travis made another small step.

A bead of hot sweat trickled down Richard's cheek.

CHAPTER FOUR

If now to this natural proclivity of men, to hurt each other, which they derive from their passions, but chiefly from a vain esteem of themselves, you add; the right of all to all, wherewith one by right invades, the other by right resists, and whence arise perpetual jealousies and suspicions on all hands, and how hard a thing it is to provide against an enemy invading us with an intention to oppress and ruin, though he come with a small number, and no great provision; it cannot be denied but that the natural state of men, before they entered into society, was a mere war, and that not simply, but a war of all men against all men.

—Thomas Hobbes, *Leviathan*

 The midday sun beat down hot enough to cook an egg on a pan lid. Travis hunched on the back of his horse, his rifle propped across the animal's withers. As he and Richard rode east over the grassy plains, he gnawed on a prairie turnip to draw strength from the starchy root and keep some moisture in his mouth. He'd

shown the haggard Richard how to recognize the plants, and they'd dug a mess of roots with their knives, but this late in the year the roots had gone woody and fibrous.

Travis kept glancing over his shoulder at their back-trail. Heat waves, like a silvered dream, shimmered across the waving grass. Weary as he was, vision could play tricks on a man. He blinked, rubbing his gravelly eyes.

I ain't sure, but this beaver's about done clear in.

Every muscle ached, his feet burned from blisters and prickly pear thorns, and worst of all, his mind had dulled as though filled with cottonwood down.

"I still don't believe you walked the horses right out of that camp," Richard said woodenly. He sat his Pawnee mare like a limp bag of bones. Dark circles hung under his hollow eyes. With each step the horse took, Richard's head bobbed loosely.

"Wal, ya see, it's like this." Travis choked down a mouthful of root. "Them Crows now, they stole these hosses pretty slick, I'd say. I figgered ter be just a wee bit slicker. Hell, coon, ye can't just up and let 'em out-Injun ye."

Richard stifled a yawn. "I thought we were going to die when that warrior woke up. You don't know how close I came to shooting him down."

"Tarnal Hell! That would have cooked our goose plumb through. Didn't yer hear me tell ye ter keep yer shot till the last?"

"That's *why* I didn't shoot him."

Travis wiped at his mouth, satisfied that no black dots —the sort running humans would make—stood out on the backtrail. "He just got up, loosened his strings, shook out his pizzle, and made water. That notion comes on a man every now and then. So, what did I do?"

"You just *stood* there!"

"Yep. I hunched down in the hoss's shadow, that Crow did his pissing—and then I let him crawl right back inter his blankets."

"You waited half the night."

"Just long enough to hear his breathing go deep and even. Then I took a step, and waited, and took another. The lesson is, Dick, that a feller can get by with a lot if'n he'll take his time and use his noodle."

Travis pulled another of the fat roots from his possibles. With a thumbnail, he scraped most of the clotted dirt off the brown skin. "I reckon I'd a loved ter have been hid up in one of them bur oaks and heard the squalls when them coons woke up this morning."

Richard craned his neck to look backward. "Are they coming after us?"

"'Course they is. Hell, we stoled their damned hosses, didn't we?"

"But they were *our* horses to begin with!"

"T'ain't neither. They's the Pawnee's, and probably the Osage's afore that, and the Sioux's afore that, and hell, who knows, maybe the Crows' afore that. Hosses get a good go around out hyar."

"But the morality of ownership—"

"Haw! I knew ye was gonna up and philos'phy at me the moment ye got yer legs back! By God, Dick, glad ter see yer turning right pert again. Reckon I was getting plumb worried ye'd up and die on me, or maybe come down with the mountain fever or something."

"What are you talking about?"

"Why, tarnal hell, coon. It's nigh onto a whole week without philos'phy. I was scared ye was ailing."

"Oh, blessed Lord God!"

"Got religion, too? Yer pap'd be plumb proud...'cept maybe about that thirty thousand dollars ye lost. Reckon that'd twist a coon's gout up something fierce." Travis cocked his head. "Wonder how old François's doing with all that money?"

Richard scowled at Travis. "Can we talk about something significant for once?"

"Ain't thirty thousand dollars significant?" He paused, getting no answer, and added, "Aw, some whore's probably cut his throat fer it by now." Travis chewed off another bite of the root. "How about Willow and ye? We never—"

"No! I want to talk about this horse stealing! I mean, these people have no moral foundations. They just steal and steal. It flies in the face of every convention of society, of...of civil order."

"Oh, they got lots of civil order. And, Dick, they don't steal—not from their own people. It's all right if'n I steal Crow hosses, 'cause they'll steal from me first chance they get. So long's no one gets caught, we'll do just fine. Wait and see. Hell, we'll probably meet up with those coons up ter the Big Horn and have us the dangdest..."

"Meet up with? You mean *these* Crow?"

"Reckon so. Hell, I got relations among the Crow."

"They'll kill us for what we've done. But, no—I mean, these are our horses. We were in the *right,* for God's sake!"

Travis waved him down, the half-eaten root in his hand. "Pay attention. I'm gonna larn ye this once. Got the wax outa yer ears? Good. Hyar's how she lays. Ye can steal from anybody ye wants to out hyar...so long as they ain't yer own people. Now, let's say ye go into a Mandan camp. You don't touch nothing unless someone gives it to ye. Ye don't *admire* nothing, because that beholds the owner to offer it to ye. Understand?"

"Yes, the rules of good manners are the same in

Boston. Well, but for the offering part. And you're supposed to comment on nice things."

"Among some Injun folk that's generally a polite way of asking fer something. Don't tell a Mandan he's got a pretty wife. Not the way yer fixing to save yer pizzle fer a holy relic."

"I'm not—"

"So, ye don't steal nothing in a village, *but,* if'n ye's a-riding through the country and happens ter spot a village off in the distance, and yer not fixing ter go in and palaver, why, who'd notice a couple of hosses missing? 'Course, they's gonna try and chase ye down ter get 'em back. And when they do, the shooting starts."

"People get killed when guns go off." Richard glanced over his shoulder as if expecting mad Crow warriors.

"Yep. Unless ye talks yer way out of it. And sometimes ye can. Now, according ter the rules, the Crow took our hosses, we took them back. Each side admires the other's bravery and skill at lifting hosses."

"It's like a giant silly game!"

"Might be ye could call it that. Ain't all life nothing but a sort of game? A feller's just got ter know the rules, Dick."

"But you can still get shot."

Travis glanced sidelong at Richard—his head had bowed, half asleep, nodding with each step the horse took. "Ye can indeed. That's part of what makes it so all-fired interesting. This country out hyar ain't fer no puff-and-struts. Ye can be free, Dick. Be anything ye wants ter, so long's ye've the courage to back it up."

Richard jerked his head up, blinking and rubbing his eyes. "I think I've heard that speech before."

"Uh-huh. Now, what's this foolishness about being a virgin? Is that why yer staying so shy of Willow? Can't stand the thought of sticking yer pizzle in where some red coon's done stuck his?"

Richard gave him a bloodshot glare. "We've had this argument before, too."

"And I ain't never got no straight answer out of ye." Travis shook his head. "Wal, what in tarnal hell are ye in love with? The woman? Or what's atwixt her legs? God A'mighty, Dick, yer about the stupidest Doodle I ever seen. There's the two of ye, staring at each other like long-lost fawns, and yer so knotted up with this virgin bed shit ye can't see what's drying up right before yer eyes."

"It's not that!"

"Then what is it? Laura? Hell, she probably thinks yer dead by now. And just what's she a gonna think when she hears ye lost thirty thousand dollars and then vanished, huh? Why, if'n it was me, I'd figger ye done skipped off ter Paris or London to live like a rich jasper, or something. And if'n ye's just up and robbed, I'd figger ye fer a stupid son of a bitch what couldn't be trusted. If'n I's as purty as ye say Laura is, I'd marry the next feller in line."

Richard's expression soured. "Don't, Travis. Don't even say it. I couldn't stand the thought of Thomas Hanson and her. Not...not like that."

"Thomas Hanson?"

"Another of my...well, friends. He's tall, muscular, with a nice smile and good family. But he uses people. He's a rake, if you know what I mean. The rumor is that he sees prostitutes. The thought of Laura and him..." Richard's head hung.

"Do tell? And ye mean ter say this Laura ain't smart enough ter know what sort of man he is? Hell, then she ain't worth shit herself."

"I *won't* have you talk about Laura that way. I intend to marry her."

"So? Is she a fool...or ain't she?"

Richard glared at him with eyes like red pits.

"Wal, I reckon she's from Boston, ain't she? And, if'n ye ain't willing to winter over with Willow, I can tell ye that Laura wouldn't be the only fool in that marriage."

Richard shook his head. "Travis, this isn't my country. I'm going back to Boston. When I get there, I'm going to teach philosophy. So, tell me. What would happen to Willow if I took her with me? Hmm? Wouldn't we be the talk of the town? Professor Hamilton and his little squaw? Can't you just imagine Willow attending ladies' teas? She eats with her fingers and wipes grease off her lips with her sleeve."

Travis glanced at the turnip in his fingers, then at the grease streaks on his sleeve, and lifted an eyebrow.

Richard's fist knotted. "They'd crucify her. And me."

"What about now? Ye've got time afore we reach the Yellerstone."

"What? Share her bed, and then just up and leave her? What kind of man do you think I am? For me, lying with a woman is a commitment. A covenant, if you will. I'm not like you. I can't just *use* her and ride off like that. I'd be no better than Thomas Hanson."

Travis took a deep breath. "Nope. I reckon not. But seems ter me, ye've made all the decisions hyar. What's Willow say about all this? She's half, ain't she?"

"She knows it's impossible."

"Maybe she wants ye anyway. Ever think of that? Or have ye been so wrapped up in yer high and mighty Bible-thumping covenants that yer forgetting she might want all of ye fer the little time she's got?"

"I am a student of *philosophy*—not quaint pastoral

Hebrew teachings as reinterpreted by transplanted Greeks. I am interested in the moral dimensions of life, *my* life." He paused. "You're disgusting."

Travis jerked a hard nod. "And I eat with my fingers. But now that ye've done throwed yer fit, maybe ye otta consider. Shoshoni have different notions about men and women. God made 'em to go together. Now, Willow's a grown woman. She knows what she's about, Dick. And I reckon that given the choice, she'd take yer Laura on head to head, and Devil take the hindmost."

Richard rode on in dejected silence, the hard set of his jaw reflecting his determination.

"Why're ye fighting so hard, Dick? Yer making yerself miserable."

Richard gave him a flinty look from the corner of his eye. "Because, Travis. Damn it, everything's slipping away from me! Don't you understand? Every time I turn around, someone wants to take something away from me!"

"Ain't no one—"

"Jesus Christ, Travis! It started the moment I set foot in my father's office in Boston. He took my studies away —sent me out here. In Saint Louis, I was robbed, beaten, tied up. August made me sign that damned indenture. You and Green have taken away my freedom to go where I want."

"But that ain't it, is it?" Travis chewed thoughtfully on his prairie turnip. It sure was stringy.

"No, it isn't! You've been mocking me for all of my beliefs. You want to destroy everything I believe in!"

"Wal, some of it's plumb silly, Dick. Like Injuns being some sort of red-skinned innocents. Or perhaps ye done fergot old Half Man trying ter split my head because ye asked him some questions about God and such?"

Richard slumped in the saddle. The anger fled just as quickly as it had come. "I just want you to stop picking at me." The haggard brown eyes had turned dull. "You don't know what it's like when everything you believed was wrong."

"Hell, maybe it ain't wrong everywhere. It's just wrong out hyar."

Richard lifted an eyebrow. "Then it's not Truth, Travis. Truth is just that—right everywhere. If I have learned anything from you, it's that life is nothing more than chaos, irresponsibility, and morality that shifts by the moment and one's present company."

"Yep, nope, and yep. Life's chaos, all right. And the way a feller acts depends on who he's with. But ye missed plumb center with that bit about responsibility. Cain't never duck that."

"But you would have me turn my back on Laura to gratify my baser instincts by bedding an Indian woman."

"Is that it? She's an Injun?"

Richard's eyes squinted painfully. "No...yes...I don't know. I'm tired, Travis, fit to fall over. I can't think now. My mind is turned to mush."

"Just tell me this. Do ye love this Laura?"

"Yes."

"And I know ye love Willow. Don't deny it, hoss. I seen it in yer eyes."

"I guess."

"Dick, hear me. Look around ye. Ain't nothing hyar but what the good Lord made. This is yer chance, boy. Ye've got an opportunity that other coons ain't gonna get. Freedom, hoss. No one ter judge ye but God. This hyar's the last chance fer a feller to live free afore the farmers come. Think, Dick. If'n ye wants ter love Willow, ye can. Hell, marry her, love her, have yer kids, and not a single scandalous whisper or cocked eye from the good pious folk.

"Don't ye see? Civilization's coming, and they's gonna ruin it all. Make it like back there." He waved randomly at the east. "But fer now, fer one shining time, it's yers, Dick. And hers, too. Don't throw it away because of what they believe back there in the East. Ye can rise above that, and I swear, ye'll never regret it."

Richard rubbed his puffy eyes and pursed his cracked lips before saying, "I don't know, Travis."

Travis nerved himself. "I did. Once. Loved, I mean. Married a Crow woman. Calf in the Moonlight was her name."

Richard straightened. "You? Married? What happened?"

Travis narrowed his eyes to keep from looking back into his memory. "She's dead. And ye otta think about that. A feller cain't see into the future. Use yer time wisely, Dick. Sometimes ye can think ye've got forever, and ye don't. It can creep up on a feller and snatch away all that's pure and fine and beautiful in his life. And when it's gone, all he's got left is the empty ache and the memories."

"You must have really loved her."

As if you'd know.

Travis straightened his backbone, and gestured with his half-eaten root. "Time's the thing. This country, lad. I had me a vision, a dream. They'll kill it, just like they kilt every other thing. They'll come in with their ways, and there won't be no more coup. No more hoss thieving. Just their damn farms and laws and 'good' folk. Won't be no free 'scaped slaves like Baptiste. No pretty women like Willow. No crafty coons like Wah-Menitu, or Big Yellow.

"Just ye wait. Come the preachers and farms, why,

ye'll have to 'fess the line, then. Wear scratchy clothes, go ter church of a sabbath, and foller the white ways." Travis hawked and spat. "Poor bull if'n I ever heard it. This coon'd rather be wolfmeat."

"Do you really think it'll be that bad?"

"Worse. Ain't nobody so God-holy boring as a farmer. 'Cepting a whole passel of farmers."

"You make it sound like damnation and Hell."

"Yep." Travis squinted into the distance ahead at the patchwork of spots that darkened the far hills. "And this coon's just seen salvation start slipping over yonder hill."

Richard shaded his eyes with the flat of a hand. "Looks like...what *is* that?"

"Buffler, coon."

"Buffalo? But they're—good God, they're covering miles! I can't see the end of them."

"Yep. Kick up that old mare. Let's go weave us a trail that'll drive them cock-eyed Crows plumb crazy."

"What if the buffalo stampede?"

"Wal, Yankee Doodle, I hope ye can hang onto that hoss's mane and keep yer seat. Fall off in that mess, and ye'll be stomped inta dust." He glanced across at Hamilton. "Seems ter me it'd be a right shame ter die, and never know what ye had in Willow."

"You always have the answers, don't you?"

"Yep. And since I met ye, I've larned ter write my name. So, tell me, have ye larned anything?"

———

Willow's agile fingers tied the last knots in the net bag she'd been weaving. Made of slender willow twigs and red cedar bark, the fine mesh would hold most of the berries she'd dried.

"Nice work," Green said, coming to sit beside her on the front of the cargo box. He sighed, wiped the sweat from his blunt face, and stared up at the broiling sun before surveying the river. The water was running smoothly this morning, only the sucking swirls breaking the glossy brown surface. Reflections of the trees and the brassy sky wavered and bobbed with *Maria*'s progress.

On the shore, the *engagés* sang *"C'est l'aviron"* as they plodded along with the cordelle slung over their shoulders. Though a good bow-shot away, their voices carried clearly in counterpoint to the birdsong and rustling leaves in the cottonwoods.

"Thank you," she said, and smiled at her bag. "I learned knots as a little girl. Playing the string game. You know, a loop. With it you can make patterns in the fingers, and then another plucks it off into other patterns."

"We call it cat's cradle."

"Cat's cradle," she said, liking the words.

Green fidgeted, running his hand along the oak deck. He traced the wood's grain with callused fingertips. "I wish you weren't planning on leaving."

She gave him a sidelong glance. "Oh?"

"Well, you're still drying berries, storing jerked meat in your pack, sewing new soles on moccasins." He waggled his hand. "Making containers. And I see you staring off to the west every night before you go to sleep."

She hesitated, smoothing the tight knots. "I want to go home, Dave. I miss my people, my mountains. My souls are not whole here. I want to hear the wind in the trees, laugh with my family, dance, and play double-ball. So, I will go when Travis and Ritshard come back with horses. One is mine."

Green sank his teeth into his lower lip. After a while he said, "I wish you wouldn't. We're two days below the Mandans. This country here, a lot of Rees have come in, driven north after Leavenworth shot up the Arikara villages. West of here, the land's crawling with Crow, maybe Cheyenne hunting parties. You'd be safer with us. We'll get you back to your people. I've given my word."

She laid the netting in her lap and studied him. "I will tell my people about your trading post. I have promised this."

"What will you tell them?"

"The truth. That I think you are a good man, but that I don't know if your White man's things are good for the *Dukurika*. I will also tell them that whether it is you or another trader, the Whites are coming and these things must be dealt with."

He tilted his head back so that she could see the small lines at the corners of his sky blue eyes and thin lips. The sun glinted golden in his beard. "*If* you make it across all that country. So many things can happen to a woman alone. Hell, the Hidatsa love to take Snake women for slaves. There's storms, white bears, fires, lightning, a thousand things could happen. A party of Blackfeet could cross your tracks."

"On the river, your boat could sink, we could be

ambushed by Rees, or lightning could kill me dead on your cargo box."

"It's that Yankee, isn't it? Richard."

She said nothing, gazing safely on the river.

"Hell, he's been trouble since I brought him aboard. There's other men besides him."

She caught the tone in his voice. "You?"

"Well...why not?"

She folded the netting in her lap. "I have seen the look in your eyes, Dave. I've seen how you watch me. Sometimes, it is as a man watches a woman he wants for his bed. At other times, I think you want me because I can help your trade. The one look I never see in your eyes is the look of the soul."

He grunted, propping his chin on a pulled-up knee. "Maybe with time. It takes a while for a man and woman to get used to each other. There are a lot of advantages to being a trader's wife. You'd never want, not for anything."

Except the soul's love.

She chased away the memory of her husband's eyes and leaned back, bracing herself on her arms so the sun could warm her. His gaze kept straying to the thin leather where her dress conformed to the rounded curve of her breasts. A man was a man. "For most women, I think it wouldn't be so bad. For me...well, I think it would make us unhappy. You would grow tired of my questions. In the end, you would hate me."

"You know all this?"

"I've read your soul. All people have a desire, something inside them that makes them who they are."

"We call it passion."

"Passion? That is my word for today. Passion. For you, passion is trade. You wish this post and what it will get for you. You wish to be treated as an important man. One that chiefs will come to see, and the *engagés* look up to. You want men to know your name."

"I will have that—and you can share it with me, become part of it. That wouldn't be so bad, would it?"

"It's your way, Dave Green. The way *puha* has made for you. Some men must be warriors, some seek Power and visions. You look for something else, to be a boosh-way. And trade is the way you will get it."

He fingered his chin and cocked an eyebrow. "All right, you know so much about me, what do you think I really want?"

Do I tell him? "Dave, perhaps..."

"Please, tell me. I won't get mad."

She met his stare, looking past the startling blue in his eyes for a glimpse of the soul beneath. "You do not see yourself. You need other men's eyes to see for you. It is that reflection you want. As other men see you, so will you see yourself."

He snorted irritably and stood up. He started back toward where Henri gripped the steering oar, then turned, as suddenly contrite. "I guess I asked, didn't I?"

She reached out and touched his leg. "That is why I would make you unhappy, Dave. You would ask, and I would tell you."

"Is that...I mean..."

"You are a good man. A man I would trust in hard times, and call my friend. Don't look hurt or angry. It is who you are, your medicine. If no one followed your path, there would be no chiefs. I think you will be a very great trader, a most important man. For that you need a chief's woman, not Willow."

He scuffed the toe of his foot on the sun-bleached oak. "Yeah, I reckon. Tell me, are all Snake women like you? Can they all see souls?"

"No. Most are happy with themselves, with the way *Tam Apo* made them."

"And you're not?"

She shook her head.

How lonely you are, Willow.

Of all the men she'd met, only Richard might have filled the hole emptied by her husband's death.

Green rocked back and forth. "Willow, I'm asking you. Please, don't go. Not yet. Not until we're closer. I can't make you a prisoner. But I'm asking, as a friend."

"I will think about it. But I must..."

At that moment, Baptiste came charging out of the trees, rifle in hand. He waved desperately, fringe swirling with the motion. "Pull up! Beach the boat!" Turning upstream, he shouted, "Fort up, boys! Rees is on us!"

CHAPTER FIVE

Hereby it is manifest, that during the time men live without a common power to keep them all in awe, they are in that condition which is called war; and such a war, as if of every man, against every man. For war consisteth not in battle only, or the act of fighting; but in a tract of time, wherein the will to contend by battle is sufficiently known: and therefore the notion of time, is to be considered in the nature of war; as it is in the nature of weather. For as the nature of foul weather lieth not in a shower or two of rain; but in an inclination thereto of many days together: so the nature of war, consisteth not in actual fighting; but in the known disposition thereto.

—Thomas Hobbes, *Leviathan*

"Henri!" Green barked. "Put in!" The patroon leaned hard on the steering oar, nosing *Maria* toward the shore. The cordelle went slack as the *engagés* threw it down and bolted back down the bank.

Green jumped flat-footed to the bow, uncoiling the

painter and slinging it toward Baptiste, who splashed into the mud, caught a coil with his free hand, and slogged shoreward through the shallows.

"Henri! Break out the guns!" Green was already scrambling back along the *passe avant*.

The boat's weight caught up with Baptiste several paces shy of the cottonwood he'd hoped to tie off on, and began to pull him inexorably backward as momentum lost the battle with the current.

Willow rose to her feet, heart racing. She scanned the trees, seeing shapes flit through the gaps. Baptiste's feet were sliding as his arms knotted and his face strained.

Wild whoops broke out in the trees. The war cries spurred the running *engagés* into panic. Henri cursed, struggling to steer. *Maria's* bow slewed out toward the river.

"I can't hold it!" Baptiste screamed as the boat dragged him toward the water.

Green dived over the side, sloshing chest-deep toward shore.

"Merde!" Henri cursed. "We are helpless!"

Willow jumped down to the deck and pulled the Pawnee bow from her pack before slinging the quiver with its arrows over her shoulder.

Toussaint, Etienne, and Louis de Clerk arrived, panting, and caught up the painter as Green waded ashore. All added their weight to the wet rope.

The yells grew louder back in the trees—then came the boom of a rifle. A man screamed in terror.

"Willow!" Green cupped a hand and shouted. "Get the guns! Inside the cargo box!"

She tore along the cleated *passe avant,* and ducked down into the darkness. There, racked along the back wall, stood the line of muskets. She grabbed up two, and scrambled up the stairway.

They'd managed to snub the painter, but even as they tied the knot, terrified *engagés* were throwing themselves into the water, flailing for the boat.

Like shadows, the dust-brown bodies of Rees slipped among the gray-boiled trunks of the cottonwoods. Slivers of arrows glinted as they arched toward the struggling men. Another gunshot banged.

"Go!" Henri shouted. "Take the guns!" He pointed toward shore.

Willow took a deep breath and jumped into the hip-deep water as the *Maria* pulled tight. The mud slipped under her feet; she struggled for balance and to keep the guns dry. Teetering on the slippery gumbo, she almost fell backward at the last moment before stepping ashore.

Green—wet and mud-splattered—ran to meet her, taking one of the muskets. He quickly checked the priming and turned to draw a bead on the closest warrior. Smoke and fire spouted when the musket boomed.

Baptiste had retrieved his rifle, leveled it, and fired.

Toussaint took the second of Willow's guns and threw himself flat on the bank to shoot.

Willow fumbled for her bow, strung it, and slipped an arrow from the quiver. Scuttling forward, she took a position beside one of the thick cottonwoods.

The last of the *engagés* had rushed past, joining the thrashing melee in the water.

"Powder!" Green shouted as he waved his empty rifle. "Henri! We need powder and shot!"

Blessed Tam Apo, *am I going to die now?*

Willow nocked an arrow, heart pounding. The Rees charged into the open, shrilling loudly, some firing rifles, others drawing their bows as they dashed to a stop, released their arrows, and charged on. How many? Ten? Twenty, at least.

A shot sounded from the boat, then another. One of the charging warriors pitched head-first into the grass.

Willow took her time, mouth dry, waiting for the right target. A young warrior sprinted headlong toward her, and Willow took her shot. The feathered shaft flew straight—right into the soft hollow under his ribs. The youth stumbled, dropping his gun and grabbing at the shaft as he cried out in disbelief.

She nocked another arrow.

Easy. Take your time.

Tam Apo, *help me.* Her hands were shaking, legs trembling. Panting, she lifted her bow, drew, and shot too quickly; her arrow whistled past a warrior's shoulder.

Slow, now. You must aim. Be sure, Willow, or they will kill you.

They might kill her anyway. But it would be a release, wouldn't it? The pain would be over.

She steadied herself. A song about *Pachee Goyo,* the Bald One, rose to her lips. As it had soothed her in childhood, so it soothed her now. She drew a bead on a muscular man who lifted a gun to shoot Green, and released, the action smooth. The arrow drove into the man's side and he screamed, gun discharging into the sky.

The blood of the Dukurika *runs in your veins, Willow. Show them. Husband! Come from the Spirit World. Help me! Steady my arm.*

She nocked another of the iron-tipped arrows, drawing the bowstring back to her cheek.

There! That one...all painted red.

The bowstring twanged as the shaft flew home, catching the Ree low, in the soft spot above the genitals. He dropped to his knees, clawing at the wood.

Now, another.

She missed as a dodging warrior skipped out of harm's way.

A bullet whacked into the tree she hid behind, splintering bark. Willow nocked an arrow, drawing and searching for her target. A Ree warrior was pouring powder into the barrel of his gun, casting anxious glances her way as he spat a bullet into the muzzle and thumped the rifle butt down on the ground to seat the load.

Is that who shot at me?

Willow shifted, sighting down the slim shaft. The warrior tapped powder into the pan and snapped the frisson shut, raising his fusee. Willow released, and the warrior screamed as he twisted out of the arrow's path.

Willow ducked back behind her tree, pulled another arrow from the quiver, nocked it, peered out from the other side as she took up the tension on the string.

He was stalking forward, a young man wearing a breechclout. Yellow paint streaked his cheeks, and a black line had been drawn down his forehead, along his nose, and over his lips and chin. A patchwork of burn scars covered his right arm. Excitement and fear shone in his black eyes as he lifted the trade gun.

Willow began to raise her bow, to draw... Too late. He was sighting down the barrel, squinting as she looked into his eye across the sights. That instant froze, eternally engraved in Willow's mind. The sounds of combat grew distant, oddly muted as she stared at her death.

He jerked and sagged in the instant before the fusee jetted fire-laced blue smoke. The boom mixed with a hissing rip as the ball cut air beside her. Willow stared, paralyzed, watching the warrior collapse onto his left side. His expression was disbelieving, his mouth rounded into an O, eyes wide as he slammed into the ground.

He floundered, trying to rise, then looked down at his leg, bent at an angle and spurting blood and meat where a ball had torn through.

In those long moments, Willow could only gape, as if there and not there.

She willed herself to draw the arrow back to her cheek, her hold wavering. Her body might have been a dream.

More from instinct than skill, she made the shot, her arrow driving deeply into the Ree's chest.

He flinched at the impact, mouth working silently as he clamped his eyes shut and tried to squirm away. One hand gripped the slim shaft, the other propped him. Then he looked into her eyes, his soul pleading with hers.

Willow swallowed hard, shook her head, and tore herself from the horror. Screams and shouts mixed with banging muskets. She plucked another arrow, and scuttled back around her tree.

Wounded Rees were hobbling away from the fighting, but here and there a man lay on the ground. She noted at least two *engagés* with feathered shafts, like oversized cactus spines, sticking from their bodies. Whimpers and frightened screams mixed with war cries and curses.

The breeze blew strands of hazy blue gunsmoke past the milling Rees. They hesitated—and Green saw his opportunity to charge forward, swinging his gun like a club. Another of the warriors jerked, head exploding, as Baptiste's rifle boomed.

Willow's last arrow grazed a warrior's back as he turned to flee.

From the corner of her eye, she caught sight of horses, two of them racing out of the trees, riders bent low, one screaming a howling war cry. *Travis!* He rode into the middle of the Rees, lowered the barrel of his

Hawken, and blew a warrior's chest open. Richard cut right, having trouble keeping his seat on the bucking white mare. Taking a chance, he tried to slide off, but was piled on his rear. As he scrambled for his feet, she saw the arrow plunge like a silver streak into his back.

No! Tam Apo, *not Ritshard!*

A cry built in Willow's throat as she dropped her bow and pulled the war club from her belt. In a dreamlike reality, she raced forward, shouting, "Ritshard!"

Richard had found his Hawken, and from a seated position, shot the warrior who rushed at him. Then he was on his feet, swinging his rifle at the Rees who closed around him.

A single warrior stopped, glanced at her, and then at Richard. He raised a short Nor'west gun, the stock studded with shining brass tacks. Pivoting on his heel, he made his choice and aimed at Richard.

Too far! Willow threw her club like a rabbit stick; the weapon—spiraling so slowly in the air—hung in her frantic vision like a thing alive. Then it thumped hollowly on the man's shoulder, bouncing up like a wounded bird and arcing into the grass.

The thunderous boom of the gun deadened her souls as she dived right, caught up the club, and rushed headlong. Sobs tore at her throat as she attacked the half-crouched warrior. His teeth were clamped, face twisted with pain. He jabbed at her with the smoking rifle. She danced to the side. He parried her whistling war club with a forearm, the impact snapping his bone.

Fury boiled within as she rose on tiptoes and swung the club again, and again, splintering the bones in his arms, crushing his face, skull, and throat.

In the comer of her vision, she saw Richard drop to his knees, an anguished expression on his pale face. She howled her rage through gritted teeth as she threw herself at a Ree who charged down on Richard with a raised tomahawk. The man saw her, slashing at her at the last minute. She blocked his first blow, barely blocked the second, and stumbled backward. His black eyes bored into hers as he lifted his hawk.

On impulse, Willow jabbed at his testicles, making him twist aside. She used a side-hand swing, as with the White man's ax. He leaped back, grinning at her, obsidian eyes sparkling with challenge. He jumped at her, feinted, and hammered her war club with an arm-numbing blow that staggered her. Like a cat, he pivoted, raising his hawk high—and a bullet hit him. She heard the meaty slap and snap of bone, watched his body jerk and collapse in a heap. He lay there, facedown in the grass. His feet slipped up and down, as if crawling, and his fingers opened and closed in the dusty grass. With each labored gasp, his lungs gurgled and rattled through the bullet holes torn in his chest wall. When he exhaled, frothy blood blew out the holes in crimson spray.

"We got 'em boys!" Travis shouted. "They's a-running, coons!"

Gasping for breath, Willow backed toward the groaning Richard, her club gripped tightly. She pulled back wild strands of hair and searched for another enemy. Her limbs shook. But the Rees had broken, fleeing back into the trees. Some carried wounded warriors, others tried to drag the dead—and gave it up as Travis whipped his ramrod from the barrel of his Hawken, primed the gun in one fluid motion, and shot one of the rescuers through the back.

As the last of them disappeared, Willow dropped her war club and crouched beside Richard. He was blinking at her, face blanched of all color. He reached up weakly, took her hand, and sighed. Then his eyes rolled up in his head and he collapsed.

"Don't die," she whispered in Shoshoni, easing him onto his side. The arrow had entered his back at an angle. During the fighting, it had snapped off just above his jacket. Willow pulled her knife and slit the heavy leather.

The iron point had cut a gash across his back and embedded in the ridge of the shoulder blade. She grimaced, steeled herself, and prodded the flesh around the arrow. The soft iron had bent when it lodged in the bone. Blood was welling up and dribbling down his back.

"Willow?" Travis leaned down beside her. His hat was gone, gray hair awry. The blue eyes gleamed with excitement, then dulled as he realized what she was doing. "Aw, damn. Not Dick!"

A gun banged behind them as Green shot a writhing warrior. The man jerked and fell limp. One of Willow's arrows stuck out of his groin.

She hunched her shoulders, stomach queasy. "Got to pull this arrow, Travis. It's stuck in the bone. He's...how you say? Out? No better time than now."

"Yep, all right."

"Hold him."

Travis rubbed his hands together and put a foot on Richard's arm. "Go fast, gal."

Willow set herself, fingers on the blood-slick shaft. She pulled slowly, harder, and still harder, watching Richard's shoulder move up and out under the bloody jacket.

"Son of a bitch," Travis growled. "Yank hard, gal."

Don't let it break.

Willow threw her weight against the arrow, fingers slipping on the clotted blood.

Richard came to and bellowed with pain, his body jumping and jerking like a spitted frog's.

"Have ter cut," Travis said.

"Dear Lord God!" Richard cried out, chest heaving. "Hurts, oh God—oh God!" He swallowed hard, lungs heaving as sweat beaded and trickled.

Another gunshot split the air and a wounded Ree was dispatched. Willow closed her eyes, nodding. "I'll cut. Hold him."

"Baptiste? Anybody! Git yer arse over hyar!"

Willow barely noticed Toussaint as the big man came and clamped his thickly muscled arms around Richard.

"Two are dead," Toussaint growled.

"Damn! Dick, she's gonna hurt like all hell," Travis whispered soothing tones into Richard's ear. "Ye ain't dying, child. Hear me? That point just stuck in the bone's all. Willow's gonna dig it out."

"Do it, Travis." Richard panted, eyes gone glassy.

Willow glanced down at the knife in her bloody hand.

His blood. My skill. Tam Apo? *Can I do this? Is my Power strong enough?*

She met Travis's questioning eyes and nodded.

"Hyar we go, coon. Hold on, Dick. Scream if'n ye got ter."

Willow sliced the skin around the shaft, and Richard made a gurgling sound deep in his throat.

"Sacré!" Toussaint hissed, looking away.

Willow used the tip of the knife like a digging stick, slipping down through the meat to the smooth iron of the bent arrowhead. Where it had driven into the bone, she used the knife to pry. Richard screamed and bucked.

"Be still, coon," Travis soothed.

Willow ground her teeth, eyes closed.

Don't think about it. You can't let yourself think. Just do it, Willow. No other choice.

She pressed the knife deeper, levering the arrowhead loose from the bone. A blood-curdling shriek tore from Richard's throat.

Sinking back on her haunches, Willow lifted the arrow free, gazing at the clotted mess of bent iron. Sunlight gleamed on bright red blood.

"We're done, coon," Travis murmured, patting the limp Richard. "Yer fine." To Toussaint, he said, "Get pressure on that hole. We got ter stop that bleeding *beaucoup rapide.*"

Willow gulped air, the world around her in extraordinary, perfect focus. Sweat trickled down her skin, and she barely heard the buzzing of the big black flies that came at the first hint of blood. "Spirit water," she said. "Travis. Bring some."

"Fer his wound."

She nodded. "Yes. You know how to tie it up tight?"

"Yep, I know." The hunter stood. "Hell, whiskey's ter be poured inta a coon, not on him."

"It healed you."

"Aw, I remember." Travis gave her a measuring stare.

"Willow?" Green called. "If you're done there, I got another one over here."

She bent down, running a bloody finger along Richard's perspiring jaw. In *Dukurika,* she said, "Live for me, Ritshard. Live."

Standing, she drew a deep breath, and started across the war ground toward Etienne, who grimaced over an arrow transfixing his thigh. Behind him sat Trudeau, blood streaming in sheets down one side of his head. As she passed, she glared her hatred at the dead Rees—especially the ones with her arrows sticking in them.

———

Travis winced as Willow dribbled whiskey on Dick's wound. He glanced at Dave Green, who stood nearby with his arms crossed. Green's blunt face betrayed his disapproval of the waste. Whiskey was a valuable commodity, not to be squandered on foolishness like wounds. But Willow insisted. If it made her happy and kept her with the boat, Dave would probably have agreed to dump it into the river.

Richard moaned and hunched as the sting brought him out of his delirium.

"Shhh!" Willow said as she bent over him. "Easy, Ritshard. The spirit water will burn the evil out of your body." Then she sang to him, the soft Shoshoni song lulling him.

"Pretty bad," Green muttered. "I've seen wounds like that turn sour and kill a man."

"Wal, 't'ain't festering yet," Travis noted.

"Hell of a waste of good whiskey," Green growled under his breath.

The grassy bank slid past as the *engagés* poled *Maria* against the current. "Two dead, three wounded. Could'a been a sight worse, Dave. All considered, we been damn lucky so far."

"Baptiste says there's more Rees up ahead." Green

fingered his square chin. "They're watching, you know. Waiting."

Travis narrowed an eye, thinking of the tension among the *engagés* as they plodded down the *passe avant* behind their poles. They didn't sing today. They were dwelling on the two graves they left behind.

Willow sighed and stood up, her gaze on Richard. Her expression had softened, betraying the ache in her heart. Travis bit his lip, thinking back, remembering the last time a woman had looked at him with such love in her eyes.

No, coon. Forget. Leave the dead buried. Your time for love is past.

Willow had turned to Etienne. He lay beside Dick, his leg bare to expose the ugly hole cut through his thigh by a Ree arrow. Trudeau sat behind, his back propped against the cargo box. Willow had sewed his scalp closed where a knife had laid it open.

"What if ye hadn't turned 'em back?" Travis asked suddenly. "Remember what happened to William Ashley back in twenty-three?"

"Yes, yes, but that didn't stop him. He took off west with what was left of his brigade. Travis, Ashley's been out trapping, making plews. We've got to reach the Yellowstone, establish ourselves at the mouth of the Big Horn. The time is now, or Ashley will have it all."

"If'n he's still alive." Travis chewed his lip. A coldness washed his soul. "Remember that dream I told ye about? The one where Immel and Jones come ter me? Warned me off from going ter the mouth of the Big Horn? Set the collywobbles ter this child's bones, it did." He remembered the look in Michael Immel's eyes, so mournful and sad. He and Jones had been killed by the cussed Blackfeet—just up from the mouth of the Big Horn.

"You were wounded, Travis. The fever comes on a man, makes him see lots of nonsensical things." Green placed a hand on his shoulder. "You're not losing your nerve, are you?"

"Hell, no!" Travis brushed off the offending hand and glared. "But in this country, a coon's got ter think. Stop thinking, stop being wary as a lamb in the lion's den, and yer gone beaver. That fight with the Rees, it could'a been a heap worse, ye know. Boats can be swarmed."

Green lifted an eyebrow. "I won't let them have it, Travis. I worked too hard for this."

"What are ye thinking, Dave? I know that slit-eyed stare, and it's plumb shore yer a thinkin' about being bull-headed, or this coon don't read sign."

"I was remembering the *Tonquin*."

"Tarnal hell, ye wouldn't!"

"Oh, indeed I would, Travis. You know the story?"

"Who don't? Jacob Astor sent the *Tonquin* 'round the Horn to the mouth of the Columbia to meet up with Stuart's Astorians. That Captain, Thorn, got too high an' mighty with the Injuns, and they swarmed the ship. Story is that after the Injuns kilt most of the crew, some coon set off the powder and blew the whole shitaree to hell." Travis shook himself.

Willow straightened from examining Etienne's leg and walked over. "He will be fine. I think he can walk in another couple of days." But worry reflected in her eyes when she glanced at Richard.

Green took a deep breath, betraying his dour thoughts. "Well, at least you're safe. Willow, thank you for your help." He gave her a sheepish grin. "I don't know what we'd have done without you."

"And maybe it's put an end to this foolishness of traipsing off fer the mountains," Travis growled.

Willow stepped past them, her long hair catching the sunlight. She sat herself on the deck, back braced on the cargo box as far as she could get from Trudeau.

Travis settled beside her and manfully avoided staring at the smooth brown leg exposed below the hem of her hide dress.

She sat silently for a while, eyes unfocused. Green stood uncertainly, thumbs stuck in his belt as he rocked back and forth.

"This isn't my place," she said simply. "By now people will have realized that I am missing. They'll be worried. My aunt, Two Half Moons, told me not to travel in the winter."

"We'll take you to your people," Green promised.

Travis caught the tightening around the corners of her mouth and asked, "Why'd ye take the chance?"

Willow shrugged. "My husband's brother, White Hail, wanted to marry me. So did Fast Black Horse, one of the important warriors among the *Ku'chendikani*."

"Among the Snakes, ain't it accepted that a man marry his dead brother's wife?"

Willow nodded. "Yes. But I did not want White Hail for a husband. I will always love him, but as *teci,* a brother —not as *kuhappi,* a husband. I knew him as a happy young man, brave to the point of foolishness. I would have soured the happiness that now dances between his souls."

"How's that?" Green asked.

She gave him a measuring glance. "Like a hide wrapped around his head, I would have smothered him. Besides, I would have been a second wife—and I can tell you, his first wife, Red Calf, hated me. To marry White Hail would have caused much trouble. I suppose that now I could have dealt with it. But not then, not with my souls hurt and grieving over my husband's death. There are times to fight—and times to leave. That was a time to leave." She smiled wryly. "I usually know when to leave."

Travis asked, "And this Two Half Moons? She wouldn't have stood up for ye?"

A bitter smile crossed her lips. "Who listens to an old woman? People are people everywhere. Packrat took me to give to his father—to pay him back for an old wrong. My people are no better than the Pawnee. Red Calf would have made me miserable." She paused. "I fear she will drive poor White Hail to his death as it is. I couldn't stay in my husband's village and watch that happen."

"It doesn't sound like you've got a lot to go back to." Green lifted a blond eyebrow.

Willow said, "Oh, but I do. I miss my mountains, the colors of the earth, the smell of the wind. And I have my father, mother, and family. My souls are dry and wilted, like poor plants under a summer sun. The plant is made well with rain, and my souls will become healthy again when I can dance the Father Dance with my family."

Green smacked his hands together. "Well, if it's dancing you need, we can—"

"Dave, I *need* the high places, to be able to see forever and reach for the sky." The longing grew in her voice. "Way up in the mountains there is a tall rock that stands up like a peg. The sides are sheer, but the top is flat. When I was a little girl, I climbed to the top and saw the world as Eagle sees it. Power filled me there, changed my life. I want to climb that rock again and reach up. Perhaps...just maybe, I can touch *Tam Apo* and..." She gazed up at the sky.

"And what?" Travis asked gently.

"Heal myself," she whispered.

CHAPTER SIX

Morality requires nothing except that freedom should not contradict it, and also that, although we may be unable to understand it we should at least be able to think of it, for there is no reason why freedom should interfere with the natural mechanism of the moral act, even if taken in a different sense. The doctrine of morality may very well hold its place, and the doctrine of nature may hold its place, too. This would have been impossible if our critical examination had not previously taught us about our inevitable ignorance with regard to things in themselves, and limited everything that we can know in theory to mere appearances.

—Immanual Kant, *Critique of Pure Reason*

Richard lay on Maria's hard oak deck, his blanket the only padding. A soul-burning pain lanced his shoulder. Etienne lay next to him, and beyond that, Trudeau sat propped against the cargo box, a bloody rag wrapped around his head. Despite

Willow's stitches, the scar would be a beauty.

What have I become? Is sanity gone from the earth?

This land was so different from Boston. Here the meaning of death had changed. By killing, he had saved Willow from slavery—saved the boat and the *engagés* from the Ree. What was right any more?

Richard shifted, the pain in his shoulder making him gasp. Thought-numbing pain. He'd spent the last couple of days in a haze of misery and bleary dreams.

But I'm alive.

The unlucky ones had been August Torme and Vincent Saint-Michel. They now lay buried in two shallow graves back at the battle site. If the coyotes didn't dig them out, the current would eventually undercut the bank and topple their bones into the river. As *voyageurs,* perhaps they wanted to be there anyway.

The fight had given birth to a grim determination in the crew that Richard hadn't seen before. Now the *Maria* was snugged to the bank by her painter, the *engagés* ashore cooking the evening meal. The breeze blowing down from the north eased some of the torment caused by the clouds of mosquitoes.

As he lay belly-down on the hard oak, hazy images slipped around behind Richard's closed eyelids: the scene on the riverbank as he and Travis rode in; the popping guns; arrows hissing through the air; and the screams of men in mortal combat. He remembered his mare going crazy, his falling off...and the angry pain in his shoulder.

He'd fumbled for the rifle, lifting it, setting the trigger and shooting the Indian who came rushing down like a wrathful demon to kill him. It remained so vivid: The gun's concussion; blue smoke billowing; and the Indian falling away, mouth open, eyes wide with shock.

He'd seen Travis shoot and bellow, crack a head with his Hawken barrel.

So I got up and fought.

He remembered the Rees circling, trying to get close enough for coup before they killed him. He'd broken one skull with the heavy rifle barrel, blocked a blow, driven the barrel into another man's face, stepped back, and knocked the teeth out of another man's mouth with the rifle butt.

Then what? He frowned, unwilling to take a deep breath. Filling his lungs turned the throbbing ache into soul-numbing agony.

Then what? Come on, Richard. You were there.

Things seemed to blur. *I fell...no, dropped to my knees, the gun...so heavy...*

...And Willow, standing over him, her bloody war club raised to protect him. Yes, that was it. The image had burned into his brain: her leather dress, wet, clinging like a second skin. Blood on her hands, spattered on her face in a freckled pattern. Her hair tumbled around her in wild raven strands. She might have been one of the Greek Furies, teeth bared in her beautiful face as she dared anyone to challenge her.

"You were magnificent," he whispered, savoring the image. "Magnificent."

"Thank ye, coon. I figgered that meself."

"Travis?" Richard started, only to have the pain drop him flat. "Damn!" God, that hurt.

"Ain't every day I get called magnificent."

Richard lifted a weary eyelid to see the hunter settling himself cross-legged and, from a leather sack, dumping out little piles of bloody hide, all bearing long black hair. Fetishes?

"How're ye feeling, coon?"

Richard closed his eye and sank into the anonymous darkness. "I think I'm ready to die, Travis. No more fights, no thirst, no running for days on end. The dead can rest—and by all-merciful God, I've never been so damned tired in all my life."

"Yer a game one, ye is. The way we figgered it, ye kilt three Rees back there. Not so good as Willow, she plumb made 'em come, she did. Now, them's some doings, but then she just ain't any old squaw, neither."

"That's a double negative."

"A duh...huh?"

"Double negative. Two no's cancel each other in a sentence."

"Hot damn, yer feeling better!"

"Go away and let me die."

"Cain't. Willow's been a-doctoring ye. She's got ye trussed up like a hog fit fer butchering. And ye otta heard the row she and Green got inter over the whiskey. Green told her no more whiskey, and she like ter lit inta him worse than them Rees did."

"What?"

"Oh, it ain't the way she's using it—though Green and me, we figger whiskey goes inta a coon instead of on him —but how much she's using. Why, that gal pours a half a gill on yer shoulder each time she fools with that binding on yer wound. Cuss me if'n I ain't sure it's helping. Ain't a lick of fever in there, and it's healing right pert."

Richard sighed wearily. "You're not the one getting it poured on you. Firewater's right. I'd rather be shot again."

"Reckon ye ain't fergot her digging that arrow outa yer back?"

Richard blinked. "Arrow?"

Travis pointed at him with the knife he was using to

scrape the fetish. "Who do ye think carved that arrow outa yer back? Willow, that's who. And she done a plumb fine job of it. Hell, I looked at that arrowhead. Took three of us—and one being Toussaint—ter dig that out. Made a hell of a hole. Now, if'n Green or me'd a done it, I'd figger ye five-ter-one fer wolfmeat by now."

Richard rubbed his cheek against the scratchy wool of his blanket. "Anyone ever tell you you talk too much?"

"If'n it was anyone, it was Baptiste or ye." The rasping sound of the knife continued.

"Willow saved me?"

"Reckon so, coon. Henri saw most of it. Said one of them Rees was gonna shoot yer lights out, and she throwed her war club. Made it shine, she did. Bounced it right off the coon's back and ruined his shot. Then she scooped it up quick like and whacked that coon down dead. Then she fought with another one until I shot a galena pill inta his lights. After that, she stood over ye like a she bear over a cub."

Richard swallowed, wincing. Breathing hurt. Swallowing hurt. He could move his feet, a little, but that hurt, too.

Richard carefully extended his chin, wishing he could lie any way but on his belly. "More fetishes? Those look pretty fresh, like they..."

It all came clear.

"Yep. Fresh batch of skunks."

"You *son of a bitch!*"

"If that don't beat all hell? I was plumb magnificent a moment ago." Travis continued to stare down his nose as he scraped human hide with the edge of his knife.

"*Damn you!* I've been wearing a man's scalp on my belt? Why'd you do that to me? To humiliate me!"

"Nope."

"You *knew* how I'd feel about it!"

"Yep."

"Why, Travis?"

"Why? Oh, I reckon I'd never seen a philos'pher with a coup tied on him."

"So, you had your joke?"

"Wal, Dick, ye just kind of set yerself up fer it. Get where my stick floats? All that jawboning about being a gentleman. Made it right interesting ter hear yer hammering on about Kant and Plato—and all the while Packrat's hair was a swinging from yer belt."

Baptiste came up from behind. "How's the sick doing?"

"Hamilton, hyar, he's figgered out about the coup."

"I'm not laughing," Richard growled.

"Why, child," Baptiste crooned, "you know, with all your talk about jumping ship and running, Travis figured you'd be hair today and gone tomorrow."

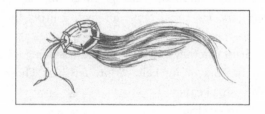

Richard gritted his teeth, reaching down with one hand to finger the long hair. Cut from Packrat's skull. *The boy I killed.* He couldn't untie it from this angle. "Get it *off* me."

The hunter gave him a mild look. "I ain't sure I'd do that, Dick. Seems ter me, that coup brung ye a sight of luck. Specially with them Sioux coons, and now, why hyar I've gone and skinned them Ree ye sent under. Hyar's three more fer yer belt. Nope. Ye wants 'em off, take 'em off yerself."

"Why, Dick," Baptiste added cheerfully, "that was one mighty fine Scalp Dance old Wah-Menitu throw'd fo' you. Soah 'nuff made the trade go slick, and the last thing we needed was that band of Teton Dakota thinking we's like that damned Leavenworth."

"If I could get up, I'd beat the piss right out of you." Richard clenched his fists despite the pain in his back.

"Best be on yer uppers." Travis chortled. "I didn't larn ye all of my fighting tricks. Now, what about these hyar Ree topknots? Want 'em tied on with that cousin Pawnee on yer belt? Reckon the Crows'll see 'em and throw a right whoopee shindig fer ye."

"Throw them overboard."

"He shoah don't seem to have no sense of high honor, Travis," Baptiste said mildly.

"Wal, now, he just ain't chipper, Mister de Bourgmont. Ye know how a coon goes a mite sour when his back's all laid open. Collywobbles the mind. He'll come around right quick soon's his meat heals."

"I'm *not* a savage!"

"Nope. Just shot the lights outa that Packrat. Danced the liver outa the Sioux. Beat the hell outa Trudeau. Run down a pack of Crow hoss thieves and snuck yer hosses back, and kilt three Rees what was gonna lift yer hair, kill yer woman, and send yer friends under. Boston doings, I tell ye. Plumb Boston!"

"Why, Mistah Hamilton," Baptiste said in a most reasonable voice, "I still ain't heard a single coon in this heah party call you 'Old Sculplock Dick.'"

Richard closed his eyes and groaned. "You wouldn't."

"Might."

He had to change the subject before Baptiste and

Travis had time to think about the Sculplock name, and how to make it stick. "What about the Rees? They've got a village up here, don't they?"

"Passed 'em." Travis looked up. "Baptiste? I'd be mighty obliged if'n ye'd fetch me pipe."

"Reckon I could. Why, I might light a bowl for myself. Dick? You want a smoke?"

"God, I'd kill for a bowl. In my possibles...wherever they are."

Baptiste's feet padded down the *passe avant*.

"So?" Richard asked. "How'd we get past the Ree villages?"

"One of the chiefs. Bear. He come down and palavered. Being a Ree, he blamed it all on one of the other chiefs. Said he'd made peace with Atkinson and O'Fallon, but he couldn't speak for the other *Nesanus*. His warriors escorted us past the Ree villages. Tomorrow we'll be to the Mandans. Safe sailing from there up past the Hidatsa villages a couple of days north."

"How long have I been lying here?"

"Three days. Willow's been keeping an eye on ye. Fever's had ye, but mostly ye've slept."

"Three days?"

"Yep."

"And Willow?"

Travis fingered the Ree scalp. "She's gonna see ye through. Then, once we're up past the Hidatsa, she says she's leaving. Going home."

Richard pursed his lips. In a low voice he asked, "Where is she?"

"Setting up camp and cooking a pot of something she dug outa the ground. Smells right keen, it does."

"She's a good woman." Richard swallowed hard. "I

wish...I wish she'd wait. You know, until you could make sure she was safe. Can't you talk her into that, Travis?"

"Nope. And I ain't gonna, 'cause she don't love me. But then, just as soon as I smoke this bowl Baptiste's bringing me, I reckon I'll go try and talk her inta my blankets again."

"Good." Richard lied and clamped his eyes shut against a different kind of pain.

"What? No lecture about what a snake I be at heart?"

Richard barely shook his head. "No. Because I don't know what's right any more."

———

Willow sat in her usual place, propped against the front of the cargo box. To either side, the *engagés* leaned into their poles, thrusting *Maria* against the sluggish current. They were singing again, spirits buoyed by their proximity to the Mandan. Faint traces of breeze stroked Willow's cheek in the mildest of caresses.

The boat moved slowly up the river, stilting along on its wooden poles. Overhead, a flight of ducks flapped past in a flurry of wings. The river seemed closely hemmed by the wall of trees that overhung the banks. The blazing orb of the sun had burned the sky white. Flies buzzed and dragonflies skimmed the water, stopping to hover over the boat before darting away. Richard and Etienne lay under a sunshade that Baptiste had rigged from a blanket, poles, and line. Both now slept, Richard restlessly, while Etienne snored happily.

Willow's head dropped lower onto her chest The sun's warmth loosened her muscles, eased the tension in her souls. The gentle rocking of the boat soothed her. The *engagés* sang:

> *J'ai cueilli la belle rose,*
> *J'ai cueilli la belle rose,*
> *Qui pendait au rosier blanc,*
> *La belle rose.*

Her souls drifted with the song, sinking away from wakefulness and into the hazy margins of sleep...

...Through the misty fragments of dreams, eyes stare at me. I know that face. With recognition comes a terrible unease; it's the Ree warrior who tried to kill me. I shot him as he lay wounded and disbelieving while pain and death crept through his body and drove away his souls.

From the hollows within, Coyote wails and mocks me. I hear shouts, gunshots. Men are running, heads thrown back as they shriek their war cries. Moment by moment, I relive the Ree battle, seeing my arrows slice through warm flesh. I see the warriors' stunned expressions as the realization of death pierces them as sharply as the arrows.

I killed them.

How heady it feels...and how hollow. Warrior's blood runs in my veins—as does the healer's. These Rees were enemies who would have killed my people. At the moment of the attack, my blood took over. Puha, *Spirit Power, guided me through the fighting, and, later, to care for the wounded.*

It swelled within me as I grasped the arrow sticking in Richard's shoulder. I look down at the blood on my hands, feel the slim shaft, sticky with Richard's blood.

Once, I would have been horrified by such responsibility for death and life. What has happened to me?

In the days before I watched my husband and son die, I would have acted differently, waited for directions rather than leaped to battle.

I have changed, loosened my *puha.*

It started with the death of my family. And I changed more while I was Packrat's slave. We fought—he and I—a battle of wills and puha. In the end I killed his Pawnee soul, broke him, and left him ready to die.

How does it make you feel, Willow, to know that you can kill a man's spirit?

A chill wind blew in her soul.

Red Calf, your brother's wife, once called you a witch, Willow. Did she see more clearly than you do?

What effect have these fascinating and dangerous White men had on me? I have seen life through their eyes and experienced their marvels. But what are they? Evil spirit beings? Or good?

When I looked into the eye of Richard's soul, he looked back, unafraid, seeking to touch my souls with his.

Pain, grief, fear, and danger have acted like fire, hardening me as flame does the point of a digging stick.

A long howl rises to mingle with my souls. The sound is very clear, as if cleaving through still and frosty air—the howl of Wolf, and all that means after Coyote's mocking laughter.

I hear your call, Wolf. You have done this to me, haven't you? You put me through these trials.

The long howl drifts away until it is nothing but echoes, and

I can see him now, staring at me with hard yellow eyes. The round-tipped ears are pricked, the broad nose quivering. His long ruff is frost-tipped, full and soft.

What do you want from me. Wolf? Haven't I given you everything?

And what about Richard? Once I saw him in my dreams, a dancing, white-mist dog. But he has changed, become something different. What is Wolf's purpose with Richard? Or, is Richard Coyote's creature? How am I to know?

As I ask, Wolf's face changes, the eyes darkening. The ruff merges into long black braids. The muzzle flattens, becoming a man's face with high cheekbones and a broad jaw. The nose is broad and strong, so familiar that I...

I know you now. *High Wolf,* puhagan *of the Dukurika.* Hello, Father. I have missed you.

He smiles slowly, keen anticipation in his eyes, as if I should know something that momentarily eludes me.

Father, where are you? Why have you come to me in this way?

But he says nothing. The smile grows wistful enough to twist the heart in my chest.

Father? what's wrong?

I know that look of his—I saw it often when I was a girl. He looks this way when something precious has been lost forever.

Who, Father? Who is lost to you forever? I don't understand.

Father's image fades. I wring my hands, pacing in my dream.

It's not me, Father. I'm coming home. You'll see. I'll be there soon. I promise. Don't mourn me.

Then I hear the laughter, and turn. My souls shrink back, and I place a hand to my breast. Packrat stands there, haughty, and behind him are the Ree warriors. I try to back away from the ghosts, but there is nowhere to flee They are pointing at me and laughing.

A sharp cry brought Willow out of the dream. She jerked her head up, and blinked. The *engagés* were looking up toward the bank as they poled the craft forward.

Willow winced, straightening her cramped limbs, and stood, shading her eyes with a flat palm as she stared up at the grassy terraces west of the river. Travis and Baptiste rode guard on the horse herd that paralleled the boat's progress. Baptiste threw his head back and bellowed a loud *"Yaaa-Hoooo!"* a call Willow had come to know meant happiness.

Travis was pointing. She followed his hand, and saw six or seven mounted Indians, who charged across the flats in a gallop. Travis and Baptiste trotted their horses out to meet them. Sunlight flashed off their rifle barrels and caught the dance of their long fringes.

Willow's first instinct was fear, for after all, anyone not her own kind was most likely an enemy—and she still didn't understand the portents of her dream.

"Who's that?" Green called from the cargo box.

"Les Mandan!" Henri whooped. "We have lived to see the Mandan!"

A joyous cry went up from the *engagés,* and they bent to their poles with new vigor.

The riders had pulled up amidst milling horses and Travis leaned out from his saddle to shake the warriors' hands.

Willow slumped against the cargo box. *Yes, I know these Mandan. They take Shoshoni women...and make slaves of them.*

She'd had enough of slavery at Packrat's hands.

―――――

The excitement could be felt, electric, like static in the air. It added to Richard's frustration as he lay forgotten on the foredeck. By craning his neck until his back pained him, he could see the *engagés* hustling back and forth from the rear of the cargo box. Busy as ants with breadcrumbs, they were rearranging cargo under Henri's careful direction. Some of the stocks would be traded with the Mandan for food, moccasins, hunting shirts, and other necessities.

Still a half-day's journey from the main village, the *Maria* lay snubbed by her painter to a cottonwood log buried like a crooked thumb in the point of a long sandbar that curled out into the river. It was a defensible position. Despite the well-known friendliness of the Mandan, Green was taking no chances. Guards were stationed on the top of the cargo box.

From his vantage, Richard could see out over corn-fields that gleamed golden in the afternoon sun. Here and there, he could make out Mandan women moving among the stalks, sometimes with black-headed children in tow.

Travis and Dave Green had ridden ahead on horse-back to talk to an American trader at Mitutanka village. A pre-scout, as Travis had explained it. A way of discovering the current disposition of the Mandan toward whites, and the critical location of the Atkinson-O'Fallon expedition.

Richard gritted his teeth and tried to move his right arm forward. Stitches of pain brought beads of sweat to his face, but he inched his arm ahead. Little by little, he managed to gain some movement, but each inch was bought with pain and tears.

If I can run down Crow horse thieves, I can stand this.

And he'd sink teeth in his lip to do it all over again.

The trick was to exercise the shoulder without tearing the wound.

I won't be any cripple.

That promise circulated around and around in his head.

He ignored the soft whisper of moccasins on the deck until they stopped beside him.

Panting from the effect of moving his arm, Richard looked up. Trudeau stood there, leering down, muscular arms crossed. The garish scab on the side of his head was peeling to expose wound-pink beneath.

"*Bonjour.* You are better, *oui?*"

"Yes, better." Richard stared up at his old tormentor through narrowed eyes. Then it hit him that both Travis and Green were gone. If Trudeau were here for trouble, did he dare call out for Baptiste?

Trudeau lifted a lip to expose yellow teeth. He fingered his mauled ear, still puckered with scars. Richard quailed inside at the memory of Trudeau's ear clamped between his grinding teem.

"You 'ave marked me, *cochonnet.*"

"You started it."

Trudeau snorted. "Perhaps I kill you, eh? I 'ave not decided." He glanced toward the stern and the working *engagés.* "Some of the others, they no longer hate you." He slitted his black eyes. "But I do. To me you are a *chien sordide.*"

Richard licked his lips and shifted, raising on his good arm. "If you want another dose of what I gave you the last time, you just wait until this arm..."

Trudeau crouched down, his face inches from Richard's. "I could kill you now, *mon ami.* Who would know, eh?"

"They'd know." Richard bit back the urge to scream for help, forcing himself to meet Trudeau's eyes.

"*Possible.*" Trudeau nodded to himself. "You 'ave changed, Reeshaw. Grown tougher. No longer a *poltron.*"

"Am I supposed to thank you for your kind comments?"

Trudeau snorted his contempt.

"Trudeau!" Baptiste barked, walking along the *passe avant.* "I reckon you got work you otta be doing."

Trudeau smiled. In a low whisper, he added, "It is not over between us." Then he rose and knotted his fists, thick muscles bulging under his shirt. With a swagger, Trudeau jerked a nod at Baptiste and headed aft.

Richard lowered himself wearily to the deck where he gasped air into his oddly starved lungs. His back prickled and ached as though cactus thorns were being pushed and pulled through his flesh. He barely noticed when Baptiste settled beside him in a swirl of fringes.

"You all right?"

"Just a little tuckered." Richard blinked at the sweat. "And a little spooked, I guess. He could have.... Oh, never mind."

"Aw, he just be struttin', showing you ain't got him cowed. He ain't gonna cause no trouble. Not after that whupping you done give him."

"My God, Baptiste, doesn't it ever end?"

Baptiste cocked his head, pensive black eyes on the corn-rich shore beyond the gunwale. "End? What? Life, coon? Hell, no. It just go on and on, like the river. Ain't no end to it till you fetches up dead."

Richard ran a thumbnail along the wood grain in the deck. "I'm tired, Baptiste. I want to go home where things are sane and normal." He paused. "I never knew how good my life was."

Baptiste studied him from the comer of his eye. "Gonna make up with your pap?"

"Make up? How can I? I lost a fortune when François robbed me. You don't know my father. He keeps a loaded musket in his office. If I turned up without the money, he'd probably shoot me dead." He swallowed hard. "He thinks I'm a failure as it is. Why remove any doubt?"

"A man changes, Dick. You have. Shoa 'nuff, you ain't the same runt I fust met north of Atkinson. You shoah yor pap wouldn't just as soon have a son as his money?"

Richard frowned, remembering those hard gray eyes. But when he looked past the eyes, and saw the sagging flesh on his father's face, the stoop in the shoulders... "I'm not sure I know who my father is any more."

Baptiste pulled his hat off and wiped the sweat from his forehead with a sleeve. Sunlight glinted in his thick mane of kinky hair. "How's you raised, Dick? Didn't yor pap take you out, larn you things?"

"I was raised, for the most part, by Jeffry, my father's manservant."

"He a slave?"

"Yes. And a good man, Baptiste. I'll free him when my father dies."

Baptiste's jaw muscles jumped as he ground his teeth. "You didn't tell me yor pap kept slaves."

Richard gave the hunter a sly smile. "Jeffry does have a single-bitted ax, but I think he considers himself too much of a gentleman to use it."

"Secret is, he better keep a good edge on it. Keen, like, you see?"

"That's my father you're talking about."

Baptiste studied him through narrowed eyes. "I ain't got no spot in my heart foah a slaveowner, Dick. No matter who."

Richard nerved himself under Baptiste's hostile glare. "It's different for them. It's...well, like they're best friends. Like you and Travis, but more."

There was no give in Baptiste's eyes.

Dear God, how do I explain this?

"They just go together, Baptiste. You'd have to see them. Jeffry—he's my father's best friend. Probably his only friend."

"And he keep his friend a slave?"

A sour feeling churned in Richard's stomach. "Listen, I can't explain it, all right? You'd just have to know them."

The bitterness in Baptiste's eyes didn't give way.

"Baptiste, I'm sorry about my father. I don't approve of keeping slaves either. But, beyond that, if you got to know him, you'd..." What, Richard? Why are you protecting him? The thought left him uneasy.

"I'd like him?" Baptiste finished. "Dick, I ain't holding it again' you none, but this child don't see past the slavery."

As if a door had swung open, and he'd stepped into another room, Richard suddenly had an entirely different glimpse of his father. He took a deep breath. "Oh, you'd like him all right. He has as much courage, craftiness, and cunning as you do. He was a brave soldier in the Revolution. And even when a ball crippled his leg, he didn't give up. His father came to America in chains—like yours did."

"But he's lucky enough to be born white."

"He was, but to have what he has today, he had to risk his life, fight for what he believed. Just like you fought for what you believed. He's got the same iron resolve inside him that you do." Richard gave him a crooked smile. "Yes, you're a lot alike. Especially when it comes to being bullheaded."

The sintering glare abated just the slightest. "You teasing me?"

"I'm betting that you wouldn't thrash a cripple, even if he was a slaveowner's son."

"Don't you never make that bet, boy." Baptiste's lip twitched with a smothered grin. "You ain't that same owl-eyed Doodle I fust met."

Richard stared absently at the wood as he thought about Phillip Hamilton. What had it cost the old man to send Richard out into the world?

It must have scared him to death. Was that why he was so unforgiving that last morning in Boston?

Baptiste shook himself. "Well, hell, I can't free 'em all."

"No, but you can feel for them, can't you?"

The hard glint had finally drained from Baptiste's eyes. "Yep, that I can." He paused. "You tell me. How does yer pap live with hisself, knowing he owns another human being?"

"It's just the way it was, Baptiste. He grew up with the notion that it was all right. But, I'll tell you what, slavery's going to simply wither away and die. My father's an anomaly in Boston, a relic, if you will."

No wonder he hated my philosophy, my rejection of his world.

"Dear Lord, that's it!"

"Huh? What you saying?"

Richard propped his chin on his fist. "What fools we all are. No matter how we want to reinvent the world, we always do it from the pieces of the past. In my father's case, he hated the British gentry enough to go to war, but down in his heart, he envied them so much that he became just like them."

Baptiste lifted an eyebrow.

"Weren't you the one who said, 'Never go against yer pap'?"

"That's afore I larned he's a slaveholder. But that's all right, Dick. I'll try not to hold yoah pap against you."

Richard gave him a sly grin. "I'd appreciate that."

Baptiste stood. "I better shinny on back and make sure them *engagés* ain't loafing. If'n Trudeau gives you grief, you just sing out, hear?"

"Thanks, Baptiste." He barely heard the hunter go.

I defended my father. And, yes, if he and Baptiste could see each other clearly, they would like each other.

Richard shook his head, and pain laced his shoulder. *Father, you old pirate, for the first time, I think I understand you.*

In his imagination those terrible gray eyes had suddenly turned oddly brittle. To his amazement, the image left a hollow feeling in his gut.

CHAPTER SEVEN

It may peradventure be thought, there was never such a time, nor condition of war as this; and I believe it was never generally so, over all the world: but there are many places, where they live so now. For the savage people in many places in America, except the government of small families, the concord whereof dependeth on natural lust, have no government at all; and live at this day in that brutish manner, as I have said before.

—Thomas Hobbes, *Leviathan*

"Where's Atkinson and O'Fallon?" Green asked. He was canted back in a handmade chair across from a stone-cold metal heat stove—not that anyone needed heat on the first day of August.

Travis casually inspected the small trading post. He and Green had ridden ahead to speak with James Kipp, the trader who lived at Fort Tilton. It always paid to scout the country first, and Kipp would fill them in on the Indian situation—chancy at best—and the army's current location. Kipp would comply, once assured that Green didn't intend on cutting out a piece of the Mandan trade.

Fort Tilton consisted of a room made of rudely squared cottonwood timbers, saddle-notched, and haphazardly chinked with pale mud. Shelving, made of everything from split planks to pegs driven into the wall and wrapped with shrink-fit rawhide, hung from each wall. Blankets, tins of oil, kegs of powder, and bales of furs were stacked, stuffed, and crammed into every cranny. The only light entered through the doorway beyond the plank that served as a trading counter, and from the rifle loopholes cut through the logs. Kegs and tins were stacked best-luck along the walls.

Travis puffed blue clouds from his pipe as he eyed James Kipp, the trader who saw to the Mandan trade for the Columbia Fur Company. Unlike Pilcher, or the Chouteaus, Tilton hauled his goods in overland from Lake Traverse, far to the east. The sober-eyed Kipp was a "hiverner," a veteran winter man who'd stuck out the hard days after the Leavenworth disaster when the Rees had made everyone on the river miserable.

He's a canny old coon. Got ter be to last it out up hyar.

Kipp puffed at his pipe, feet up on a pressed bale of beaver. His leather pants had gone grease-black, contrasting to his newly made doe-brown moccasins. He wore a red flannel shirt, the collar unbuttoned to expose curly hair.

Kipp looked down his nose at the blue smoke rising in whorls, and said, "Atkinson and O'Fallon? Aw, they're up palavering with the Crow. They were here. When they weren't fighting with each other over every damned thing, they were making treaties right and left."

Travis relaxed. The worst fear had been that they'd be here, among the Mandan. Travis caught Green's eye, thinking, *Wal, Dave, leastwise we don't have ter run fer the boat, and drop back downriver till we can find us a hiding hole.*

"Fighting with each other?" Green asked, face like a mask. "You mean Atkinson and O'Fallon?"

Kipp slapped his leg as he laughed. "Yep. Atkinson give a bunch of gifts to the Mandan—but O'Fallon, why he's a fire-eater to start with, he wanted to wring some apologies out of Four Bears fer letting his young men side with the Rees when they shot up Ashley back in twenty-three. Atkinson and O'Fallon got so het up at each other they went at it with their dinner forks till the camp aides pulled 'em apart."

"Do tell?" Travis pulled at his beard. *If the leaders is busy fighting amongst themselves, they might not pay much heed ter rumors about a keelboat on the river.* "But they still made new treaties? How'd that work?"

"Like you'd expect. Everybody sat down to a big feast, then they squired that Peter Wilson around. You heard about him?"

"Uh-huh," Green growled. "The fancy new Indian factor or some such. General Clark sent him up to help pacify the river after that mess Leavenworth made of the Ree villages."

"Hell!" Kipp jabbed with his pipestem. 'Told everybody he's the new subagent—special for the upper river. He's a damn politician. Saint Loowee thick, if'n ye ask me. Mark me, boys, he'll take right smart care of the upper river...a-sitting in a damn office on Walnut Street!"

"Got any idea when they might turn downriver?" Green asked innocently.

Kipp sucked at his pipe, and shrugged. "Depends on how long the river Crow can keep convincing them to give out presents and foofawraw. Couple of weeks. Heard tell they wanted to make the mouth of the Yellowstone. More of that crazy talk of an army fort there."

"Army on the upper river?" Travis shook his head. Fool's business, fer sure. "They couldn't even keep them riflemen down ter Cantonment Missouri from starvation. Fort Atkinson's barely hanging on as 'tis. Talk is, they's gonna move the fort south, down toward the Blue somewhere. How in hell can they supply a fort up hyar? Injuns would plumb laugh themselves silly when them soldiers started eating their boots along about February."

"Reckon yer surefired right, coon." Kipp scratched his beard. "Aw, I don't know what the hell good they'd do. Look at what happened to you. Fresh damn treaty, ink ain't even dried, and the Rees jump yer boat."

"But Bear showed up the next day." Green waggled a mocking finger. "Said it wasn't his boys that hit us."

"...And got the ever-loving shit shot outa 'em," Travis added. He was watching Kipp poke a dirty finger into his mouth. He used the digit to wiggle one of his yellow teeth. "Can't trust a damn Ree, I tell ye. Fight ye one day, wipe yer blood off, and ask ye in fer dinner and a squaw the next."

"They're treacherous, all right," Kipp agreed, staring thoughtfully at the tip of his damp finger. "But, hell, they all are. Assiniboins kilt a couple of Mandans the other day. Party of Yanktonis run off a bunch of horses belonging to some Hidatsa. The Hidatsa talked a couple of Cheyenne into going along fer revenge. They ran across a party of Cree coming in to trade, and damned near killed 'em all. Now everybody's scared the Cree is gonna come down, and maybe join up with the Yanktoni. Who knows who's gonna die?"

"Some things never change," Green said, chuckling.

"But I'll bet Atkinson and O'Fallon are just happy as little larks at a bug hatching, making treaties right and left."

"Which are good until the feast is over, or the next party of Sioux ride across the horizon." Kipp laughed. For a moment, he made a face as he prodded his errant tooth with his tongue, then added, "Only a madman would try and make sense out of the upper river. Hell, I've seen times when the Mandan didn't have anybody else to kick, so the Amahamis picked a fight with the Mitutankas."

Travis sucked his lips, squinting at Kipp's mouth. *I could just up and pull that loose chomper of his. A pair of tongs and a good yank, and hell, it'd come out right smart, it would.*

"Ain't that the truth," Green muttered. "Hell, I heard about an Assiniboin chief got so carried away double-dealing, shifting alliances, and taking advantage that he found out he'd declared war on himself."

"So, what happened?" Kipp asked, the tooth momentarily forgotten.

"Why, he couldn't resist the opportunity to get one up, so he shot himself in the back, then his right hand hacked off his left just as it reached up to lift his scalp."

Travis slapped his knee. "This hyar Pete Wilson figured this out yet? That these folks like killing each other fer no reason?"

"Nope. Like I said, he's a Saint Loowee puff-and-strut. He's all blowed up with making peace treaties." Kipp knocked the dottle out of his pipe onto the dirt floor.

Then Kipp cut tobacco and tamped it into his pipe. The whole time, his tongue played with that tooth.

'Course, if'n it didn't come loose, a coon might need ter take his patch knife and pry it out by the root.

Teeth were always a problem. But then, God had

figgered that dodge out early on, which was why he put so cussed many in a feller's mouth to start with.

"Half yer stockade posts look fresh-planted outside in the palisade," Travis noted, to take his mind off the tooth.

"Yep. Moved 'em up a couple of weeks ago. Moved the whole post. Wanted to be a hair closer to Mitutanka village. Figgered I's a goner a couple of times these last years. Probably would have been, if old Four Men hadn't taken me clean into his lodge."

"Mandans are generally good folks." Green cocked his head. "Which brings us to the here and now."

Kipp lifted an eyebrow. "Yer not after my Mandan, are yer?"

"Nope. That's why we come here first. Travis told me you were a coon to ride river with. His word is good. Dealing straight, Kipp, we're going to spend a couple of days here. Rest the crew."

"Uh-huh." Kipp sucked at the offending tooth like it was rock candy. "And next spring they's gonna be another batch of blue-eyed babies born, and I'm gonna have to hear that damned crap about lost Welshmen again."

"That still flying around?" Travis asked.

"Goes clear back to Evans fifty years ago, or some such thing." Kipp turned his head and spat impressively in emphasis. "Some damned fool is born every day, ye know." He gave them a level glance as Travis, in vain, inspected the spittle for the tooth. "And then what, Dave?"

Green leaned back, taking a deep breath. "Then we head upriver."

Kipp studied Green. "How far?"

"Long ways." Green spread his hands.

"Three Forks?" Kipp glanced at Travis. "Naw, Trav. Yer

not that fool-stupid. Not after what happened to ye up to the Great Falls, and then Immel and Jones atop that. Ye've a heap more sense than that."

"We'll let ye know where we end up," Travis said with a grin. "That's plew to poor kit, I do swear."

"Sure, Travis." Kipp nodded reflectively. "Let me know when ye get there...and leave *my* Mandan alone."

"I give ye my *word*. Now, will ye let me yank that damn tooth *outa* there?"

Kipp gave him an oddly confused look, as did Green, who'd evidently missed the tooth entirely.

"Hell, no!" Kipp thundered. "Yer lucky enough I trust you around my Mandan, let alone around my damn mouth! It's my tooth and I'll do her as I will." He jabbed with the pipestem again. "And it just so happens that fiddling with it gives me something to do of an evening."

"Your Mandan trade is safe," Green said. "But you'd better be making plans, James. The Company's gonna be coming upriver after you. Pilcher's been licking his lips, and Chouteau's been dickering with Astor."

"Tilton and me, we got hyar first," Kipp claimed.

"Yep," Green said. "But the price of plews is going up. The big outfits have their eyes on the upper river. No telling who will stir up who. Things fall apart here, come on upriver. You never know—in this country, a coon might need a warm post to hole up in. That, or he could bet on which Injuns is fighting which other Injuns this week."

"Not on your life. Hell, just in the time we been talking, the Yanktoni's brokered a peace with the Ree and are planning on wiping out the Crow, who've just made an alliance with the Assiniboin."

"And ye can live like this?" Travis blurted.

"Well," Kipp mused as he returned to sucking his

tooth, "Injun trade is like three-card monte. A coon never knows which card'll turn up where. So far, Tilton and me, we've been watching the ace, and turning the right card up."

"Yep," Travis said thoughtfully. "But some coon will always come along with slicker fingers, and the dealer will slip ye a deuce."

And he couldn't shake the memory of the dream he'd had. The one where Lisa, Immel, and Jones had told him not to go to the mouth of the Big Horn.

———

The sun burned in a red-orange ball over the rounded bluffs west of the river. The slanting light softened the grassy slopes. Drainages lay in shadow, dark bur oak and brush creating the illusion of veins in the meat of the earth. Tasseled corn gleamed in the Mandan gardens, tall above squash and bean plants. The golden glow on the rounded Mandan houses within Mitutanka village cast a magical illusion of wealth and peace.

The Mandan had built this, their largest village, on a spur-like ridge that stuck out into a loop of the Missouri. With sheer bluffs and water on three sides, the location was defensible, and could be easily approached only from the southwest. Richard stared out from where he lay on the *Maria's* deck. The evening breeze carried faint cries and laughter from the village, and the dry scent of grass and eternity down from the western plains. He'd been out there, beyond the river, in the endless waves of golden grass rippling in the wind. In that vastness, he'd walked under the eye of God.

Was it really me who ran down the Crow? He could recall the fever of his aching muscles, the wretched thirst, the crushing fatigue. *But I made it. Travis kept me going, made me reach down inside to find the will to go on.*

On the bank, upside-down bull boats, like wounded turtles, cast humped shadows over the track-stippled mud. They'd made their landing here, upstream from a creek the Mandan called "Washing-the-Dishes." Just beyond that creek, his horses grazed, guarded by three Mandan boys.

One day in Boston, in the comfort of a drawing room, he would look into a crystal glass of sherry and tell the tale to a rapt audience of ladies and gentlemen. Would they believe him?

But he'd done it. Recovered his horses. That stubborn ember of pride burned bright through all the other confusions filling his head.

Willow rounded the corner of the cargo box on silent moccasined feet. He watched her, so lithe and graceful. A white woman didn't walk with that sinuous balance.

He smiled up at her. "I thought you'd be at the feast. That chief, the one they call Four Bears, is feeding everyone. They're going to dance, I hear."

"I came to see how you are before Travis and the others come." She dropped to her knees beside him. Her thoughtful expression betrayed a subtle sadness.

He eyed her warily. "Is something wrong?"

"I went with Travis and Green when we arrived here today. There, in the village, I saw several women. Slaves. Some were *Agaiduka,* another was *Ku'chendikani.* I knew her family."

Richard pillowed his chin on a knotted fist and stared out at the sun. It was sinking slowly behind the darkening irregular horizon. "Maybe we could buy them? Take them home?"

She raised her face, hollowness in her eyes. "They

would not go. They have children here, different lives to live. I talked to one who has been adopted into the Awatixa clan, and has bought rights into the White Buffalo Cow Society. I think these women have become more like the Mandan, and less like the Shoshoni."

She looks beautiful in the evening light.

He watched her, trying to engrave the sight into his memory: how the glow accented her bronze skin; the sleek black hair in regal cascades over her shoulders; slim hands clasped in her lap; and her eyes, so large and dark under the perfect brow.

Willow said, "Before I was taken from the mountains, I would not have believed that people could walk so many different paths. Richard, is it so impossible for us?"

He ran a finger along the wood grain of the worn deck. "I don't belong here." The warm lights of Boston, the gaiety and laughter of old friends called to him. "This isn't my place, Willow." He imagined himself in black broadcloth, standing at the lectern. Before him sat rows of bright-faced young men, eager to learn. "I have a different life back in Boston."

She sat silently, head bowed.

"Would you rather that I lied? Told you it would all work out? And then have me leave? Listen, life used to be so clear. I knew right from wrong. My philosophy books gave me everything I needed to make decisions about life. I knew who I was, and what I was. Where I fit into the universe." He pulled at his long hair. "But nothing that I believed seems right any more."

"Maybe it wasn't really right in the beginning."

"Everything has become hopelessly tangled. Willow. I have to find Truth again."

"And this Laura? The woman in Boston? Is your heart for her?"

He ground his teeth for a moment, then said in a wooden voice, "Yes...because I have to believe I'll marry her. If I don't, I'll lose the last of what my life was, and what I want it to be." He glanced at her. "Do you understand?"

She nodded stoically.

Voices carried on the evening air, followed by the plank rattling. Travis appeared around the cargo box at the head of a group of young Mandan warriors: muscular men, bare-chested, with bright face paint that accented fierce obsidian eyes. "Howdy, coon. Time's come ter feast and dance."

"What?" Richard gave the hunter a wary look; the warriors lowered a rolled buffalo hide to the deck and spread it out.

"Honor guard!" Travis said proudly. "Fit fer a wounded warrior. C'mon, coon. We're going ter a shindig."

"Travis, I"—strong hands reached down and lifted him onto the robe—"but...wait!"

"Hush now, coon. Yer a guest. And do me a favor. Don't moan or groan, no matter how it hurts. These warriors here, they's Black Mouths, soldiers. Each of 'em's been through *Okipa*. That's a ceremony where they run skewers of wood through their bodies. Then they hang till they pass out and send their souls to the Spirit World. Powerful medicine fer only the strongest and bravest. C'mon. And Willow, ye come, too. Uh, as Dick's wife. Otherwise, he'll have ter fight off all the young women wanting ter lay with him."

Richard winced as the stalwart warriors knotted their hands in the buffalo hide and bore him off like a haunch of meat. All in all, it wasn't too painful, except when they thumped him against the cargo box while crossing the *passe avant*.

"Where are we going?" Richard demanded as the warriors threaded their way through the bull boats.

From where Travis and Willow followed, the hunter called, "We're headed up ter Mitutanka, lad. I told ye. It's feast time, and a Scalp Dance ter boot. Celebration fer blizzarding the lights outa that sneaking bunch of Rees that jumped us downriver. As of today, Mandans is at war with the Rees. 'Course, that could change tomorrow, so we'll shindig tonight."

"What do you mean, change tomorrow?"

"This hyar's the upper river, Doodle. Alliances switch faster than cards in a New Orleans poker game."

Richard glanced up at the muscular men carrying the buffalo robe. They looked lean and dangerous, smiling and muttering among themselves in their sibilant tongue. Black Mouths—the warriors who policed the Mandan camps. They looked like savages all right, each bare chest lumped by hideous scar tissue. Nor did they seem to understand the severity of his wound; they flew across the uneven ground at a run.

Just one misstep, a trip and fall, and his back would split open like a mush melon. In resignation, Richard closed his eyes and considered the "wife" business. Travis would come up with something like that—and just after he'd been telling Willow about Laura.

They wound up the trail, past the palisaded wall, and into the village, a maze of rounded lodges, each built within mere feet of its neighbor. He might have been floating in a sea of huge earthen bubbles. After several twists and turns, Richard was totally confused as to their direction.

Square-roofed doorways jutted from the curving walls, some with children or old folks sitting on the roofs.

These spectators called down to the bearers, and were answered by the warriors' laughing calls.

A dog yapped at one of the warriors' feet. A hollow thump, and the cur vanished into the shadowed ways, yipping its pain.

"Where are we going?" Richard called. "Hey! Let me down!"

One of the warriors said something in Mandan, but the progress continued at the same breakneck pace.

"I might just as well be a log, for all you care." Richard gritted his teeth as pain shot through his back.

Then they burst into an open space. Through the folds of the buffalo robe he saw an odd column of planks around a cedar tree, a beaten-dirt plaza, and what looked like a chopped-off lodge. Then they charged headlong into a square doorway, and the timbers of the entry passage flashed past. The interior of the great lodge was crowded with Mandan seated shoulder to shoulder.

The Black Mouths slowed to march ceremonially down a narrow aisle to the center of the lodge and laid the robe gently to one side of a bonfire. Green and Baptiste sat beside a scarred Mandan chief. The Black Mouths nodded to him and smiled, before retreating through the crowd to places beside the door.

Gasping with relief, Richard took in his surroundings. Perhaps seventy feet in diameter, the interior was spacious. The log roof arched high overhead, and between the sooty rafter logs he could see the wicker-work of branches that bore the heavy earthen covering. The whole was supported by four vertical tree trunks centrally placed. Stringers ran from each trunk to rafters that ran down like rays to more stringers supported by short perimeter posts. In the highest arc of the roof a huge smokehole opened to the purple light of evening.

Directly beneath it, the bonfire crackled and sent sparks upward.

Nestled between the perimeter posts were the beds; each consisted of a leather-hung cubicle, something like a small four-poster. Through openings in the sides he could see the thick sleeping robes. After some of the miserable nights he'd spent in the rain, they looked remarkably snug.

The Mandan watched him with curious dark eyes, the burble of voices making a din. Equal numbers of men and women were present. The place smelled of smoke, leather, dust, and human musk.

Travis and Willow crossed the lodge, and all eyes turned to follow their progress through the throng. Willow walked with a stately elegance, like a queen among the masses. In the firelight, her hair gleamed, and her blanket was held tightly to her slim body. She seated herself beside Richard and quickly checked his wound. The tension in her face added to his own.

"How's the ride?" Green asked. He gave Richard a mild look, pipestem drooping from the corner of his broad mouth. The booshway was sitting cross-legged on a buffalo robe, his billowy white shirt unbuttoned at the collar. Baptiste sat on the other side of two Mandan chiefs, talking to one with a series of rapid hand signs, his white teeth flashing in a smile.

"Fast," Richard said uneasily.

"Figgered ye'd not want ter miss this," Travis told him as he settled between Richard and Green. "What with yer dancing down ter Wah-Menitu's, this otta be plumb easy. Hyar, ye can sit 'em all out."

The chief beside Green stood, and the babble dissipated into silence. A woman walked forward, her long-fringed dress snow white, glistening with a wealth of beads. She presented the chief with the biggest pipe Richard had ever seen, the stem a full five feet in length. The chief took it reverently and offered it to the cardinal directions. The woman in white snared an ember from the fire and lit the heavy stone bowl. He puffed a cloud of blue and began to speak in the sibilant Mandan tongue.

"That coon's called The Four Men," Travis whispered. The Four Men was large, almost overweight. He had a round face, prominent cheekbones, and a long, thin nose. His hair was greased and stuck through with feathers. A fox hide draped over his shoulders like a mantle.

"And the man beside him? The one decked out in the claw necklace and shells? He looks important."

"He is. That jasper's called *Mato-Tope,* Four Bears, the most powerful chief among the Mandan. He's a heap good friend ter have in this country."

Four Bears wore a decorated buffalo robe over his shoulders, and a breechclout with a quilled flap hanging down almost to his knees. The tops of his moccasins were beaded in colorful patterns. A huge bear-claw necklace hung over his scarred chest. A pendant of silver lay beneath. The man's hair was long, oiled, and curled back at the top of the high forehead. Those eyes, dark and shining, might have belonged to a bird of prey.

"Yep," Travis said. "He's a heap of warrior, old Four Bears is. Kilt a Ree in his own lodge once."

"I'm more at ease already," Richard muttered, turning his attention to the speaker. "What's The Four Men saying?"

"Oh, all the usual. About what fine friends us whites is. How we shot Hob outa the Ree, and come hyar like warriors."

Food was carried in by women and placed before

them on wooden platters. Richard stared at the lumpy
balls with misgiving.

"Four-in-one, they call it." Travis said. "Eat up, Dick.
T'ain't more than corn, squash, sunflower seeds, and
beans."

Next, steaming portions of roasted buffalo hump and
whole tongues were laid out in mountain sheep-horn
cups. The flaky white meat in the wooden bowls was
sturgeon. Richard's stomach growled. He hadn't realized
just how hungry he was.

All around him, people were eating, laughing, dark
faces shining. The hubbub grew louder.

Richard licked his fingers and glanced at Travis. 'This
business of Willow being my wife. It's really for her
protection, isn't it?"

It was Willow who answered: "No. For yours. The
Mandan offer their women to honored guests. Travis
thought it would make you uncomfortable. If I am here
as your wife, you can avoid lying with a Mandan woman."

Richard made a face, and cast uneasy glances at the
crowd of Mandan surrounding them.

"It is not your custom," Willow said. "But it is theirs,
and you are a guest."

"Reckon if'n ye get an offer, Dick"—Travis was
chewing on a joint of meat—"ye might want ter refuse
politely, and offer to pray fer the feller and his wife. I
reckon ye can do that fer 'em."

"Anything you say. But why do they offer their
women? A different form of prostitution?"

Travis ran a sleeve over his greasy mouth. "The way a
Mandan figgers, a successful man has medicine, Spirit
Power. One way a lesser man can get some of that power
is ter lend out his wife. When she lays with the first
feller, he shoots power inter her. Then, later, her man

lays with her and sucks it up. What's the word? Transfers?"

Richard reached for another of the four-in-one balls. He bit into it, savoring the sweet taste. "A transfer of power? But at what price?"

"Folks all got their own ways," Travis replied, already eyeing the young women in the back of the room. Richard followed the hunter's appraising gaze. He stopped in mid-chew, food forgotten. The women wore nothing but decorated buffalo robes—some painted and tasseled, others beaded—over their shoulders.

"If you keep staring like that, your eyes will fall out of your head. Just like they did from Coyote's," Willow remarked dryly.

Richard barely caught the raising of her eyebrow. Her displeasure seemed to be with him rather than the Mandan.

Green continued to talk and laugh with Four Bears, the trader apparently fluent in Mandan.

Richard chewed thoughtfully, trying to imagine how Kant, Hegel, Rousseau, or Locke would have reacted had they been placed in his circumstance. It was so easy to brand the Mandan as savages, licentious in an animalistic way, and dismiss them.

But when I look around, I just see people. Laughing, smiling people—as I'd see at a festival in Boston were it not for the clothes and the setting.

Despite himself, he couldn't help but study the waiting women, seeking to understand the thoughts in their heads.

"Ye might not want ter stare," Travis warned. "They'll be thinking yer interested."

"Prostitution is payment for services. I'm still having trouble accepting the idea that a man would just *offer* his wife."

"In this case, it's religion, Dick. Wal, ye'd best not go a-philos'phying 'em." Travis dropped his gnawed bone and used his knife to slice off a thick chunk of the tender tongue. "Just be polite and pray fer 'em." Then the hunter grinned. "Reckon I'll take up fer ye."

Richard stared at him.

Travis chewed innocently, the scars twitching as his jaw muscles worked.

To change the subject, Richard asked, "What was that column of planks outside? It looked like it had a tree in it."

"It's an altar," Travis said. "The way the Mandan tell it, back just after the world was created. Lone Man—he's kind of like Adam—saved the people. It seems that a huge flood come. Wal, old Lone Man, he built a palisade around the people. Built it high enough that the water didn't come over. Saved everyone. Nowadays, ye'll not enter a Mandan village without seeing that little pillar. The tree inside is the sacred cedar. That represents Lone Man. Mandan make offerings to it. Pray there."

"And the oblong lodge with the flat face?"

"*Okipa* lodge. That's where these coons have their big spree. They calls the buffalo there, do their torture. Mandan believe the *Okipa* keeps the world healthy."

"Real torture?"

"Reckon so. They starve themselves, sweat and sing,

set out the skulls. When the time's right the bravest young men are skewered and hung from thongs, like deer from a meat pole. The whole time, they're a-praying to God. It's a test of courage. Finally, a warrior, he passes out, and if'n he be worthy, the Spirits take his soul away fer a vision. In the meantime, the Foolish One—sort of like the Devil—he's driven off, and the world is set right."

"A renewal?"

"Reckon so. Powerful medicine. I seen it once." Travis shook his head. "Ain't no way ye'd hang me up there like that."

Richard studied the scars on the Black Mouths. How could any man bear such pain?

"I know what yer thinking," Travis muttered through a mouthful of four-in-one. "But, tell me, what's a better gift ter God? A prayer? Any coon can pray. Injuns figger the only pure thing ye can give to power is part of yerself."

"The Greeks and Romans used to sacrifice a goat, or chicken."

"Huh!" Travis shook his head. "Seems ter this coon that it's the chicken makes the sacrifice. Nope, Dick, thar's only one thing in the world that's wholly yers, and it's you." Travis gestured. "Look around. Here and there ye'll see folks short of their little fingers. They cut 'em off. An offering to power. Seems ter this child, there's a heap of them Bible-beaters back in the settlements could larn a thing or two from Injuns. Now, if'n yer ready ter hang yerself by the thongs, or offer a piece of yerself, that's an honest gift ta God, I tell ye."

"Maybe." *And to think I once believed that I understood human nature.*

But, his contrary self replied, isn't the *Okipa* nothing more than a form of crucifixion? And all the more holy by being self-inflicted? From a philosophical perspective, how did one reply?

Professor Ames, his fellow students, they had all debated morality, ethics, the nature of God, man, and the world with such clarity. But here, so far up the Missouri, those ideas had become as murky and fluid as the very river itself.

He glanced down at the scrap of human scalp hanging at his belt. Every time he'd made a resolution to remove it, his will had failed him. What had happened that he wore a man's scalp on his belt—and carried three others in his possibles? Was this person really Richard Hamilton from Boston? Had he once sat in lecture at Harvard, and bowed so gallantly over Laura Templeton's hand in an ornate parlor?

In the middle of this huge Mandan lodge, surrounded by people, he felt barren and isolated. Tonight, men would offer their wives to other men in a system of belief beyond his comprehension. These smiling, warm people hung their warriors from skewers through the flesh. Yet they had brought him here to be honored for bravery.

I am supposed *to understand! I am a philosopher, a student of mankind and thought.*

From the past, Thomas Hanson's voice mocked: *"...If you really think creatures like Indians are human. Are they, Richard?"*

Was that it? Indians were just a kind of sophisticated beast? His gut crawled at the suggestion. He had touched Willow's soul, felt the Power in the one-eyed stare of Lightning Raven, the Sioux *wechashawakan.*

"Indians—and all the primitive races, for that matter—are beasts. They can't be tamed. Just like wolves and foxes can't be domesticated into dogs. They can only make way for civilization with its nobler institutions." Thomas Hanson's voice, from

that long-ago Boston parlor, droned on in Richard's memory.

Despite their incomprehensible beliefs, look as he might, Ricahrd couldn't see the beast in any of these Indians. At least, no more so than among his white compatriots. And there sat Willow, easily the most beautiful woman in the country. When she looked at him, he could see the hurt in her eyes, because he would not allow himself to touch her.

Beside her sat Travis—a truer friend than he had ever had. But a gap was opening between them.

It's inside you, Richard. From the dim halls of memory came the words of Professor Ames: *"It is within man to seek truth in a world of chaos, to establish a framework within which a man can interpret and deal with the world, with his fellows, and his God. That search is called philosophy, gentlemen."*

Premonition stirred deep in his soul—a sense of impending horror, as if the very Fates were pulling him toward a dark and terrible tempest. The cold fringes of the black storm were brewing just beyond the realm of perception.

And when it breaks, it will destroy all that I was.

And maybe kill him in the process.

The image of the cedar tree surrounded by its planks lingered in his mind. A refuge against swirling waters. But the only thing it contained was the wooden representation of a lone Mandan hero.

CHAPTER EIGHT

In nature, not only is the interplay of forms unrestrained and unlimited in contingency, but each figure by itself lacks the concept of itself. The highest level to which nature derives its existence is life, but as only a natural idea this is at the very mercy of the unreasonableness of externality, and the individual vitality is in each moment of its own existence entangled with an individuality which is alien to it, whereas in each expression of the spirit is encapsulated the instant of free, universal self-relation. Nature in general is justly determined as the decline of the idea from itself.

—Georg Friedrich Wilhelm Hegel, *The Philosophy of Nature*

"Woman of the People." Shoshoni words interrupted Willow's thoughts as she watched the Mandan dancers.

Willow turned to inspect the newcomer who'd walked up behind her and now settled on crackling knees. She was an old woman, perhaps of forty summers. Her glossy braids were still jet black and hung down in front of her rose-beaded dress with its fine fringe, but years of winter winds and summer suns had engraved and burned her face. Lines curved down from the corners of her eyes to surround her chin. They were intersected by starburst wrinkles from the corners of her nose and mouth until her face looked like sand-scoured wood. Squat and sturdy, she had the look of the *Ku'chendikani*.

"Greetings, woman. May Wolf shed his blessing upon you," Willow replied in her tongue.

The elder cocked her head, squinting. "Huh, I know that accent. But it's been so long."

"*Dukurika.*"

"Ah!" The woman clapped her hands. "So, a Sheepeater! They say you are not a slave, but travel with the Whites. This is so?"

"It is. I am Heals Like A Willow. The daughter of High Wolf, of the Rock Sheep clan. My people live in the Powder River Mountains, but sometimes we join our cousins in the Owl Creek Mountains across the Big River."

"Yes. I recall. Here, I am called She Sews the Roses. But once, among the People, my name was High Mountain Rose. My father was *Agaiduka* and my mother was *Ku'chendikani.* Then the Crows, the *A 'ni,* took me when I had no more than ten summers. I lived with them for several years before they traded me to the Amatiha Hidatsa. A young man took a liking to me. I've been here ever since."

She doesn't ask if I know her relatives. It's as if her people have ceased to exist.

Curiously hurt, Willow returned her attention to the gyrating dancers who shuffled and stomped in a circle around the center posts. With a high-pitched yip, they all leaped and twisted, landing on crouched legs in time to the beat of the big, round drums.

"Quite a dance," She Sews the Roses said, watching the sweat-streaked warriors panting and whirling around the four support posts and its fire. "They do this for you...in your honor."

"Then we are most honored." Willow waited, aware of the woman's sly scrutiny of herself and Richard.

"It is said that you killed some of the Arikara yourself. Many people here are talking about that. Only a very brave woman would act like that."

"Wolf guided my hand and gave me courage."

"And you have no obligations to these White men? None of them own you?"

"No."

She Sews the Roses rubbed her callused hands together and pursed her lips. After a moment, she said, "I have been asked to ask you. Would you stay here?"

Willow lifted a skeptical eyebrow. "Stay here?"

"That man"—She Sews the Roses indicated Four Bears with a twitch of her lips—"is a very powerful chief. He has watched you over the last couple of days. He does not believe that you are married to this wounded White man. I am told to tell you that he would make you very comfortable, give you many presents. Honor you and make you his wife."

"Why doesn't he ask me this himself?"

"He cannot speak your language, and he's worried the White men might become angry."

Willow crossed her arms. "Why would he want me? I'm nothing but trouble. Just ask the White men."

She Sews the Roses laughed and slapped her dress in a very Mandan way. "You ask that? Look at you! Young, strong, too beautiful to be an *Aitani* Snake woman. And you have killed warriors in battle. Taken scalps! When you walk, every man in the village watches the way your hips sway, how your breasts fill your dress. They talk about your hair, and how it looks in the sun. You have filled their imagination with fire, Heals Like A Willow, and they would feel themselves burn inside you."

Willow glanced at Richard, oblivious on his robe beside her. He was watching the dancers, face somber. She knew that look; he was wrestling with his soul again.

"He's kind of skinny," She Sews the Roses said, jerking her head at Richard. "And he looks like he doesn't see much of this world."

Willow cocked her jaw. "He sees more than most. Do you always judge a man by his muscles?"

"Come, girl, be sensible. A man's a great deal like a horse, you know. You can just tell by looking at them: the shoulders; the line of the back; how hard their rumps are; the power in the legs; the size of their testicles—those things. This one, well, even if he's White, he still looks like he'd gaunt up and fall over the first time you needed him to do anything important. And what sort of children would his seed grow? Spindly-legged things, sickly whiners with hollow eyes. You know the kind."

Heedless of Willow's narrowing glare, She Sews the Roses spread her arms wide. "So, what *do* you see in him? Not wealth. He's not even a trader, just an *engagé*. Four Bears, now, he'd make you a rich woman. A favorite wife. Give you a place by his side and anything you wanted. You would sleep on a white buffalo robe...be looked up to by every person on the river."

Willow glanced over at Four Bears, who picked that moment to meet her eyes. They stared, measuring each other, probing and challenging. In the process, she read his soul, understanding all that drove him.

"I do not think so," Willow told She Sews the Roses. "I will stick with my skinny White man. And as to what I see in him, if you can't feel his *puha*, then you would never understand if I told you."

"Power? *Him?*" She Sews the Roses made a face. "Very well. But you're making a mistake."

"Am I?"

The elder wrung her hands, nodding seriously despite swaying to the beat of the drums. "A mistake, yes. Even if you don't go with Four Bears. You surely don't want to go back to the mountains, do you? Stay with us, girl. These people, they will make you one of them. It's a better life. A woman's worth more here. You'll have status, and a say in the council. You can own property, a house, fields, and corn. You can buy rights to Power—own part of the sacred bundles, even join the White Buffalo Cow Society."

"My place is with my people," Willow said, catching sight of Travis as he came strutting through the doorway. He was followed by a young woman who ducked away to an expectant young man. The two bent their heads together, whispering excitedly. Travis started toward them, a new pair of moccasins in his hand. He grinned crookedly, a sparkle in his eyes.

Richard watched with a wooden face. The hunter made his way through the dancers, doing a little jumping and yipping of his own. Grinning, he settled on his haunches and slapped the moccasins down beside Richard, crying, "Hyar's a gift, coon. Fresh made."

"And where did you get them?" Richard asked wearily.

"Why, from that lass's young buck, coon."

"Travis, I don't think I can—"

"It's Mandan custom." Travis glanced up, winked at Willow—and noticed She Sews the Roses. His expression froze, wariness cooling the twinkle in his eyes. With barely a hesitation, he added, "'Course, I got me Bear Power along with being a great warrior, so this coon gets a little more than a squeeze ter his pizzle."

Richard made a face and rubbed the bridge of his nose. "I'm glad for you—I really am."

Travis shot another glance at She Sews the Roses and added, "Yer just not catching on quick enough, Doodle. They's others a-sneaking in from the sides, and yer blinder than a fire-burned buffler bull."

"I'm what? What did you say?"

Travis met Willow's gaze and shook his head. "I said, ye don't know shit, Dick."

Richard nodded in slow agreement. "Well, for once I can't help but agree with you. I've got a funny feeling, Travis, like I'm on the verge of making..."

A young man leading a robe-covered young woman stopped before Richard, nodded, and spoke softly in his tongue, an expectant tone in his voice. The young woman stared self-consciously at the ground.

Travis translated. "Dick. He wants ter know if'n ye'll lay with his wife. He says it would be an honor to the both of them."

Willow watched Richard from the corner of her eye.

Richard swallowed hard as the white-tanned robe slipped open to expose the young woman's body. From the barely budded breasts and the smooth brown skin, Willow doubted she was more than a year beyond her first menstruation.

Richard took a deep breath, and made a futile gesture with his hand. 'Travis, tell her...tell her that I can't —wounded."

Travis chuckled, but spoke solemnly in the Mandan

tongue. The young man nodded, and clutched his wife's hand.

"All right, coon," Travis growled out of the side of his mouth. "Ye'd better pray fer 'em. And do it up right pert, hear?"

Richard winced, teeth gritted, as he sat up. Sweat began to bead on his face, from the heat in the lodge as well as the pain of his exertion.

"Dear Lord God!" he cried out. "Grant this young man and woman big medicine! Impart unto them the knowledge of Plato, Aristotle, and, yes, most of all, Saint Augustine. Let them know forbearance of the flesh! Render judgment unto them with the same authority and sanction as would be rendered by Saint Bernard of Clairvaux!"

"Who's Saint Bernard of Clairvaux?" Travis asked.

"Christian mystical philosopher. All of his life he looked forward to climbing the ladder to Heaven and watching the damned sinners falling past him into the pit."

"A treasure of a man, I'm sure," Travis agreed.

"They made him a saint."

"That happened ter lots of coons. Think of old Saint Louis, now, he's some, he is. Got a whole damned city named fer him." Travis turned back to the waiting Mandan, speaking rapidly.

The young man nodded, and with a flourish, removed the beautifully beaded robe the young woman wore. This he folded very carefully and laid it before Richard. He gave Travis a satisfied smile, a look of accomplishment in his eyes. He said, "There, see. My integrity remains triumphant, and through rational action, I have achieved a moral outcome for all involved."

The youth turned and led the naked girl over to Green, who sat conversing with Four Bears.

Richard's grin faded as the trader glanced up, eyes gleaming, and rose to take the young woman's arm. Willow watched Richard's face fall as they walked past and the naked girl gave him an excited smile of gratitude.

"Ye were saying...?" Travis asked mildly.

"Are you sure about this one having Power?" She Sews The Roses whispered into Willow's ear. 'Take my word for it, go to Four Bears. At least he's a man!"

———

Far to the west, beyond the treeline at the river's edge, the stark white of roiling thunderheads contrasted with the hot blue sky above and mocked the black depths below—now partially obscured by silver skirts of rain sheeting across the far horizons of grass.

Willow was familiar with such storms; in the blackness beneath those soft clouds, wind, hail, and violent rains hammered at unwary victims, filled the drainages, and flattened all but the most sturdy of shelters. Lightning carved the heavens in streaks as thunder blasted and tumbled away into the distance.

Today, because of the storms, the wind was right, and *Maria* sailed upstream before the rushing breeze. They were being drawn into the storm, and a premonition of danger lay curled within Willow's souls.

Richard sat hunched on the coiled painter, his back bare to allow the wound to breathe. She had checked it that morning, satisfied with the dark scab surrounded by crusted yellow. The White man's spirit water had worked again—despite Green's scowling reluctance to use it thus.

Whites were funny that way. They insisted on drinking it, which only made their souls burn and their thoughts turn foolish.

She stepped past Richard and leaned down, arms braced, to watch the keel slice the murky water in a hissing rush. *Maria* surged ahead like a living thing. Willow could sense the boat's soul, even though the Whites scoffed at the idea.

The wind blew her hair out in a fine mist of black strands. The sail groaned and popped, the wooden mast complaining. For once, the *engagés* rode atop the cargo box. Some slept, recovering from their "rest" among the Mandan, while others tended to their mending. Several gambling games were being played, accompanied by shouts and curses.

On shore, Travis and Baptiste would be trotting the horses through the rolling hills beyond the river's bluffs, out where they could spot trouble before running afoul of it. Too many enemies filled this country. In that sense, Green's advice had been correct.

So, you stayed, silly woman. Here you are, your souls hurting.

Dreams of Richard filled her restless sleep, his smile shining for her, a dancing light in his brown eyes. Her body ached for his, longing to join with him as a man and woman should. She had come to love him, and condemned herself in the process. No matter how she sought to delude herself, he had committed himself to

Boston, to his Laura, and to the notion that this world held no possibility for him and Willow. Ache for him as she might in her dreams, he would never share her bed.

Would it have been better to have taken a horse, chanced the Sioux, Assiniboin, Crow, Ree, and Hidatsa? And beyond them lay the Cheyenne, the Atsina, Arapaho, and Blackfeet. Like hungry coyotes, they filled this lush grassland with its endless herds of buffalo, antelope, and elk. Here—at least in summertime—a person would be hard-pressed to starve to death. So much game, and prairie turnips and ground bean grew everywhere.

She looked to the west, past the storm, and in her mind's eye imagined herself floating, rising up past the riverbank that slipped so gracefully behind them. Out there, beyond the trees, over the endless rolling grass, the land would become broken, cut by steep drainages that carved sharply twisted channels into the pale clay. The bluestem grass would give way to patches of sagebrush, to isolated stands of limber pine and juniper. Out there the sky would lose this dull, lowland blue to become deeper, crystalline. In the distance, stark against infinity, her mountains waited. Her souls rushed toward those pine-green slopes, where flinty granite underlay beds of quartzite and the softened curves of overhanging sandstone. A swelling joy filled her when she thought of those high peaks, of the rich aroma of pine and fir. She could hear the sibilant wind in swaying branches.

Eagle soared there, drifting out from the cliffs over dizzying heights.

That was her land, the home of her souls. There she would find herself again. Only in that high country could she hear *Tam Apo's* echoed voice in the breeze, see His pulse in the rippling waters, and feel His strength in the defiant rock.

Soon, Heals Like A Willow. Soon.

One of the *engagés* on the cargo box laughed raucously. Her reverie snapped like a dry stick.

She turned, pulling her gleaming hair back from her cheeks, and walked over to settle against the cargo box across from Richard where he perched on the coiled painter. The heat from the planks massaged her tense back, and she leaned her head against the oak.

Richard glanced uneasily at her. "Travis says that Four Bears asked you to stay with him."

"Yes."

He fumbled with the scalps tied on his belt. The sun had turned his pale shoulders ruddy. "Did you think about staying?"

She tried to see into his lowered eyes. "I did. He offered me many things."

"Well, if he offered so much..."

"He didn't offer me his soul."

"I see." He pursed his lips, the frown deepening.

"Richard, what happened to you? Green has a word, he calls you 'brooding.' What does that mean?"

"It means self absorbed to the point of distraction."

"I don't know those words." English was so hard. She felt lucky enough to have finally managed the "ch" in Richard's name.

"It means I don't know the answers any more. Not about life, about my father, or myself. Is it so wrong to believe in one man for one woman? Travis, Green, and the rest fornicate with any squaw that comes along! For God's sake, why?" He glared at her.

Uneasily, she answered, "If God did not make men to lie with women, why do you have a pizzle and I have a cunt?"

"*Where* did you hear that word?"

"That is what the *engagés* call my—"

"I—I know. Never mind, I...Willow, just promise me. Don't *ever* use that word. Not around civilized men."

She closed her eyes in disgust. "How can I understand your trouble when you won't even talk to me about it? Does this offend the Power of your damned philos'phy?"

He gave her a misery-laden stare, finally whispering, "No. I mean...it shouldn't." He paused, gesturing with his hands. "Something's happening to me, Willow."

"It's the Power in your soul, Richard. It looks for a way out."

"Power? That's magic...superstition. I don't believe in that kind of nonsense."

"You want everything to fit the way you believe. It's like seeing a fish and trying to make itself into a bird. I can't understand you. What makes your way right, and everyone else's wrong?"

He gave her a hostile stare. "Four thousand years of rigorous philosophical dissection, debate, and discipline."

She took a breath to still her growing anger. "Different people have different truths. No one truth is better than the others. If you wish to know the Mandan, listen to their stories. In the Mandan village I heard the story of Black Wolf, one of the Mandan heroes from the beginning times. He went out and killed the monster Four Stripes. To do so the Old Ones turned him into a woman, and Black Wolf lay with Four Stripes to lull his suspicions. Afterwards, as Four Stripes slept, Black Wolf killed him. The Old Ones turned him into a man again, and he started home. On his way back to his people, the Sacred Grandmothers told him that a young woman should couple with a powerful man, and then when her husband lay with her, she would give that power to her man."

"Willow, you can't compare a story with truth. Something in the universe must be ultimate. Absolute. That's what I've lost"

It is hopeless. He cannot, will not, understand.

She rolled the fringes on her sleeve between slim brown fingers. "You're wrong, Richard. Stories are full of truth. That's the Power they have. They are more than just the words. The stories live, and have Power all their own. They carry the souls, take them places and teach them things." She paused. "And what does the White man's God say? Are there no stories?"

"Of course we have stories. Adam and Eve. They lived in simple purity in the Garden of Eden. Eve ate an apple and obtained knowledge. In the process, she found out she was naked, and covered herself. When God saw her and Adam wearing clothes, he knew they'd eaten the forbidden fruit and cast them out of the garden. That's it."

"There must be another story. Does Eve never lie with Adam?"

"Well, yes, but the story doesn't exactly tell about it."

"Is she the only woman in your stories?"

"No, there's Mary, the mother of God. But she's a virgin. Jesus, her son, is born through immaculate...uh, by God's will. No man lies with her. Willow, believe me, there are no sexual unions in our stories. None. Even Mary Magdalene never lies with Jesus."

Richard's frown deepened, and she could see his soul quickening, the gleam that thrilled her growing in his eyes. "Dear Lord God, there's no female element! That's one of the big differences."

"I don't understand."

He made a fist, thumping his knee. "No sexual stories. No female element to the stories. We don't talk about it...we never have. The celibacy of the priesthood, the virtues of the virgin marriage bed, original sin, all of it goes back to that epistemological framework." He gave her a quizzical look. "But what does it mean for us as a people?"

Willow stared out over the wind-rippled water. "It means you keep your women in houses like you do your God. Your Boston-God stories don't have women." She gestured around them. "I have heard Travis say this country is too dangerous for White women. You have been so blinded by your White God, you cannot join with a woman when you desire her. You are so trapped that you even hate your friends when they join with women. You have said you cannot take me back to Boston, that they will not understand."

"No, it's not—"

"I don't believe you, Richard." She cringed from the cold futility within her. "You claim to seek Power and knowledge. I have seen the thirst in your soul, and I have respected that. But now, I wonder if I was wrong."

"Willow, listen. Before I came here, everything was clear and concise. Right was right, and wrong was wrong. But everything I believed, it has all turned to shifting sand. I just have to find the way, is all."

It's hopeless, Willow.

She steeled herself. "You've said that over and over. You will never find it, Richard. If someone tells you a new truth, you will call it a silly story. You deny the *puha* within you, and call it nonsense. You are like Coyote, who cast his eyes into a tree so he could see from the heights—but only blinded himself. I am sorry for you."

She stood. Feeling absolutely wretched, she climbed onto the top of the cargo box. The *engagés* had been watching the exchange with amused eyes.

From behind her, Richard called, "Willow, please come back."

Too late, Richard. I've had enough.

She ignored him as she stalked through the curious *engagés*. Her hand on her war club, she dared one to smirk, or make one of their pizzle-in-hand gestures. None did.

Green stood beside Henri at the steering oar; his face beamed with pleasure as the wind tugged at his baggy white shirt. At the sight of her smoldering glare, his smile disappeared.

"Green," she said calmly. 'Tomorrow morning, I am taking my horse. I will be returning to my people."

"Now, Willow"—he raised weather-browned hands in mollification—"you know this country is crawling with hostile..."

"I am *leaving*." With that, she jumped down on the stern where Toussaint and de Clerk were playing eucher. Boiling with rage, she settled herself to watch the wake spreading out in a rippling V.

CHAPTER NINE

The study of truth is partly hard and partly easy. A proof of this is the fact that no one man is able to grasp it adequately. However, not all men entirely fail. Each says something about the nature of the world, and though individually he adds little or nothing to our understanding of it, but from the combination of all, something considerable is accomplished. Thus, as truth seems to be like the door which, the proverb says, no one can fail to find, in that respect our study of it is simplified. But the fact that we can have some notion of it as a whole, but not of the particular part we want, shows it is difficult. Perhaps, too, the difficulty is of two sorts and its cause is not so much in the things themselves as within us. For as the eyes of bats are to the brightness of daylight, so is the reason within our soul to things that by nature are the clearest of all...

—Aristotle, *Metaphysics*, Book II

"Now, what's all this foolishness about?" Travis asked as he stepped out of the darkness into the glow of Willow's small fire. She'd built it out beyond the boatmen's camp and placed her bedding and packs under the spreading branches of a grizzled old bur oak.

She looked up at him, dark eyes gleaming in the firelight. Her slim fingers stroked a willow stick she'd been smoothing with a sandstone abrader. When finished, the straight white wood would make an excellent arrow shaft. "I am leaving in the morning, Travis."

He scratched his bearded cheeks, grunted, and swatted a mosquito. "Baptiste and me, we cut fresh sign out in the hills today. Thirty, maybe forty hosses ridden Injun-file. 'Course, a feller cain't tell much from tracks alone. Warn't no travois drags, Willow. All warriors."

She said nothing.

He added, "Reckon we had us this palaver a time or two before. Ye knows how the wind blows out hyar, and she's a mite dangerous...specially this time of year. It's war season."

She shot him a sidelong glance, and returned to her work. How pretty she looked with the firelight accenting her graceful cheeks and the softness of her lips. Her long black hair spilled down over her shoulders, so rich and glossy he longed to reach out and touch it.

Willow took a deep breath, tilted her head back, and exhaled wearily. "I cannot stay here any longer, Travis. I have only been fooling myself."

"Uh-huh."

All right, coon, how'n hell are ye gonna handle this?

He squatted down on his haunches, pulled out his pipe and makings, and tamped tobacco into the bowl.

"And the worst thing is, I don't know how it happened to me. I am *Dukurika*—a woman of the mountains. He's a skinny White man with hair on his face. His skin is like a dead man's...one who's been floating in the river. You've seen such a corpse? The skin is that color of white. So, in the name of *Tam Apo,* why do I want him to touch me? Why do I want him to share my blanket?" She clenched both fists. "*Why* does he fill my dreams at night?"

"Dreams, huh?" Travis used twigs to snake an ember from the fire and lit his pipe. Injuns set a heap of store on dreams. Over the years, that had rubbed off on him—like his Immel and Jones dream that kept recurring night after night.

"Dreams—yes." Her slender hands absently caressed the smoothed wood. "I see him with me, walking in the mountains. We hold each other and look out from the high places. Together, we share the hunt, then laugh as we cut up the meat...enjoy that rich smell of a freshly killed elk.

"And at night, we lie side by side under a warm buffalo robe. The fire crackles and sends its sparks up to join the stars. The nights are glass-clear up there, not like these plains. You can see so many more of the star people, like white frost on the black sky. Richard and i are together beneath that sky and talk of a great many things: of God, and Power, and the curious things men think and say."

She shook her head. "But it will not be that way, Travis. Something is not right inside him. Maybe it's that Whites only have one soul? I don't know."

"Willow, keep in mind—"

"Yes, I know. He has grown stronger in the ways of a man, but he has lost the way of the soul. Do you understand?"

"Yep. I reckon."

"I would help him find it again, except he will not

open himself to the search. He has his way—and will accept no other."

Travis sucked at his pipe. "I just saw him over to the boat. He's all-fired anxious ter talk to ye."

"I do not wish to talk to him." She looked up. "I have no more words. My souls still ache from the death of my husband and son. I cannot ache for Richard, too. I do not have enough of myself to give away any more. Not like this, not day by day." She closed her eyes. "Among my people, we believe that unfulfilled dreams will cause the souls to sicken and die. It is happening to me, Travis."

"Aw, I'm sorry, child." Travis handed her his pipe while he considered options. Problem was, he didn't have a whole lot of sympathy for the knothead Doodle.

She puffed, blowing the smoke toward the oak branches overhead.

"Ye might want ter at least hear what he's got ter say. He seemed—"

"No."

From the way she said it, that seemed like the kit and kaboodle. Travis rubbed the smooth scar tissue on his nose with a nervous finger, squinting out at the darkness. Buffalo wolves howled an eerie duet out on the grassy hills. "I'm a curious coon. I heard tell that Green asked ye ter take up with him. Then Four Bears made ye an offer. Does it have ter be Richard? Most Injun women would jump at the chance to marry white."

"I'm not like most women, Travis. I want more than White man goods, robes, horses, and a share of a chief's status." She handed his pipe back gloomily. "In all of my life, I have known only two men I could share my souls with. One, I married. He's dead because I couldn't save him. And Richard will not share his soul with me because his God has blinded him."

"Huh?" Travis cocked his head. "Ye lost me there, gal."

She studied him with those dark, depthless eyes. "You can know a people by their stories, Travis. I have learned this of you Whites: in all of your stories, there is no woman to make up half of the world. Richard told me of Adam and Eve, of Mary. There are no other women in any of the stories—at least, none who is important. And none of the women lie with men. Among my people, Coyote lies with women all the time. He even carries a spare penis, just in case. The Pawnee, the Rees, the Mandan, all have stories about women and men, coupling, creating life and the world around them. Tell me, when your God creates the world, does he couple with a woman to do so?"

Travis rolled his pipestem in his fingers. This wasn't an angle on God that he'd ever thought about. "Reckon not."

"Are any of the heroes saved by a woman?"

"Nope."

"And there is no coupling?"

"Nope."

"This is not balanced, Travis. No wonder you Whites think you have only one soul."

"And just how many should we have?"

"My people believe two. The first is the *mugwa*, the life soul. The second is *navuzieip*, the free soul."

"Free soul?" He squinted at her. She wasn't gigging him, just for fun, was she? Making jokes to see how far he'd go?

"The soul that leaves your body and wanders when you dream."

"I guess I'd always figgered that was just me imagining." But the dream he'd had down by Atkinson still chilled his gizzard. Michael Immel and Robert Jones had come to him, warned him about trouble at the mouth of the Big Horn.

Willow's words drew him back to the here and now. "Mother Earth and Father Sky, each is half of Creation. Tell me, why would your God be male if there was no female? Why would he need a pizzle and balls? Wouldn't you think such a God would be neither? Like a rock?" She sighted down the straight arrow shaft, then glanced at him. "I think maybe you Whites don't know shit about God. I don't understand how you can be so clever with things like boats, and guns, and glass, but so blind and confused about God."

"Now, I don't hold with a lot of Bible doings, but we ain't confused," Travis growled irritably. "Not at all. God just, well, He is, that's all. And—and just 'cause ye think *we're* confused ain't no reason ter go running off to get *scalped!*"

She gave him an irritating, knowing smile. 'Travis, I have learned what I came among you to learn. *Tam Apo,* Our Father, must be much like your God, but beneath him is *Tam Segobia,* Our Mother. He has Wolf and Coyote as helpers. *Tam Segobia* has Water Ghost Woman and her helpers. Women fill our stories—maybe not as many as among the river peoples, where women own the houses and men belong to their mothers' clans, but they are there. And we have a voice in our councils.

"You Whites trap your women in houses to have your children. But I think I understand why now...and why Richard cannot share himself with me." She reached over and tossed a broken branch onto the fire. "I pity your people, Travis. They will never be whole."

He rubbed the tobacco-stained pipestem with a callused thumb. Just how did God expect him to answer that? "This child's been a heap of places, gal. Seen me a heap of sights. Some of what yer saying is fire in the pan; some's damp powder. Whites is folks like any others. Reckon they's some cruel—but so's Injuns, or this child ain't seen squat. Now, the good book our Lord gives us teaches folks to turn the other cheek, to show charity to the weak and hurt."

Her eyes flashed. "I think that is a lie. What did you do to the Shawnee? How do you treat your slaves? Even the belly-crawling Pawnee adopt a slave into a family. Do Whites? I've heard the stories Baptiste tells."

"Well, hell, whites is plumb nice compared ter Black-feet, or Rees, or—"

"Good, bad, it does not matter. You don't understand what I am saying. Your souls are half empty."

He scowled at the fire, scratching for an answer and coming up completely blank.

She tucked her knees up and propped her chin on them to watch the fire. "Richard will always be White. I will always be Injun. He is a man. I am a woman—a thing to be kept."

"Maybe. Hell, I don't know what he's gonna be. Willow, he's come a long way from the skinny runt what François dumped on deck that night. He's come right about, he has. Taken coup, stoled hosses, larned a thing or two."

And why the hell am I defending him? He's been like ter drive me crazy since that Ree fight.

"Those are warrior's skills, Travis. What of his soul?" She rocked back and forth, her delicate face framed by that gleaming raven hair.

"Soul? What in Hob do I know about souls?"

"Enough, Bear Man. You see more than you admit. He says he seeks to know the world; but he cannot until he looks within himself. Not just for courage, but for balance and understanding. His *puha* is struggling to come out, and he struggles just as hard to keep it trapped. I told him once that he couldn't 'think' his way to God. Maybe I was wrong. Maybe the White God can be known only by thoughts; but if that is so, it is a very different god from *Tam Apo,* who must be known here." She touched her chest.

Travis scratched his ear. As palaver went, this one was turning out poor beaver. "Ye ain't like any woman I ever knew, red or white. Reckon ye'd drive a coon plumb berserk."

"The way I did Packrat?" Willow raised an eyebrow and smiled grimly. "My father is a *puhagan.* I am his daughter. Among the *Dukurika* we keep the old ways— the ways from before the coming of the horses. My father taught me to ask hard questions. We are not like the *Agaiduka* and *Ku'chendikani,* who are starting to believe more like the Crow, Blackfeet, and Arapaho."

"Yer father, huh? Reckon he got a handful a-raising ye, girl."

"He did." She smiled wistfully. "During the late winter nights High Wolf, my father, told the old stories. The ones about the time after the Creation. Then we talked about what they meant. Why did Coyote do everything he could to pester Wolf? What did it mean when *Pachee Goyo* was carried away by Cannibal Owl? Why are *Nynymbi* and *Pandzoavits* magical, and most people are not?"

"*Nynymbi? Pandzoavits?*"

"*Nynymbi* are the little people, guides to the water world, the ones who shoot magical arrows into people and cause sudden sharp pains, or trip them when they're walking in the forest. *Pandzoavits* are the rock ogres, with sticky hands covered with pine sap. When they catch lone travelers, they grab them and put them in baskets they carry on their backs. Then they run home to eat their catch." She smiled. "I was a full woman before I finally confronted my father. I told him I had never seen a *Nynymbi*, or a rock ogre, never felt their power, and didn't really believe in them anymore."

"Uh-huh. And what did he say?"

"High Wolf nodded and smiled at me. That's when he told me that *Nynymbi* were real only so long as we believed in them. That was a very important lesson for me, Travis. I believe in the *Nynymbi* and *Pandzoavits,* and use power to guard against them; but unlike Richard, I believe in them because I *want* to."

"And that makes a difference? Wanting to?" He stared hollowly at the pipe, way out of his depth with such things.

"A heap of difference." She slapped at a mosquito that landed on her shin; the arrow shaft lay forgotten beside her. "Answer me this, Travis. Who needs who? If God did not believe in people, would people be like plants in darkness, and wither away and die? Or, if people did not believe in God, would God slowly waste into nothingness and die?"

Travis stared absently into the fire, trying to track his way around her slippery question. "Damned if I know, Willow."

She stretched then, her lithe body supple and provocative in the firelight. "Perhaps you should think about it, Bear Man. Then you would know why believing because you want to is so important."

"Tarnation! I'm the wrong coon fer telling this to. Go talk ter Dick about this hyar God, and such."

"I don't think his soul would hear the question, or feel the answer."

Travis knocked the dottle out of his pipe. "Just promise me ye won't ride off tomorrow."

"So that Green can have his Snake woman to help with the trade?"

"Nope. So I can get ye home safe. Reckon I'd not want ter dream about ye laying out there in the grass, scalped, wolf-chewed, and rotting in the sun."

"I will think on this. But I do not promise, Travis."

———

The camp slept. A great horned owl's *hoo-hoo-hooo* carried on the night; water lapped at *Maria's*, hull, and night insects chirred and buzzed in the darkness. Richard lay on his stomach. He slept restlessly, his left leg drawn up, his right arm tucked close to his body. Though his wound might be healing, his soul ached. Perhaps he heard the yipping cackle of the coyotes on the near shore and the piercing rejoinder of the wolves to the south. Or was it just the dream?

I feel no fear, only a dull emptiness, like the hollow-stom-ached longing that comes from perpetual grief. As I walk up Park Street. and turn left onto Tremont, my steps echo. Boston is unusually quiet on this somber gray morning. The clouds hang low in the sky, brooding, and look ragged where wisps trail beneath.

The cobblestones are wet and grimy, gritty under the soles of my boots. Bits of trash soak in the puddled water.

Something is wrong. I glance anxiously at the shop windows. They gape back at me, and when I stop and peer inside, I see nothing. Only featureless gray. No familiar floor, ceiling, or walls —just a foggy emptiness.

The buildings are nothing but shells. When I tap my fingers on the wet brick, it sounds hollow. Rapping my knuckles on a stone wall, I get a wooden sound in return. I try a door this time, hammering on it with my fists. It's not right, somehow, and when I grip the doorknob, it doesn't turn, doesn't even rattle. I look closely and discover that the door isn't real, but painted onto the wall.

A suffocating anxiety filters through my chest. I back into the middle of the street and shout. "Hello!"

The call echoes into the blanket of silence.

I turn, running headlong to Hanover Street and round the corner. Everything seems familiar. I crisscross the street, racing from window to window. Each building is a sham—a false front beyond which lies that unsettling gray nothingness.

In the middle of the street, I cup hands to my mouth, hollering, 'Is anyone here?'"

Silence answers.

I cock my head. Even in its quietest moments, one can hear something in Boston: the breeze in the rafters; sea gulls; a slamming door; cart wheels on the paving. Now my ears fail to catch the slightest whisper. Not the creak of a timber or the scurry of a mouse.

It isn't just the silence. Nothing moves but the wounded clouds drifting eastward. No pigeons, no birds, not even flies. I look up: no slips of smoke rise from the chimneys.

My heart begins to pound. Something is terribly wrong. I sense rising danger, brewing like a witch's cauldron. I break into a run, dodging left onto Union, panting as I fly down the silent *street. I veer onto Charlestown Street, sprinting now, for something pursues me through the silent city.*

Throwing a look over my shoulder, I see a darkness settling over the empty hulls of buildings. The miasma rolls toward me, devouring the city as it comes.

Dear Lord God, what had become of all the people? Will? Laura? Jeffry? Father? Are you gone? Dead?

I run faster. Fear prickles along my spine now, goading me to greater effort. It's coming...coming...I dash onto Causeway and run onto the Charles River Bridge. The planks boom beneath my boot heels.

In the middle of the bridge, I stop, for the Cambridge shore is murky and uncertain. I turn: All of Boston has been engulfed by the pall. The skyline can barely be discerned, the buildings no more than dark squares. No light burns in that sullen twilight; no sound is heard. It is as if the city never was.

Fear runs bright within me. I'm panicky, frantic to run. with nowhere to go. "What happened here? I don't understand!"

"What did you expect?" Professor Ames steps out of the gloom behind me. "You didn't think Boston was real, did you, Richard?"

"Not...real?"

Ames stares wistfully at the darkened city. The mild blue eyes have turned glassy in his ruddy face. He's a small man, frail-looking, with snowy hair, and as usual, dressed in black. "You still don't understand, do you?"

"I must find Will and Laura. My father's in there and he..." I bury my face in my hands, crushed by the realization of what I've done, how much I've lost. "He trusted me, sir. And I failed him. He'll never forgive me for this...Never."

"It's not there, Richard," Ames says gently.

I look out between my fingers. The only thing that remains is a dark haze, like billowed smoke from a range fire.

"Not there?" I stagger forward, arms wide. Even the Charles

River Bridge abutments have vanished. I stand on a bridge to nowhere.

"It never was." Ames's voice fades.

"But, sir! I was there...and so were you that last night at Will's, when Laura and I..." I turn back. Ames is gone.

My mind reels, like a drunken man's. I reach out and steady myself on the weathered wooden railing. All that remains is the bridge. The haze covering Boston swirls and darkens to sackcloth. When I look over into the water, it isn't the Charles that I see but the murky Missouri with its flotsam and foam.

My limbs are suddenly weak. Boston, where is Boston? It couldn't just disappear like that.

"It was there," I insist, looking back. The haze lifts, and I catch glimpses of virgin forest. The treetops are barely visible in the darkness.

"I don't understand." Where am I to go? What am I to do?

Harsh laughter makes me spin around. Lightning Raven, old One-Eye, the Sioux wechashawakan. sits on a buffalo robe, bathed in firelight. I am afraid of this old man. I first met him in my dreams, and then face to face in Wah-Menitu's village. He fixes me with the scarred socket of his empty eye. "It is all illusion, White Coyote. You—and your philosophy None of it is real here. I watch you, and you become more and more like Inktomi, the Trickster. You fool yourself because you are a coward."

I back away. The bridge is gone, and the river runs just behind my heels. "No, I'm brave. I fought Trudeau, stole my horses back. I fought the Rees, and Packrat."

One-Eye's face twists with disgust—and fills the world. 'Any man can fight and die, White Coyote. You are afraid to look at truth. Afraid of what you might discover."

He drifts there in the air and as I watch he changes. His back arches, malformed and hairy. The sagging face is taking on a canine look, eyes, two of them now, yellowing, piercing me. The long lip lifts to expose wolfish teeth.

I back into the water, stepping down from the bank. The wolf leers down at me, death and violence in his eyes. Fear drives me out into the current. I stagger back and forth, arms flailing for balance.

I sense the wolf's intent—to tear my flesh from my bones. It will eat me alive. The current is tugging at me, wrapping around my legs and drawing me backward into deeper water.

The wolf leaps—growling—and, with nowhere to go, I twist and dive into the black swirling water. Thrashing and kicking, I am sucked down, ever deeper, my lungs fit to burst. I whimper fearfully as I'm whirled around and around.

I've got to find the way out...got to find...

Richard jolted awake, gasping for breath. Safe—he was safe on *Maria's* deck. The fear slowly melted from his veins while a cool breeze caressed his skin. A gaudy sun had just cleared the eastern horizon to cast bloody light over the dark-shadowed land.

Boston an illusion? He rubbed a hand over his sweat-damp face. The dream remained so clear, as if lived rather than spun from phantasms. A Power dream, Willow would have told him.

Willow!—He had to see her, talk to her.

Am I a coward? Is that it?

Birds riddled the morning with intertwining songs, their music alive in the branches. Richard willed himself to sit up and stare out at the river; the water looked placid in the crimson light.

But no matter how smooth the surface, strong currents run beneath.

A man could float along, mistaking the whirls and eddies for reality on life's journey to the sea of death. But dive down below and he would truly know the current's power as it jetted in endless passage.

Boston: a place of caged bears, all ignorant of the

reality beyond the bars. What was it Professor Ames had once said? Something about a building, and walls...It hadn't made sense at the time, and Richard couldn't remember. Well, it would come back to him.

Boston—his world—where men constantly erected new bars to imprison themselves. They called the bars religion, philosophy, morality, law, or ethics, and the worst thing was that they never saw them for what they were: artifacts based on illusion. Not ultimate reality.

Richard moved slowly, deliberately, to remove his blanket. He gasped, not at the healing wound, but at the sunburn on his shoulders. The pain reassured him. That —unlike the city of his dreams—was palpable.

After all those months of patient lectures by Travis and Baptiste, he could finally understand what they were trying to tell him about freedom, and life.

Jaw clamped, Richard braced himself on the cargo box as he emptied his night water over the side. He'd lain on the deck for long enough.

One careful step after another, he made his way to the plank and tottered down to the camp. Smoke rose in blue twists from the *engagés'* breakfast fires. Men sat on rumpled blankets, smoking their long-stemmed pipes while they talked over the last of their watered-down coffee. Tin pots clanked as they were collected for the day.

Richard nodded to Toussaint and Simon as he passed their fire. Trudeau ignored him, as did de Clerk and the rest. At Travis's fire, the beds were already rolled, the saddles missing.

Richard studied the crushed grass, picking the trail through the bur oak and ash, to find the cavvy. Baptiste talked soothingly as he saddled the hammer-headed roan.

Travis had picked up the white mare's front hoof, inspecting a cut on her fetlock.

"Good morning," Richard said.

"Yor up?" Baptiste asked. "I guess Willow's doctoring did you some good. Hell, I never seen a coon heal that fast from a wound like that."

"She's some, she is," Travis agreed, lowering the hoof and slapping the mare reassuringly. He straightened and studied Richard through neutral eyes.

"Where is she?" Richard looked around, expecting to see her ghost through the trees like a brown wraith, her bedroll under one arm, her packs secured by the other. "I really need to talk to her." Richard noticed that Willow's horse was missing.

'Too late, coon. She done lit out fer her people. Packed up afore dawn, saddled her little brown mare, and headed fer the mountains." Travis absently scratched the mare's ears. Baptiste had crossed his arms, head tilted. He watched Richard through hard black eyes.

Richard stared dumbly. "What? This is a joke, right? Another trick you're playing on me? Look, I've got to tell her something. It's important, Travis."

"Too late," Baptiste said gruffly. "She's done left, Dick. Ain't no trick to it. She pulled her stick."

"I don't…I mean, you didn't just *let* her ride off?"

"Wal, what did ye expect? That we'd tie her up and threaten to shoot her?" Travis demanded. "She's free, Dick. Ye freed her yerself back when ye raised the Pawnee."

"She can't leave. Not now. Not when I've—"

"She's *gone,* I said." Travis stepped closer, blue eyes cold as winter ice. "Because she wanted ye…and ye didn't want her. Not as a woman, anyway. Hell, I tried to talk her out of pulling her traps, spoke fer ye—Hob hisself knows why—but she'd made up her mind. And rightly so, I reckon."

"We've got to go after her." Richard eased his good shoulder against one of the trees to support the sudden weakness in his legs.

"Nope," Travis replied curtly. "Baptiste run a scout up the river last night. Atkinson and O'Fallon is about three days upriver. We gotta find a place ter cache *Maria*. By the time we get that done, Willow's gonna be long gone. She's gonna be riding careful, hiding tracks."

"But you could follow her, Travis. You're the best there is at working out tracks."

The scarred hunter gave him a grim smile. "Maybe. But we got the boat ter take care of. Dick, hear me, now. We're on the upper river. Ain't no friends out hyar. Understand? Assiniboin, Yanktoni, Atsina, Blackfeet, Cheyenne—any of 'em will take the boat."

"But you can't just leave Willow alone out there!"

"She's a growed woman," Baptiste said coldly. "She knows this country, Dick. She ain't no pilgrim."

Richard wrapped an arm around the tree, steadying himself with something stable in a world suddenly shaken. "What if they find her out there?"

"Then they'll rape her fer a while and lift her topknot after they's through." Travis spun on his heel, but not before Richard saw the strain on his face. "I ain't a gonna think about that, Dick. I got a boat ter get upriver. Now, come on, Baptiste, we ain't got all day."

Mute, Richard watched them pack, grab up their rifles, and climb into their saddles. Then they hazed the rest of the horses out of the little clearing. Travis hesitated at the break in the bur oak, touched the brim of his hat, and clucked his horse onward.

Richard rubbed the back of his neck, and made his

way to Willow's camp. He bent down to run his fingers over the flattened grass where her bed had been. The fire still held warm embers, faint ribbons of smoke rising from the ashes.

A sickness lodged in the pit of his stomach. *My fault... all my fault.*

CHAPTER TEN

Adam, though his rational faculties be supposed, at the very first, entirely perfect, could not have inferred from the fluidity and transparency of water that it would suffocate him, or from the light and warmth of fire that it would consume him. No object ever discovers, by the qualities which appear to the senses, either the causes which produced it, or the effects which will arise from it; nor can our reason, unassisted by experience, ever draw any inference concerning real existence and matter of fact.

—David Hume, *An Enquiry Concerning Human Understanding*

 Travis lay in the grass beside Dave Green and Henri. The booshway growled angrily under his breath as he glared at the river beyond the mat of buffaloberry branches. Henri had his pipe clamped between his teeth; the bowl was stone-cold. Despite Green's growling, the patroon remained calm, staring out at the river's main channel.

Travis gave Green a sidelong glance. The booshway

wore a baggy white stroud shirt, a felt hat pulled low on his blond hair. His blocky face had a hard set, blue eyes narrow as he glared at the world. His thick fists were clenched.

Travis worked his chew from one side of his mouth to the other, and spat a brown streak with enough accuracy to knock a grasshopper from a spike of bluestem. Dave was fit to kill, all right.

The patch of buffaloberry where they lay concealed them from observation. They'd found the perfect place to hide the boat. Behind them, *Maria* was screened from view by a wall of young cottonwoods. They'd pulled her into an old loop of the river, cut off now, and mostly silted in. To the north, grassy bluffs—worn down by countless seasons of wind and storm—had turned tawny in the late August sun.

"We'll be fine," Travis said. "The boat's outa sight. Ain't nothing to give us away to Atkinson."

"It's not Atkinson and O'Fallon." Green shook his head slowly. "Though it'd be hell if they caught us up here without a permit."

"Willow?"

"I'm going to reach out with these hands"—Green's outstretched thick fingers curled—"and choke the life right out of that skinny little Doodle bastard!"

"Now, Dave"—Travis swatted at a big bottle fly—"she's free. Ye agreed to that way back this side of Fort Atkinson. Said she's a guest, remember?"

"Why didn't you stop her?" Green demanded, his square face reddening with anger. "You had the chance. Don't you know how important she is to us? Damn, man, she can bring in the Shoshoni. Think of the opportunities that squaw represented. And you...you just *let her go?*"

Henri's mustache twitched, but he kept his expression bland.

Travis's eyes followed the fluttering path of a little blue butterfly that wobbled past his nose. "She ain't just a squaw, Dave."

"Now, what in hell does that mean?"

Travis rolled his chew and shifted away from the stiff grass prickling his side. "Reckon she's a friend of mine."

"Then, why in hell did you just let your *friend*—and an opportunity that could save us years—ride off into the plains? Don't you—"

"Because I set store by friends, Dave," Travis replied coldly. "Or maybe ye've a short memory on that account?"

"Easy, my friends," Henri said, studying the river.

Green ground his teeth. "No. I haven't forgotten, Trav."

Silence stretched. A flock of siskins twittered in the overhanging cottonwood branches, playing among the triangular leaves.

"So." Green relented. "She made a friend out of you?"

"Uh-huh." Travis squinted across the river. She'd be down there, someplace. Far to the south, cutting across country, keeping off the skyline, running shy of the waterholes and creeks to avoid human hunters. "Never met a woman like her afore. Seems ter me, Dave, that we otta cross our lucky stars that her type's as rare as it is. Too many Injun women like Willow, and we'd be in a fix fer sure up hyar."

Henri tapped wistfully at his cold pipe and added, "I know that one, she is like the fox, cunning and quick. And she fights like the panther when cornered. If anyone can cross the plains, it is *ma petite Willow*."

"Well, I sure never met a woman who could see as

clearly as Willow did. That queer look she'd give a feller...
I guess I believe her when she says she's looking straight
into your soul." Green shifted, curious. "You ever try and
take her? Offer to marry her?"

"Nope." Travis worked his chew and fingered his rifle.

"Why not? She was the match of Calf in the Moonlight, that's sure. Or did that warn you off?"

"Nope. First off, she and Dick was making eyes at
each other. Another reason was she didn't give me no
sign she's interested in the likes of me. Last of all, I don't
reckon no coon with sense would go pushing himself off
on her. She kilt the last red bastard did that."

"Hamilton killed him."

"He just finished the job she'd started. Mark me,
Dave. She had that Pawnee kid right where she wanted
him. You told me yerself how he was plumb spooked at
Fort Atkinson. Said he was crazy enough to try and ride
off on a hobbled hoss. She done that to him. Claims she
drove him insane—and this child believes it. Only coon
hyar could have had her was Dick."

"Yep. And I'm going have his sorry hide just as soon
as the damned army floats past. That white-arsed
Doodle's going to wish he'd died clear back when he had
the scours." Green clenched a gnarled fist to make his
point.

"Leave him be, Dave."

"*Leave him be?* Not on your—"

"Leave him be." Travis poked Green with a hard
finger.

"Damn you, Travis, sometimes I don't understand
how your head works. Just let him alone? After he soured
the deal with Willow? It was his stupid, bull-headed
idiocy that drove her off. Hob take him! A woman like
that...and he just ignored her."

Travis spat one last time, then plucked the chewed quid from his mouth, studying the toothmarked leaves before flinging it out into the nodding sunflowers that grew to his left. "How come ye quit playing cards with me?"

"Got tired of getting skinned down to my bones. Tarnal hell, if I played for money with you, you'd own this whole shitaree—boat, barrels, and muskets. I can't pull nothing over on you."

"Then trust me, Dave. I seen the look in Dick's eyes when he figgered out that Willow'd gone fer good. He ain't looked that bad since the night François dumped his sorry carcass on deck. Leave him be...in fact, be nice as Hob. Reckon he'll do just fine a-twisting his own tail. Hell, the way he blames hisself, if'n he was Christ, he'd be pounding the nails into the Cross."

Green considered, a grim smile curling his hard lips. He fingered his thick blond beard. "All right. I'll let him alone."

"Good."

"I don't know why I let you talk me into these things."

Henri chuckled to himself.

Travis pointed down at the bend of the river. Baptiste came toward them at a dead run, skirting wide of the spiky green rushes in the marsh bottom. "Lookee yonder. The way Baptiste's moving, Atkinson and his soldiers is just round the bend. Reckon I'm gonna Injun over and make sure the *engagés* stay put."

Green's fists clenched. "All right. Try not to shoot any if you can help it. Last thing we need is for the army to hear a shot."

Travis grinned, backing away. "Ye know me. If'n I'm ary a thing, it's careful!"

"Oui." Henri added. "And sneaky as a Comanche in a trader's horse herd."

———

Some long-gone storm had blown down a giant cottonwood. In subsequent years the bark had sloughed off to expose the smooth wood to sun and weather. Time had silvered the bare trunk, which now served as home for ants, spiders, and field mice, and made a perfect seat for Richard Hamilton as well.

He sat hunched in the midday sun, using a long stem of grass to slap aimlessly at bugs, grass spikes, or simply nothing as the mood struck him.

Maria lay grounded on the mud behind him while the *engagés* sat in clusters in the shade of the cottonwoods. The day of rest would have been a delightful respite, but for the muggy heat, the biting flies, and the sense of desolation that possessed him.

In the beginning, he had expected to see her come riding in, head high, raven braids bouncing as she pulled her mare up. Then, ever so regal, she'd give them that knowing look and fall in on one side of the horse herd.

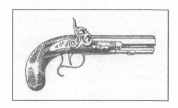

But the distant horizon had remained empty. Nor had she appeared out of the tree-filled bottoms with their brushy cover.

Face it, she's gone.

The thought turned over and over in Richard's mind. Each time it did, the soul-sickness expanded, eating more of him.

Sure, he was supposed to think of Laura, of how they would marry eventually, but Laura lived in a different world, one Richard couldn't be sure existed any more. Here, on the river, he dreamed of Willow, and forbidden love.

How did you make such a mess of this?

He closed his eyes, remembering the first moment he saw her, sitting straight and proud on Packrat's horse.

I shot him dead to protect you. Willow. Blew his chest open.

She'd been hurt, and he'd held her, carried her, marveling at the softness of her body.

"The first time I ever held a woman." He slashed bitterly at a ladybug, missing the insect but knocking it off the half-eaten leaf it had been laboriously crossing.

How close he had come to surrendering to her that day above the Grand Detour. He'd been bathing in the clear water, enjoying the sunlight sparkling off the ripples and warming his bare skin. What horror he'd felt when he looked over to see her standing there like a goddess. He could recall every detail—how the sunlight had caressed her, the way her hair glinted. Yes, and the way the water had beaded like diamonds on her dark skin. Somehow, in the talk that followed, they'd drifted together, responding to the caress of the water, and each other.

Why didn't you do something?

Slashing at the grass again, the stem broke. He rolled it between thumb and forefinger, scowling. "Because she was an Indian...and I was a fool."

"First his woman leaves him, and now he talks to himself," Trudeau's voice intruded.

Richard jumped to his feet, wincing at the dull ache it caused in his back. Trudeau stood several paces away, white shirt rippling in the breeze. Mockery filled those dark eyes. Off to one side stood Toussaint, arms crossed.

"Go away," Richard said wearily.

"Go away? Like your woman, eh?" Trudeau laughed, shook his head, and sauntered off toward the other *engagés,* his fingers tapping the grass spikes as he went.

Toussaint studied Richard with veiled eyes. "Trudeau, he's still bitter, Reeshaw," Toussaint made a Gallic shrug. "A man ees no more than he ees."

As the big *engagé* trailed off in Trudeau's wake, Richard plucked another grass stem, looking closely at the tiny veins in the rough green leaves. "A man is no more than he is. *Cogito, ergo sum.* God, does that mean I'm going to be a fool for the rest of my life?"

"What's that, coon?"

Richard shook himself, surprised that Travis had stopped behind him. "Is everyone sneaking up on me?"

"Nope, just walking normal like." Travis cocked his head, careful eyes on the *engagés.* "But ye was so all-fired interested in that stem of grass, I could'a lifted yer topknot clean, and ye'd never have known a thing till the breeze was blowing acrost yer skull."

"Did you come here specifically to harass me?"

"Nope. Come ter do a head count on the *engagés*...and it looks like they're all hyar."

"Green ordered Toussaint to keep track." Richard winced as he swiveled his shoulder, surprised at how much more he could move it today. "He's a strange man."

"Yep. Come from Montreal, way back when. Story has it that Toussaint come home early one night and caught his wife in bed with his best friend. Supposedly he kilt 'em both, threw lamp oil on everything, and set the whole shitaree afire. Trouble was, he had two twin daughters, little babies in a crib. They burnt, too. Now, some folks might forgive a man fer burning his wife and her lover, but not them baby girls."

"Did he ever say why he burned the girls?"

"Not ter me, he didn't. I ain't never heard him talk about it. Story tells it that he burnt 'em because he warn't sure they's his daughters. But that's just story."

Richard rubbed the back of his neck, glancing skeptically at Toussaint. "I can't believe it. The man saved my life that time the bank caved in and pitched me into the river. I would have drowned but for him. And he always seems to be concerned with doing the right thing."

"Uh-huh. Wal, if'n yer gonna fall in the river and drown again, don't go sleeping with his wife first. He might not pull ye out next time."

"Just once I wish you'd—"

"Come on, coon." Travis turned on his heel, the Hawken balanced in his right hand. "I figger ye'll want ter see this."

Richard glanced warily over at Toussaint, who now lounged against a cottonwood, chin propped on his callused hand as he watched three-card monte being played on a blanket. Killed his wife? *A man ees no more than he ees?*

Richard shook himself and followed in Travis's tracks. They wound through the cottonwoods, then down toward the willows. Travis raised a hand for care, and led the way into a copse of cottonwood saplings just up the bank from the roiling water.

Richard crouched and followed Travis into the concealment of the trees. "What are we doing?"

"Atkinson and O'Fallon is coming. They're just

yonder, round that bend." Travis studied Richard from the corner of his eye. "Ye thought much about them?"

Richard sighed. "It would be a fast and safe trip back to Saint Louis, wouldn't it?"

"Yep."

"Wait a minute. Why are you bringing this up? I said I'd stick with you until the mouth of the Yellowstone. We're not there yet."

"Ye ever think about what happens when ye get there?"

"Yes. I take a horse and ride for Saint Louis."

"Uh-huh. So, tell me, Dick. What're the chances that ye'll make it—a lone white man—two thousand miles through the dead of winter, with the temperature at forty below, snow drifted higher than an elk's ass, and ten thousand Injuns all fit ter lift yer outfit and hair first chance they get?"

Richard exhaled wearily, dropping his head into his hands. "I don't know. Damn, Travis, I'm not even sure I care anymore. But, I... Just a moment, this is lunacy. Why are you doing this? What do you care? You're tempting me, damn you. Why? What game are you playing?"

Travis fingered the scars running across his face as he watched the river. "I ain't playing no game, Dick. I'm giving ye facts, is all. And I reckon I'm a mite curious. How are ye gonna choose? Coming round that bend is General Atkinson, nine keelboats, and hundreds of soldiers. Ye'll be back in Boston in time fer Christmas— and nary a chance of getting yer hair lifted on the way."

"And the other way?"

"Ye'll stick it out on the boat...as an *engagé*. Sweating and pulling yer way to the Yellerstone. I reckon it'll be the end of September by the time we get there. Probably be the first of November by the time we make the mouth of the Big Horn. Ye won't have safe passage down the river fer another year—and then it won't be no nine keelboats full of soldiers."

"Salvation or Hell, is that what you're offering me? Who are you, Satan in the wilderness?"

Travis smiled grimly. "I been called worse."

"I don't get it. You've laid a trap in this, haven't you?"

"Nope. It ain't no skin off my arse no matter what ye choose."

"If Willow hadn't left, you wouldn't be doing this, would you?"

"I reckon not."

Richard rubbed his sweaty face. That's when he saw the coyote watching him intently from the thick grass. The yellow eyes seemed to bore into his, measuring and weighing. But he didn't have time for coyotes. "I don't understand."

"Call her a test, Dick. Philos'phers take them, don't they?"

A test? To see if I'm stupid enough to stay, or smart enough to go? It had to be something deeper than that. Travis Hartman never did anything simple or superficial.

"Is it that you want me to go? That you're mad because Willow left? Look, I didn't force her to ride off, Travis."

"Nope. At least, not at gunpoint." The hunter cocked his head as if listening. "Tell me, Dick, do you love her?"

Images of Willow filled his mind, the firelight on her face at night, her slender hands so graceful, the endless depths of those large dark eyes that seemed to have looked into eternity. How whitely her teeth flashed when she smiled.

And Laura?

She's become a myth, Richard. As much an illusion as Boston. Face it, she's a dream.

Richard cleared his throat. "Yes."

Travis pulled his rifle up beside him and chewed thoughtfully at the fringes of his mustache. "And if n ye could get her back, would ye?"

Richard nodded, unwilling to make the vocal commitment that his soul screamed

"Wal, coon, she's upriver." Travis jerked a thumb. "That is, if'n she makes it safe back to her people. More than one man around hyar is ready ter choke ye dead fer making her leave. Me, I understand her reasons, and I figger I understand yers. Ye made that choice, and now, by God, ye'll live with it."

"Then, you're telling me this because you *want* me to leave?"

Travis's blue eyes were cool. "This hyar's yer Yellowstone, Dick. I'm just making ye choose early because it's the smartest thing. If'n ye want ter go home to Boston now, ye'd be best ter take Atkinson's boats. But, when ye makes that choice, ye'll live with it fer the rest of yer life."

Richard closed his eyes. "But if I go with you...there's a good chance I'll be killed up there." The *wechashawakan* had as much as promised it that night at Wah-Menitu's village. But he'd also promised that the answers lay upriver, and hollow emptiness back east.

"I reckon if'n I's a philos'pher, I'd take Atkinson's boats back."

"Just once I'd like to see you be wrong for a change."

"Last time I's wrong, I got half my guts carved out and had ter have yer likes sew me shut."

Richard grinned in spite of himself. "So, let's say I go with you. What are my chances of finding Willow?"

Travis shrugged. "Baptiste and me, we figger it's fifty-fifty that she makes it home safe. She ain't no pilgrim, that's certain. The way she had it figgered, she'd cut straight southwest to the Little Missouri, stick ter the uplands, sneak down ter water at night, and make about twenty-five miles a day. More'n that, she'll wear that little mare down."

"If no one catches her."

"There's always that."

The pesky coyote's stare still fixed on Richard. Didn't the creature have enough sense to steer shy of men?

"I'd have stopped her if I'd known. Travis, I would have thrown myself at her feet and begged forgiveness for all the stupid things I've said and done. God, I hate myself. What a hypocrite I've been. Talking about Truth—Truth from the narrowed blinders of a silly Bostonian. I've been wrong all along. Arrogant in my ignorance."

"Would ye fix it?" Travis reached into his possibles for his tobacco. He cut a chew off the twist and offered it to Richard.

"If I could." Richard studied the brown plug, and shook his head. "Everything we accept as true, it all comes from Greek, Roman, and Judaic foundations. Christian thoughts and dogma were built upon them and have shaped everything we believe. But it's only true in Boston. Not here. You tried to tell me." He swallowed hard. "Willow tried to tell me.

"She's a one fer that, she is. The night afore she left, she asked me about God. She asked, 'If God doesn't believe in us, will we die? Or, if we don't believe in God, will God die?' And she said it was really important to know what you want ter believe. Now, that took me some figgering, 'cause I reckoned that ye just believed what ye was supposed to. Hell, this child never wondered *why* he's supposed to."

"She confronted me with the same epistemological challenge."

"Huh? Epissed..."

"Epistemological. The study of how we know what we know."

"Ye didn't use that word on her, did ye?"

"Of course. I think I mentioned eschatology as well."

"Esskat...Shit! No wonder she left."

"But that's the root of—"

"Shut up, yonder's Atkinson."

Richard crouched lower behind the branches. The first keelboat had rounded the sinuous bend in the river. It was following the main channel as it came into view. The brown boat's reflection elongated on the glassy blue surface. A second boat rounded the curve, and then another, and another.

On they came, rushing headlong down the river. Driven by human-powered paddlewheels, they seemed to fly across the water. Blue-coated soldiers lounged on the decks and cargo boxes. Some relaxed on bales; others occupied themselves with card games, mending clothes, or cleaning equipment.

"Hell of a fleet, ain't it? Not even Manuel Lisa ever got so many boats upriver. And ain't them paddlewheels some?" Travis spat, then pointed. "Lookee thar! William Ashley, by God. And them coons in the buckskins, why, I seen them up ter the Platte last year. Tarnal hell, look at them packs of beaver!"

Richard squinted at the brown bundles lined up along the cargo boxes. "That's beaver?"

"Uh-huh. And ye can bet they's more prime stuff cached in the cargo boxes. Hell, old Atkinson shoulda had lots of room by the time his soldiers ate their way upriver and he give away all his presents. Ashley's a rich man, coon. That's a lifetime's wealth right afore yer eyes." Travis paused. "Lessen, of course, he up and gives the like away to François and his boys."

Richard bit off a quick retort, and Travis chuckled. The boats were moving fast, water boiling at the bows. With all those soldiers, that much power, it would be a safe trip. And not all would be lost. Talking with Ashley and the others, Richard could learn enough about the fur trade to repay at least a little of what his father had lost.

"If I want to leave, I can just up and run out to the edge of the river?"

Travis shook his head. "Wait until tonight. Ye can take yer white mare and head downriver. I'd reckon ye'll make their camp by morning."

"They'd ask where I came from. I'd have to tell them something—and Green doesn't have a trading permit. I couldn't lie, Travis."

"Nope. But then I know ye, Dick. If'n ye give yer word that ye won't tell 'em nothing about us fer a couple of days, we'll be so far upriver they won't come after us. By the time we take fur ter Saint Loowee, it'll be blowed over. Hell, maybe ye could talk ter old Red-Hair Clark and smooth it out fer us?'

"My father has a great deal of influence. It wouldn't... my God, what am I saying?" He watched the boats shoot past. They had to be making close to six knots.

They watched in silence as the line of craft rounded the cottonwood-lined bend of the river and vanished as if no more than a mirage.

The swelling emptiness in Richard's chest expanded; he lowered his forehead onto his hands. For long seconds, he was content to hear the rustle of the leaves, the chatter of the birds, and the humming click of the insects.

Dear Lord God, what am I going to do? Which direction do I go from here?

He tried to quiet his milling thoughts. All those arguments on ethics, on responsibility, on man in nature, seemed no help to him now. The answer, the thing he was looking for, lay just over the mind's horizon. There, in the blackness of imagination. If only he could reach out just a little further...stretch that last bit and lay ahold of...

"Damn it."

"They's past, coon," Travis said, laying a gentle hand on Richard's wounded shoulder. "Wal, it's yer decision ter make."

Richard lifted his head, blinking, more soul-sick than he'd ever felt. "I've made it."

"Do I need ter saddle yer hoss?"

"Nope. But I changed my mind about that chew. Cut me a piece. I think I need it."

Travis gave him a wry smile. "Glad ter have ye aboard, Dick."

"Yes, well—then why don't I feel so good about it?"

The hunter straightened, stepping out of the cottonwoods to stare after the army boats. "Because, coon, I knew ye wouldn't."

Richard glanced over at the tall grass. The coyote had vanished as if he'd never been.

———

At the top of a rise, Willow pulled her horse up, watching her backtrail in the slanting light of sunset. The whole world might have turned to soft gold as the tawny grasses glowed in the yellow light. Undulations in the land created soft shadows and honeyed contours that grew ever fainter until they met the darkening blue of the northeastern sky. The heavens rose like a glassy dome, a fitting cap for the majesty of the vista.

Nowhere in that infinity of grass did she see more than scattered bands of buffalo and antelope. Her horse stamped, flicking ears and tail at the bothersome flies.

Willow reached out to pat the mare on the neck, whispering, "And to think I don't like horses."

An ear swiveled in her direction.

"You and me, we are going to be friends for a while. At least until we reach the mountains. After that, who knows? Perhaps I shall turn you loose in the meadows."

Willow clucked her mare forward, winding down from the high bluff into a hollow. Spikes of grass made a hissing sound as the mare broke through their virgin ranks. They pattered off the bottom of Willow's moccasins, seeds knocked from the bristling heads.

So much grass, ridge after ridge, as far as the eye could see.

Following the lay of the land, Willow crossed a divide and worked her way down into a shallow valley as the sun turned gaudily red, flattened on the dark silhouette of horizon, then sank behind the distant bluffs.

Just after sunset, she made camp in a patch of chokecherry and wild plum. A small fire, barely enough to see by, satisfied her needs. The night was pleasant, and she needed only to warm a tin cup of water for tea. The rest of her meal consisted of dried berries, pemmican she'd traded for among the Mandan, and slivers of jerked buffalo meat.

Unrolling her blanket, she leaned back against the saddle and watched the night sky darken. Frosty specks of starlight twinkled and grew ever brighter.

The air carried the scent of dry grass, brush, and leaves. Occasionally the breeze would tease her with smoke from her dying fire, now burned to faint red embers.

The mare crunched contentedly on grass, molars grinding loudly in the newly fallen silence. Somewhere in the distance, buffalo wolves howled into the gloom, to be answered a moment later by a band of coyotes, their yipping calls higher, mocking, the way Coyote had mocked Wolf since the beginning of time.

The familiar stories of her Shoshoni people brought her comfort. Coyote and Wolf, always in opposition. Wolf, ever so responsible, dedicated, and obsessed with duty. Forever crossed by Coyote, the Trickster, who sought shortcuts, gratification, and trouble.

She sipped her mint tea and stared into the starry maze of night. "How did I act? Like Wolf, responsible, and prudent? Or have I tricked myself?"

As a child, she'd looked up at the night sky, conjuring patterns among the stars. And tonight, as she did so, she could see Richard's face, his eyes, nose, and mouth, shaded into reality by the longing in her souls and the dusting of starlight across the heavens.

He'd be in camp by now, staring into a fire as Travis and Baptiste smoked their long-stemmed pipes. The *engagés'* fires would be flickering in the background as soft French songs rose on the night.

What is he thinking? Am I in his thoughts the way he fills mine?

She emptied the last of her tea, setting her cup to one side. Such a useful thing, a tin cup. Travis had given it to her.

You made your choice. Willow. You must live with it.

It hadn't been so hard. She'd simply saddled up and ridden out. The longing for Richard, and the companionship of Travis and Baptiste, had only begun to hurt. In the coming days that gnawing ache would try her souls.

She crossed her arms, seeing a star streak across the sky and vanish. "Yes, it will hurt. But only for a while." As the distance between them grew, so would the ache fade.

"In the end," she promised herself, "it will be much kinder for you than suffering each day—so close to him, and so far away."

She resettled herself under the blanket. "Good-bye, Richard. May *Tam Apo* watch over you, and help send you back to your Boston."

Then tears blurred her vision of the stars.

CHAPTER ELEVEN

Moral virtue is not implanted in us by nature; for nothing that derived from nature can be metamorphosed by habit Thus a stone that naturally must fall downwards, cannot be habituated or taught to rise upwards, even if we tried to train it by throwing it up ten thousand times. Nor again can fire be trained to sink downwards, nor anything else that follows any single natural law be habituated or trained to follow another. It is neither by nature, then, nor in defiance of nature, that virtues are nourished within us. Nature gives us the capacity to receive them, and that capacity is perfected by habit.

—Aristotle, *Nicomachean Ethics*

The days of September wore away under enamel blue skies, warm winds, and amber sunlight. The land had changed, the last stands of green ash left behind them. Cottonwoods in solid ranks lined the floodplain now, groves of bur oak only dotting the higher drainages. The

Missouri ran almost clear—a man could see the bottom as he wrestled the heavy cordelle through rush-and-cattail-clogged shallows.

They pulled across the mucky confluence of the Little Missouri, and passed the mouth of Little Muddy Creek. Several times, small bands of Assiniboin rode down from the uplands to trade. Each time, Green bartered trinkets, powder, and ball for buffalo robes, thick moccasins, and sections of pemmican-filled buffalo gut.

"Laying in fer winter," Travis remarked when Richard asked about it.

The night air brought a new crispness, one that tingled the skin and quickened the heart. How different the chill was—not the sapping damp cold of the woodlands, but cold that gave a fellow a sudden slap.

Like an ox, Richard labored on the cordelle, sparing neither his body nor soul. He drove himself, heedless of his injured shoulder, and then harder and harder as he healed completely and the scab fell away from the puckered scar.

At first, Trudeau had snorted, commenting about a booshway Yankee who couldn't even keep a squaw. Richard ignored him, but as his body hardened, Trudeau fell silent.

I bear my own cross, Richard told himself, bitter at the irony, for his cross was made of bristly hemp, his Golgotha forever around the river's next bend.

He had the time to think now, for the endless toil was mindless. The river had finally washed away his foolishness. Time and again, his thoughts turned to Philip. By now his father thought his only son dead.

First Mother, and now me. How deep is the wound in his soul?

Every ache, every blister and trickle of sweat that ran down his bent back, came in the penitent quest for self-forgiveness. He'd stagger forward, coaxing more out of his fatigue-numb flesh.

A philosopher? No, a fool. And an arrogant one at that.

Muscles popping, he'd throw himself into the pole, trying to shove *Maria* upriver by sheer force of body and will. He welcomed the pain as the pole bruised his shoulder.

If I can chase down the Crow, I can endure this.

He could envision his father, incomplete, and adrift. Like a dim reflection of his civilization, he had nothing but a shield of masculinity left.

Panting, he'd wipe stinging sweat from his eyes and glance over at Travis where he sat his horse at the edge of the cavvy, the Hawken resting crossways on the saddlebow. Over the distance, their eyes would meet. The flicker of understanding passing between them.

Then Richard would redouble his efforts, seeking to peel the cleats off the *passe avant* as he pushed the boat upriver. The other *engagés* might not have existed, phantoms among whom he worked.

Blind, everyone, was blind. *But I have the first faint images of the vision.*

At night, he'd eat all he could hold, drink the last of

the watery coffee, and seek his blankets. Then, despite the thick haze of exhaustion, the dreams would come. Fantastic images of Willow, her warm lips parting, dark eyes gleaming, soft strands of raven black hair curling around her perfect cheeks...

She danced in the sunlight, naked, full breasts swaying, water gleaming in silver droplets on her smooth brown skin. Around she spun, arms like wings as she rose and fell to the rhythm of French songs. Her dark eyes sparkled with a diamond intensity.

"I have the answer, Ritshard," her sensual voice told him. "It is here." And she pressed the hollow between her breasts. "The truth is here, Ritshard."

He reached for her—only to have her drift away like smoke on a soft morning breeze.

"Tell me! Please!" And he chased after her, nearly berserk with the need to hold her, to tell her it would all be fine in the end.

"I love you, Ritshard." Her distant voice caressed his soul. Then she faded like a chimera. Panic rose, timed to the beat of his heart, driven by a premonition. Subtle tentacles of horror tightened around him, invisible and shadowy.

He ran then. And ran, and ran, as he had in pursuit of the stolen horses; but the entire time, down in the root of his soul, no matter how hard he ran, he knew he was too late.

Finally, staggering with exhaustion, he topped one of the grassy knolls and found her.

She lay sprawled on her back in the grass, bloody sockets where those lustrous brown eyes had been. Her wealth of shining hair was gone, the skull caked with blackened blood. Her lips— dried by the hot wind—had pulled back from broken teeth. Maggots writhed in a gray-white ball where her tongue should have been.

Arrows pierced both of her breasts. Her nipples had been

hacked off. The edges of the ragged wound in her belly had curled up and hardened, but he could see where they'd pulled her intestines out and strung them around for the coyotes and ravens.

My fault.

The words would echo around his head. He bent down to kiss her sun-dried skin. As his lips touched her, a shadow blotted out the world. Terrifying, it lowered itself over him, and a horrible chill settled into his soul until he could only bury his face against her wind-dried flesh...

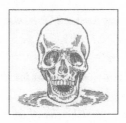

Gasping, he awoke to stare around the silent camp. Any regret for his aching muscles, for the blisters and exhaustion, had vanished. And with sunrise, he rose again, ready to pull or push the boat onward, alone if necessary.

That night, he would dream it all again.

————

Leading Richard's white mare, Travis rode the gray gelding down toward the line of *engagés* who cordelled *Maria* against the current. Like obstinate mules on a towline, they threaded through the marshy shallows, splashing and singing, as ragged-looking a crew as had ever ascended the river. At the end came Dick, back bent, head down, driven by that stubborn will.

Travis made a quick scout of the grassy flats leading up from the river. To the north, the bluff had been cut off sharp, and one day, some fool like Atkinson would build a fort on that level high ground. But, God willing, not for many years yet.

The wide floodplain to the south of the river rose in a sloping ridge. Here and there, cairns of white rock had been piled: ancient Injun signs that rose above the autumn yellow grass. Tufts of cloud sailed serenely from the west, schooners of white against the high blue.

Fat prairie dogs with sparkling eyes stood at the mounded entrances to their holes. With each shrill bark, their tails flicked. The year had been a good one for prairie dogs, and if these critters were this fat, so were the buffalo.

A badger broke cover from one of the holes, its fur shaking in time to its waddling, bow-legged run. The blizzard of barks and squeaks went silent as the prairie dogs dived for safety.

Travis checked the pack behind his saddle, then clucked his horse to the edge of the flat beside the cordellers. He shifted, hearing the saddle leather complain, and called out, "Hyar! Dick!"

Richard left the line of curious cordellers and slogged through the rushes and tall grass. The Doodle had gone plumb to hell, ragged, dirty, face smudged, beard matted with filth. Sun-browned skin and hard muscle showed through rents in the shirt.

"Come on, Dick. Hyar's yer hoss. Climb up, coon."

Richard studied the white mare, noting the saddle with his rifle and possibles tied across the bows. "I've got work to do, Travis."

"Fer now, yer doing it with me."

Richard slid a muddy moccasin into the stirrup and swung onto the mare. Travis tossed him the lead rope before kicking his gelding around and into a trot for the high ridge.

"This wind, coon," Travis called over his shoulder, "it's mountain wind. Ain't a thing atween us and the Shining Mountains. Take a sniff. Ye can smell it. This hyar be the last step. God's country starts at the mouth of the Yellerstone. Ye'll see. Wild, unkept. Full of bears and painters and buffler. Nothing soft about it, not like downriver."

"I didn't notice much that was soft downriver, Travis. In fact, some of the country was pretty hard."

"Huh! Ye'll see, Dick."

"My name's Richard."

"I think I heard that afore." Travis crested the rounded top of the ridge and pointed. "Thar she be, coon. Take a look."

At the base of the bluff, a sinuous ribbon of water wound its way out of the south to join the broad Missouri. Even from this distance, the water looked clear, inviting, somehow fresh and pristine. In the floodplain, the cottonwoods rustled with the wind, some of the leaves already turned bright yellow.

"The Yellowstone," Richard said reverently.

"I ain't been here since twenty-three. Last time I saw her, the ice was breaking and Perez, Sal Smith, ol' Jacques Lejeuness, and me was taking a pirogue full of fur south ter Saint Loowee." He gestured around. "'Course, all this was snow-covered, colder than a bat's ass. And this wind what feels so warm and dry today, she's a-blowing like the gates of Hell swung open, fit ter freeze a man's piss afore it hit the ground."

Richard slouched on the mare. "Did I ever tell you that you have a unique way with words?"

"Nope. C'mon." Travis booted his gelding and led the way down into the broad floodplain. Buffalo chips, bleached light gray, dotted the short grass that crackled dryly under the horses' hooves. Travis sniffed, detecting the moist smell of the Yellowstone.

"This hyar, she's a mite of a dangerous place." Travis glanced around. "A heap of coons has gone under hyarabouts. Kilt by Blackfeet, Sioux, Assiniboin, Atsina, and anybody else passing through. This country around the mouth of the Yellowstone, it's open ground, claimed by the River Crows, Blackfeet, and the Assiniboin, and even sometimes by the Hidatsa."

"You said Immel and Jones were killed on the Yellowstone." Richard's eyes had narrowed as they neared the outermost of the cottonwoods. "Was that around here?"

"Upstream a mite. Hell, lookee thar" Travis pointed to a big bundle resting in a cottonwood. Brown, a little longer than a man, it lay on a platform that had been laid across a crook in the branches.

"What is it, Travis?"

"Dead man wrapped in a buffalo robe. Tree burial."

Richard frowned, slowing his horse. "Whose?"

"Crow, most likely. Can't tell without dragging him

down. He's gone beaver. Best leave him rest." Travis trotted his horse across an old river channel, hooves clattering in the rocks. "Death can come right quick in this country, Dick. A coon's got ter be on his uppers. Cain't take no chances, can't let yerself go—or the next thing, yer topknot's gonna be dangling from some Blackfoot coup stick."

"Are you trying to make a specific point?" Richard looked back over his shoulder at the lonesome corpse.

"Yep."

"Well, why don't you try saying it outright?"

They rode across the shallows and onto a gravel bar in the Yellowstone. Travis slid off his horse, tying the animal to a half-buried log that had drifted down to lodge there.

Richard stepped down and tied off his animal as Travis waded out into the river and drank deeply. He sucked down the cool water, happy with the familiar taste. Water trickling from his beard, he said, "Come on, Dick. Drink up. This hyar's mountain water."

Richard followed, mud washing from his worn moccasins and frayed hide pants. As he drank, Travis studied him, noting the dullness in the eyes, the smudged dirt, the stoop to the normally straight shoulders.

"All right, Dick. Peel yer clothes off 'n that sorry carcass of yers."

Richard squinted at him. "What?"

"I said, peel, coon. Yer gonna wash up. Hell, ye smells like a hiverner, and yer all gone ter shit—and poor doings at that."

"I'm fine."

"The hell ye are! Yer crappy! Filthy, broke down like a runty camp dog. Ye ain't even wearing yer coups any more. Why? 'Cause yer all punky inside. It's eating ye,

Dick. All that blame yer heaping on yerself. Well, by God and Hell, yer done with it hyar!"

"I said, I'm fine."

"Skin yerself, pilgrim." Travis gestured with his rifle.

Richard's fists knotted. "I'm going back to the boat."

"No, ye ain't." Travis balanced on his toes. "I brung ye hyar ter fix yerself. Yer carcass ain't a-going nowhar's until ye've made peace and cleaned up."

"You can't stop me."

"Wal, Doodle, it seems ye left yer rifle on yer saddle. I didn't." Travis cocked his gun, the click loud. "I can stop ye fer good, right hyar."

"Go ahead."

Travis shouldered his rifle, settling the sight blade on Richard's right eye. "Take a close look, coon." Despite the muted sound of the river, the click of the set trigger made Richard flinch. "Now, yer just a hair from dead. A mite of pressure from my finger, and old 'Meat-in-the-pot' hyar will raise ye certain. Take a look down that barrel, now. That's death, Dick."

Richard swallowed hard. "Travis? Why...why are you doing this?"

"Figgered to larn ye a lesson." And at that, he lowered the rifle, pulling the trigger as he caught the cock with the crook of his thumb and set it at half-cock. "Yer fixing ter get yerself killed anyway. As yer friend, I could make it quicker than the Blackfoot would."

"You wouldn't have shot me."

"I don't point no rifle at no one lessen I'm ready ter kill him." Travis tilted his head. "Now, Dick, ye've had time to punish yerself. It's over, hyar and now. If'n it ain't, I'm gonna shoot ye dead and leave ye fer wolfmeat."

Richard sagged then, looking uncomfortable.

"Dick, I ain't got time fer this nonsense. We're on the

Yellerstone now. Baptiste and me, we need another man ter help keep watch and guard the hosses. Look at ye! Yer trying right hard to ruin yerself, Dick, and I ain't gonna have it, that's all."

Richard lowered his head, water rippling around his ankles. "It's all gone hollow, Travis. I've been purging myself. That's all."

"I reckon a feller needs that on occasion. But time's come to ante up."

Richard paced back and forth, gesturing his futility. "Dear Lord God, Travis, I'm just beginning to understand how smart Willow is. She asked questions I've never heard before, challenged the very foundations of what I believe, what my people believe. But, do you know what? They'd throw her out of Boston! Call her a savage! Is that just? Is it ethical? Hell, to them she's nothing more than a greasy squaw!"

"You know she ain't. If'n they don't in Boston, I reckon that's their loss." Travis fingered the sight on his rifle. "But I never had no truck with them ignorant puff-and-struts."

"Everything they believe is wrong. All of it."

"Wal, ain't it all right fer some folks ter believe one way, and other folks ter believe another?"

"No! Don't you see? Not if you want to know ultimate Truth. It's like..." Richard's brow furrowed, then his eyes lit. "Of course! That's the example Professor Ames used. Travis, think of a building. Our people see the north wall and we call it God. The Mandan see the south wall, and call it God. The Shoshoni see the east wall, and Rees the west. Each calls its wall 'God.' But which is the real God? None—they are only sides of God. What a philosopher wants to know is the whole of God—all the walls, the floors, the hallways and closets and roof. That's the ultimate Truth."

Travis cocked his head. "Maybe."

"I was taught to believe that the north wall was all there was. We've accepted that for over two thousand years. And we've made assumptions based on that acceptance. From each assumption, we've made *other* assumptions about right and wrong, good and evil, duty, honor, and sacrifice. Like weaving a tapestry of how the building should look, each thread elaborating the nature of God and world. Now, the whole tapestry has come unraveled. I don't know which assumptions are correct any more."

"So, why are ye pushing yerself so?"

"Because I'm ashamed of my hypocrisy. Willow must think I'm a complete idiot."

"Hell, she only stayed as long as she did because of ye, ye knothead!"

"And if she dies out there? Damn it, Travis, I have nightmares about it, of her lying dead, scalped, and rotting."

"She's a full-growed woman, coon. Snake Indian down ter the center of her bones. And, hell, even if they catch her, she'll make it through. She's got a heap of sense. Damn it, Dick, is it so hard fer ye to trust her?"

"I...hell, I don't know."

"Wal, I do. Now, listen. This country's hard. Sometimes folks die. That's life, boy. Real life, not the Boston-be-safe-in-a-cage kind. She knows what she's doing."

"If I could only apologize, tell her how much I love her."

"Do it when ye sees her in the mountains, coon."

"If I see her in the mountains."

"Wal, acting like ye are now, I ain't sure yer gonna live that long."

"Me? She's the one out alone."

"She's got sense. You don't. Now, skin yerself and start scrubbing."

"And if I don't?"

"Wal, any coon wants ter go moping about in this country's nigh dead, so I ought just as well shoot ye hyar. First time yer out picking up firewood, a-feeling sorry fer yerself, some Blackfoot's gonna sneak up and kill ye. Why, if'n yer as good as dead, I might as well save ye the trouble of waiting. And this way, there ain't no chance of somebody who's depending on ye being let down, neither."

Richard narrowed his eyes. "That's not reason enough to shoot me, Travis."

"Ain't it? I'll be honest with ye, Dick. *I'm damned tired of fooling with ye.* Hear? Look down south there, damn ye! Immel and Jones died just a mite yonder. That's good enough fer this beaver. Now, if'n it ain't fer ye, well, I reckon we'd have ter figger which side of the building ye was seeing and which I was. Then we'd have a palaver over ethics—and in the end, I'd still shoot ye dead."

Then Travis smiled cynically and added: "Of course, there's the matter of the bet I made with Green and Baptiste."

"Bet? What bet?"

"I said I'd cure ye or kill ye—and bet a hun'ert prime plews on the outcome. Which, when a feller comes right down to it, makes all them walls yer talking about a mite frivolous."

"Maybe I'm making a career of being a fool."

"Wal, a coon's got ter do something with his life."

Richard kicked angrily at the water. Then he took a deep breath, pulled off the ragged remains of his shirt, stepped out of his moccasins and pants, and splashed into the water.

————

Willow followed a southwesterly course across hilly country cut by a cat's-cradle maze of drainages. The soil here came in many colors, yellow, bright red, and sometimes streaked in white, gray, and blue clay layers. Oaks crowded the bottoms while irregular patches of limber pine, juniper, and ponderosa timbered the higher slopes. Buffaloberry, serviceberry, and squaw currant matted the draws and covered cool streams. She knew where she was now, in the broken country just north of the Black Hills.

She traveled along the hillsides, sometimes leading the brown mare when the deer trails became too narrow. Off to the south, high-rising plumes of blue-brown smoke marked a fire racing across the grasslands. One set by lightning, or a human hand?

Let's just hope we don't meet them.

Nor were humans her only fear. A mountain lion had almost cost her her horse that morning. The lion had screamed less than a bow-shot above the trail she followed. Only by sheer willpower, and a little terror-mustered strength, had she been able to hold the mare. Her other great dread was bears. This was perfect bear country, the sleek beasts haunting the berry bushes with their ripened fall bounty. Each time they crossed a bear trail, the mare rolled her eyes and stamped. As long as Willow didn't surprise one, she and the horse had a chance to skirt wide and avoid a confrontation.

Willow ducked under the slanting branches of a giant chokecherry, her mare bulling through with a crackle of branches and more than a little sidestepping.

"Don't you try that with me on your back," she chided, "or I'll cut your throat and eat you myself."

The mare huffed her sides, nostrils distended as she studied the slope below. Two gray wolves slipped through the tall dry grass and disappeared into the buffaloberry thickets.

Willow kept to the deer trail, moving slowly. Every so often she'd stop, generally in the shadow of a limber pine, to study both her backtrail and the nearest high points. Those hilltops worried her. There, high above the surrounding country, enemy scouts might lie in wait.

Warriors used such heights to keep an eye on the entire country. Like eagles, they watched for buffalo, elk, or antelope. To pass the time, men flaked their fine arrowheads from obsidian, chert, or quartzite. Sometimes a young woman would accompany her man, and while they talked, she'd work on weaving, making a basket or net, or perhaps painting designs on leather.

But more than game could be spotted. So could enemy warriors, loose horses—or a vulnerable woman traveling alone.

And if I'd been traveling this carefully, Packrat would never have captured me in the first place.

She tossed her braids back and stepped over a deadfall. The trail skirted a patch of rosebushes, the spiny branches ripe with rosehips. Reaching out, Willow was able to pluck several and eat them. Since reaching the hills, she'd traveled on a full stomach—wild turkey one night, sharp-tailed grouse the next. Each day's forage provided chokecherries, wild plum, and the myriad of berries.

She rounded the side of the hill and stopped to stare out across the irregular bluffs. Far to the west, beyond the Powder River, high thunderheads obscured the horizon; but here, closer, was a landmark she recognized.

A half-day's ride to the south, a colossal pillar of naked gray stone rose from the rumpled land. Long grooves, like the grain of a tree, lined the sides leading up to the flat top. A dense forest of pines grew in the detritus at the base of the slope.

The giant monolith was called *We'shobengar,* a place of terrible Power. Among her people it was forbidden even to point at it, lest terrible *puha* be unleashed against the offender. Many peoples told the story of how a pretty girl was promised to Grizzly Bear in marriage. But when she grew into a young woman, her heart settled on a young man of her people. To avoid her fated marriage, she and the young man eloped.

When Grizzly Bear heard that his bride had fled, he pursued her in anger. Being a spirit animal possessed of great Power, he soon chased down the young couple. The girl and her lover took refuge at the top of the high pillar of rock, just out of Bear's reach. The giant grizzly scratched and scratched, cutting those long grooves in the sheer rock, but he could not reach the lovers.

The beautiful young woman and her handsome young lover were not allowed to escape, however. The giant grizzly moved into the rock, living there as he waited for his bride to try and climb down. In the end, only the vultures were happy, for the trapped lovers finally starved to death. And ever since, the spirit of the grizzly had lived inside the Bear Lodge, waiting through time for his wife to descend.

Willow massaged the back of her neck as she studied the tall pillar. *You see? Things could be worse, Willow. You could be trapped up there with Richard. The only way out to be eaten alive by the bear, or eaten dead by the buzzards.*

The southern flank of the hillside offered some protection for her movements. She studied the slope, picking the route with the most cover. From here, she would veer eastward, cross the head of the Little Missouri, then the Little Powder River, and finally the Powder River itself. After that, the Powder River Mountains lay only two hard days' ride to the west. If she placed herself correctly, she could slip right up Crazy Woman Creek on the old elk trail.

And then I will be home. Tam Apo, *guide me. I'm so close.*

But then, because Coyote had fooled around with the beginning of the world, that's when unexpected disaster was most likely to strike.

She smiled wryly. "We'll just take our time, horse. Travel smart. That's the way to make it home."

The mare stamped, and ducked her head to rub her rope halter on a foreleg.

"Evening is coming. If we can cross this last creek and climb the other side of the valley, we can be out in the flats by nightfall. Then, if the moon holds, we can be far out into the sagebrush before it becomes too dark to travel."

Taking a deep breath, she gave the mare a jerk and started her careful descent of the hill.

Maybe it was only nerves, but she kept glancing at *We'shobengar,* unable to shake the feeling of eyes watching her every move.

Licking her lips, she patted the Pawnee war club at her side, and checked to make sure she could swing her bow down and that her quiver hung ready at hand.

Easy, Willow. You're just worried, stirred by We'shoben-gar's *dark Power, that's all. Relax, take your time, think. You'll make it.*

If only she hadn't thought about Coyote, and the tricks he played on people's hopes and fears.

CHAPTER TWELVE

The causes and means by which any virtue is either produced or destroyed are the same; and equally so in any pan. For it is by playing the harp that both good and bad harpists are produced; and the case of builders and others is similar, for it is by building well that they become good builders and by building badly that they become bad builders. If it were not so, there would be no need of anybody to teach them; they would all be born good or bad in their several crafts. The case of virtues is the same. It is by our actions and dealings between man and man that we become just or unjust It is by our actions in the face of danger, and by our training ourselves to fear, or to courage, that we become either cowardly or courageous.

—Aristotle, *Nicomachean Ethics*

Phillip barely allowed himself to breathe. His heart was pounding painfully in his chest.

Dear Lord, pray that this man has answers.

Blue smoke curled up from Charles Eckhart's cigar as he sat in a chair across from

Phillip's cherrywood desk. The ship's clock tick-tocked the hour: well past six. Eckhart looked rumpled and travel-worn. He kept glancing around the office, at the Charleville musket, at the fireplace and globe, and the huge leatherbound Bible that lay open to Leviticus.

Through the French window behind Phillip, the faint glow of late afternoon sunlight slanted through the smoky haze that drifted up from Boston's endless chimneys. Out in the Commons, boys were playing and running.

Phillip nerved himself. "Thank you for coming so far, Mr. Eckhart. What...news?"

Eckhart puffed out a cloud of smoke and shook his head. "My regrets, sir, but I haven't anything pleasant to report. I enlisted numerous agents in Saint Louis, but we uncovered nothing. Several rumors came to our ears, one about a man named François who had recently arrived in Saint Louis, and flushly at that. He had been involved in nefarious dealings in Illinois and might have obtained ill-gotten gains there. Before we could approach the man, however, he was found floating in the river, his throat cut."

"Hardly conclusive," Phillip grumbled, watching Eckhart intently. He fought the urge to massage his tense chest.

"We agree, sir. It was, however, the most likely avenue of inquiry at the time. I mention it only to assure you, sir, that I followed out every possibility. My sources in Saint Louis included Mr. Blackman, of course, as well as General Clark, Colonel Benton, and Mr. Ferrar, all note-worthy gentlemen, and all most anxious to help ascertain your son's circumstances."

In the silence that followed, Phillip carefully reordered his desk, squaring the ledgers just so, placing the British officer's button in line with the inkwell and quills. Hope welled suddenly. "And the chance that he absconded?"

Eckhart puffed and exhaled, smoke rising in a plume. "My opinion—and the one I am submitting to the company, sir—is that he was the victim of foul play. Up until the time he stepped off the boat, he was a model courier. Suspicious of everyone, standoffish, and private. Of all the passengers, I made the greatest effort to gain his confidence, and he proved most disagreeable. Nor did his behavior in any way draw attention to the fact that he carried money. Rather, he acted the way a boorish scholar should."

"But something happened," Phillip insisted. "I want to know what."

"There was one incident." Eckhart studied the ash on his cigar. "Your son claimed that someone had left a human head in his room the night before we reached Saint Louis. I heard this from a fellow passenger, who'd heard it from a crewman on the *Virgil*. By the time my investigation led me to this information, the *Virgil* had departed from Saint Louis. Since that time, I have contacted the *Virgil's* captain, and he confirms that a human head had indeed been left in Mr. Hamilton's quarters. At the time, he thought it a practical joke since the young man was so socially disagreeable—frontier humor being what it is. That may indeed be the case, or it might have something to do with your son's disappearance."

Phillip removed his glasses and took a deep breath. "And my son? What are the chances that he's alive?" There, it was out. Pay the devil his due, he'd finally have an answer.

Eckhart's gaze narrowed, cigar smoke rising like lazy serpents around his nose. "I can't tell you with certainty, sir. Man to man, however, the chances are that he's dead, buried, or sunk in the river. That someone, somehow, caught wind of that money and waylaid him."

My God, my God, what have I done? Oh, Richard. I'm so sorry.

Phillip closed his eyes. Completely forgotten, the wire spectacles bent double in his knotted fist.

————

Following the Yellowstone south, the *Maria* might have entered another world. Beyond the cottonwoods, the broad floodplain stretched to badlands of eroded clays, narrow channels, and soft soils that grew scabby little plants barely worthy of the name.

At night the *engagés* marveled at the petrified wood Travis and Baptiste brought in from their hunts. On one excursion they located the petrified bones of some large animal. Most were too big to carry, but one—Richard recognized it as a vertebra—would have dwarfed the biggest of horses. It, too, was solid stone.

"From before the Flood," Green whispered, shaking his head. "Damnation, all the times I been up and down through here, I've seen the petrified wood, but the animal bones? Tarnation, that runs a shiver down my backside."

That night the men burned the fires brighter than usual, and more than one slept on his rifle while dreams of monsters filled his head.

The Yellowstone was as stubbornly different from the Missouri as the Missouri had been from the Mississippi. In places, gravel banks and braided channels ran so shallow that *Maria* had to be grasshoppered across the shoals to deeper water. The crew would construct a huge

A-frame of cottonwoods, and the frame was winched forward in one giant step—the boat hanging beneath—before the tackle was reset and the process repeated. On such days, all hands worked like dogs.

"By God, I'll be happy to be done with this," Travis growled, as he wiped a muddy sleeve over his muddier face. "She's nigh to two hundred miles from the mouth down ter the Big Horn. Hob's balls, I ain't never seen the river this bad afore."

Gravel bars weren't the worst. For the first time, Richard saw rapids. Here, the cordelle was run out, and *Maria* was drawn ahead with tackle and a makeshift capstan.

A sweating Toussaint told Richard: "And what you see here? Poof! This ees not whitewater, *mon ami*. For this, we would not have to portage even a canoe *d'maître*."

"Will there be that kind of water further up?"

"Somewhere, I'm sure. The *Roche Jaune,* she starts in the mountains, *oui?* Where there are mountains, you will find whitewater. But this boat, *Maria?* She will not go so far. She is made for calmer waters, not like the canoe."

One early October morning, Richard awoke to find a thin scale of ice on the top of his cup. Thick white frost lay on the grass, and the air had a glasslike clarity. As the breakfast fires crackled, he huddled in his blanket, puffed out his breath, and looked up at the Cottonwood leaves.

The number of yellow ones wobbling on the morning breeze surprised him.

"Geese'll be headed south," Travis remarked over his steaming coffee—if the thin brown liquid could be called such. "Surprised we ain't had snow."

"Snow?" Richard wondered.

"Yep. I seen snow up hyar first of September. She's holding back a mite this year."

"That's worrisome," Baptiste said, head thrown back to study the enamel sky. "Warmer the fall, the colder the winter. Mark my words, coons, we're gonna have us a hell of a cold one."

"Forty below," Travis muttered, then threw out the last of the grounds from their pan. "Tarnal Hell, I wisht like Hob that old Dave would be a mite freer with the coffee on a morning like this."

"If'n he's much freer," Baptiste rejoined, "ye'll be without come the mouth of the Big Horn. Hell, only reason he brung any was just ter keep the *engagés* from slitting his throat and stealing his outfit."

True to Travis's words, the next day the first waves of geese, herons, loons, and pelicans cut the afternoon sky. Thereafter, endless honking, piping V's winged southward.

A relentless wind was blowing out of the west the day they finally reached the mouth of the Powder River.

With savage fury it spattered the miserable line of *engagés* in cold rain. To the west, a sullen cloud bank darkened into blackness, and promised increased fury—one with teeth of snow. A blizzard of yellow cottonwood leaves fluttered past as the wind ripped the last of the glorious fall colors away. Naked now, the land turned brown and gray.

Richard hunched a shoulder to the brunt of the biting wind and slashing rain. Only ceaseless exertion countered the growing cold as they waded through opaque, chalky water at the Powder's confluence. Forlorn yellow leaves bobbed on the surface. Splashing chest-deep, the men cursed and ground their teeth, calling encouragement as their feet churned the soft mud under the main channel.

To the right, chop covered the Yellowstone, driving whitecaps onto the rounded cobbles in the low channel.

"Doesn't this wind ever let up?" Richard yelled, wiping at his wet face.

"*Non*." Simon craned his neck to shout back along the cordelle. "Sometimes she get much worse, *oui?* Blows like this for days until you wish to cut off your ears just to still the howl."

"And tonight," de Clerk promised from behind, "you will discover a new meaning of cold, *mon ami.* Smell the wind. That fresh crispness, *oui,* that is snow. First it will rain—enough to soak us through. And then the snow comes. Wet, melting, and, oh, so miserable!"

"I can hardly wait." Richard clawed his way up the slippery far bank, cramped fingers around the gritty cordelle. Feet braced, he pulled with all his might as *Maria* steered wide around the shallow mudbars at the Powder's mouth. On deck, polers battled the wind, shoving the keelboat against the blast.

Soaked, cold, muddy, and wretched as he was, Richard

hesitated long enough to stare up the Powder's mucky channel. The water looked solid, like paint, and the banks were covered with cottonwoods and willows. Nothing much marked it as special, but its headwaters formed in Willow's mountains.

Was she there, even now, walking along the streams that would eventually flow to this spot?

Please God, make it so.

De Clerk's predictions for the night's weather came true. The brunt of the storm bore down on them, driven by the west wind. In the light of a sputtering fire, Richard watched a slushy rain fall like flickering silver arrows. Behind a hastily constructed wall of brush, he huddled in his wet blanket like a sodden turtle. No songs rose to duel with the storm, no laughter, jokes, or jests. The other *engagés* crouched over their feeble fires, trying to protect their fragile source of heat.

"How do, coon?" Travis asked, as he appeared out of the inky night and hunkered down beside Richard. "How's life on the river?"

"Wet, cold, and wretched," Richard replied, prodding his smoking fire with a damp stick. Overhead, the wind roared through the trees, pelting them with half-frozen water.

"Reckon so, lad; but fer nights like this, ye'd not know ter appreciate them warm, sunny mornings when everything's fresh green and the meadowlarks is trilling."

"I'll try to remember that" Richard hugged himself, desperate to keep some warmth in. "I've just been thinking, is all. Look at us. We're conquering the world, taking civilization around the earth. Isaac Newton has discovered how the universe works, exposed the hand of God in the clockwork precision of science with its mathematical perfection. A new freedom is blowing around the world; old orders are falling. Napoleon taught us that the age of despots is passed. So, if civilization has produced all of these good things, how can the philosophical framework be flawed?"

"Damned if I know."

"Damned if I do, either. And I'm not sure I ever will. The world's just so big, Travis."

"Seems ter me, ye've started to see the whole beaver. Remember when we talked about that?"

"I do, and it seems like a lifetime ago. I want to apologize for being such a boor. You've been right, Travis, about so many things." Richard glanced across at his friend. "Why on earth did you stick with me? It would have been easier to just let Green, or Trudeau, or the river kill me."

Travis wiped at the scarred ruin of his nose. "It was that day when Green pulled down on ye with that pistol. Ye looked right into that barrel, and there was fire in yer eyes. I just figgered I'd take the chance, and hell, once I did, I just couldn't let ye whip me and prove me wrong."

Richard shook his head. "You've the patience of a saint, Travis Hartman."

"Me? Ha! They's men out hyar what call me a devil. And some call me a bloody heller. Saint, now, that's some. Ye just needed out of the cage, Dick."

Richard stared up at the dripping black heavens. "I've still got a long way to go. It's like arguing with yourself. You can always win because you anticipate your own answers." He paused. "When we get to the mouth of the Big Horn, I'm going after her, Travis."

"Is that a fact?"

"I'm free, aren't I? I have to go and find her. There are things I have to tell her."

"And then what? Just talk about philos'phy and ride

off when ye finally figger out ye can't pin God down like a butterfly on a board? Tell me, Dick, ye just going to ride in fer a nice chat and ride out of her life again?"

I'll cross that bridge when I reach it.

Then he imagined his father's face, heartbroken with grief. "Travis, no matter what, I have to go back. I left some unfinished business in Boston. You understand that, don't you?"

"Be a man and don't go hurting her no more."

Richard nodded, rainwater trickling coldly down around his face. "Whatever happens between us, Willow and I will figure it out together."

"It won't be easy."

Richard turned his head toward the south, now obscured by blackness, storm, and cold. "No, it won't. But then, wasn't it you who told me that nothing in life is easy?"

———

When Heals Like A Willow saw the riders, she should have turned her mare's head west, hammered her in the ribs, and ridden as if the rock ogres were chasing her. Instead, she left her horse hobbled and sidelined in a steep-walled gully and crawled out to scout them. She lay in the bottom of a shallow drainage—little more than a depression screened by short sagebrush—and watched as the file of horsemen approached. Even if one had looked her way, he wouldn't have thought the scanty cover shielded so much as a jackrabbit.

The warriors passed silently, black silhouettes against the evening sky. They rode arrogantly, the way warriors did when they had nothing to fear. Willow knew that cut of clothing, those decorations and adornments: *Pa'kiani,* the dreaded Blackfeet.

They followed the ridgetop across the brittle caprock Willow had just crossed. Here the shale had been burned to a dull red color, no doubt from some antic of Coyote's just after the Creation. The land was covered with such outcrops of rock, interbedded with layers of coal in bands of gray, black, and bright orange-red. The stone was not without merit, for it could be chipped into useful—if soft —tools, and in this land chert, quartzite, and obsidian were scarce.

Willow emptied her mind so that no part of her *mugwa* would touch one of the Blackfeets' souls. Nevertheless, she tensed when, one by one, they crossed her route, oblivious to her previous passage.

Then she saw the bunched form tied to one of the last horses. The captive was followed by two young men, both hard-eyed, their hair blowing wildly in the west wind. Each carried a trade musket, butt-propped on his rawhide saddle, ready to be leveled and fired. One wore a red blanket tied loosely around his shoulders, the other a buffalo robe. Neither took his eyes from the captive. The prisoner bounced along, defeat reflected in his sloped shoulders and sagging back. Despite the biting wind, he wore only fringed buckskin pants of *Ku'chendikani* design.

His hands and feet were expertly bound; his blood-matted hair whipped in the wind.

He turned his head then, squinting westward toward the distant Powder River mountains—and Willow jammed a fist into her mouth to stifle a sudden gasp.

She hardly recognized the battered and bruised face so similar to her dead husband's. White Hail's left eye had swollen shut, and the dark lump on the right side of his jaw implied it was broken. Bruises, or dried splotches of blood, mottled his cheeks, ribs, and shoulders.

Willow lowered her head to the dirt, breathing deeply as she struggled to quiet her panicked souls. So, the premonition hadn't been for her but for her brother-in-law, White Hail.

And what will you do now? He is surrounded by more than twenty warriors.

She lifted her head again, watching as they rode off into the twilight. The wind continued to pull at her, flapping her dress and tugging at her hair as she lay in the narrow drainage.

She shot a glance over her shoulder to the west. Darkness was coming soon, the distant mountains obscured by silver-wreathed gray clouds. The bite in the wind promised bitter temperatures.

Would the *Pa'kiani* ride on? Or would they find shelter in some nearby winding gully, or under the lee of a hill?

Willow rose carefully, scuttling forward across the crumbly dirt and chipped rock. She eased up to the ridgetop—careful not to skyline herself—and watched as the now shadowy figures turned off and rode down the lee side of the ridge.

It's impossible! I can't take him away from them.

The wind battered at her, trying to knock her off her feet. Willow used the last of the dying light to take her bearings. To the west, the land dropped away, cut by thousands of drainages that reminded her of a maze of roots all woven together from the stem of the Powder River. To the east, it opened into undulating hills capped by red humps of burned shale.

But to the northeast, a bluff slanted out at an angle. The *Pa'kiani* had just disappeared in that direction, and what better place for fleeing warriors? From the heights, they would be able to scout the country prior to leaving in the morning. The tilted caprock would provide some protection from the bitter wind, and the horses would find sufficient grass on the slope below the rocky point. Such places collected large snowdrifts in the winter, and consequently grew excellent grass in the spring as well as tall sagebrush for fires.

A smart woman would ride off.

Willow chewed nervously at her lips. She hated the pang in her heart. White Hail had always been kind to her, his adoration and love shining in his mischievous eyes.

"He was foolish to ride off to find the Mandan," she told the wind. Red Calf would have been behind it, goading him to bring her trinkets with which to adorn herself. Women could be such fools.

Willow turned her steps toward where her horse was hobbled, and added, "Just as I'm foolish enough to go and try to save him. The *Pa'kiani* will no doubt kill us both in the end."

And if they do, the Pa'kiani *will leave my corpse lying around for the coyotes. Since my* mugwa *will be free to wreak havoc, I will find Red Calf, and make her suffer until she dies.*

———

Borne on the capricious wind, white flakes of snow drifted out of the black sky to settle on White Hail's clay-cold skin. Shivers wracked him; they antagonized his bruises and aches rather than warmed his battered body.

He lay bound, hands tied uncomfortably to his ankles. The clever *Pa'kiani* had trussed a stick between the knots so that he couldn't manage to wiggle his fingers close enough to untie them. Then they'd staked him to a sagebrush so that he couldn't chafe the thongs on the rocks.

White Hail shivered again, and wondered how long it would take him to die. He'd always been tough, capable of enduring cold and heat, privation and exertion. The *Pa'kiani* would make his death as painful and horrible as they could. For White Hail's part, he would have to use all of his resolution, every small grain of courage that he could muster. Prisoner though he might be, he'd give them not one mouse hair of satisfaction.

The war between *Pa'kiani* and *Ku'chendikani* was a very old one. In the time of White Hail's grandfather, the Shoshoni had obtained horses from their *Yamparika* Comanche cousins and ridden out on a war of extermination. Like a huge pack of wolves, they'd swept up from the south, murdering *Pa'kiani,* chasing them ever northward, and collecting coup on the way.

The *Pa'kiani* had fled north in terror and defeat. But in the process, they had obtained horses of their own, and way up in the north, they had met the British traders who gave them a deadly new weapon. Armed with the White man's guns, they swept back south, defeating the Shoshoni in battle, overwhelming camps, murdering men, women, and children—invincible.

Almost too late, the Shoshoni had met the Americans, and now struggled to obtain guns of their own. At present, the powerful *Pa'kiani* were checked—barely—but the Shoshoni bands had been pressed back into the mountains, into remote strongholds where ambushes could blunt *Pa'kiani* superiority in firepower and numbers.

And I had to fall prey to these vermin.

White Hail swallowed the grunt of pain his latest bout of shivering invoked. The snow was falling faster now, spinning down in fluffy flakes to melt and trickle down his numb skin.

What I'd give for a blanket. Tam Apo, *please, give me courage. Show me the way to die well, and give these* Pa'kiani *weasels nothing more than the coup they've already taken from me.*

White Hail shifted, stifling a groan. The snow fell so thickly he could barely see the sandstone cliff they'd camped beneath. A lookout huddled up there, keeping guard—as if he could see anything through the darkness and falling veils of snow. Two other youths slept by the horses, ready to spring to life and wake the rest of the warriors who lay wrapped in their blankets like logs among the sagebrush.

Even if I could get loose, how would I escape?

The thought slipped around in White Hail's stumbling mind. The *Pa'kiani* slept on their weapons. The only way he could kill would be to bash his victim's brains out with a rock, and the sharp-eared *Pa'kiani* would hear that.

White Hail, accept it. You are dead. The spirits have turned away, brought you bad luck from the moment you began this crazy journey to the Mandan.

A terrible bout of shivers left him gasping for breath. He tried to swallow, but the grating ache in his jaw just hurt worse.

Would Red Calf miss him? She would give him three moons, then she would take the baby and look for another man to keep her.

Will you so much as shed a tear for me, Red Calf?

Lying in the dark, shivering to death in agony, he could finally face the truth: Heals Like A Willow had tried to tell him so many months ago. Red Calf would barely grieve. She had already cast her eye on Fast Black Horse, preferring to be his third wife rather than White Hail's first.

White Hail cocked his head. Had he heard something, or was his muzzy soul slipping loose from his body? A man imagined things when he was close upon death.

So many mistakes. White Hail tried to see through the twirling snowflakes and the black clouds, wondering if his brother were there, waiting for him.

Will you pray for me, Brother? Call my mugwa *to you? Please, Brother, I don't want my souls to roam around all alone, hated and feared, doing horrible things.*

'Too many mistakes," he whispered wearily, trying to shift his position. The action speared pain through his side. The *Pa'kiani* had taken him completely by surprise—caught him sound asleep just before dawn.

I didn't even lay a hand on a weapon.

Which was why he was still alive. Instead, they'd jumped on him, muscled him down, and bound him. Then, for hours, they'd counted coup, beating him with clubs, willow sticks, and rocks, and burning him with hot sticks from his campfire. And in the end, they'd taken him along as a trophy on their ride northward. They would take him to one of their villages, beat him to death, scalp him, and feed his mutilated body to their dogs.

If I live long enough. He smiled, the movement of his lips tormenting his swollen jaw.

He couldn't defy the bone-chilling cold much longer. Each flake of snow that melted and trickled down his side drained off that much more of his heat. *Tam Apo* willing, he would be dead by morning. Either that, or so disoriented they would have to kill him.

Don't let me cry out. Don't let my mugwa *grow so tired I lose control of myself. Not in front of these spit-licking dogs.*

But it could happen that way. A man did foolish things in delirium. He wept, shamed himself, and whimpered.

Tam Apo, *help me.*

The wind gusted and twisted, snow now falling in wreaths. Good. If it kept up like this, he would be stone dead in the morning. The Blackfeet would kick him around, cut off his scalp and genitals, pull out his intestines, mutilate his body, and ride off. When they went, however, it would be without the satisfaction of hearing White Hail beg.

"Come on," he whispered to the storm. "Kill me."

"You can die later," a familiar voice—a woman's, barely audible over the wind—whispered. "For now, be very quiet or they will wake up and kill us both."

At the corner of his vision, a low, snow-mounded shape moved ever so slowly. White Hail squinted and blinked, then succumbed to the shivers again, half-wondering if the apparition would still be there when his vision cleared.

Yes, there. He scowled, watching as it hunched over his bound hands and feet. His legs had grown so numb he barely felt the thongs part.

"We must go slowly, *teci*, quietly," the voice told him in the language of the People. "Can you stand?"

White Hail stared, trying to comprehend. "Where are we going? Who are you?"

"Shhh!" Then a warm hand reached out, feeling his forehead, his chest, and arms. "You are very cold. You're not thinking clearly. Very well, White Hail. This is a test of your manhood. If you are a brave warrior, you will stand, and make no noise. If you are little more than food for *Pa'kiani* dogs, you can stay here and grovel at their feet like a maggot in rotten meat."

White Hail steeled himself, groaning in spite of his attempt at silence. His legs failed him at the last instant, but she caught him, supporting his weight.

"Easy...easy, White Hail," the woman whispered.

Carefully they took a step, and then another, picking their way through the sleeping warriors as snow fell in skirts of white that obscured the world.

"Willow?" White Hail wondered. "Heals Like A Willow, am I dying? Is this my *mugwa* leaving my body?"

"Shut up!" she hissed.

He clamped his jaw—and regretted it instantly as pain seared the right side of his head. If anything, the ache cleared his thoughts enough that he could concentrate on keeping his feet. Heals Like A Willow! His befuddled mind struggled with the reality. But where had she come from? How had she found him?

Is this real, or a trick? A part of death I just don't understand?

They were climbing now, heading straight up toward the point. White Hail frowned, unease prickling somewhere deep in his thoughts. This was wrong, somehow, but he couldn't find his way through the veils of fog that filled his head.

Dangerous, so very dangerous, with the *Pa'kiani* sleeping all around them.

Now they were working their way up the steep slope, around boulders, one step at a time. They paused periodically when agony raced through his bruised ribs and aching joints.

They climbed higher, up where the wind whipped around, right up under the sandstone ledge.

"This way," Willow whispered. "I have a horse. We'll get you up on top, and..."

They were climbing over the last of the cracked sandstone now. Snow covered the rocks in a fluffy whiteness that illuminated the ground enough for him to see his dark legs against the snow. They had to crawl over the top, each movement a spear of agony, and then they were up, gasping, she from the exertion of supporting his weight, he from the horrible pain. The wind savaged him, beating his numb skin with snow—and immediately to his right, something, a snowy lump, moved as if alive.

And then White Hail remembered. They'd just crawled over the rim—right in front of the *Pa'kiani* guard who'd been placed on the high point. With a stifled cry, White Hail threw himself on the guard in a last desperate attempt to save them.

"Stop that!" she whispered. "He's already dead. I killed him first."

"Willow? Is it really you?"

"Yes, *teci;* now be quiet. Take his blanket and clothes. Then I'll see if I can steal you a horse."

As he prodded the corpse, she drifted away into the storm.

Willow. Here. Perhaps *Tam Apo* had heard after all.

CHAPTER THIRTEEN

War itself requires no special motive but appears to be an integral part of human nature; it even passes for something noble, to which the love of glory impels men quite apart from any self-centered urges. Thus among the American savages just as much as among those of Europe during the age of chivalry, military valor is held to be of great worth in itself, not only during war (which is natural) but in order that there should continue to be war. Often war is waged only in order to demonstrate valor; thus an inner dignity is attributed to war itself, and even some philosophers have praised it as an ennoblement of humanity, forgetting the pronouncement of the Greek who said, "War is an evil inasmuch as it produces more wicked men than it takes away." So much for the measures nature takes to lead the human race, considered as a class of animals, for her own purposes.

—Immanuel Kant, *Perpetual Peace: A Philosophical Sketch*

The big coyote sat on a rocky knob and watched the six horses and three blanket-wrapped riders pass below. His buff-gray coat ruffled in the cool breeze; the bushy tail curled around his delicate feet. He might have been a king, so majestically did he perch on the height, surrounded by blue-green sagebrush with its waving spikes.

Richard couldn't take his eyes from the animal. He felt wary of that piercing yellow-eyed stare, those pricked ears, and the rapt attention with which the creature watched them file by.

Baptiste led the way, then Travis, and finally Richard. They traveled Indian-file, following a small creek up into the highlands south of the Yellowstone River. Each led a packhorse, the panniers piled high. Ropes tied in diamond hitches secured tarps, or manties, that protected the goods from rain and the rigors of travel.

Tall sagebrush, some as high as a horse, choked the narrow bottoms, and the white limbs of cottonwoods rose against the gray sky. The hills around them had a chapped look, prickly with scrubby sage, rocky outcrops, and waving spikes of tall grass.

Richard thumped his white mare in the ribs with moccasined heels and rode up beside Travis. "Did you see that coyote up there?"

Travis glanced sidelong at the skylined creature, and nodded. "Yep. Curious old coon, ain't he? Probably figgering he'll just Injun into camp tonight and chew every single bit of harness and rigging on these saddles into bits."

"They do that?"

"Yep. Sneaking thieves. I've heard tell they like the leather cause of the hoss sweat, the salt taste. That, and hell, coyotes is just ornery. They'll chew packs, steal food, anything they can get away with."

Richard couldn't shake his unease. Why did the creature watch them with such intensity, as if a spectator at a great event?

"I wish he'd go away," Richard declared.

Baptiste pulled his horse up, and turned in the saddle, head cocked. "Coyote makes powerful medicine fo' the folks out heah. They calls him the Trickster."

Travis hunched on his saddle, spat over the off-side, and squinted up at the coyote. "That true, ye flea-bit varmint? Ye a-waiting ter trick us? Wal, I'm telling ye, don't go ter no trouble, lessen we raise ye, hear? We ain't no Injun coons. We's white! And a heap more trouble than yer likes is fit fer."

Baptiste narrowed an eye. "Who's white?"

"We is," Travis insisted. "That's if n I decides ter count yer mangy hide in with our august and noble company."

"August and noble? Where'd you heah that?"

"Why, I been a-listening ter Dick, hyar, and improving my elocution."

"It ain't working," Baptiste growled.

Richard ignored the banter and kept his attention on the coyote. He might have been stone, so still did he sit.

"Willow told me that among her people, Coyote caused all kinds of trouble at the beginning of the world." He fingered his rifle, oddly reassured by the smooth wood and cold steel.

"Yep," Baptiste agreed while the breeze flicked his long fringes. "Crow tell stories about him, too. They call him Old Man Coyote." Baptiste narrowed his eyes, turning his attention from the coyote to Richard, then back. "Raises yoah hair, does he?"

Richard started to nod, then shook his head. "It's crazy. I'm sorry, just tired, that's all. Maybe it's the weather."

"No, tell us," Travis said softly, as his gelding dropped its head to crop.

"Nothing." Richard flushed, suddenly self-conscious. "It's irrational. I'm spooky, that's all."

Good God, I'm an educated man, and there's nothing up there but a hungry old coyote that's never seen a white man before. "Come on, let's go"

Travis and Baptiste traded looks, then the black hunter kicked his animal around and jerked the pack-horse in line. Travis followed as Richard dropped back to his place.

From his high rock, the coyote watched them go. His only movement was the flick of an ear, almost a parting gesture.

Richard clamped down on the stirring unease within. Since coming to this wild land, some part of him that he'd never known had come to life. Was it just intuition, or the stirring of his vivid dreams and the building sense of premonition? The tension kept him alert, his eyes scanning the sage-clad ridges to either side.

This trip had come on him suddenly. Baptiste had ridden in the night before, cold, wet, and mud-spattered, with the news that he'd spotted a Crow hunting party a day's ride to the south.

"About time," Green had cried, warming his hands on the crackling fire before his tent. "I've been half worried the Crow had left this country."

Baptiste had accepted a steaming tin cup from Henri, sipped the watery coffee, and told them, "Wal, Long Hair and his River Crows was palavering with Atkinson and O'Fallon. After they done broke up the council. Long Hair talked the clans into heading south to make their fall hunt on the Tongue. Soon's they lay in enough buffler, they's gonna head down to the mouth of the Powder fo' winter camp."

"You told them we were building a post at the mouth of the Big Horn?" Green rubbed his jaw nervously, an eyebrow raised.

"Yep. They said they's glad the white generals fulfilled their word so fast. I told 'em we'd be ready to trade just as soon as we could get a post up. Maybe another moon. Figgered it might be better to keep 'em away until we get buildings up."

Green frowned for a moment, then nodded. "Yes, I suppose you're right. They'd steal us blind."

"They's Crow." Travis chuckled.

"Since they be making a hunt," Baptiste continued, "I told 'em we might send a party to their village. Trade there. Dave, we're a gonna be needing robes, moccasins, and such right quick. Specially with this weather turning. That, or yoah *engagés* is gonna freeze."

That same night they had filled the panniers with powder, lead, skinning knives, glass beads, cloth, and other foofawraw. Then, in the blackness before dawn, Travis had toed Richard in the side, "C'mon, coon. They don't need yer stringy carcass on the cordelle today. Let's go meet the Crow."

So Richard had thrown back his frosty blankets and stumbled over to help load the recalcitrant horses. He'd picked up his rifle and possibles, and, at the last minute, tied his coups onto his belt. From the river, they had cut south, wound through the pine-covered hills with their outcrops of sandstone and shale, and found the drainage they now followed.

Richard pulled his blanket tighter about his shoulders. Glancing back, he could still see the coyote watching them from that solitary pinnacle.

Easing up beside Travis, he asked, "Tell me about the Crow. You said they'd rob us?"

Travis smiled grimly, the scars rearranging themselves on his face. "Given half a chance. I've lived with them." He paused wistfully. "They're related to the Hidatsa, and they know the benefits of having whites fer friends. Especially with the Blackfeet on one side, and the Sioux, Cheyenne, and Arapaho on the other."

"What sort of people are they?"

Travis stared off into the distance. "Wal, coon, they's unlike any ye've met. And, tell the truth, after yer reaction ter Mandan, I figgered I'd bring ye along just ter see yer philos'phy reaction ter Crow doings."

"Meaning you expect me to be appalled."

"Wal, they got their notions. Now, when it comes to laying with women, they don't hold back. They figger it's just plumb natural ter chase each other's wives."

"Surely there must be some sense of fidelity?"

"There is. Most Crows marry and stick ter it. Of course, they got themselves a kidnapping ceremony every year where they steal each other's women. But, Dick, ye got ter quit judging folks based on white ways. These Crow, I reckon they're the most friendly of folks. Give ye the shirt off'n their back."

"As well as their wives."

"Sometimes."

"Travis, what about the children? How do they feel, not knowing who their father is? What kind of life can they have, knowing they're most likely bastards?"

"Don't matter to 'em. Among Crow, thar ain't no such thing as a bastard. Children belong to the mother, to her clan. And there ain't no one loves children like the Crow. Hell, most Injuns out hyar, they go to war and kill their enemies—men, women, and children. Not the Crow, they kill the enemy warriors, take the women and kids, adopt them into the tribe, and make 'em Crow."

"Seems to me, they couldn't turn their backs on them."

Travis shrugged, careful eyes on the country. "I've met Blackfoot women who was taken over the dead bodies of their husbands who wouldn't go back ter the Blackfeet after living with Crow fer a couple of years. No, Crow are a heap different. Women own property, and even get adopted into the sacred societies with their men."

"But they're all thieves. What good are the fruits of labor if another can take them away? It flies in the face of every philosophical principle. From Aristotle to Hegel, it's become an established fact that property, and its protection, is a human fundamental."

Travis shrugged in response to Richard's lifted eyebrow. "Whose property? Among Crow, everything belongs to the clan. Take the medicine bundles, now. A man can buy the right to part of a bundle, and he takes care of it, but it still belongs to the clan. A man only owns his weapons, and of course, his hosses—at least till the Blackfoot steal 'em. When he kills meat, he can keep the best parts, but the rest belongs ter the clan. Ye see, they work together, feed each other, share things in a way we'd call stealing."

"I don't understand about the clans."

"Clans hold the people together. These are River Crow. Most of 'em is Whistling Water, Streaked Lodge, and one clan called the Piegan—but *don't* confuse them with the Blackfoot. The Kicked-in-the-belly, the Filth-eaters, and Sore-lips are mostly Mountain Crow, and live farther west. According ter Crow lights, people are like them clumps of driftwood that pile up along the river, all tangled together. And, since yer all so fired interested, no man will lay with a woman belonging to his clan. They figger that ter be incest."

"And Long Hair is the chief?"

"Yep. But not like among the Pawnee and Arikara. He ain't a chief because his pap was. Take old Long Hair—a character, he is—he ain't got no authority over another Crow. He can make decisions, all right, but the other Crow only obey if'n it suits them. They call him Long Hair because he carries his hair in a little box that he straps on like a pack. Says he'll have Power so long as he don't cut his hair. Most of the Mountain Crow, now, they follow old Rotten Belly. He's a quiet sort, hard to figger, but smart as all Hob. Story is Rotten Belly and Long Hair locked horns a while back and split the tribe."

"Sounds like anarchy."

"Huh?"

"Mass confusion."

"Nope. They trust a leader—or his medicine Power. The clans really have the authority. Them and the societies."

"And these societies, are they like those Black Mouths I met among the Mandan?"

"Wal, the warrior societies are like...like the Freemasons. All men of a certain age who patrol the camps. Every year a different society is given responsibility to oversee the hunts and keep order in camp. Let's see, there's the Half-Shaved Heads, the Foxes, the Big Dogs, and Muddy Hand societies. Some societies, like the Hammer Society, is fer young men. Others, like the Raven Society, fer old men."

"It sounds worse than Boston." Richard thought back to the rigid social circles of his youth, to families like George Peterson's who would only receive people of a certain standing.

"Maybe. Then ye've got the sacred societies, like the Tobacco Society. Tobacco is a medicine plant ter the Crow. They think it was the first plant ter grow after the world was created. The Tobacco Society oversees the planting come spring and they're the keepers of the rituals. Takes years of study ter larn the songs and the dances, and the who-does-what."

'Then I guess pretty much everyone has to be in a society?"

"If they'll take ye. Some folks pay ter join societies that are responsible for things like the Bear Dance or the Horse Dance. All them societies got rules. They don't just run around like a bunch of crazy chickens."

"But which society controls the others?"

"None of 'em. Everyone's equal except for certain times and duties."

"It sounds crazy."

"To white notions, maybe, but it suits the Crow just fine. Never knew such a bunch of happy folks." Travis squinted up at the sage-covered hills. "They're free, Dick. They just do as God and the spirits tells 'em."

"And hope the Blackfeet don't scalp them."

"There's always that. But in this country, that's just the way it is. Red or white."

"Why, Travis? Peace would make everyone's life easier. Can't they all get together and sit down in council—Blackfeet, Sioux, Crow, and all the rest—and make a treaty that would let them live without constant war?"

"The traders would like that. But, nope, I don't reckon so. Men make their name in war and hoss stealing. Thinking about it, they ain't that all-fired different from them kings back in Europe. Folks is too proud. Hosses is too tempting."

"But free? I wonder, Travis. How can you be free when you're probably going to die tomorrow?"

The hunter cast a sidelong glance. "Ain't that when a coon's about as free as he can get?"

Baptiste called over his shoulder, "If'n' you's to ask the Crow, they'd say it's just the way the world was made. Goes clear back to the Creation when old man Coyote was swimming around in all the water. He got a duck to bring up mud, and he made the world. Then, being Coyote, he called a meeting of all the animals and they got inta a hell of a squabble. Old man Coyote and his younger brother started stealing women, raiding, and so on. He taught such things to the Crow, and the world's been squabbling ever since."

Richard shook his head. "Coyote, again. It seems like he's always trouble."

"Yep." Travis tensed as four mule deer—does and fawns—broke from the trees and bounded gracefully up the slope. "That old coyote still bothering ye?"

"I feel...as if something's wrong. I don't know why."

"Uh-huh, wal, keep yer eyes peeled, coon. Willow said ye had Power, and in this country it pays ter heed hunches. Baptiste and me, we'll keep an eye skinned."

———

They were called the Gourd Buttes for the plants that grew along their lower slopes. Visible all across the Powder River basin, they made an excellent guide for a traveler. Also, from those heights, a scout could see anyone passing, or locate the large herds of buffalo that roamed the basin's grasslands.

Willow, leading the way for White Hail, chose to pass far to the north, following drainages, staying low off the skyline. For White Hail, it was all he could do just to keep his seat on the stolen *Pa'kiani* mare. She still caught occasional glimpses of the flat-topped buttes as she steered her course westward from the crossing of the Powder River. They had just topped the divide into the valley of the Crazy Woman. The snow which had blown down with such vengeance had now fallen victim to warm sunshine. The yellow or gray clays turned to mud from the melt; it balled on the horses' hooves.

Despite the warmth, that crisp undercurrent of fall lingered in the air, and strengthened with the night as the temperature fell below freezing. Ahead of them, the Powder River Mountains glowed whitely in the sunset. The glory of snow-capped peaks gave way to the cool pine-green of the steep slopes with their rocky uplifts.

Willow led the way down into a draw where a seep flowed out of a coal seam. The willows and cottonwoods that grew there stood bare over a carpet of brown leaves.

White Hail clung to his mare, a white-faced roan with a swayback and bowed legs; not the finest of the Black-feet horses. In the tension and danger of the rescue, evidently quality hadn't been the highest of Willow's priorities.

She helped White Hail down and hobbled the animals, then began the task of snapping dead branches from the cottonwoods and inspecting the ground litter for dryness.

White Hail slumped onto the ground in exhaustion. He'd taken a warm buffalo robe from the dead lookout, and now wore it wrapped around his shoulders. The swelling on his jaw had dropped, but his mouth felt like a stranger's. The lower jaw no longer lined up with the upper, and missing teeth added to his dismay when he moved his tongue around. Scabs had formed on his burns and cuts, and the bruises on his ribs and shoulders had dulled into yellow and purple splotches. He hurt all over —both in body and souls.

"I still cannot believe it's you," he said thickly.

Willow frayed grass stems and tipped a bit of charred tinder into the starter. Her strike-a-light clicked when she struck flint to steel. Blowing the spark into flame, she fed twigs to the flicker of fire, and told him, "It's me, *teci*. But I'd rather bet on gaming pieces than the luck of being at the right place at the right time to rescue you again."

"Luck? Maybe my Power isn't broken. Maybe my Spirit Helper sent you my way. Nothing happens without reason." He swallowed painfully, crawling down to the seep. He scooped out leaves. When the water had pooled, enduring the pain, he drank and resettled himself with his back against one of the cottonwoods. "I still don't know how you did it—got me away, I mean."

Willow wiped her hands on her dress, satisfied that the fire was started, and untied her pack from behind the saddle. "They did not expect trouble. Only a fool would be out in such a storm. The snow was falling so thick, and the guards were so cold, it was easy."

He glanced away, fingers tracing the lines of a stick he picked up. "How did you steal that horse? How did you sneak it past the guards?"

She opened her pack, pulling out her little metal pot

and dipping it full of water from the hollow he'd dug. "I used that ax. Slipped up behind them and split their heads open. It didn't make as much noise as I thought it would."

He winced, raising fingers to his swollen jaw. "I wish you'd told me that you'd already killed that guard on top of the hill. I looked pretty foolish wrestling with a dead man."

"Ummm, and the worst is, given your condition, even dead he might have won." She shaved dried meat and berries into the water before putting it on to boil. "And then you wouldn't have that nice warm buffalo robe to wear."

In silence, they watched the last of the day turn to twilight.

As the light failed, a distant band of coyotes wailed.

"White Hail, how did you happen to be out here? What were you doing?"

He tapped his stick on the leaves. "I was taking ten horses to trade with the Mandan for White man's things. Since the baby was born, Red Calf has been saying that she's no longer beautiful." He stared woodenly at the dirty leather covering his knee. "The birth was difficult. I waited the proper time, but when I joined her under the robes, she would not have me. Said she was not ready. I waited...and waited some more, but still she would not couple. Then, one day, I saw her with Fast Black Horse. She was admiring his warhorse, talking about how sleek and powerful it was. How it was a true stallion, capable of filling a mare."

"And what did Fast Black Horse say?"

"He said that such a horse was for only the finest of mares, for mares that would run free, full of spirit. It was the way he said it."

"Yes, I know," she replied wearily. "And you decided that by making a trip east, you could bring back riches and prove yourself worthy of her again. You are a fool, White Hail. She's not worth your life. I think your brother would tell you to go home and throw her things out of your lodge."

"But what of the child? My son is beautiful, Willow."

She stirred the fire and added more wood, then braced her arms on her knees. "For now, he needs her milk. Let him suck and grow. When he is ready to take a name, Red Calf will be with child again, and you can claim your son. Two Half Moons can watch over him while you're away hunting or stealing horses. She'll make him into a human being."

"She's old."

"A child will give her a reason to get older."

White Hail rubbed the back of his neck and made a face. "Why do you always have the answers, sister?"

"Because, unlike most, I think in, and out, and around problems." She gestured. "It isn't hard to do, brother."

He grunted in defeat, then asked, "Are you sure the Blackfeet will not track us?"

"By the time they could see well enough, snow would have covered our tracks. We kept to the ridges, and then dropped down into the valley bottoms on rock outcrops. Unless they want to waste a great deal of time circling, I don't think they'll follow. And, if they do, by the time they cut our trail, we'll be far ahead of them."

She shrugged. "And think, brother. Their prisoner is escaped, and even worse, three warriors are dead. They will think their medicine is broken, and *puha* has deserted them. What's left but to hurry home in disgrace?"

He twirled the stick in his fingers. "They'd been on a long raid...far to the south. They fought our *Yamparika* cousins, lost many men and horses. I think you are right; they'll keep going north. Their war leader, his Power is bad. I do not think he will lead another party of *Pa'kiani* warriors."

Willow shrugged. If the Blackfeet wanted to go south to fight with the feisty Comanche, it was better than having them raid the *Dukurika* or *Ku'chendikani.*

White Hail glanced at her tin pot, at the knife and ax, and the Pawnee war club. Then his gaze strayed to the metal buckles on the saddle and the bow and quiver. "Enough about me, Heals Like A Willow. Tell me about these things you have. About the metal—and the Pawnee weapons. And, tell me, are those not scalps sewn to the seams of your dress?"

As the stew simmered, she told him of leaving the *Ku'chendikani* and how the Pawnee warrior Packrat took her prisoner, about her travels eastward, and her meeting the Whites.

"Ah! A White man saved you?" White Hail's eyes went large. "Did you glimpse his Power? Are they not as great as I have said?"

Sober-eyed, she cocked her head. "His name is Richard. I looked into his eyes...saw his soul."

"What is this tone in your voice, sister? I'm not used to hearing it. Tell me."

She fiddled with the fire. "Another time. You need rest."

"You could tell me while I rest."

From the look in his eyes, he wouldn't relent. He listened as the night fell cool and clear around them. She told of Travis, Green, the *engagés* and the *Maria.*

"This is ready to eat." She handed him the tin. "Do not chew. The bone in your jaw is not ready for that. It's bad enough that you talk. Just swallow the meat whole. I cut it into chunks small enough that you won't choke."

She continued her story as he sipped and watched her, alternately startled and awed by the things she described.

When he'd emptied the tin pot. Willow took it, refilled it with water, and made a stew for herself. As it cooked, White Hail stared thoughtfully at the patterns of twinkling stars glowing overhead.

"At least you understand their Power, *papinkwihi.* You see, I was right. They are magical."

"They are *men!*" she flared. "And I have come to know them for all that they are. White Hail, do not make yourself into a fool over them the way you have over Red Calf."

He stiffened, stung by her words.

She didn't relent. 'There is no other way to say it. At least, not a way that you will take seriously. *Tèci,* they are men, no better or worse than any others. They are bringing many things to our land. Some are good, others are bad. It is up to us to find a way to take what is good, and avoid what is bad."

"And if the People will not believe you?"

She shook her head, stirring the fire with her stick. "I don't know. I'm afraid that too many of our people think as you do, that the White men, and their goods, are Powerful and good. But tell me. White Hail, did you know that in the beginning, the White trader comes with wonders, but when he finally leaves, there is only death?"

"I do not believe that."

"You may believe what you will."

"The traders want peace. I have heard them say so."

In English she remarked, "I didn't know you talked

their tongue." At his puzzled look she repeated her question in Shoshoni.

"You have learned their language?" White Hail's amazement gave her ironic amusement.

"And more."

"And you still believe they are bad for us?" He shook his head. "Willow, what would you have us do? Go to war with them?"

Willow stared down into her stew, watching the steam rise. "No, Brother. For all the danger and death they bring to their friends, the vengeance they take on their enemies is even more horrible."

He frowned into the firelight.

She finished her stew and began to repack.

"What are you doing?"

Willow rose and retied the pack to her saddle. "The Blackfeet are behind us somewhere. Who knows what other enemies might be out here? If we keep to the ridges, we can go that much farther before dawn. By this time tomorrow, I want to be at the base of the mountains. From there, we'll follow the foothills south, and then up the forks of the Powder River. We should find the *Dukurika* in the canyons on the other side of the mountains."

"The *Dukurika*?" He stood skeptically. "I'm not going up there."

"As you wish, *teci*," she said. "You have a horse."

Through veiled eyes, he studied her. "Heals Like A Willow, you are a very different woman from the one I knew. No, I think I will ride along—and perhaps learn what has happened to you. You have told me many things, but I think there is a great deal more that you aren't telling me."

"Perhaps."

"Did one of the White men give you his Power? Is that what happened? Was it this Ritshard? Why are you so secretive?"

How strange that you should ask that, White Hail.

"Richard gave me nothing." She bent down, unfastening the hobbles. "Come, I will help you onto your horse. We have a long way to ride tonight, so save your strength and stop asking questions."

"I can get on my own horse, *papinkwihi*. And I have a lot of questions to ask you."

"We will ride in silence," she ordered, heeled her mare around, and turned her back on the valley with its little seep and dying fire.

———

The River Crow had placed their village in the wide bottoms of the Tongue River. The cluster of parchment-brown tipis blended with the grass and freshly fallen Cottonwood leaves. Richard, Baptiste, and Travis inspected the village from a cobble-strewn flat on one of the sagebrush-dotted terraces, a good seventy feet above the floodplain.

A haze of smoke rose from the smokeholes to hang like blue mist among the winter-bare cottonwoods. Unlike the Sioux lodges, the Crow extended the poles almost twice the height of the intersection point, giving their lodges an hourglass look. From the pole tips, bits of colored cloth, horsetails, and other streamers hung like flags.

Out in the hills to the east, the horse herd grazed. So many animals! Richard couldn't count the number. The huge herd had to cover several square miles.

"My sweet Lord, I guess stealing horses does pay off."

"And they's the best," Baptiste agreed.

The day had warmed, bright and sunny. But here and there, on the north slopes of drainages, patches of snow still clung to the shadows.

"Right time of year to hunt," Baptiste remarked. "Meat will cure plumb fine fo' winter."

"Uh-huh, and ye'll do yer best ter eat 'em outa all they've kilt, too, won't ye?"

"Reckon so." Baptiste's white teeth flashed in his dark face. "Now, what say we goes on down and stir up the dogs some."

"Stir up the dogs?" Richard asked.

"Ye'll see," Travis rejoined.

Even as they rode down the loose slope, people were turning out to watch. So did an incredible number of dogs, who, upon catching sight of the strangers, charged forth barking and yipping.

Over the tumult, Richard could hear the camp crier calling out the arrival of visitors.

What followed was a melee of shouted greetings, cacophonous dogs, and squealing children. Richard had all he could handle just controlling his excited horse, hanging onto his rifle, and keeping a grip on his pack-horse's lead rope.

They entered the camp like lords returning from the Crusades, winding through the village in a parade of women, children, and men. Before each lodge, a brightly painted shield, decorated with feathers and strips of fur, hung on a tripod.

Dismounting, Travis gave orders concerning the packs, each of which was immediately taken under guard by several young men bearing fur-covered sticks. When some inquisitive Crow came too close, he or she was first warned, and then whacked.

Travis explained: "Camp police from that society I told ye about."

Richard couldn't help but gawk. He was surrounded by brown faces; some were painted, and occasionally one was tattooed around the chin or on the forehead. Children were everywhere, apparently as wild as ferrets, for none was rebuked by their parents as they charged around, or mobbed the traders, pulling at clothing, laughing, and shoving.

Panic seized him as he looked around. A sea of Indians surrounded him. Everywhere he looked, impenetrable black eyes stared back. They shoved against him, tens of hands touching him, prodding, pulling at his possibles and groping his flesh. Coupled with the sense of foreboding came a sudden realization that there was no boat to run to, no armed *engagés* to protect him.

"I hope they're friendly. If something goes wrong, what happens to us?"

"They'll slit yor throat, plumb shoah, and you ain't a gonna have but a split second to worry about it!" Baptiste cried, and laughed in a way that sent shivers up Richard's back.

He was suddenly plagued by the way that coyote had watched so intently—like a witness from an Old Testament account.

CHAPTER FOURTEEN

Spirit is the *self* of the actual consciousness, to which spirit stands opposed, or rather which appears over against itself, as an objective actual world that has lost, however, all sense of strangeness for the self, just as the self has lost all sense of having a dependent or independent existence by itself, cut off and separated from that world.

—Georg Friedrich Wilhelm Hegel, *Phenomenology of Mind*

 At a shouted order, the din subsided and the crowding Crow parted for a burly warrior. He carried another of the staffs, this one curved over at the top to form a crook, like a shepherd's, from which dangled feathers and scalp locks. He wore fringed leggings and a breechclout. Numerous scars puckered his bare breast and shoulders. Richard had seen the like among the Mandan. More of the scarifying torture?

The warrior stopped at the edge of the crowd, his

haughty face breaking into a smile as he recognized Travis and Baptiste. He'd plaited his hair into a single braid that hung down his back. The forelocks had been roached high and curled back above a smooth forehead. His black eyes sparkled, a smile coming to his lips.

"Travis!" he cried, and stepped forward, hugging the hunter with enough vigor to make Travis groan.

"Two White Elk!" Travis pounded the man on the back. "By God, coon, ye be a sight fer sore eyes."

"So're ye," the Crow responded. "My heart sings." And then he launched into a string of Crow talk, his hands flying in the sign language of the Plains.

"Reckon ye know Baptiste de Bourgmont." Travis turned to Richard. "This hyar be my friend, Dick Hamilton."

Two White Elk studied Richard thoughtfully, noted the coups on his belt, and wrapped Richard in his arms. Richard's ribs creaked and his breath tried to slip past resisting lips. The man smelled of smoke and grease, and kept chattering on in Crow.

"Two White Elk says yer most welcome," Travis translated.

"My pleasure," Richard managed to wheeze as Two White Elk turned him loose to crush Baptiste to his breast

"Time to smoke and make palaver," Baptiste called as he produced a twist of tobacco.

The center of a flurry of activity, they were led through a maze of lodges to a tipi painted with antlered animals that Richard decided were elk. Tendrils of smoke still rose from white ash in a firepit in front of the lodge. Willow-frame backrests were produced, set around the firepit, and covered with soft buffalo robes. Travis settled himself in the first one, acting all the while like a lord among vassals.

A young woman appeared out of the crowd, a long beaded sack in her arms. This, she ceremoniously handed to Two White Elk. Even as Richard seated himself, the soldiers were calling orders, gesturing with their sticks. The rest of the Crow settled themselves cross-legged around the margins.

From the corner of his eye, Richard saw their packs being brought and laid beside the elk lodge.

In a sudden stillness, Two White Elk withdrew a long pipe from the beaded bag. He cut tobacco from a twist, and, with a crooked finger, tamped it into the bowl of the redstone pipe. When he had finished, he raised the pipe and sang a prayer before offering it to the heavens, the earth, and the cardinal directions.

Lit with an ember from the fire, the calumet passed from hand to hand until the participants had smoked. Then Two White Elk stood, speaking eloquently.

"He's telling everyone about his coups, the hosses he's stole, and the other great deeds he's done," Baptiste explained. "Now he's telling everyone about Travis, and how he's a great warrior and friend of the Crow, and that we should be treated as honored guests."

Even as the speech continued, buffalo and mountain sheep-horn bowls filled with steaming meat were brought. To Richard's delight, each of the whites was offered his own steaming buffalo tongue on a wooden platter.

Baptiste indicated the roasted tongue. "Special honor."

"I'm all for that," Richard replied, stomach growling. The feast began in earnest, and he stuffed himself with the delicate tongue, hump roast, and pemmican.

Tea was brewed, a subtle flavor of mint and raspberry soothing to the taste. All the while people chattered amiably; children continued to scurry through the crowd like mice. The conversation between Travis and Two White Elk never let up. For the most part, they seemed oblivious of the others, like the best of friends.

"Where's Long Hair?" Richard asked.

"Out hunting buffler," Baptiste managed through a full mouth. "They killed a bunch a couple of days ago, and they's looking fo' another herd. If'n a rider comes in, this whole shitaree could be on the move in half an hour."

"They can take down the village in half an hour?"

"Yep. And if'n they's to get a good kill, they'll need to. Have to race the wolves foah the meat."

Travis was talking seriously with Two White Elk, his hands adding to his stumbling speech.

Seeing Richard's interest, Baptiste added, "Crow ain't an easy language ter larn. I can just pick up occasional words, and that's only 'cause I larned some Hidatsa. Crow split off from Hidatsa a time back."

"Two White Elk spoke English."

"Yep. But just what little he larned from Travis."

Richard watched the people, meeting their inquisitive stares, trying to fathom the things going on in their heads. Individual men and women kept coming up to talk to Travis. The hunter greeted many with hugs, calling them by name like old friends.

At last, the packs were brought forth, and Travis stood, raising his hands and calling out. When he had their attention, he made a short speech in the sibilant Crow tongue. Immediately, half of the circle of spectators vanished, hurrying off toward their lodges.

"Told 'em what we'd come to trade foah," Baptiste said.

The Crow reappeared bearing robes, sections of buffalo gut stuffed with pemmican, and parfleches of jerked meat Some of the women brought moccasins tied on strings like dried herrings.

"Come on," Baptiste said, rising. 'Time to work. You and me, we unpacks and guard the goods. Don't let no Crow run off with nothing. Travis will call foah what he needs as he needs it."

The soldiers kept the Crow in some semblance of order as they crowded around. As Richard had seen Green do so many times, Travis seated himself and took charge. Richard untied the manty and did as he was told, growling at the unruly children who tried to sneak little brown hands into the packs. A good-humored soldier helped to fend off the more obnoxious of the kids.

As the stock of powder, lead, cloth, beads, and needles shrank, another, larger stack of robes, moccasins, and other goods grew beside it.

When the sun finally slanted over the western horizon, Richard was more than ready for the trading to end. To his knowledge, only two bars of lead and four tin cups had mysteriously vanished from under his eyes. For the life of him, he couldn't tell who had pinched them.

As evening softened the camp, they tied their plunder together, lashing it tightly with sinew rope.

"Soldiers will guard it." Travis stretched his back, glancing at Two White Elk. "Come on, reckon it's time ter enjoy Two White Elk's lodge, have a smoke, and eat a little."

"We done good," Baptiste said, grinning at the plunder.

"How are we going to carry all that? We only brought three pack animals."

"Don't worry yor head none, Dick. Travis done traded old Two White Elk fo' more hosses. 'Sides, we're gonna need 'em afore spring." He slapped Richard on the back. "Come on, let's fill our bellies."

Richard and Baptiste saw to the final packs, making sure they were securely tied and under guard. The evening chill was settling as they pulled the lodge flap aside and stepped into the tipi.

Two White Elk called out the Crow welcome, *"Kahe!"* when Richard ducked through the door flap. Then he was shown to one of the seats in the rear behind the firepit. Two young women sat to one side, each nodding at him and giggling, talking about him in Crow. An older woman crouched behind them, head cocked to their talk as she watched Richard with curious eyes. Travis was already seated, talking and laughing with Two White Elk. Baptiste was also greeted with a *"Kahe!"* when he finally ducked through the flap.

The lodge was roomy, perhaps six paces across. The poles rose to the soot-blackened smokehole above, and a fire crackled in the central pit. A rawhide rope was tied off at the intersection of the poles and ran down to a peg driven into the ground behind the firepit. The rope anchored the lodge from blowing over in high winds. Amazed, Richard decided that no less than eighteen hides, artfully sewn together, made the cover. A liner had been tied a third of the way up the inside poles for insulation. It, too, was decorated with brightly painted buffalo, horses, and geometric figures. Bundled robes for bedding, and stacked parfleches, were tucked against the liner sides. The tripod and shield now stood inside the doorway.

The usual horn bowls were laid out, each brimming with its treat. "I'm not going to have to eat dog again, am I?"

"Nope." Travis grinned. "Crow don't eat dog."

"Good." Richard stared down into the bowls. "Uh, I'm not going to regret this later, am I?"

"According to Boston ways, maybe. But 'tain't nothing ye ain't already et."

A constant stream of visitors flowed through the lodge. Most settled around the sides to listen as Travis, Baptiste, and Two White Elk talked about old times.

How unlike the drawing rooms of Boston. Here, the camaraderie seemed palpable. Most of the conversation ended in uproarious laughter, Richard could only smile in ignorance. The women, unlike those of the Sioux, joined in, often interrupting, adding their comments. The only curiosity was the old woman who sat behind Two White Elk's wives. She talked to everyone, but never even deigned to notice Two White Elks—nor he her.

"What's in yor noodle, Doodle?" Baptiste asked once.

"I'm thinking that they don't seem like savages."

Baptiste nodded. "More like family."

"Yes."

"Now, ain't that an amazement." And Baptiste gave him a conspiratorial wink.

"What about the old woman?"

"Her? She's Two White Elk's mother-in-law. Them

two girls in front is her daughters, Two White Elk's wives."

"They don't like each other?"

"They think each other's shining."

"But they don't talk."

"Nope. Among Crow, a man don't never talk to his maw-in-law—lessen he buys the right."

"That's crazy."

"Makes a heap of sense to this chile." He paused. "But then, I never had no maw-in-law."

Richard bit his lip. Damned slavery. To change the subject, he asked, "He married sisters?"

"Uh-huh. I reckon it's easier that way. A stronger bond atwixt families. The girls know each other. Ain't so much jealousy atween first and second wives."

"How perfectly...logical. I wonder why we didn't think of that?"

"Didn't have no Crow philos'phers, coon."

The night wore on. His stomach full, warm in the fire's heat, Richard nodded off, soothed by the babble of voices. A life like this, it wouldn't be so bad, would it? As he dozed, uneasy fragments of dreams slipped around his head. In most of them, Laura Templeton was giving him a hard-eyed squint. She stood with her delicate hands braced on her hips, and the expression on her beautiful face boded no good.

A toe in the ribs brought him awake, yipping, "Laura, damn it! I didn't do anything." He stared owlishly about.

Travis grinned down, the scars a demon's mask in the firelight. "Didn't do what?"

"Nothing!"

"Ye gonna sleep thar, coon? Or would ye like some of these soft blankets that New Moon Rising's laid out fer ye?"

Richard jerked upright to see that the lodge had been transformed. Bedding now surrounded the walls, and a young woman watched him with curious eyes. She knelt on the buffalo robes she'd just unrolled. The thickly furred hide looked wondrously inviting.

Richard sighed. "I'll take those robes, all right. But I must go outside first."

"Yep. Me, too." Travis led the way, ducking out into the cold night. Their breath clouded white as they walked out toward the edge of camp. The lodges looked magical, the thin hide glowing, lit from inside like giant lanterns.

Richard unlaced his pants and sighed as he relieved himself. "Such a pretty night."

Beside him, Travis grunted. "Uh, coon? That gal, New Moon Rising? She's fixing on warming yer robes fer ye."

"You mean with hot rocks? Like a fire brick wrapped up and put at the bottom of the bed?"

"I reckon with herself. She's fixing ter spend the night with ye."

Richard's urine stopped in midstream.

"Wal, I said I'd ask ye."

Richard puffed a frosty breath, and continued to empty his water. "Do I have a way out of this?"

"I figgered maybe fer just one night—and not really knowing her—ye might be considering a change. It wouldn't hurt nothing. She's not like Willow—I mean, no attachments or obligations or nothing."

"Travis, trust me on this, please?"

"I'll tell her it'd be bad fer yer medicine. But ye might give her something. I saved a couple hanks of beads and some other foofawraw in my possibles ter give Two White Elk and his family fer gifts."

"Thanks, Travis."

Richard laced his pants, and together they walked back. The rich smells of woodsmoke, cured leather, and horses filled the night air.

"Makes me feel right at home," Travis said wistfully.

"Baptiste said you lived with the Crow for two years."

"Yep."

"And...you took a wife?"

"Yep."

"Sounds like you don't want to talk about it."

"Nope."

Outside the lodge, Richard steeled himself, taking the string of beads Travis offered. He ducked inside where New Moon Rising still knelt on the robes. Two White Elk lay under the robes with one of his wives. Baptiste's curly hair was visible above his bedding—and so was a Crow woman's long shiny hair.

Richard swallowed, and approached New Moon Rising. She smiled up at him. An inquisitiveness filled her dark eyes, her lips parted to expose white teeth.

"I...I can't Right now, it would be bad for my medicine. But, here, I offer these beads for your kind...um, offer."

Travis spoke gently, translating to Crow.

New Moon Rising nodded, the glow of expectation ebbing like a winter tide. Richard handed her the beads, and she touched him ever so briefly in the exchange. Then she stood, and without a word, slipped out.

The old woman tied the door flap closed behind the girl, and settled herself in the bed beside the entrance. Richard rubbed the back of his neck, growled to settle his churning emotions, and pulled the robes over him.

Meanwhile, Travis settled himself in the bed where Two White Elk's second wife lay, and began shucking off his clothing. Richard gaped, on the point of blurting out a protest, then forced his eyes closed as Travis tucked himself in.

It's Travis's business...and Two White Elk's. Go to sleep, Richard.

As the firelight flickered on the lodgepoles, a female giggle made Richard start. Then someone sighed with an import he had never heard before.

In desperation, he rolled himself over, used his fingers to plug his ears, and wished desperately that he could think of anything except Willow, and how she'd looked that day on the river.

———

Willow and White Hail climbed a long, rocky slope that led up into the Powder River Mountains.

The trail they followed was old, so old that the People's stories said it had been made just after the Creation. Among the *Dukurika*, it was known as the Ghost Way. Travelers passing this way placed a rock on each of the cairns that lined the route. To do so was to recognize the spirits who guarded the way. So many stones had been piled that the cairns had grown to the size of a small lodge. So many rocks, so many travelers.

How many years had passed since the first stones were laid?

Willow paused to let her Pawnee pony catch its breath. She slipped off the animal's back and turned to look out across the valley behind them. The Red Wall—a long sandstone hogback that ran north-south at the base of the Powder River Mountains—rose to the east, and gleamed in ocher magnificence under the morning sun. Out beyond the Red Wall, sharp ridges dotted with pine and juniper gave way to the Powder River Basin's distant buttes and drainage-cut ridges. There the Gourd Buttes rose like slumbering blue sentinels, the last bulwark before the horizon lost itself in the hazy distance.

Sagebrush and patches of scrubby mountain mahogany grew out of the slanting rock. Just to the north of their path, the sheer-walled canyon of the Middle Fork of the Powder River sliced deeply into the mountain's heart, exposing layers of limestone, clinging pines, and fallen rock. In the tree-thick bottoms the river ran clear and cold, dashing white over boulders.

The bulk of Black Mountain jutted against the southern horizon, a huge hump of uplifted rock running east-west She had passed odd to the south of it as Pack-rat's captive. That road down the Platte had taken her to Richard—and to the lonely ache that rode in the depths of her souls.

"You look sad, sister." White Hail slipped down from his horse's back. Some of the strength had returned to his legs, but his jaw was healing crooked. He gazed off across the basin as he emptied his water.

Willow shrugged and bent to pick up a stone the size of her fist. She took several steps uphill, and tossed the rock onto a cairn marking the Ghost Way. "My hurts are my own, White Hail."

"Come," he said, leading his horse up next to hers, "I can walk for a while. It will do this *Pa'kiani* beast good to rest." He raised an eyebrow. "If only you could have stolen that white gelding the war chief rode. Now *that* was a warhorse."

"Perhaps I should have left you with the *Pa'kiani.* You could complain to them." She started forward, leading her mare toward the next of the rockpiles, searching the ground for a suitable offering.

"Forgive me. Willow, what hurt are you hiding under this blanket of bitterness and anger?"

"What goes on within my souls doesn't concern you."

He sighed wearily as she located and tossed a rock high onto the next cairn. It clattered as it settled into place.

"Do you recall that once you called me your friend? No? I remember that day very well. I had come to ask you to be my wife. You said you could never marry me, but that I would be your *teci* forever."

"Yes, I remember."

"That man, the one you called brother, is speaking to you now." He studied her anxiously. "Or have the Whites witched you with their Power? Is that it? Some evil they shot into you like a *Nynymbi* arrow?"

She picked up another rock as they climbed, hefting it in her hand. Cold from the night before, it chilled her fingers. "Ease your worries, Brother. No evil White Power was shot into my soul."

No, indeed, I did this to myself.

And she tried to ignore Richard's soft brown eyes as they stared out from her souls. If she allowed herself the freedom, she could sense Richard's gentle kindness. So close, so sweet and beckoning, that she wished nothing more than to let herself fall into that warmth and drown.

"I have seen such a look in your eyes before, Willow. The last time it was tainted with grief for my brother's death." White Hail led his horse around a patch of mountain mahogany and jerked at the lead rope to keep the swayback from stopping to crop grass. 'Tell me, was it a man who did this to you? Was it this Ritshard who bruised your souls? Did you love him?"

She picked up another rock so he wouldn't see her face.

"I think it was him," White Hail continued neutrally.

Willow tossed the rock onto the next pile. "Shouldn't you save your breath for the climb?"

"Shouldn't you share some of the burden bearing down on your souls? Perhaps both of us would climb with more energy."

She led her horse around the remains of a juniper. A lightning strike had blackened the branches and trunk.

"Are you afraid of me, *papinkwihi?*" White Hail asked. "Do you think I would judge you harshly? Or perhaps you distrust me so much that you think I would tell everyone your secret?"

"No, not that."

"Then tell me, Willow: will you keep this thing inside you until it festers and fills your *mugwa* with poison?"

The breeze had begun to tease fitfully as the morning warmed. A small herd of deer rose from their beds among the mountain mahogany and watched, ears wide, before they turned and bounded away.

Oh, Willow, what harm will it do? "Yes, I loved him."

White Hail climbed beside her, face tilted up to the morning. She watched him furtively, waiting for some reaction.

"Having a White man for a husband would not be such a bad thing. A woman could do much worse."

"It wasn't a matter of wealth, White Hail."

"He didn't want you?"

She closed her eyes for a moment, seeking some sense of inner peace that eluded her. When she looked out again, the world appeared just as callous. "He didn't want me."

"Another wife?" This time White Hail picked up the rock to toss onto the next cairn.

"Yes...another woman."

"He could have married you, too. As I've told you, being a second wife isn't so bad."

"He didn't *want* me for a wife, White Hail."

"Then he was a fool."

"He wanted something called Boston."

"Is that a kind of White man's Power?"

"No, it is a place far to the east where a great many White men live. He is from there, and he wants to go back. He told me stories about it, about people living in lodges built on top of lodges, of giant boats that the wind blows back and forth across a mighty water they call ocean. The pathways between the houses are even covered with stone so one's feet don't get muddy." She shook her head. "I'm not sure I believe all the things I heard, but I don't think he lied, either."

"So, go with this Ritshard and see if it's true."

"He said his people would not like me, that I wasn't White. And, White Hail, the Whites, they own things—even their women. They put them inside their lodges and never let them out. That's why you have never seen a White woman. Why no one you know has ever seen a White woman. They even keep their god in a building. It's called church."

"Indeed? I never would have thought." He shook his head in wonderment. "How incredibly Powerful they must be if they can keep God in a building. This building, is it very big?"

"I saw buildings at Fort Atkinson. They are much bigger than the Mandan lodges—but big enough to hold God? Perhaps the White man's god is not very big."

"He must not be very Powerful." White Hail picked up another rock and gestured toward the sky with it. "*Tam Apo* needs all of the sky to hold him. *Tam Segobia*, Our Mother, fills the entire earth."

"The White men have no *Tam Segobia*. In the White stories, their god created the earth and all the animals. He created man, but only as the last thing did he create a woman—and then she acted like Coyote, tricking their first man, Adam, into God's disfavor."

"That's what they believe?"

She picked her way carefully through a thick patch of sagebrush. "On my souls. I think that's why they distrust women so. I heard stories from the *engagés,* stories about something called original sin. Because a child is born from a woman's vagina, its soul is unclean."

White Hail reached up to rub his sore jaw. "I have seen the Whites among the Mandan. They seem to couple with a great many women. And among the *A'ni,* they have a reputation for all being 'young men,' meaning they take any chance they can get to couple with a woman."

"It is so," she agreed. "I saw them. Many would have coupled with me if I'd let them; but it is different. There was a Frenchman named Trudeau. He wanted to lie with me more than any of the others. The look he gave me was the one a warrior gives a captive woman. An enemy look. Do you understand what I mean?"

"Maybe." White Hail gave her a hard-eyed glance. "This Ritshard looked at you that way?"

She struggled for the right words. "No. He wanted me, White Hail. Not as a possession, or a conquest. But he feared me at the same time, as if...I were a trickster, like this Eve woman in their Creation story."

And, like a pattern in cat's cradle, a piece of the puzzle suddenly came clear. *Oh, poor Richard. Your people have misled you so completely.*

White Hail tossed a rock as they passed another cairn.

"How appropriate," Willow whispered. 'This is a sacred trail, a way of climbing the mountains in search of Power. For myself, I am finally beginning to understand."

"That this Ritshard is a fool?" White Hail said sourly. "I need climb no mountains to know that, Sister."

"Not a fool, White Hail. If you had been born and immediately had one of your eyes covered, one of your ears plugged, one of your nostrils sealed with pine pitch, and one of your arms tied up, would you know the world the way you now do?"

"Of course not! Don't be silly."

"Richard is not a fool, teci. He searches like a *puha-gan*. I've seen the Power in his soul, but his White ways have crippled him. Not like I just said, but in his soul. I understood part of it, but not all. Not until just now."

"So...you would go back to him?"

"I can't, Brother. The day before I left, I explained the problem to him. If he is truly to become *puhagan*, he must free his soul from the entrapment it was born into."

"Do you think he will?"

Willow picked up another rock, hefting it in her hand as she continued to lead her horse up the long trail. She felt good today: lungs working just hard enough to breathe deeply but not pant; the exercise warming her sufficiently to balance the cool breeze; strength and agility filling her legs. With a perfect toss, her rock clattered into place near the top of the next cairn.

"I don't know. I think he will need to shed more of his old self first, much as the buffalo shed an old winter coat. Until he does, it will smother him."

They climbed in silence then, and Willow was more than aware of White Hail's periodic looks. Finally, he told her seriously, "I am going to kick Red Calf out of my lodge."

"That is the first sensible thing I've heard you say in a long time."

"I would like you to move into it when she is gone."

"Your sense was short-lived."

He was watching her from the corner of his eye. "Are you waiting for this White man, this Ritshard, to come to his senses?"

"No," she lied. And then she told the truth: "He will not come for me. He must go back to Boston. It is a need deep within his soul. One that will never let him rest until he fulfills it."

"And what if I told you I yearn like that for you?"

"I'd say you had better go back to Red Calf. She'll only kill your body. In the end, I'll kill your souls."

After a pause he asked, "The way you talk...does this Ritshard only have *one* soul?"

"That is what the Whites believe. Everything is singular. One soul, one god, one truth, one right way. It's as if they see life with only one eye—despite having two in their heads."

"How strange...and frightening, too. I can't imagine. If the *navuzieip* and the *mugwa* were joined into one, how could they dream? I'd think they'd go crazy—like two people trying to talk out of one mouth."

"They *are* crazy, *teci*. Crazy like Coyote. Never pity

them, but watch them constantly. Think of a rattlesnake in a bush. You can never trust it."

White Hail walked in thoughtful silence, and finally asked, "What will you do? You're a young woman, Willow. Are you going to keep all the men who desire you at an arm's length? My brother is dead. This White man is far away, and not coming to seek you out. Are you going to live alone?"

Her gaze followed an eagle that circled high overhead. "For now. I need to be alone in the high places, listen to the wind, watch winter come to cover *Tam Segobia*, and let my souls heal themselves."

———

We're almost there! Dave Green had dreamed, hoped, and prayed for this day, and now, after nearly three thousand miles of winding, treacherous river, he was about to live it.

He could not have wished for a more perfect day: the sky was a throbbing blue vault overhead; the sun shone golden and warm on the tawny grasses. A mild breeze coasted softly down the valley of the Yellowstone, and the air smelled of river, juniper, and pine mixed with the pungency of sage. Flocks of gray-capped finches rose in a mob as the *Maria* passed the high bank where they'd been hunting for seeds.

"We should see it any time now," he muttered, pacing nervously. His heart was pounding as he shifted from foot to foot.

The *engagés* sang, voices spirited as they poled the keel-boat against the current. Henri wore a constant smile that curled up his thick black mustache.

As they rounded a bend, he could see the familiar

opening in the south bank. "There it is, boys! Feast your eyes!"

Ululating cheers broke out as the *engagés* looked up from their toil.

Made it! Made it, by God!

Dave knotted a fist and shook it Looking down at the current, he could see where the murky waters of the Big Horn ran parallel to the clear waters of the Yellowstone.

"Steer wide," Dave urged Henri. "There's probably mud-banks just out from the mouth."

"*Oui, bourgeois.*" Henri was chortling like a giddy boy, his white teeth shining.

"Take a good look, boys!" Green whooped. "That's the mouth of the Big Horn! Let's bring her in in style!"

With a shout, the *engagés* bent to their poles with renewed vigor. *Maria* shot ahead.

Green paced anxiously back and forth as he had during every tense moment on the journey up the river. The wild whoops had stopped, the *engagés* now calling encouragement to each other as they panted and set their poles into the main channel's gravelly bottom and shoved the boat forward.

"I have hoped that I would live to see this day. *Merci, mon Dieu,*" Henri said reverently as he caressed his steering oar and watched the wide mouth of the Big Horn. At the margins of its discharge, swirls and eddies marred the smooth surface.

"We all have, Henri." Green smacked a balled fist into his palm. "By the Blessed God in Heaven, I had my doubts. I guess even a fool gets a little luck every now and then."

"*Oui,* and only two men dead. We had a charmed voyage, Dave." And at that Henri crossed himself.

The Big Horn's broad swell of murky water silvered in

the sun. Like a conquering hero, Green propped his fists on his hips to look up the meandering channel with its willow-lined banks giving way to cottonwoods and brush.

There is the doorway to my empire.

Tan sandstone outcrops rose on either side of the wide valley, their slopes dotted with pine and juniper. His heart was swelling in his chest as he danced a happy jig and turned his attention back to the Yellowstone.

"It's not far now, boys," he called down to the sweating *engagés*. "Right up there, see? That high bank. That's the spot we've been waiting for!"

He strode to the front of the cargo box, barely able to contain himself as he studied the landing. The Yellowstone's sloping bank had grown over since the Missouri Fur Company had abandoned Fort Benton three years before. Where once the feet of Immel, Jones, and scurrilous old Bouche had walked, only tall yellow grass and rosebushes remained.

Green gave the signal, and Henri leaned into his oar, heeling the *Maria* up against the bank. Trudeau picked up the painter, looping the coils around his shoulder. Taking a short run, he spanned the narrowing gap in a mighty leap. The man's moccasins made a hollow thud on the bank; he scrambled ashore, followed immediately by Toussaint. Together they lined out the painter, tying it off to a worn cottonwood that had served the same purpose since Manuel Lisa himself had chosen this spot for Fort Raymond, back in late fall of 1807. After being abandoned for years, Joshua Pilcher had rebuilt the post in 1821 and renamed it Fort Benton.

"Tie her fast now," Green barked. "Wouldn't want her to float clear back to Saint Louis without us!"

"*Oui, bourgeois!*" Toussaint laughed as someone tossed him the stern line.

Green studied the high brush with a narrowed eye. *I wish to hell Travis was here. It'd be just my luck that having come this far, there's a big band of Blackfeet the other side of the rise.*

Then he shouted for attention. "Now, let's not forget where we are, boys. Henri, break out the rifles. Trudeau, you set up guards and make a scout as soon as you get a musket. Keep an eye peeled out there!"

Able hands slid out the plank, settling it in place. Henri smacked the toil from his hands, sighed, and ducked down into the cargo box. One by one, he handed the muskets up to Green, who passed them to Etienne, and then on to the others.

"All right," Green said, as Henri handed him his old faithful Hawken. "Let's see what remains of Fort Benton. Now, I want a keen eye peeled, boys. At the first hint of Injun sign, sing out—and I don't want anyone to wander off. Keep within sight of your companions!"

Green led the scramble up the slope and onto the flats. How many years had it been since he'd stood here, a young *engagé,* so full of hopes and dreams?

Well, David, today you've come back. And it's yours, all yours.

He hefted his rifle and walked forward, past the weather-gray stumps with their ax marks. The grass rustled beneath his boots as he followed the familiar path. The place looked sadly desolate. Most of the palisade had fallen down, and the cabins were nothing more than burned-out shells.

Henri stopped beside him, peering around owlishly. "Some of the logs can be saved."

"Yep. We'll have to pack a bunch more in." Dave glanced up at the cobalt November sky and sniffed the warm breeze. "It's fine weather. But it won't last." He stepped over the fallen palisade and took stock. "I'd say build a blockhouse first. That will give us defense and shelter from the blizzards at the same time."

Toussaint came at a trot, the usual sad expression on his face. "*Bourgeois,* we 'ave found old firepits. The ashes, they are long cold, three, maybe four months. From zee rocks piled inside, they are *les Indiens.*"

"But nothing fresh?"

"*Non, bourgeois.* Trudeau, he see old platforms in zee trees to the west, but the bodies are no longer there. He thinks they are old."

"I wish Travis and Baptiste were here," Henri muttered. "I would sleep better."

"*Moi aussi,*" Toussaint agreed.

Green slapped them both on the back, and shook his head. "For the moment, Travis is better off where he is. And we're going to need those Crow supplies a heap more than three more rifles here. Toussaint, we've got three, maybe four hours of daylight left. Let's get camp set up. But first, I want some of these old palisades dragged up for a breastwork. Tonight, we'll have us one hell of a feast, two gills of whiskey per man, a little dancing and singing, and then, by God, tomorrow, we go to work on the post."

"*Oui!*" Toussaint's expression brightened; calling orders, he walked off toward *Maria.*

Green took a deep breath, inhaling the rich fragrance of the land. "God damn the naysayers, I'm here! At the mouth of the Big Horn—and before the rest of the insiders like Astor, Chouteau, Pilcher, and the others."

Henri slapped him on the back. "I'll go and see to the boat, Dave. There is much work to be done."

"Yes, a lot of work."

But for now, I've beaten the odds. Green tightened his grip on his rifle. *And, as God is my witness, there's no one who can take it away from me now. If it comes to war, I won't be licked by man, beast, or weather!*

His steps light, buoyed with exuberance, he walked across the narrow neck of land and stared to the south.

Travis? No matter what I tell the rest, I wish you were here with me, old friend. You be careful down there. I just got a feeling, hear?

CHAPTER FIFTEEN

So many things are now clear to us. Now let that honest fellow speak out, I will say, now let him answer my question. He does not believe in the beautiful by itself, he will have no perpetual model of perfect, unchangeable beauty, but he believes in a myriad of beautiful things. This is the son of sight-fancier who will not brook being told that the beautiful is one, and the just is one, and so forth. Here, then, is my question: "My good man, of all these beautiful things, is there a solitary one which will not sometimes appear ugly? Of all these just things, will one never appear unjust? Of all these pious things, will one never appear unpious?"

—Plato, *The Republic*

 Richard awakened to tickles and itches. Still mostly asleep, he reached up, scratched, and rolled over. A pinprick of pain made him scratch yet again. The annoyance awakened him enough that he recognized the

sounds of the village—and remembered other sounds from the night before.

God would have spared Sodom and Gomorrah had he known about the Crow.

A tickle traced across his face, but this time his quick fingers captured the tiny creature. In the thin dawn light, Richard stared at a little black speck barely larger than a...

Dear Lord God, it's a louse!

His stunned brain couldn't accept what he was seeing. Not until the scalp over his right ear began to tickle.

He crushed the tiny vermin between the nails of his thumb and forefinger. His hair seemed to burn now, and tickles were born all over his flesh, along his legs, around his testicles, on the soft skin of his sides.

I can't believe this.

Pulling back the covers, he noted that only the old woman was up, tending the fire as she boiled something in a dented copper kettle that smelled delicious.

Richard tiptoed to the doorway, slipped out into the chilly air, and greeted the crystal morning with less than abundant enthusiasm. His breath puffing, he shivered and followed the path down toward the slow current of the Tongue River.

Every man has his vulnerability, the thing, or circumstance, they can't abide. For some it might be leeches, for others, ticks or spiders. That day on the Tongue, Richard discovered that his was lice. Perhaps it was being raised on Beacon Street, but the very idea that he'd been infested with the filthy buggers just set his gut to crawling.

I've got to be rid of them...now!

In a panic, he hurried across the frost-crusted grass.

Several young men were already splashing about in

the water a hundred yards downstream as Richard scowled at the pink horizon. His breath whitened in the chill air. The ground under his feet had frozen hard. With deepening dread, he slipped out of his clothes.

He waded bravely into the shallows and gasped at the numbing cold. Sloshing out into deeper water, he dived in. At first the terrible cold shocked his nerves. Then it began to eat into his very core.

Holding his head underwater, he scrubbed his hair vigorously, rooting his scalp with frantic fingernails. Tarnal hell, the critters couldn't take cold like this, could they? Surely it would stun them to death, drown them.

Soap, oh, Heavenly Father, what I'd give for a good bar of lye soap!

Lungs laboring, muscles knotted, flesh shivering and goosebumped, he got his feet under him and stood in the hip-deep water. Beneath his feet, the mud was gooey for the first couple of inches, but rounded river cobbles beneath provided solid footing.

To his surprise, the air felt even colder than the water.

"Another dousing won't hurt," he told himself firmly. "Right." Better to turn blue and die of pneumonia than to have lice. He dived in again, bubbles gurgling around his ears as he scratched and scrubbed.

When he could stand it no longer, he surfaced, teeth chattering. He barely noticed the rosette sky, the magnificent orb of the rising sun, or the dappled shadows on the sage-covered hills. Rubbing water droplets away, he blinked at his cold-pimpled skin, searching desperately for little scurrying beasts. He caught one down deep in the mat of his pubic hair, gleefully pinching the defiler between his nails. But, if there was one...

He ducked himself again, this time clawing at his

crotch, scratching and flailing to dislodge any unwelcome invaders. The cold had become unbearable.

Enough. Richard, any more of this and you'll freeze to death.

He stood up, thigh-deep in the river, rubbed water from his eyes, and bent over despite wracking shivers to pick carefully through his pubic hair. *God damn! I've never been so cold in all my life!*

But, lice! Dear Jesus, a man had to draw the line somewhere. He'd curled over until he could see the underside of his cold-knotted scrotum and continued the hunt for tiny insect bodies, unaware at first that another body was in the water beside him.

Richard glanced sideways to find New Moon Rising—naked herself and dripping wet—bent over as he was,. Her neck craned as she stared, curious to see what he'd been so intent on. In a straightforward tone, she asked him a question. Her mild brown eyes reflected frank curiosity.

For a moment, he stood as if rooted.

Nor was she the only one. The current had carried Richard fifty paces down from where he'd left his clothes, and five other young women were in the process of either disrobing or wading out to join him and New Moon Rising.

"Oh, good God!" Thrashing through the water, he stumbled and fell, flailing. He found his feet, coughing and sputtering. When he looked back, the young women were still standing there, silently watching him.

———

"Graybacks, huh?" Travis asked as their horses picked their way across a sage-covered bench and began to climb a long gentle ridge. The notion of Richard with lice pleased him immensely—but the tale wasn't half as entertaining as the stories the Crow girls were telling about him down at the river. It seemed they had trouble with the English word "Richard" so they were calling him "Looks for His Balls."

With a straight face, Travis said, "They can devil a man half to distraction, I'll tell ye."

"Don't I know it." Richard stared glumly at him, absently scratching his flank as he rode along.

"Looks like you needs 'nuther hand, Dick," Baptiste observed. "You got one foah the reins, another to hang on to yor shooter, but one shy fo' the scratching, coon."

Travis chuckled, and fought the desire to do a little scratching of his own. "Yep. Why I reckon best medicine fer graybacks is ter boil these hyar clothes. They's a smudge can be made out of larkspur and fir sap. Ye can trade fer some when the Mountain Crow come in. Burn it and the soot'n kill the varmints. In summer, ye can burn it and the smoke'll keep the skeeters down."

"What about now, Travis?" Richard demanded. "I tried drowning and freezing them to death."

Travis could not help but smirk. "Hell, it might have worked, coon. But ye run outa that river so fast, and crawled right back inta them clothes of yern. Why, the onliest thing graybacks likes better than a man's hair is the seams in his duds."

Travis patted his Hawken and looked back over his shoulder at the pack string. He'd saved a trade rifle to barter with Two White Elk for the four additional pack-horses that now followed them. The Crow nags, backs covered by their packs, were tail-hitched to the Pawnee horses. All in all, it was a damn fine trade. And if worse came to the worst, and they didn't get a good hunt before deep cold, they could eat the horses.

"What did Two White Elk tell you?" Richard asked suddenly. "You and he talked a lot."

"Oh, lots of things. About the Blackfoot, about what old friends had counted coup, about who'd married who and who'd divorced who. Who'd been killed. That sort of thing."

"Travis...can I ask something personal?"

By God, hyar it comes!

Travis raised an eyebrow and shot a knowing look across at Baptiste. The comer of the black hunter's lip curled in disgust

"Ask what? About the phil'sophical importance of graybacks?"

"No. I mean...well, you and Two White Elk's wife. Isn't he your best friend?" Richard's face looked like a mask, as if he were trying desperately to act unconcerned.

"Son of a *bitch*!" Baptiste roared, slapping a hand on his thigh with enough fury to spook his horse into a quick sidestep. "I'm gonna wring his damn Doodle neck!"

Richard looked plumb panicked as he gave Baptiste the sort of glance a condemned man might.

Travis chuckled. "Relax, Dick. I bet that neck-chopper yonder that ye'd ask about it first chance ye got."

"But I..."

"Bet him twenty prime plews, I did. And by Hob's balls, Baptiste, they'd better be right prime."

"They'll be as prime as any upriver, you miserable duck-fucker."

"What's a duck-fucker?" Richard's nervous gaze slipped from Travis to Baptiste.

"Feller what cares fer chickens and the like on board ship." Travis nodded at Baptiste. "That old slave there, he ain't about ter let me forget I's a sailor once before I got religion and skipped over the side in New Orleans."

"Go on," Baptiste cried in disgust. "Answer his question. But, holy hinges of Hell, Dick, stop costing me money. Just fer once, can't ye let somethin' happen without asking questions about it?"

Richard looked sheepish, his fist knotted on the reins.

Travis glanced sideways at Richard. "Two White Elk, he's my brother, Dick. Crow do that. Adopt each other. Wal, Two White Elk and me...let's just say we got a heap in common. Things we share that are special to just us."

"I could tell."

In steely tones Travis said, "No, I don't think you could, Doodle. And right hyar and now, I ain't about ter discuss it with ye. Ye've not earned that right, and I ain't sure ye ever will."

Travis pounded heels into his horse's ribs and cantered on ahead, letting the crisp breeze chill the heat out of his anger.

He don't know no better, coon. It's different fer him, a Boston boy that never had to wipe the snot out of his own nose.

Travis sighed wearily, letting his horse slow and cool out as he neared the ridgetop. It didn't do for a man to charge headlong over a hill, not in this country. Even if an Eastern Doodle had driven him half to distraction.

Travis let his horse walk over the crest and gazed on the snow-capped peaks to the west. Yep, there they were, worthy of their name, gleaming in the light. The sight kindled something happy down inside him. Since ascending the Yellowstone, bits and pieces had been coming back to him. Fragments of memory that he'd pushed out of his head. Seeing Two White Elk had opened the gates, releasing the flood.

Now he looked out at the country, taking his time to inspect every ridge and gully, mindful of any irregularity. Dark clumps of buffalo spotted the breaks down into the Big Horn. That would bear remembering, depending on how long it took to reach the river's mouth, where, hopefully, they'd find Dave in the process of rebuilding Fort Benton.

If the weather held, the *engagés* could cobble together some sort of shelter, and he, Baptiste, and Richard could shoot enough meat to get them through the deep cold. A warm spell generally opened the country around the end of January or first of February. The chinooks would blow and give them another chance to hunt buffalo in addition to the deer, antelope, and small game that could be collected around the fort.

Travis sucked the sweet air into his lungs, savoring the odors of sage, earth, and grass. So fresh, why, nothing could compare. The spirit of the sky, soil, sun and stars, the rocks and plants, surrounded a man—the very essence of what it meant to be alive.

The hollow clopping of horses' hooves intruded, and Travis paid no heed as they rode up next to him. He simply raised an arm and pointed. "Yonder."

"What are they?" Richard asked. "Clouds?"

Baptiste chuckled, teeth flashing. "He do take all."

"The Shining Mountains, Dick. Part of 'em at least. We call 'em the Big Horns."

Richard fixed on the distant mountains like a pointer, his fingers tracing the curved cock on his rifle. "Willow's mountains? So high? Why are they white?"

"Ain't you never seen no mountains afore?" Baptiste asked.

"Well, some." Richard rubbed his jaw. "Around Pittsburgh and along the Ohio River."

"He ain't never seen mountains," Travis confirmed. "Not shining ones, anyway. And yep, if'n Willow's alive, that's where she's headed. Hell, she otta be there by now."

"And this river running down the valley in front of yor nose"—Baptiste pointed—"is the Big Horn. And just yonder, to the north beyond them bluffs, is where we otta find Green and the boat."

Travis tarried, eyes on the distant mountains; the memories, so long suppressed, began to boil up inside him. For a brief instant he lived with Moonlight again. Once more he could enjoy her smile, the laughter in her eyes, the way she held him and teased him by plucking at the hair on his chest with her nimble brown fingers. She'd been so small and elfish, an imp of a thing with an insatiable appetite for fun. He closed his eyes. He could see her looking up at him after they'd made love. He'd place his hands just so, on each side of her head, marveling that such a tiny slip of a woman could wield such power over him.

They'd had two years together. Some of them right over yonder, at the foot of those mountains, and up in the gentle pine and fir slopes of the Pryors. A man could live like that...if only for a moment.

But I never knew those two years were going to have to last me all of my life.

"Travis?" Richard's voice cut through the dream.

"Huh?"

"That's the third time I asked you."

"Asked me what?"

Richard scratched under his arm, squinting curiously at him. "I thought you were the one who talked about being on your uppers, about not locking yourself in your head."

"Yep, wal, Travis, he's a fine one foah giving advice," Baptiste said dryly. "But he ain't always a one to take it."

Travis gave Baptiste an evil scowl. "Ye got something ter say?"

"Just that we ain't getting no closer to camp a-sitting up heah." Baptiste winked, and smiled. "Maybe Dick and me, we'll mosey on. Catch up with us when you will, coon."

Richard gave Travis a skeptical glance as the horses filed past, but for once he held his peace.

Travis had to rein in his horse, the animal anxious to follow the others. The breeze hissing through the short sage and grass seemed to carry her whisper to his lonely ears.

"Yep, wal, gal. I do shorely miss ye."

Impatient, the horse whinnied, shattering his tranquility with the surety of an ax through river ice.

"All right, damn ye." Travis let the horse have its head, taking one last look at the Big Horns, so clear and clean in the distance.

———

Generations of *Dukurika* had camped in the overhang high on the canyon wall. Sometime in the distant past, perhaps just after the Creation, the limestone beneath the sandstone caprock had been undercut, leaving a big hollow that ran back into the mountain. Since the overhang had a southern exposure, it received sunlight all year long. The rock was warmed during the day, and radiated heat throughout the night. Because the camp was high on the hillside, it remained warm when the cold air settled in the canyon bottom. Down there , in the shadowed depths, the *Dukurika* cached their deep-frozen meat supplies.

The camp was protected from both the west and north winds. Water could be had by climbing down to the creek. Wood was plentiful, with juniper and limber pine on the slope below, and lodgepole and fir forests above.

Mountain sheep wintered on the slopes to the east, nibbling the bitterbrush and cinquefoil. Elk used the grassy flats below for winter range, and mule deer liked the brush-filled draws and pawed through snow for last season's forbs.

Willow had found High Wolf's band at the shelter, right where she'd expected. Early that afternoon, she had picketed the horses on the rim above, and led an uneasy White Hail down the precarious trail through the caprock. Nervous flutters had filled her stomach when she called out their arrival.

The youth called Felt the Fire had poked his head around a rock outcrop and asked who was there. At Willow's answer, he'd vanished, to be replaced an instant later by Eagle Trapper, who cried out in happy amazement, clapped his hands, and rushed out to hug her.

Somehow she had survived a blizzard of questions, hugs, jokes, and proddings. The dogs had barked, the children had squealed, and her parents had beamed. The telling of her adventures had lasted from the time she arrived, all through the afternoon and evening, and now extended into the night.

I am home.

After all the upset that began with the death of her husband and child, she was once again high in her beloved mountains. She sighed as she looked up at the night sky. In the high mountain blackness, the stars shone with a brilliance she'd missed out on the plains.

A roaring fire crackled—lively sparks dancing up into the cold air—and illuminated the sandstone cliff above the camp. A framework of poles and hides—enough to protect bedding and packs—had been built behind the drip line and across the rock overhang.

Willow stood before the fire, a soft-tanned white mountain sheep robe over her shoulders.

One by one she studied the familiar faces cast in the flickering yellow light. This year's camp consisted of three extended families of High Wolf's small band.

High Wolf, her father, the band's headman and *puha-gan,* perched on an angular slab of rock, his favorite dog, Star, at his feet. White Alder, her mother, sat cross-legged on an elk hide to High Wolf's left, a glossy bearskin robe over her shoulders. White Hail—an honored guest—sat at High Wolf's right. White Hale's *Pa'kiani* buffalo robe was pulled tight against the night's chill. Rock Hare, Willow's brother, sat beside his wife. Red Squirrel, who suckled her infant son under a fox-hide cape. Marmot and Pika, their two boys, five and four years old, cuddled together under a soft bear robe and watched with gleaming eyes.

Next in the circle was Many Elk, High Wolf's long-time friend and companion. He had been like an uncle to Willow. His wife, Lodgepole, sat beside him, covered with a finely tanned sheep hide. Their son. Black Marten, and his wife, Sweet Grease, shared a buffalo robe with their three children.

Beside them, filling out the circle, were Eagle Trapper and Good Root, also old friends of High Wolf's. *Tam Apo* had smiled upon them, for their five children had all lived; the eldest, Felt the Fire, was ten, while little Flicker, the youngest, still nursed and slept in a fur-lined cradleboard. The band's pack of dogs lay along the margins of the shelf that dropped off into the canyon.

In celebration of Willow's arrival, a feast of succulent sheep and baked ricegrass cakes had been prepared. The empty dishes—cut from the boss of a mountain sheep's horn—had been licked clean by the dogs and now lay empty before them.

Willow finally brought the long story of her adventures to a conclusion: "From the Spirit Trail, we crossed the mountains. The snow is still passable beneath the peaks. And here we are. I am home."

"These things you tell us"—High Wolf shook his head, fingers scratching Star's neck—"they seem almost impossible."

Willow's father was an old man. After forty-five winters, his hair remained thick, but silver streaked the black; he braided it tightly into two queues that hung down either side of his broad face. A thin, straight nose ran from strong brows and accented his prominent cheekbones. Good-humored eyes looked out from deep sockets, the comers crinkled in crow's-feet from squinting across snow fields and into cold winds. His heavy jaw ended in a pointed chin that gave his face a triangular look.

He wore a finely crafted sheephide coat, the leather tanned maiden-soft, and tailored to his broad shoulders and muscular arms. Zigzags of lightning, Power lines of thunder, and images of wolf and mountain sheep had been painted on the white leather.

"Nevertheless, I tell you the truth," Willow replied.

"She does indeed," White Hail added. "Upon my soul, I swear it."

High Wolf said. "My grandfather saw the first metal knife when he was a a boy. It had been brought here by the *Newe,* carried up from the Spanish lands in the far south. He was told the White men were Powerful spirits who worshipped a terrible god. When my father was a boy, he was told other white men lived off to the east, as well. When I was a boy, we learned of the British, living far to the north. And then John Tylor came and married a *Dukurika* wife, but he said that only now and then would a trader come."

The old *puhagan* shook his head. "Now, daughter, you say the Whites are coming here to stay for good. Not just passing, through like the Astor men that I have heard tell of. But you have seen them. Lived with them? Is this good or bad?"

Willow used her toe to nudge a juniper log further into the fire. "Like any men, they are both good and bad. I'm afraid my words will not be believed, but I insist that we will come to grief if we treat them like spirits instead of like ordinary men. They have things we need—and many that we do not."

"Willow and I disagree on this," White Hail said. "The White men bring us great wealth. Wondrous weapons to destroy our enemies, and better axes and knives. You've seen the beads they bring. How they are lustrous and gleam in the sunlight. Their metal kettles never break. I've seen paints of unbelievable brightness and color, metal needles that never dull. So many things we need."

Willow shook her head. "They will make us no wealthier than our enemies, and the guns they trade, they trade to everyone. We will obtain nothing from the White men that every other people will not receive. The trap is that White Hail is partly right. We must have guns to balance the advantage given to the *Pa'kiani* and *A'ni*."

Many Elk tugged at one of his long braids. "Why do we need guns? We are not warriors, Willow. The way it is now, when the *Pa'kiani* come, we simply disappear into the forest. We know the hidden ways and can vanish like mist. They travel on horses...and only on the main trails. The only thing to be gained by fighting is an opportunity to have a funeral for someone you love. Then a person must live in grief for the rest of his life. Winning a fight does not bring the dead one back."

White Hail stiffened slightly; but then, *Ku'chendikani* and *Dukurika* had never really understood each other's concepts of war. Among the Sheepeaters, honor came from the hunt, not from scalps and raids.

"The White men come for furs," Willow stated. "For now, that is all they want."

"Is that so bad?" High Wolf frowned as he stroked his

dog. "If they come here, we can give them furs for their metal pots and knives and axes."

"The fewer things we trade them," Willow insisted, "the better off our people will be."

White Hail made a face—then relented under Willow's scowl.

Willow's mother was short and broad. Despite the eight children—only two had lived—that White Alder had borne High Wolf, the years had been kind to her. She still looked young enough to be Willow's older sister. Now she said, "These White men things you talk of. Like the iron knife you have, Willow. I would like an iron knife like that."

She pointed to the few glass trade beads worked in among the bone and quill-work designs that decorated the bodice of her sheep-hide dress. She had accumulated them, one by one, over the years. "These are very good beads, and unlike dyed quills, the colors do not fade. If these few things are good, then perhaps many of their things are good."

"Mother, *Tam Apo* gave us everything we need. It's all here, in our mountains. As long as we avoid raiders and fighting, we might not need guns. We kill enough in our sheep drives on the ridges. We know the ways of brother elk in the timber, and catch enough of his kin in our snares for food and hides. We do not need horses and guns to shoot buffalo when we can trap them in our surrounds and pens. While the Plains people must move constantly to feed their horses, we stay in one place and harvest roots, berries, and grass seeds in late summer. Our food can be cached for later use because we don't have to move it with us all the time."

"Yes, yes, we know these things," Eagle Trapper said as he absently ruffled his son's hair. "We have argued it with our *Ku'chendikani* cousins for years. But what about these White men? If they can make such tools as your iron ax, what else can they make? You have told us about the big wooden lodge that floats, and the giant log lodges. I would like to see these things."

Her brother, Rock Hare, nodded. He'd looked skeptical as Willow related her story. "I, too, would like to see these things. I have seen guns. For a long time I have wanted one. To know that the White men are bringing such things here, near our mountains, makes me think I might go down and get one from them."

Willow sighed wearily. Rock Hare was four years older than she, and had always seemed invincible, all-knowing, and capable. Now he acted pitifully innocent and vulnerable. When had that changed?

Willow asked, "Why do you want a gun, Brother? What will it get you that your bow will not? Remember the winter of the big snow? We had crept up on six deer in the willows. You told me you would kill them all. And one by one you did, the only sound the twang of your bowstring, and your sharp arrows striking flesh. With a gun, Brother, you would have killed only one deer. At the bang, the others would have run."

He raised a mocking eyebrow. "I suppose you know *all* about guns, Sister?"

"I know of them. Travis persuaded me to shoot one when he was teaching Richard to shoot. I will stick to a bow, and kill silently. And, Brother, when I run out of arrows, I will make more. When you run out of powder for your gun, you must go to the White men and trade them as many hides as they ask for more powder."

"In saying this," White Hail agreed, "Willow is right. Only the White men can make gunpowder and bullets. I have seen *Ku'chendikani* trying to mix their own powder from bark, charcoal, fine-ground bone, all sorts of things. Nothing works. You *must* trade for powder and balls with the Whites."

"Are they all bad?" A pensive Eagle Trapper rested his knobby chin on balled fists. "Are none of their things good? If this is so, I think we should just avoid them altogether. But I know the Whites have traded with the *Ku'chendikani*. Nothing terrible has happened to them."

Willow studied them, trying to read the effect of her words. "Many of the Whites' things are bad, yes, but not all. Let me tell you about their spirit water."

White Hail's eyes gleamed and be smiled wistfully.

Willow continued, "It has wonderful qualities. I poured some on a White man's wounds. They healed cleanly, without forming pus and hot flesh. But the White men do not use it for this. Instead, they drink it, and it makes their souls crazy. It turns a wise man into a fool."

"Then we would not want it," High Wolf agreed.

Willow shrugged. "Are you sure? Remember the time when Half Bear was hurt? The elk was supposed to be dead, but jumped up at the last instant and gored him. The wound angered, and grew hot, dripping and stinking from the evil that entered it. Half Bear's *mugwa* was driven from his body and he died horribly. I think I could have healed him with the spirit water."

"How?" High Wolf demanded, his *puhagan*'s interest piqued. "What Power does it have?"

"I don't know. Maybe it drives the evil spirits from a wound the way it drives the good sense from a man's soul when he drinks it"

High Wolf stared thoughtfully at his dog. "Then that would be a good thing."

"My people," Willow pleaded, "you must be very

careful with the White men. They are unbelievably clever. They aren't like us. They don't think the way we do. In the beginning, they give gifts: pots, iron needles, strike-a-lights, little things that amaze and delight.

"The first thing we, as *Dukurika*, will do is show these wonderful things to our friends. And, as is proper and polite, when our friends marvel, we will give the gift to them. And they to someone else, and so on. This is where the White man is so very clever, for in the trail of the gift, I will always want another strike-a-light or another mirror like the one I gave away. Like thirst in the alkali flats, the desire will grow. But the next time the White man comes, he will not give away the wonderful things. At that time he will say, 'Trade! I will give you a strike-a-light for a beaver hide.'

"And, my people, the thirst will have grown so powerful, you will take your hides down and give them all to the White men so that you have many strike-a-lights to give to all of your relatives."

"And the next time the White men come, all these people will trade." High Wolf nodded his understanding. "These White men are clever indeed."

Willow raised her hands. "Never underestimate them. Respect them, but never trust them. They act like Coyote in the beginning times. As long as you always understand that you are Wolf, and they are Coyote, you will do well with them."

Everyone around the circle was nodding thoughtfully, remembering the Creation and how Coyote always caused trouble. Everyone but Good Root, who watched her with suspicious eyes. She'd always been one of those aggravating sorts, a woman who used words like little splinters, never hurting her victim outright, but always sliding something irritating under the skin.

Men who act like Coyote?

Richard's eyes watched from her memory. No, he'd never tried to trick her. He'd always been incomprehensibly honest—at the same time he tricked himself.

Was he on his way back to Boston, traveling downriver even as she stood here?

What will you think when you pass all those places we saw together, Richard? Will you remember me at the site of the Ree battle? At the Grand Detour? Or the camp where you shot Packrat?

CHAPTER SIXTEEN

But it is manifest that this imaginary right of slaying the defeated in no way results from the state of war. Men are not enemies by nature, if only for that reason that, living in their primitive independence, they have no mutual relationships sufficiently durable to constitute a state of peace, or a state of war. It is the relationship of things, and not of men, which constitutes war; and since the state of war cannot arise from simple personal relations, but only from real relations, private war—war between man and man—cannot exist either in the state of nature, where there is no settled ownership, or in the social state, where everything is under the authority of laws.

—Jean-Jacques Rousseau, *The Social Contract*

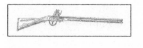 Richard rode last in line as they traveled north down the broad valley of the Big Horn. Travis was in the lead; he'd been unusually quiet since leaving the Crow village. Baptiste walked his gelding to one side of the pack string, his rifle cradled on the saddle before him, wary eyes missing nothing.

The Big Horn River flowed down through a broken

brown land of jutting sandstone ridges, accented by the speckled slopes where limber pine, juniper, and ponderosas grew. Patches of sage mottled the hillsides and flats, contrasting to the autumn-tawny grasses that swayed with the perpetual wind.

The river itself wasn't much, at least, not to Richard's eyes. After all the months on the Missouri, the terrible toil to reach this place, he'd expected something magnificent. Instead, he saw an unremarkable course of placid, silt-murky water that lazed indolently between cottonwood-rich banks. Greasewood patches interspersed with tall grasses, and stands of sagebrush covered the broad floodplain. On the whole, the land appeared rocky and dry. The nights were clear and nippy, while the days warmed slowly as the sun climbed its winter arc across the sky. When the air warmed, however, the wind picked up, until by late afternoon it roared over the rocky outcrops, moaned in the trees, and hissed through the sage. Richard rode hunkered against the blast, eyes in a squint.

Even so, the land had an essence, a raw presence he couldn't define. Not the somber, threatening antiquity of the Eastern forests, but something primal that hearkened to a language of the bones as well as the senses.

How odd that the earth could speak in such different tongues. Rifle in one hand, lead rope in the other, Richard studied the notion. In Boston, he couldn't have conceived that the land lived, that it could be felt. Grass was grass, a tree a tree, and dirt...well, what could one say about dirt? Abstractions that defied any meaningful relationship beyond the dialectical "me—it."

And what would his friends at Fenno's say about such a notion?

They'd laugh me out of the tavern.

As he would have once done to any fool who made such a ludicrous postulation.

Yet here I am, suddenly aware of what cannot be.

Or what his people would not accept.

And does that go so far as to encompass a Crow man sharing his wife with his best friend?

What was too much in this land of wild excess? Some dilemmas had a great many horns. His gaze roamed the endless sky. An eagle hovered in midair, suspended by the powerful currents that blew up the eastern bluffs. How magical: a floating dot of life against the infinity of blue.

He'd crossed a perceptual chasm: Boston on one side, the wilderness on the other. Each mutually incomprehensible. Boston—rational, ordered, and chaste, so carefully compartmentalized and predictable; the wilderness— intuitive, lusty, upredictable and anarchic in its savagery and violence.

In Boston, a man could take his leisure in a lamplit drawing room, a fine glass of brandy at his side, and read Kant. Kant had meaning there, so safe and sound behind a fortification of brick, walnut paneling, and French windows.

But where did a man find a philosopher for the wilderness? Not even Thomas Hobbes wrote in a language eloquent enough for the serpentine grace of the river, the razor-sharp clarity of the night sky, or the eider mantle of sage-rounded hills. Nor did Hobbs understand the visceral dialectic of man in the wilderness; not nasty, short, brutish, and mean, but defiant in victory or painfully broken in defeat—with all the vibrant stages in between.

Since I've come here, I've but barely begun to understand.

Fear now cut as keenly as broken glass. Contentment was a coveted thing of brevity; but when he had it, it ran warm and full in his soul. Joy, sorrow, love, and hate, each had been honed until life hung upon their pointed spikes, pierced through.

How did a man communicate gut truths like those to Professor Ames, or Will Templeton, or George Peterson? One might as well explain "yellow" to a blind man or Mozart to the deaf.

If this new reality is only perception, how do you know it's true?

He smiled grimly, avoiding the epistemological trap that would lead him to chase his tail around and around in endless circles.

The coyote gave him a start. The creature stood sky-lined on the ridge, quartered to the wind that whipped its tail and ruffled the long gray-brown fur. The ears were pricked, and even over the distance, Richard could feel those measuring yellow eyes.

What on earth would possess a coyote to—

A hollow boom rolled through the hills, like fading thunder across the sky. Even the earth seemed to shake.

"What the hell?" Baptiste pulled his horse up, listening as the sound rolled away.

Travis reined in. The pack string slowed, shook, and began to nibble what grass they could reach past their tail-hitches.

Richard cupped a hand to his ear, catching only the ripping of grass and the grinding of equine molars above the sounds of wind in the sage.

Finally Travis shrugged. "Wal, she's a funny country. A feller hears them booms every so often. And groans sometimes, too. Especially at night when yer laying with yer ear ter the ground. It's like the old earth is a-talking ter ye."

"I heard a boom like that," Baptiste agreed. "Down

on the Cheyenne River, it was. Way out in the badlands. Just a big boom—and the sky so clear and hot"

"Hell, remember back in eighteen hun'ert and eleven? We's nigh ter Saint Loowee and the whole goddam ground bucked and reared. Earthquake, remember? Hellacious thing that was. Trees all knocked over, and the very sand underfoot a-welling up like water."

"I ain't nevah fo'getting that," Baptiste agreed fervently. "Heard they's places the Mississippi even ran backwards after that."

Richard nibbled at the corner of his lip. That sense of unease had begun to creep back into his soul. This time he didn't scoff, but pulled his mare up from her grazing and urged her alongside Travis.

The scarred hunter was searching the surrounding hills, careful blue eyes intent on the rimrock, on each patch of trees.

"Didn't sound like a shot," Richard said. "But...there's something—"

"Uh-huh."

"Aw, I reckon it's just the spirits," Baptiste said. "A feller hears funny sounds out heah."

Travis shot a quick glance at Richard. "Got an itch in yer gut?"

"Just a feeling, kind of like something's gone wrong."

"Willow said ye had the makings." Travis reached up to scratch his beard. "Baptiste, I'd say we're no more than six, maybe seven miles from the Yellowstone. Reckon we'd best trot these mangy hosses on down. Skin yer eyes, coons. Let's go fast, but let's be savvy. If'n thar be trouble, we'd best see it afore it breaks on us."

Baptiste's wary gaze had been searching for threats. "You really think they be..."

But Travis had booted his bay gelding and was already

trotting forward, grass and cottonwood leaves rustling under the hooves.

Richard circled around to come in behind the string with their bouncing packs. Baptiste rode past, eyes narrowed, mouth grim, rifle clutched in one powerful black hand. When Richard glanced back at the heights, he saw nothing more than sagebrush quivering in the wind. The coyote had vanished as if it had never been.

A tightness began to build in his chest as they trotted grimly onward. Travis rode like a hunting wolf, using the cottonwoods as cover, threading his way through thickets of willow and fording the shallows when oxbows of the Big Horn blocked their way.

If anything, the wind seemed colder as it rushed down from the west. It moaned around the buff sandstone caprock and whispered secrets among the pines. The tall grass lashed at the soles of Richard's moccasins, and hissed around the fast-moving horse hooves. In his imagination, the whole world might have been calling a warning.

"Use your head," he muttered to himself. "Nothing's wrong."

They'd reach the mouth of the Big Horn and find Green and the *engagés* refurbishing the old Missouri Fur Company post. In the end, it would turn out that he'd done another silly thing in a long line of silly things.

Travis slowed as they broke out of the trees. He pointed at the squared headlands that opened into the distance. "Yonder's the mouth of the Big Horn."

"I ain't heard nothing else, Travis," Baptiste called, his rifle still at the ready. "Ain't seen no sign, neither."

"Nope." Travis didn't sound convinced.

For the fifth time, Richard checked the priming in his rifle, then patted his powder horn and bullet pouch. In the process, his hand brushed the scalps, and their silken touch sent a tingle along his backbone.

"How do you want to do this?" Baptiste asked. "Ride right down the middle of the valley, or choose one side?"

"Down the middle, I reckon." Travis squinted at the distant trees that marked the Yellowstone. "If'n she's trouble, we'll pitch in."

"Don't heah no shots," Baptiste replied. "Ain't nothing wrong, Travis. You be hoodoo shy. Skittish as a one-eyed hoss."

"Maybe."

They started forward again, Richard's mouth dry. Even the burning itch of a louse bite over his left ear could be forgotten.

Travis used a gravel-bottomed ford to cross the Big Horn one last time. The horses splashed through belly-deep water, and buck-jumped up the far bank. Then Travis wound through the sage to a deeply rutted buffalo trail, leaning wide to study the ground. "They's been hyar," he muttered, voice hushed. "Reckon that's Toussaint's footprint—or this child ain't seen sign."

"How old?" Baptiste asked.

"Day...maybe two."

"Well, they made it safe this far."

"Uh-huh. On yer uppers, coons. Fort's just yonder." Travis kneed his horse forward, half-crouched, rifle ready.

Leaving the sage, they rode through a patch of chokecherry and serviceberry and into an abandoned camp. Green's tent stood amid smoldering firepits. Here and there, rolls of blankets and other packs lay, some kicked about.

Beyond the camp, part of a buildking had been constructed, the walls three logs high. Logs, freshly hewn, scarred with yellow notches where the axes had cut, waited to be rolled up and into place.

Richard barely noticed. *Engagés* lay here and there, sprawled like rag dolls. Too many bristled with arrows. Their colorful clothing was blood-splotched and torn, and flapped and rippled as the wind blew along dead flesh.

"Dear Lord God." Richard swallowed hard. He heard the metallic click as Baptiste cocked his rifle. The horses stamped, wanting to shy from the flapping clothing and the smell of blood and violence.

"Blackfoot," Travis announced in a flat voice. With his rifle, he pointed to a half-naked man pitched face-first in the grass. A bullet had blown a gaping hole through his back to expose bits of spine, ribs, and shoulder blade.

"They didn't pick him up?" Baptiste wondered, glancing around nervously.

They followed the route of the battle down from the partial construction, over the edge of the terrace, and onto the riverbank. There, the scene became macabre. The dead lay as they'd fallen, transfixed by arrows, bludgeoned, or shot, but Richard saw the first piece: a head. The face had been peeled away; the neck was nothing more than stringy knots of tissue.

He'd seen the like once, decayed and worried by rooting pigs. And again, later, when François had left it in his room aboard the *Virgil*. Richard's stomach twisted at the thought.

"What the hell?" Travis pointed at a shattered arm, the flesh mutilated, as if wolf-chewed.

"God damn," Baptiste whispered, eyes fixed on a pair of legs that dangled from the spreading branch of a cotton-wood. One of the legs hung oddly, as if the bone had been smashed; trails of intestine hung like a strand of gray rope from the remains of the hips.

"It's as if the hand of God ripped him in two and tossed him up there!" Travis shivered, his blue eyes oddly glazed.

Richard slipped off his horse, stepping carefully over one of the dead *engagés*. A bullet had caught the man in the groin, and he'd thrashed on the ground for a short time before a hatchet split his forehead open. The eyes blood-streaked, Louis de Clerk stared emptily at the sky, pupils still wide as if in disbelief.

Richard had to nerve himself to pick up a piece of wood. "Milled," he said, running his hands over the splintered piece. "Oak. I know the grain of it. I lay on it long enough while my back healed. This is oak, Travis. A piece of the boat."

Travis paled, clutching at his saddle for support.

Baptiste stepped down, ground-reining his horse as he inspected the brutalized remains of a dead Indian. "Sweet Jesus. This coon's full of splinters."

"Keg over there," Baptiste called, pointing at part of a smashed flour barrel. "What the hell happened? Damn it! *What the hell happened heah?*"

"Green blew up the boat," Travis said woodenly.

"Huh?" Richard turned, a shredded length of cloth in

his hands. He stared at the frayed fabric, aware of the splinters, of the acrid smell of burned powder.

Travis rubbed his face, looking as old and tired as Job. "Blackfoot hit 'em by surprise. Probably snuck up on their bellies, crawling through the sagebrush. Everyone panicked, ran for the boat.

"Green got 'em lined out, but too late. Them's the red bastards ye see shot. When they swarmed the boat, Dave ducked below, probably hid down behind the powder with a strike-a-light. He waited till the Blackfoot was all aboard...and blew the whole damned shitaree."

"Sweet Jesus," Baptiste murmured, sinking to his knees. He just stared at the ground with an empty gaze.

Richard stepped over what looked like a bloody lump of heart and lungs. A jellied leg lay to one side, the thigh bone splintered like kindling. He stared down at the river, running placidly with its smooth-swirling water. Only the litter on the bank looked out of place.

"Damn it, Davey," Travis whispered, and slipped off his horse, stumbling, legs gone weak. Richard looked over to see tears, like tiny diamonds, on his scarred cheeks.

None too steady, Richard climbed back up the bank, along the line of dead. There lay Toussaint, as if he'd slumped down and fallen over. No less than six arrow shafts stuck out of his big body, most broken off before he died. A rifle was still clutched in his hand, the stock shattered, but around the big boatman lay three Blackfeet, their heads crushed.

A soft groan, barely audible, came from the willows just west of camp. Richard approached on cat feet, recognizing the trail for what it was. A man had dragged himself along here, bleeding, mashing the grass flat.

At the edge of the willows, Richard crouched, rifle

cocked. Every so cautiously, he stepped into the grove, following the wounded man's route.

He was lying on his stomach, young, little more than a boy. His right arm was a mangled mass of coagulated blood and broken bone, matted with dirt, leaves, and grass stems. A splinter of oak, like a stiletto, was driven into his lower back, and from the bloody smears, the boy had tried to pull it out.

The Blackfoot boy moaned again, glancing up. His black eyes might have been cast of glass. In that moment, Richard read the boy's soul: panic, shock—a terrible, naked disbelief.

Richard raised his rifle as he looked into those haunted eyes, and, as if in a dream, set the trigger and shot the boy through the head.

He never looked back as he turned and retraced his way to the clearing. He'd poured another charge and was seating his bullet on its patch when Travis came running up.

"Whar at, coon?"

"Just one," Richard said, awed by the control in his voice. "Back yonder."

"Might be more," Travis stared around anxiously, rifle clutched like a lover. His mouth was working in a slack-lipped way. Bright panic glittered in his eyes. "Might be...more."

"Travis?"

The hunter's hands were shaking, the eyes unfocused.

"*Travis!* Take a scout." Richard rammed the ball home. "Check for sign."

Travis nodded, shook his head, and took a deep breath. "Damn...damn..." And then he strode away, waving the all-clear to Baptiste who'd covered them from under the lip of the bluff.

Richard watched him disappear into the sagebrush, then carefully primed the pan and snapped the frisson closed.

What now? Oh, Lord God, what now?

"Don't think about it," he told himself, willing his soul to be as empty as the Indian boy's had been.

Trudeau had died hard. He'd been shot in the back, low down above where the spine joined the hips. As he'd tried to crawl away, some warrior had driven an arrow through his back and pinned him to the ground before Trudeau's scalp had been cut off. Just enough strength had remained that Trudeau could claw at the grass, but not free himself. From the scraped soil, uprooted grass, and the dirt-packed fingernails, he'd hung on until just before their arrival.

"God damn!" Baptiste kept saying in a fragile voice as he walked from body to body. "God damn 'em all!"

Richard slowly shook his head as he looked over the camp. *This is like a dream, Richard. This can't happen.*

Travis emerged from the sagebrush, expression strained. "Got tracks. I make it four of them. Two is carrying one, and the fourth ain't no daisy. He's dragging a leg." He choked down a swallow. "Blast must'a panicked the hosses. They's afoot."

"Let's go get 'em." Baptiste turned for his horse.

Richard rubbed his face; how hot he felt. He made himself walk steadfastly as he caught up his horse and vaulted into the saddle.

They took the trail back toward the bluff, and located where no less than twenty horses had been held.

"Make it five," Travis said, indicating the ground. "Kid. Probably a horse guard on his first raid."

"Guess it's his last one," Baptiste said, a savage glitter

in his eyes. His jaw muscles had bunched under that smooth ebony skin.

"I reckon so," Travis rasped. His knobby knuckles were moon white where they grasped his Hawken too tight.

———

Travis stared into the flames of the Blackfeet campfire with unseeing eyes. He felt like a senseless husk—like an old log so rot-punky inside that he'd gone hollow. Nothing rose out of his soul. Not anger, or rage, or even grief.

The night pressed down on all sides, cold and silent but for the sounds of the river. Nothing stirred him, not when he looked at Baptiste's slack face, or at Richard's— their eyes fully as blank as his own. The three of them just crouched there, staring into the dancing flames, night-blind, and none caring a damn.

Travis glanced at the Blackfeet corpses still lying where they'd fallen. The panicked warriors had made no effort to hide their trail as they fled westward, scrambling up over the bluffs, sliding them down steep hillsides, and staggering hard across the flats. Dashing pell-mell upstream for the fast-water ford that would let them cross the Yellowstone and escape northward into their territory.

The two wounded had slowed them. In the end, no doubt refusing to believe in the existence of any pursuit, they'd camped in this sheltered cove, surrounded on three sides by rimrock.

I wouldn't have believed anyone would follow, either.

Travis traced fingertips along the ridges of scar tissue on his face. The flames wavered and leaped, burning patterns on the back of his eyes.

Travis had placed Richard on the right and Baptiste on the left. Slowly, carefully, they'd crawled through the sagebrush, and there, hunched over the fire, the Blackfeet seemed as dull and spiritless as the hunters who surrounded them.

It was too easy. They's already beaten—Power broken. At the first shot, they could do nothing else but jump up...ready to die.

They'd barely fought, jabbing with their guns, slashing with bows, as three White rifles blasted the night. The wounded man hadn't even tried to stand, but lay like a wilted flower, accepting death. One of the boys, the horse guard most likely, had charged off in panic and run plumb into Richard.

Travis glanced over to where Hamilton, wrapped in his blanket, stared owl-eyed into the flames. *Was that really ye, Dick? I'd have never believed ye'd bash a boy's brains out like that. And nary a flicker of an eye.*

Nor had Richard stopped there. He'd come roaring in out of the night and beaten the wounded warrior to death with his rifle. Then, lips back, teeth clenched, he had whipped his knife out and bent down. The keen blade had slid around the top of the skull, parting the connective tissue as Dick peeled the scalp off. Holding it high in the firelight, fist gripping the hank of hair midway, he'd watched it bob and sway in the breeze.

Laughter had choked in his throat—the kind a crazy man made—and he'd turned back to the first Blackfoot and repeated the deed.

To look at him over the fire now, Richard appeared as hollow as Travis felt. A man with nothing left inside.

Travis rubbed his eyes, afterimages of the flickering fire burning in his soul.

It warn't just Dick, coon. Ye were a mite berserk yerself. A calm—like ice in yer soul. Mindless, because God damn, it happened to ye again! Just like in the dream. They told ye, "Don't go ter the Yellowstone." They come to ye down just this side of Fort Atkinson and warned ye.

He shivered and threw another piece of wood on the fire. It popped, sparks twirling up.

It had happened here, real close, probably within a rifle shot of where he now sat. Immel and Jones had been this close to Fort Benton when the Blackfeet ambushed them, killed them, cut their bodies to pieces, and left them for the wolves to scatter.

Travis glanced at the dead again. Maybe these were some of the same Blackfeet that had killed Immel and Jones. *Just like the seasons, it all comes around.* But he hadn't listened.

And what if he had? Would Green have believed a dream? Turned back on Travis's word? Not a chance in Hell.

Travis chewed at the callus on his blood-caked thumb. *Maybe some things are just fated to be, no matter what. Just like Calf in the Moonlight and me. Or Dick and Willow. Or Green and the Blackfoot.*

Baptiste had finally roused himself enough to kick dirt over the tacky stain where a Blackfoot had bled out, then unrolled his blankets. He didn't even look at Travis as he lay down and settled his blanket over him. Cradling his rifle to his side, he pulled his hat low over his eyes—a dark shadow of a man blending into the night. Of them all, Baptiste had been the most sane, thirsting for revenge, driven by anger and frustration.

But, Dick, now. He'd been different. Not a stitch of emotion, as if his soul had shut off. Just like back at camp where he'd shot that kid.

Never seen a coon so cool, Dick. Just like ye done killed men all day long. Part of a job, like hoeing weeds in a garden.

Images—like all the others that haunted him—came trooping out of Travis' mind: Dave Green, the young *engagé,* pulling his first boat upriver for Manuel Lisa. Shivering out in the snow on the Little Missouri. Plotting, dreaming, seeing a future, like a mirage—shimmering, wavering, a vision of the mountains so far away.

But when the picture come clear, Davey, it wasn't like ye wanted.

How sure Dave had been that night in Saint Louis. Half a world away, and not a year passed. But Dave Green would dream no more. How many pieces did that much powder blow a man into?

Toussaint, Trudeau, Henri, the others...gone. All gone. Travis sucked idly at his tongue, watching the fire leap and dance. *Manuel Lisa, Michael Immel, Robert Jones, William Issom, Andrew Brown...no, stop it. Damn, Travis, yer list could go on forever.*

So much death. He shook his head. *I know more dead men than live ones.*

He glanced up at the dancing stars, the Milky Way splotching the darkness like a pale band across the sky. "Was it so damn bad? Hell, all Dave wanted ter do was take a boat up and make a little trade. Son of a bitch, it just don't make sense."

"Never does," Richard said.

Travis looked across and met his eyes, gleaming like an animal's in the firelight. "Ye otta be asleep."

"You, too."

"Can't."

"Me neither." Richard rubbed his hands nervously and looked around at the dead Blackfeet, at the bloody curve of skull where his knife had cut the scalp away. He'd done it quick and clean, as if he'd been cutting off men's hair all his life.

Travis threw another piece of wood into the fire, noticing that Baptiste's breathing had deepened. "Back at the boat...I mean...wal, the camp. Thanks fer keeping my head on, Dick."

"Keeping your head on?"

Travis pulled at his beard while the greedy flames licked up around the wood. "There's times a man goes plumb crazy. Loses all his sense. Reckon I's headed that way today. I'd just wandered around, getting crazier and crazier till...Hell, who knows? Anyhow, thanks for telling me ter go cut fer sign."

Richard shivered, tucking his blanket tighter. "I told myself it was a dream. I knew it was a lie, but it was so easy to believe. Why is that?"

"How the hell should I know?"

"I'd just wake up, and the boat would be waiting for us." He puffed a frosty breath up toward the stars. "But it's not. And everyone's dead. Green. The *engagés*. So I killed them, Travis. The boy in the willows...the warriors here." He squinted quizzically. "I thought I'd pay 'em back, make it right. But...but, it's not right. Is it?"

"Maybe. I don't know."

"I keep trying to understand. What happened, Travis? Tell it to me. Make it rational. It is, isn't it? We're not just animals, are we? We *do* think. We do have reasons, don't we? This didn't just happen for nothing."

Travis took a deep breath. "I reckon we all had reasons. Green wanted ter trade…make his name on the river. To the Blackfoot, that boat was more wealth than they'd seen in years. The warriors who take a whole boat, why, they's gonna be sung about fer years. Marry who they want and become chiefs. That's reasonable, ain't it?"

"Yes."

"And Dave, he makes a mistake. Maybe he puts the wrong coon on guard. Maybe he figgers that he's safe, that no enemies will come until he's forted up. No matter, the Blackfoot hit the camp. Dave's a quick one. He sees it's all lost, so he ducks down below deck and waits. Maybe he's wounded, but he lets as many of them skunking Bug's Boys climb aboard as he can, and then he strikes his spark and boom! If'n Dave can't have it, ain't no Blackfoot gonna get rich off'n Dave Green's sweat and blood."

"But to blow it all up?"

"Ain't the first time." Travis scratched his chin, remembering the *Tonquin*. "It's a hunch, Dick. But I figger he's wounded, knowing he's gonna lose it all anyway. Folks get a mite crazy when a dream dies right in front of 'em."

"I guess."

"And then there's us. We come riding in, and it's all gone. Friends are dead. The boat's blown ter hell. Just dead men and splinters a-laying all around." He watched the firelight, trying to block other images: old friends gone to rot and bones, a pretty young Crow woman smiling up at him, reaching for him with soft, warm, and loving arms. That spark of life growing inside her womb…

I went crazy fer a long time, then.

"I've done this before," Travis whispered. "But that time, there warn't no Dick to give me something ter do."

"Before?"

"When they killed my Calf in the Moonlight—my Crow wife. Cut the little baby out of her belly. I warn't there, Dick. Out hunting, ye see. Then—like t'day—I found her. I got real crazy that time. Did things...things I don't want ter remember."

For a long time they watched the fire leap and crackle, the sparks dancing upward and winking out like stars dying in the night sky.

"When dreams die," Richard said hoarsely. "We're good at that, aren't we? Killing dreams, I mean."

"Reckon so."

———

The weather had turned blustery and cold. Richard, Travis, and Baptiste had picked up what they could salvage from the campsite: axes, powder horns, rifles, and twists of tobacco. Bits and pieces of stuff were scattered along the shore, including strap iron that could be traded as raw material for arrowheads, some hanks of beads that hadn't broken, gun flints, two lead ingots, a couple of tins of tallow, and several slightly frayed bolts of cloth. All in all, they could make packs for only six of the additional horses they'd managed to catch up. Of the twenty-some the Blackfeet had lost, they found twelve.

Where disbelief had once driven him, now a terrible despair closed in around Richard's soul— like a fog on Boston Harbor. He acted mechanically, picking up bits of this or pieces of that. Some stubborn remnant of conscience insisted that the dead should be buried, but

Travis declared, "They's wolfmeat now, Dick. Ye'd dig for days to cover 'em, and by Hob, the second ye's outa sight, the wolves would dig fer days to uncover 'em again. Best let nature have 'em, the way God intended."

So he'd let the corpses lie, and tried to ignore the ravens that landed on the bodies at every opportunity, and the coyotes that slunk back and forth in the night.

"Where to?" Baptiste asked as they mantied up the last of the packs.

"Downriver, I guess," Travis decided. "Go back and maybe winter with old James Kipp among the Mandan."

Baptiste leaned on his horse, arms hanging over the saddle. "Huh, wal, I reckon that Green told me ten percent. I's a partner, Travis. Reckon as surviving parties, half this plunder's mine."

Travis squinted, considered for a moment, and nodded. "Reckon so. Dave would have wanted it that way."

Baptiste stared up at the clouds, the cold wind tossing his long woolly black hair. "I been thinking I'd take my share and maybe mosey back to the River Crow. A night of soft woman next to this coon set right, it did." He paused. "Yo'all could come along."

Travis glanced at Richard. "How about ye, Dick? Whar to?"

Richard fingered the reins he held, glancing idly

around the desolate flat. Four ravens stood over a hole they'd pecked in Toussaint's belly. They were cawing outrage at a fifth over some raven insult.

"I think I'm going south."

"South?" Travis asked. "Going ter find Willow, are ye?"

Richard nodded. "I have to see her before I head back. And then, well, I remember something you told me a long time ago, Travis. That if I ever got lost, all I needed to do was follow the rivers east of the mountains and they'd take me to the Missouri. Well, the Platte heads just down south of Willow's mountains, doesn't it?"

"That's a heap of empty, hostile country." Baptiste looked dubious. "Dick, whyn't you come winter with the Crow? Hell, come spring we'll travel back to the Mandan with 'em. You can catch a boat downriver from there."

"That's a sight of sense." Travis looked unsettled himself.

"If I travel overland, I'll be in Saint Louis by spring," Richard insisted. "And, like you said, it's all empty country." He smiled sheepishly. "Besides, the sooner I get back, the sooner I can send a message to my father. Let him know I'm alive."

"Uh-huh—and François?"

"If he's still around, I guess I'll just have to settle up, now won't I?"

"Remember that be city." Baptiste pointed a finger. "Them white folk, they don't take to no murder, no matter how fitting."

Richard shrugged. "Oh, I suppose I can figure a way without getting myself hung. Remember, I'm a gentleman."

Baptiste gave him a toothy grin. "Yep, wal, don't use no ax on him."

"South ter the Snakes, and then east along the Platte," Travis mused. "Hmm. Mind the company, Dick?"

"What?" Richard turned to stare at Travis.

"You crazy?" Baptiste jerked a thumb over his shoulder. "They's a right warm Crow village four day's ride yonder, piled high with meat, surrounded by warriors, and chockful of women ready to hop inta yor blankets, and you wants to go riding off into the Plains in winter?"

Travis scuffed his moccasin on the hard ground, watching as it scraped the grass away. "Wal, Baptiste, I'll tell ye. I'd consider it, but while ye was a-slipping yer pizzle inta that gal, Two White Elk and me got ter talking about old times. Calf in the Moonlight was Two White Elk's sister. Now, maybe I could find that again... and maybe I couldn't. He treated me like a brother. Even give me one of his wives—as a Crow does to blood kin. But, coon, my heart's been hurting since. Ye understand?"

Baptiste made a face. "Aw, hell, it ain't the fust time we've split up. Come on, then. I'll ride on down to the mouth of the Greasy Grass with y'all. See y'all that far at least."

"Done." Travis stepped into the stirrup and threw a leg over.

Richard frowned and mounted, taking only one look back at the Yellowstone and the broken dead who lay there.

CHAPTER SEVENTEEN

I am not permitted even to assume God, freedom, or immortality for the sake of the necessary practical employment of my reason, if I cannot deny speculative reason of its pretensions of transcendent insights, because reason, in order to arrive at these, must use principles which are intended originally for objects of possible experience only. If, in spite of this, these principles are applied to what cannot be an object of experience, it really changes this into an appearance, and thus renders all practical extension of pure reason impossible. I had therefore to deny knowledge in order to make room for faith.

—Immanuel Kant, *Critique of Pure Reason*

Heals Like A Willow sat on a spire of rock that jutted up from the Powder River's Mountains' western flank. From this aerie, she could see across the basin to the south and the greater basin to the west. The Owl Creek's Mountains, like a rocky hump, divided them. The river called

Pia'ogwe, or Mother River, emerged from its sheer-walled canyon in the Owl Creek Mountains and flowed between blood-red ridges on its way north to the Yellowstone. Beside it was *Pa'gushowener*, the Hot-Water-Stand, the big hot springs Green had talked about.

Farther across the basin she could see *I'sawean,* the Coyote's Penis, the tall guardian peak that marked the beginning of the snow-capped basalt cliffs beyond. The Wind River's Mountains stood like jagged teeth bared against the distant blue horizon. Her people did that. Named mountain ranges for the rivers that flowed out of them.

Down in the broad basin to the south, Packrat had captured her en route to this high point. Her goal then had been to grieve for her husband and son. She could finally release the hurt. Not only could she ache over the loss of her husband and baby boy, but she could conjure Richard's gentle eyes, and what might have been between them. Past and future pain, all reconciled at once.

My souls are still wounded.

Why hadn't scars formed? Would they ever?

Perhaps it was because she had failed to heal her husband and infant son. That was, after all, her Power.

I healed Travis, Richard, and the others. And, like a puha-gan, *I used my Power to destroy Packrat's soul.*

Willow tucked her sheephide coat tight. The chill wind blew bitterly across these heights.

She sensed him before she heard his careful approach. The way was treacherous, a difficult climb. A slip would mean broken bones at the very least.

She allowed the vista before her and the Power of the land to soothe her souls. How old had she been? Seven, perhaps eight summers the first time she'd climbed up here to see what it was like. Perhaps that was when

Power first entered her souls and set her on the path she'd followed.

His clothing rasped on the rock, and he grunted as he pulled himself over the lip. She refused to look at him for the moment, allowing her dream soul to float on the distance.

He waited patiently.

Finally she said, "You're not as spry as you once were."

"No. And when it really gets cold, my joints ache."

She smiled and took her father's hand in hers, marveling at how warm he was. He wore his decorated sheephide coat, warm leather leggings, and a beaverhide hat from which his gray-streaked braids had escaped.

She told him, "I think you need to sweat more. You know full well that the older you get, the more tiny evils slip into your bones. I think it's the small things, Father, that build up and lead to old age."

He settled himself beside her in the brunt of the wind. "You're cold, girl. About to freeze up here."

"My body, yes. But my souls feel a special warmth. I've missed this. *Tam Apo's* presence is here, His breath on the wind. His soul in the sun. And what does *Tam Apo* cover? There, beneath His magnificence, is the whole of *Tam Segobia,* Our Mother. From here I can begin to understand Her Power, the beauty of Her soil so like skin, the plants like Her sleek hair, and Her bones in the very rock. The Power here, Father, is that the two halves of the world come together."

High Wolf glanced suspiciously at her from the corner of his eye. "Did I ever tell you that my children came out backward? The son I wanted to become *puhagan* is only interested in his family. The daughter that I expected to fill my life with grandchildren is so tightly wrapped in Power that she even frightens me."

"Do not fear me, Father. I would never harm you."

He rested a hand on her shoulder. "No, girl. I know your heart...or at least I think I do. Sometimes, though, Power can do terrible things. *Pa'waip*, the Water Ghost Woman, has been known to grant women Power. Some use it to have babies. But sometimes a women have used it to shrivel men like green grass in the heat of a fire."

"That is not my Power, Father. *Pa'waip*'s Power comes from deep underground in the water world. Mine comes from the sky world."

"I know. But, Daughter, the lesson should never be forgotten."

"You've always been wise. And besides, I gave you a grandchild. His death still wounds my soul."

High Wolf's nostrils quivered as he scented the wind like a hunting wolf. "Snow is coming." After a pause, he asked, "What happened to your family, Heals Like A Willow? We heard very little about it. Only rumors that came up the trails during the trading season."

"They both came down with a fever, sweating and delirious. I did all I could, all I knew to do. I used sage, phlox, and blazing star tea. I built a sweat lodge, and tried to sweat the spirit of the sickness from them. Their bowels loosened and ran like water. I sang for them, and the *Ku'chendikani puhagan* came and performed a sucking cure, removing *Nynymbi* poisons. Try as we might, their *navuzieip* drifted away, and their *mugwa* followed. All that was left for me was their corpses, Father."

She hesitated, then looked at High Wolf. "The one thing I didn't do...I didn't send my *mugwa* to bring them back from the Land of the Dead. That's why they died."

His gaze sharpened. "Nor should you have, Daughter. A woman—especially a young woman who bleeds every moon—does *not* send her soul anywhere."

Willow bit her lip, and jerked an uneasy nod.

High Wolf sighed. "I'm glad you did nothing foolish, *peti.*" A pause. "Willow, death comes and goes. No one knows the way of it. Your mother bore me eight children. I have you and Rock Hare—the rest are dead. One day, I will die, and eventually, so will you. Coyote decided that for us just after the Creation."

"Yes, I know," she said ironically.

The crowsfeet around his eyes tightened as he squinted into the distance. "What is this other sadness you carry within you, girl? You guard it very well, but I can sense it. I think White Hail knows, but he is honorable and will not say. An interesting man, this White Hail. Married to another, but in love with you. It would be proper for you to marry, become a second wife for him."

"I can't marry him. Father. The mating wouldn't be right. Not for him or for me."

High Wolf grunted a simple assent, giving her a sidelong glance. "And this other sadness? You are very skillful at avoiding answers when it comes to that."

She sighed, rubbing her hands together inside her sheep-hide coat. "He was a White man, Father."

"Ah?"

"His name is Richard Hamilton, a man from a place called Boston."

"He is Powerful?"

"Yes, but not trained." She turned. "I looked into his soul, Father. Down deep inside, into the *mugwa,* and he looked back. Not in fear, but with curiosity. Do you know how many men can look into a woman's eye of the soul without fear?"

"Not many, I'll admit. Did he sicken? Go weak? Show signs of being a two spirit?"

"No. He only grew stronger."

"Then what happened?"

So she told him, starting at the beginning where Richard shot Packrat, following all the way to the last discussion she had with him.

"The fact is, Father, that Richard could not see beyond his people's beliefs. The Whites have a God—a father who created the earth. But he did it alone without any mother like *Tam Segobia*. I might not have understood, but it was the same argument that I used to have with Slim Pole."

"And Ritshard did not respond as the *Ku'chendikani* do? That *Tam Apo* has His own mysterious reasons for making the Creation as He did?"

"No." She frowned. "That is one of the things that attracted me to him. Ask a question, a serious question, and he loses himself in the search to answer it. Down in his *mugwa,* he has the roots of a great *puhagan.* But the White ways have blinded him, separated him from himself with something called 'reason.' The Whites believe they can 'think' their way to God." She waved out toward the spectacular vista. "They don't understand that God must be sought in the heart and souls."

High Wolf cocked his head, and Willow could read his expression well enough to know he was skeptical of her attraction.

"Father, you need not worry about me. He is far away, on the river north of the mountains. He will not be there long. His heart is telling him to go back to Boston."

"Once before," High Wolf reminded, "I was worried by a young man. That time, my daughter ran off to the *Ku'chendikani,* and my souls wept. I do not know Boston, but I fear it is farther away than the places *Ku'chendikani* travel."

"Yes, Father. A great deal farther." She placed her hand on his. "But you need not worry this time. Some mountains cannot be climbed. In this case, he is White and I am *Dukurika*. We are separated by a vast distance, greater than that between sky and earth."

High Wolf raised an eyebrow. "But, if you will remember, Daughter, in the *Dukurika* story, *Tam Apo* and *Tam Segobia* joined, and in their mating created the world."

Willow nodded, brushing a tear from her eye and blaming it on the bitter wind. "Yes, but you will also recall that they were torn apart, which is why today earth and sky are separate. And, if the story is true, they will be separate until the end of time."

———

Richard, Baptiste, and Travis camped that night on a grassy flat where a small creek ran into the Big Horn. The packs were arranged in a circle around the fire, rude fortifications in the event of attack. The horses stood in a makeshift corral at the edge of the firelight, heads hanging. Holding eight horses was one thing; holding twenty was something else.

Richard sat hunched, a blanket over his shoulders as he ran a cleaning patch through his rifle. "I still have trouble believing it happened."

"Yep." Baptiste rubbed his hands together, the callused skin making a soft sawing sound. "But ol' God sure got Hisself a belly laugh outa us."

"God?' Richard wondered.

"Ain't He the one supposed to know if'n a sparrow fall?"

"Reckon so," Travis said tiredly. "Wal, if'n it was God, He played hell, all right."

They sat in silence, the only sounds those of the night and the fire. Richard loaded his Hawken and rammed a ball home. The wiping rod clicked as he ran it through the ferrules and into place. He just sat there, feeling the polished wood, pressing his thumb on the barrel keys and lock.

"It's like being cast loose." Richard stared vacantly. "The boat was always waiting for you. When you reached the boat, there were men you knew. Food. Safety."

"Yep," Travis muttered. He lay back, staring up at the starry sky. In the far east, a half moon glowed, a hazy ring around it.

Richard shook his head. "How funny. You know, I keep thinking it's all a mistake, that we're going to go back. Find *Maria* tied off on the bank, and Green, and Henri, surly old Trudeau, Toussaint and the rest, all acting just like nothing happened." He rubbed his fingers along the browned barrel. "But I know it's a lie. They're really dead."

When had the boat become so important? Once, he'd hated it—and the men who worked it. He scratched at a louse bite under his arm. Of all the anchors in his life, only Boston had meant as much to him as the *Maria*.

But I spent a lifetime in Boston.

"Wolfmeat, fer sure," Baptiste agreed, still rubbing his hands. "Wolfmeat...just like we'll be one day."

"Or worm meat," Travis added. "Depends on where ye goes under. Fer me, I'd a heap rather be wolfmeat than worm meat. Now, a feller dies back in the settlements, they dig a hole and cover his carcass up. Hell of a thing, being dumped down in the dark damp dirt to rot and feed worms. Not this coon. I want my bones scattered around in the grass and sunlight."

"Wal, you still get turned to shit one way or another, be it wolf or worm." Baptiste rubbed his hands harder, the muscles at the corner of his jaw jumping and wiggling.

"They took me prisoner," Richard said absently. "Carried me off and made me work like a convict at labor. So, why do I miss them so much?"

"Ye made a place, Dick." Travis slipped his pipe from his possibles. He shaved tobacco into the bowl, tamped it, and lit a stick in the fire to start it. He puffed and passed the pipe to Baptiste, who took a pull and passed it in turn to Richard.

"Made a place?" Richard watched the blue smoke curl upward before passing the pipe back to Travis.

"Reckon so." Travis puffed, then blew streams of smoke through his ruined nose. "Hell, remember that first day when Dave was gonna kill ye?"

Richard nodded.

"Wal, ye warn't worth shit then, Dick." Travis tapped his teeth with the long pipestem. "But I saw fire in yer eyes and give ye a chance. Tarnal Hell, coon, ye made ye a place. Worked up plumb from the bottom, ye did."

Was that it?

Baptiste said, "Feller's life changes when he finally becomes a man. Ain't no going back after that. Like dropping a glass bottle. It can't be undropped."

"I sure miss them." Richard reached for Travis's pipe

and smoked the last out of the bowl before knocking out the dottle and reaching for his tobacco to refill it.

"Yep, wal, hyar's to ye, Dave." Travis raised his cup, though it held only tea made from rosehips they'd collected.

"To Dave," Baptiste assented, lifting his cup.

"To Dave, and all the rest," Richard amended, raising his own empty cup.

"Old Henri could sure make a tongue stew," Travis said wistfully. "And that cussed Simon? Damnation, that corn-pone he cooked fer breakfast, that was some. It was."

"Warn't nobody could sing like Louis de Clerk." Baptiste smiled. "And that Etienne, why, he's a pulling fool on the cordelle. Never seen his like."

"Good men all around." Richard relit Travis's pipe and drew, the bowl glowing red. He puffed the smoke out and handed it to Baptiste.

"Remember when Jean-Paul snuck that snake inter Eppecartes's bed?"

Richard smiled, images flashing through his mind. "And old Toussaint? Remember him in the Ree fight?"

"He's some, he was. Took a heap of them Bug's Boys with him back on the Yellerstone, too," Baptiste reminded them. "I hope I go under like that, dragging a heap of 'em with me."

As they talked, Richard saw the men, one by one, their faces reflected in the fire, bits of laughter, a remark recalled.

I received something from each of them.

He thought of Trudeau, back broken, pinned to the ground by a bloody arrow. How he'd hated Trudeau, the bully, the womanizer. And in the end, he'd fought him fist to fist, and won.

I couldn't hate him. Not after that.

And Toussaint? To think of Toussaint was to remember muddy cold water, the collapsing bank, splashing and floundering, and Toussaint's strong arm clamping on from behind to tow Richard to shore. But he'd burned his wife and children? *A man is no more than he is.*

Then there was Green, indomitable, willing his boat ever onward. A tragic figure fit for Euripides. He'd built the dream, nurtured it, and turned it into reality despite insurmountable odds. Green had placed a fortune at risk, defied and defrauded the government, outfoxed the competition, the river, and the Indians to haul his boat all the way to the mouth of the Big Horn.

What thoughts passed through his head as he hid down there, wounded, maybe dying, in the hold? Did he hate the Blackfeet warriors leaping onto the deck? Or were his last thoughts on the gruesome irony of having come so far, made the final destination, only to lose it all?

"Damn," Travis said. "Damn it all."

———

They parted at the mouth of the Greasy Grass, a shallow stream that rolled out of low hills. On its marshy banks, Baptiste shagged out his horses and packs. He clasped Travis to his breast in a bear hug, the two of them looking into each other's eyes, sharing a communication Richard suspected went clear to the quick of the soul.

"You all sure you don't need no more of these hosses?" Baptiste indicated the cavvy. Eighteen animals milled, heads up, ears pricked as they watched the animals Travis and Richard had led aside.

"We got more 'an enough for us and our plunder,"

Travis told him, slapping his back. 'Take the rest. Trade 'em ter the Crow. That many critters would just get in our way."

"Dick?" Baptiste stepped over, his rifle in the crook of his arm. He took Richard's hand in a powerful grip before drawing him into a hug. 'Take care, coon."

"You, too. And, Baptiste, thank you for everything. All the things you taught me. I won't forget...ever."

"Watch old Travis for me." He paused, eyes questioning. "Hell, you could just ride over to the Crow for a spell. You don't gotta go chasing down after the Bad Lodges "

"The who?"

"The Snakes. Crow calls 'em Bad Lodges 'cause of the wickiups they make sometimes."

"It's something I must do for myself. For Willow."

Baptiste gave him a fond grin. "Wal, Dick, you's always welcome in my lodge."

"I don't suppose you'd ever call me Richard?"

"Reckon not."

"Somehow, I thought you'd say that. God go with you."

"Yep. You, too, Doodle." And at that Baptiste turned, walked to his horse, and stepped lithely into the saddle. He touched the brim of his big black hat with a finger. "So long, coons. Watch yer topknots!"

Travis shouted, "Watch yers!"

Baptiste snaked up his lead rope and turned his horse, driving the cavvy toward the ridgeline that would take him east to the Tongue River divide. He'd laid claim to a powerful white gelding taken from the Blackfeet. His long fringes swayed with each of the horse's dancing steps.

"Just like that?" Richard asked, stunned by the quickness of it.

"Just like that," Travis agreed. "He'll be around. Seems I never could shake him fer long. Not since that night down ter Louisiana. By God, imagine that. Him a-hiding up in that tree just over my head while them slavers swarmed all over."

"I'll miss him."

They mounted up, fighting the horses, who wanted to follow their fellows. Richard kicked his mount ahead into the hill-cradled valley of the Greasy Grass. As they rode, he concentrated on any sign of disturbance. The enormity of their situation had finally come home to him.

We are alone out here, two thousand miles from Saint Louis. There is no one but us. Travis and me. No rescue, no reinforcements, only us.

Any mishap could spell disaster: a broken leg; a wound like the one the Ree had given him; a disorienting fall; getting horse-kicked. Anything.

If I die out here, no one but God will ever know.

He glanced up at the faint white haze of high clouds that had blown in from the west. The air had a feel to it, an expectant stillness. "How far to Willow's people?"

Travis had been brooding, expression pinched, a bitterness in his blue eyes. "About a week or two. Depends. I ain't exactly sure. I been around them mountains, but never up inter 'em. I know they's only certain trails what go up. Willow said something ter me, once—

that her folks generally wintered on the southwest side of the mountains. Now, we're on the northeast, so I guess we're just opposite of where we need ter be."

"So we should go right over the top?"

A ghost of a smile bent Travis's lips. "Reckon not. That's about as good a way as any ter freeze yer arse ter death. Up high, there, the snow's deep enough to bog a hoss. And a feller cain't make his way across the passes. Nope. I figger the best way is to circle around the base of the mountains and come up from the south, up through the hills."

"Hills? Don't all mountains have hills around them?"

"Not these. Ye'll see. 'Cept on the south, they's sheer rock walls that climb right up inta the sky. A coon's got ter know the trails. Trust me, I figger it's best to go around."

"It's going to be a cold trip, isn't it?"

"Reckon so." Travis grinned then, the first time since the disaster. "Ye'll be a hiverner by the time ye make her back ter Saint Loowee, Dick."

"We're in a fix, aren't we, Travis?" Richard glanced around at the hills. The north slopes were timbered in dark patches of ponderosa pine. On the flanks, tawny grass waved in the wind, speckled here and there with sagebrush. A sense of loneliness welled from the cold land, the wind, and the impotence within that tried to smother him.

"Huh? A fix? Hell, we're right chipper, Dick. We got two good mounts and four packhosses full of goods—and the right trade stuff ter boot. We got good Crow-tanned robes, pemmican and buffalo jerky, tobacco, more'n enough powder and lead, and a stack of guns. With them doings, we can nigh trade fer the moon. Nope, ye ain't in a fix until ye've lost yer possibles, and yer afoot in the snow. That's when she's Katy bar the door."

"What do you do then?"

"Then it's cat-scratch." Travis rubbed one of the scars on his cheek. 'To tell the truth, Dick, ye do whatever ye can. Most of all, ye think! Use yer noodle. Most important thing is to stay warm and dry. Next most important thing is to keep yer belly full. Third, make ye a shelter. Anything to cut the wind and cold, even digging it outa the snow." He chuckled. "Larned that from a Cree, I did."

"What about frostbite?"

"That's a killer, Dick. I had an old Assiniboin tell me once that he lived by wrapping himself up so thick in hides that he flat couldn't freeze. But most of it is ter use yer smarts. Break yer knife? Use a sharp rock. I seen Injuns make cutting tools outa the damndest things. Figger this: rock cuts; bark and twigs make cord; wood burns; and hide and hair covers. Travel when ye can, and hole up when she's too damn stormy."

"What do you eat? I mean, if the ground is covered with snow?"

"Anything ye can," Travis said. "Meat's meat. Rose-hips, dried berries on branches, hell, I even heard tell of stripping pine bark and eating the inside."

"Well, let's not go quite that far, shall we?"

"Reckon I'd rather have fat cow any day."

CHAPTER EIGHTEEN

It is therefore neither absurd nor reprehensible, neither against the dictates of true reason, for a man to use all his endeavours to preserve and defend his body and the members thereof from death and sorrows. But that which is not contrary to right reason, that all men account to be done justly and with the right. Neither by the word *right* is anything else signified, than the liberty which every man hath to make use of his natural faculties according to right reason. Therefore the first foundation of natural right is this, that *every man as much as in him lies endeavour to protect his life and members.*

—Thomas Hobbes, *Leviathan*

Light flakes of snow twisted and tumbled from the gray skies as Willow stopped on the rimrock above the camp; a tightly strapped bundle of firewood hung on her back. For long moments she looked out over the canyon, taking in the beauty. Snow dusted the dark green trees on the far side with a tracery of white. The wind had sifted snow into the crevices and cracks of the caprock, accenting the buff sandstone. From high up the canyon, a lone wolf howled—a reminder to the world of Wolf's frustration with Coyote during those early days of Creation.

She took a deep breath, drawing the familiar scent of rocks, juniper and pine, and moist earth into her lungs.

Home. The only place she'd ever truly belonged. As a child she'd scampered over the rocks, hidden in the hollows, and explored the meadows of these mountains. The plants that grew from this soil, the animals that lived here, all had fed her growing body. The solitude of the high points, the roar of wind through the trees, and the patter of rain on the rocks had filled her ears. She'd been charmed by the mixed colors of the earth, and the interplay of shadows in the distance. Here she had first heard the voices of *Tam Apo* and *Tam Segobia*.

She resettled the heavy firewood and picked her way along the narrow path that led down the base of the rimrock. The path wound about like an outrageous serpent's trail, climbing over spalled rock, dipping down around clumps of juniper. It finally ended at the rock overhang where High Wolf's band had made their isolated camp.

They didn't always live like this. In summer the *Dukurika* gathered in large groups. Memory of the great ceremonials brought a smile to her lips. As a child, the excitement had built with each step traveled toward the dance ground, until she thought her breast would burst open. What a magical time it was, filled with food, games, magic tricks, warm days of play and long summer nights before roaring fires. And so many people. The throng had seemed to include everyone in the whole world.

The most important dance was the "Stand Alone in Thirst Dance." For four days and nights the men danced, fasted, and waited for a vision. Some prayed for the gift of Power, or courage, or skill in the hunt. At the same time the dancers offered thanks to the spirits of the animals and plants that had fed them, and asked for continued grace from the spirits.

Before Willow's birth, the "Stand Alone in Thirst Dance" had been brought to the *Ku'chendikani* by Yellow Hand, the great *Yamparika puhagan*. High Wolf himself had danced to the sun twice.

When people weren't dancing, they were trading, or gambling. Young men found pretty girls to impress. When they impressed well enough, and when the families were in agreement, marriages were made. Or, if there were problems, a young man and woman eloped to make a life for themselves.

Willow smiled at the memory of a young man dressed in finely tanned buckskin leggings. How broad and muscular his shoulders had been. The sunlight had glowed blue in his long black hair. He'd had a rainbow-colored abalone shell gorget at his throat. But the most important thing had been the depth reflected in his eyes.

He had taken her hand, saying in his *Ku'chendikani* accent, "I have heard of a Powerful young woman among the *Dukurika*. I had heard that she was the most beautiful woman anywhere, and that her name was Heals Like A Willow. I am hoping that you are she, for if any woman could be more beautiful than you, my eyes could not bear to look at her."

She had laughed at that, her heart dancing with his. "And if you have heard of Heals Like A Willow, Buffaloeater, you know that I'm considered odd, dangerous, and most men will have nothing to do with me."

"I've heard such tales," he asserted, a smile on his lips. "But having looked into your eyes, I think they were the bitter declarations of men who were simply unworthy of your beauty and spirit."

I loved you from that moment on, husband.

Who would have guessed they would have only a few glorious years?

Willow walked into camp. The dogs lay curled in furry balls, their tails smacking the cold ground as they watched her with kindly brown eyes.

"I miss you, husband." She rolled her shoulders where the load had stiffened them, and searched about for her ax. White Alder had admired it in *Dukurika* fashion, and Willow had graciously surrendered it. How did one say no to one's mother? From White Alder it had gone to Lodgepole, and then to Red Squirrel, and the last Willow had seen of it, her brother, Rock Hare, was carrying it. The same had happened to all the rest of her belongings—all but the Pawnee bow, arrows, and war club.

Rock Hare was tall, lithe, and handsome. He wore a thick coat made of bearhide and sheepskin leggings that ran down over high moccasins. He sat with his back to the rock, a pile of juniper bark to one side. This he shredded, drawing the stiff bark over a stick to separate the fibers. After picking them apart, he placed the threads on his thigh, twisting them around and around into a firm strand. The next fibers he twisted the other way. When he had three strands, he braided them into the length of cord he was making.

"What are you doing?" Willow crouched next to him.

"Making another snare, Sister." He glanced at her.

"This one shall catch the cottontail who has been making tracks down in the berry bushes in the canyon bottom."

"Where is the ax? I'm going to cut down some of those snags on the canyon rim. We could throw the trees over the edge; what doesn't snap when it hits the rocks, we can cut up with the ax."

"Good idea. I think the ax is next to my bed."

She stood, traced her way inside the shelter, and located the ax in the dim light. Not until she stepped outside did she notice the abused edge. Not just dulled, it had been bent and gouged.

"Rock Hare?" She stalked over to where he worked. "What did you do with this? How did this happen?" She thrust it toward him.

Nonplussed, Rock Hare studied the ax, and then her. "How did what happen?"

"This edge, you silly packrat! Look at it!"

His eyes lit then, and he smiled. "It's a wonderful thing I discovered about the ax. When you strike rocks with it, sparks fly! Eagle Trapper and I tried making fires by hitting different kinds of rock with the ax, but it didn't work. A strike-a-light is better."

The slow anger continued to build. "You will sharpen it again, Brother."

"All right. When I am done with my snare."

"Now, Brother."

Mild surprise showed in his eyes as he realized the extent of her anger. Scowling, he took the ax and studied the edge, a frown lining his forehead. "This is iron. A big piece. How can I sharpen it?"

"With blocks of sandstone, the same way you grind wood, antler, or slate."

He glanced suspiciously at her. "But this is iron. It's a lot harder than wood or antler."

"Then you had better get to work, because it will take you a long time."

"I don't have any sandstone blocks big enough for this. And I'm not sure what kind I'd need."

Willow narrowed her eyes to evil slits. "Then you had better go and find out, Brother. Sharpen the ax. We need it for cutting wood, and if you ever hit a rock with it again, I'll burn your bedding!"

He rubbed the back of his neck, watching her suspiciously. "You wouldn't dare."

"Wouldn't I? What kind of fool uses a valuable ax to hit rocks...and just to see *sparks*!"

"You don't tell people what to do in this camp, *Sister*."

"When it concerns things like the ax, I do, *Brother*."

"Well—go back to your *Ku'chendikani,* or your White men, then. Order them about like children."

"Sharpen the ax, and it will be forgotten, Rock Hare." She met the flash in his eyes, overcame it by force of will, and glared fire into his souls until he glanced away.

"All right. I'll sharpen the ax. Now, go away and leave me alone." He made a shooing gesture with his hand.

Willow took a deep breath and shook her head. "I'm sorry, *paci*. Perhaps it's my fault. I should have told you what to use an ax for. It has a special spirit, one that's used for chopping wood or bone. Not for rocks."

"I'll sharpen it." Rock Hare nodded curtly, as if to convince himself.

"All right. It's forgotten between us. I'm going for another load of firewood. With the storm coming, we'll need it. Do you remember how we'd make a big fire and tell the winter stories about Coyote and Wolf and the Bald One? We'll do that again, just like in the old days."

"Yes. It will be good." He smiled his relief that the ax affair was over.

Willow retraced her way to the path that led out onto the rimrock.

"He just didn't know," she told herself as she walked back into the trees. All the dead branches within reach had been broken off by previous hands. As a result, Willow had to extend her search. By the time she'd accumulated another load and followed the path back to camp, twilight had settled on the land.

High Wolf crouched over one of the fires, laughing and talking with Many Elk. Eagle Trapper and Black Marten were inspecting arrows, discussing which feathers needed replacing in the fletching, while Felt the Fire led the children in a round of the string game.

Cat's cradle, Willow thought as she unloaded the wood from her tired shoulders and inspected the pile. The women had brought in enough to see them through several days.

Now, as the evening meal cooked, the women huddled over a game of four-stick-dice being played on a blanket.

From the intent expressions, a wager had been made, the stakes high. The dice—made of split willow stems, the pieces nearly finger-length—were tossed against a round rock placed on flat piece of rawhide. The score was determined by the number of dice that landed with the red-painted flat side up.

A cast was made, the dice clattered on the rock, and Good Root howled in misery as Lodgepole clapped her hands and yipped victory.

Counting heads, Willow turned to White Alder. "Mother, where is Rock Hare?"

Her mother looked up from the game with a frown. "He went with White Hail. They're down in the canyon somewhere. Rock Hare made a new snare. He took it down to set it."

"Did he sharpen the ax?"

"What?"

But Willow knew. She took a moment to calm herself, before hunting down the ax—right where Rock Hare left it, as dull and bent as when she'd given it to him.

"God damn you, Rock Hare."

"What was that?" Many Elk asked, as he studied the binding on one of his stone-tipped arrows.

"It's a White man's curse. Somehow, it fit."

"Who were you cursing?" Lodgepole gave her an uneasy glance as she reached for a beautiful white leather coat that Good Root reluctantly surrendered.

"No one, *pia*." Willow used the kin term for "Mother" to placate. "I was upset because Rock Hare didn't sharpen the ax."

"He's a man," Lodgepole replied, as she rose and tucked the coat over her arm.

Good Root muttered to herself as she stepped over to the hides, pegged and stretched for tanning. Her fingers probed the brain and urine mixture that coated the elk hide. Satisfied with the results, she pulled the pegs loose, then rolled it into a tight bundle.

"That's a good hide." Lodgepole studied the thick roll with calculating eyes. "Big bull. Had antlers like trees. But that hide, almost pure white. I've never seen such a white elk."

"And you'd like to gamble for it, wouldn't you?" Good Root gave her a lopsided squint. "Not likely. Not until your *puha* changes."

Willow hefted the ax, remembering the *Pa'kiani* skull she'd split with it. And now Rock Hare used it to smack rocks just to see the sparks fly?

"Willow?" Lodgepole laid a gentle hand on her arm. "I've seen that expression on your face before. Calm down."

"I told him I'd burn his bedding if he didn't sharpen this."

"Oh? And where would Red Squirrel and the baby sleep? Out in the snow with Rock Hare?" She made a chiding sound with her lips. "Willow, he's a man. God made them to be lazy in everything but hunting. Look around you, girl. Even *Tam Segobia* holds up the sky. If men didn't have women to look after them, you know they'd all die. Oh, sure, they'd hunt all the food they could eat—and then freeze to death in the first storm because they didn't have anything to wear."

Willow ran gentle fingers over the ax head, remembering the river and the *engagés,* all so busily occupied. They'd worked like ants, toiling and sweating, pulling that huge boat against the current. No ax went dull in their camp. No rifle was left uncleaned.

"Willow?" Lodgepole asked. "Did you hear me?"

"Yes...I did. I was remembering the White men, is all."

"Do you want to talk about it, child? I can see the longing in your eyes."

"No, but thank you, Aunt. You wouldn't know what I was saying. I think a person must stand between two worlds to see either clearly. Perhaps...perhaps that is what he needs."

"Who? Rock Hare?"

"It wouldn't hurt him to pull a boat for a while. But, no, I was thinking of another. One who seeks the ways of the *puhagan,* but has been kept from the way by a blindness worse than Rock Hare's."

"Rock Hare isn't blind. You're talking in riddles, Willow."

"No, Aunt I'm speaking very clearly. Now, if you'll excuse me, I have to go and see if I can find the right size sandstone blocks to sharpen this ax before the snow covers everything and the light is gone."

———

The cougar screamed in the middle of the night. The sound terrifying. Close. Richard bolted upright, grabbing for his rifle with mittened hands. Travis growled like an animal, thrashing out of his blankets and leaping to his feet.

The horses blew and stamped, tossing their heads in panic. Richard heard the picket rope snap—and the horses bolted into the night. For what seemed an eternity, their pounding hooves faded into the darkness.

"Good God, Travis, what kind of beast screams like that?" Richard grabbed up his rifle, earing the cock back as he peered anxiously beyond the circle of packs.

"Painter!" Travis cried as he danced from foot to foot and swung his arms at the darkness. "Go on! Git outa hyar! Git, now!"

Richard swallowed hard, heart hammering as he

waited for God knew what. His only security came from the rifle. But what help would that be? The cat, seeing so well in the darkness, could be upon him before he so much as raised the gun.

Still growling and muttering to himself, Travis stomped around cursing, then bent down and stirred the fire. He fed bits of frozen sagebrush to the glowing coals. The gusting wind ebbed and flowed, picking up now, whistling down from the heights to savage their lonely camp.

With the first feeble fingers of flame, Richard's panic finally drained away, but he didn't let loose of his Hawken gun.

"Damn cat," Travis cursed, leaving the fire to check the frayed picket rope. "Hell, they don't cotton much to hoss flesh, 'cept maybe the foals come spring."

Richard exhaled the last of his fear, and added, "That sound...horrible, like a scream from Hell."

"Yep. That's a cat all right." Travis returned to hunch over the fire. "Reckon we got a couple of hours afore daylight. Then we've got ter run down them fool hosses."

"The painter? He won't come back, will he? Try for us?"

"Painters ain't much on man flesh. Oh, they'll take ye, given half a chance, but not like a griz. Nope, painters prefer deer, rabbits, smaller stuff that don't fight back. 'Course, they'll take a dog, child, anything easy."

Richard rubbed his head and shivered against the cold invading all the places his blanket had been keeping warm. "We don't seem to have any luck at all, do we?"

"These is just runaways. 'T'ain't like they was stoled."

Richard shrugged into the buffalo coat he and Travis had sewn from the Crow hides they'd traded for, and pulled his hat from his possibles. And such a hat it was.

Travis had cut a patch of hide in the shape of a simple cross, then sewed three of the seams together to make the body of the cap, and rolled the fourth piece into a furry bun for a bill. It didn't look like much, but the woolly buffalo fur was warm. If a bit prickly on the skin.

Another gust of wind blasted the camp, tearing flames right off the fire.

"Until i came to this country, I never knew the wind could blow with such fury."

Travis bent down to shave jerky into a tin pot. "Generally when she blows like this it means a change in the weather."

"Snow? You mean, more than we've had?"

"Yep. Best eat up, Dick. I reckon it'll be a long, cold day. Come daylight, we'll find the hosses and I reckon we'd best make tracks fer the Tongue River bottoms. Hole up down there until the storm breaks."

Another gust of wind howled through, spattering them with bits of blown sand and snow. "Willow's people, they wouldn't be camped out here? Along one of the rivers?"

"Not Sheepeaters. They's mountain folk. No, from what I know about Sheepeaters—and it ain't a whole lot —they'll stick ter the hills. That way, ain't no Blackfoot war party's gonna catch 'em. They tend ter country where most folks don't go."

Richard watched tendrils of steam blow away as the stew began to cook. "What about our packs, Travis?"

"Leave 'em sit. They'll be fine until we get the hosses. Hell, them mangy beasts won't be more than a mile or two. We'll come back and pack up.

"And hope the coyotes and wolves don't chew all the lacings to pieces."

"Yep. There's always that. Reckon we'll piss around

'em first. Mark the camp with man-scent ter keep 'em off."

"Mark it?"

"Wolves and coyotes, ye see, is respectful critters. Mostly. Until their stomachs gets the better part of their manners."

With the first haze of dawn, they peed a circle around their camp. Richard hung his possibles around his shoulder—making sure he had a full day's supply of jerky—and checked his Hawken before they started off. The horse tracks were easily visible through crusted patches of snow, and where the hooves had bruised dry grass or marred frozen dirt.

"Thar's that coon's sign." Travis pointed to a big cat track.

Richard placed his mittened hand alongside the track. "How big would you say?"

"Six, seven feet long. Maybe two hundred an' fifty pounds. He ain't a very big one."

"I don't know. I've seen a lot of cat feet in my day. They don't grow 'em like that in Boston."

"Do tell?"

The wind continued to pound at them as they trotted across the rolling ridges and grass-filled draws where the horses had run in blind panic.

"Whoa up!" Travis called, slowing and bending to study the snow at the head of a deep gully. "What in Tarnal Hell? They split up hyar. Four's gone off ter the right, two's ter the left."

"Is that bad?"

Travis shrugged, staring down the valley. "Depends on how the draws run. You go left, I'll go right. They'll probably be bunched up at the first side canyon, looking at each other over the gully. That, or they found a place where the banks caved in and crossed so's ter tie up again."

Richard nodded, following along the left side, studying out the tracks. Little wisps of snow were blowing down out of the heavy sky, the wind biting at any bit of exposed flesh.

At the first side canyon, there were no horses. Richard could see where they'd stood, no doubt whin-nying back and forth to their friends on the other side of the sheer-walled gully. The piles of horse manure were stone-cold to the touch, outsides frozen. Hours old.

"Which way'd they go?" Travis shouted.

"Up there!" Richard pointed to the east where the gully had to head.

"Mine went on south." Travis shot a nervous glance up at the scudding clouds. "Camp's up at the head of this draw. I'll meet ye thar."

Richard licked his lips, looking uncertainly up the winding drainage. "Are you sure?"

"Dick, we gotta catch these hosses afore it really starts ter snow. Watch yer backtrail. I'll see ye soon. They ain't gone that far. But if'n ye really gets lost, head on south. Make ye a camp on the Tongue River. North side. I'll find ye."

Richard shivered, then with a wave, he turned to follow the horse tracks that headed up the side canyon. The snow was patchy here, most of it piled behind the sagebrush like white cones, and drifted along the north slopes.

The tracks changed from a trot to a full run. Probably panicked at being separated from their fellows. Richard pushed himself to a brisk walk to keep warm. For water, he scooped up the crusted snow, crunching ice crystals.

Near the head of the gully, the horses had bolted

across the drainage and headed southward again. On the snowy slope, Richard saw yet another set of tracks, those of a big dog. And then another cut in, and another.

Wolf pack! He made a face and studied the snow that blew past, not in small flakes but big ones, and a lot of them. They were starting to stick in the hollows.

Richard cursed and charged up and out of the little valley, chasing the tracks. "Damn wolves! What are you doing? Just running the horses for the hell of it?"

A full-grown wolf couldn't take down an adult horse, could he? The tracks led across ridges and shallow gullies. Wolves would play with animals, run them just for the sake of running.

Except this didn't feel right. It had an ominous sense about it, as if the wolves had been working the horses with a purpose. He checked the Hawken's priming, ensuring it was still dry.

Snow began to clot the folds of his buffalo coat, and he had to keep the lock of his rifle dry. The trail drew him onward: a hoof scar here; a set of pockmarks in the old snow there; a bruised sagebrush. With an odd satisfaction, Richard trotted along, reading the sign with a sense of authority.

He crossed another of the ridges and descended into a broad valley, the treeline like a gray mat in the haze of blowing snow. They'd be down there, in the trees, out of the wind. By now, the wolves should have broken off to seek easier prey. Yes—the trees, that's where the horses were. They were Indian animals, used to camping on the rivers.

He could feel the leaden ache in his legs as he hurried down, and his breath was coming short.

Slow down. Catch your breath. Travis always said not to overheat and sweat in the cold.

Snow fell across the valley in lacy veils that turned the entire world into a chiaroscuro of pale shadows. Snow crunched underfoot as Richard passed beneath ghostly branches.

Searching for fresh sign, he crisscrossed and found what looked like tracks, now no more than snow-filled dimples. He glanced backward at his tracks through the trees. Should he go back?

Travis wouldn't. He'd see it through. Besides, the horses had to be somewhere close.

Richard wavered, listening, the silence so complete he could hear the rustle of snow crystals falling. The wind had dropped to a mere breeze.

I should go back.

But what if the horses were just a short ways away? Travis would chide him for getting so close and turning back.

He pushed onward, soon realizing the dimples weren't horse tracks. A wolf yipped off to his right, and Richard turned, heading into the wind. He'd not gone far before he saw the wolves, five of them occupied with a bloody pile of...

"You sons of bitches!" He leveled the Hawken, eared the cock back, set the trigger, and shot the big gray wolf that stood atop his favorite white mare. At the report, the wolves jumped. The big gray yelped, whipped around to bite at his side—and staggered sideways, stiff-legged, to fall and thrash in the snow.

The other wolves vanished, slipping away soundlessly into the trees.

As Richard reloaded, he could see them, watching from cover. He approached the dead horse warily and studied the torn carcass. The ground here was mucky, an old beaver dam that had silted in and frozen. The horse had been driven into the soft soil where it bogged, unable to kick, and the wolves had ripped its belly open.

Richard rubbed his wet face and groaned, then glanced at the dead wolf. "Damn you. Maybe you took my horse, but I killed you and I'll take coup, you bastard."

Richard narrowed an eye, appraising the thick pelt. Images of a warm wolf coat filled his mind. Loath to leave it, he still had to find the other wayward horse. It wouldn't take that long, and the loss of a horse deserved some recompense. He pulled his knife, flopped the wolf onto its back, and slit the belly open.

The task of skinning took longer than he anticipated. As snow fell, he pulled the last of the hide loose and rolled it into a thick bundle. Using tendons cut from the wolf, he tied it tightly and threw it over his shoulder.

With a last shake of the head, he sadly inspected his mare. "Goodbye girl. Breaks my heart, but if God's just, your soul now runs with the wind and dances among the stars. Sorry I didn't get here sooner."

The big flakes of snow melted as they landed on the wolf's pink carcass. He gave it a kick and started back through the trees. If he kept the wind to his left, which should be west, it would guide him back to the north.

The world had turned to snow, and the wolf had been a big animal. How long had it taken to skin him? His tracks were nothing more than dimples.

Richard stared around in the haze, trying to pick his direction. Then the wind changed; fine snow filtered down in swirls. Which way?

One way's as good as the next.

He started forward, beating snow from his coat and rifle as his feet crunched in the new-fallen blanket. No matter how far he walked, it seemed that he never broke out of the trees.

I'm headed up or downstream. I've got to go right or left to find the slope.

He'd walked under the black lump in the tree before he recognized it; a shiver traced down his back. Burials. One, two, three...Jesus, at least ten that he could see through the falling white veils. Each of the corpses had been wrapped in a robe now mounded with snow. The subtle stench of death carried down to Richard's nostrils.

He turned, uneasy at the number of dead he'd walked so carelessly beneath. "Good God." His heart thudded as he carefully backtracked until he'd passed beyond them.

Chewing his lip, he cut right, away from the burial ground. Whose? Blackfeet? Crow? Arapaho? Would any of them show much mercy to a lone White man walking among their ghosts?

"I'm sorry," he called to the silent dead. "I didn't mean to disturb you."

And then he fled, charging headlong through the trees. Frantic only to escape, to put as much distance between himself and the silent corpses as he could.

Crossing a low spot, he slipped and tumbled. He stared anxiously at the ice he'd exposed, and realized he was on a frozen pond.

Dear God, if you fall through, you'll freeze! Treading carefully, he could hear the ice crackle underfoot. Grasping willows, he pulled himself up on firm ground, and charged onward, half expecting the sound of ghosts in pursuit.

"Silly," he gasped under his breath. "You're being foolish. They're dead, Richard. Just like passing through a cemetery."

But the dead in a cemetery are safely underground. You don't have to smell them, see their bodies.

He nodded to himself. "Right...and maybe the folks that stuck them up there heard the shot when you killed the wolf. So, fearing the dead might be irrational, but their living relatives might just find a dead horse and a lone White man's tracks mighty interesting."

That thought inspired him to hurry through the falling snow. His belly rumbled, and every so often he'd cup up a snowball to chew for water. Was it his imagination, or was the light dimming?

That was when he came to the river: cool dark water interspersed with patches of snow-covered ice. But which river was it? The Tongue?

"Well, for God's sake, don't cross it."

And with that, he continued onward, seeking a way through the trees, and from there, into the uplands that would take him back to camp.

The sky grew ever darker.

CHAPTER NINETEEN

As men, therefore, are so slightly acquainted with nature, and cannot agree about the meaning of the word law, it would be very difficult for them to agree on a good definition of natural law. Accordingly, all those definitions we encounter in books, besides lacking uniformity, err from being derived from several kinds of knowledge which men do not naturally possess, and from advantages they cannot comprehend, as long as they remain in a state of nature.

—Jean-Jacques Rousseau, *Discourse on the Origin and Foundation of Inequality Among Mankind*

Travis spent three days in complete misery while the storm blew itself out. Most of the time he huddled under his blanket, nursing the small sagebrush fire for warmth. Occasionally, when the wind lulled, he'd shake the snow off his blankets and check the horses. They were picketed with their tails to the brunt of the storm—and looked just as miserable as he.

"That'll teach ye ter go a-tearing off when a painter screams." He'd look off to the south, hoping to see a half-frozen Richard staggering toward camp.

Then the storm would pick up and he'd return to his blanket, and memories of other storms he'd waited out like this. The one that ran through his head most often was the time with Dave Green so long ago on the Little Missouri.

"Huh, funny how things go around, ain't it?" he'd ask the spectral images that surrounded him in his blanket shelter. Wasn't it curious that each of the faces he saw in the embers of his fire belonged to a dead man? But look as he might, he didn't see Richard's there.

"Poor damned Doodle." Travis shifted, feeling the weight of the snow. He'd propped up the blanket with his ramrod, and now lifted a comer to make sure he wasn't buried so deep he'd suffocate.

So, where had Richard gone? Travis had found five of their six animals just before the heavy snow began to fall. The only missing animal was Richard's white mare—and Travis had half expected to find that the mare, with Richard on her, had beaten him back to camp.

"Wal, coon. Hyar's ter hoping yer a-waiting down ter the Tongue."

Aye, but can that poor Doodle survive the likes of this?

The unspoken question rolled around in Travis's uneasy soul.

On the fourth day, the cold awakened him. He poked up through his snowy warren and stared around in the predawn pink. Overhead the sky was vividly clear, the air so sharp it prickled the nostrils with each inhalation.

"Deep cold," Travis whispered, looking at the

hunched horses. They stood together in a clump, shivering with their heads down. They'd eaten the grass down to dirt, and tramped the manure-filled snow.

"C'mon, coons," Travis told them. "Let's get the packs on yer cussed backs and make our way down ter the Tongue. See if'n by some chance of fate old Dick's still alive and waiting fer us."

He kicked the packs from the snow, rolled his ice-stiff blanket, and chewed a thick stick of jerky as he packed the horses, careful to knock as much ice as he could from their backs before seating the load.

A finger after sunup, he swung into the saddle and squinted around. The land looked soft and virginal under the endless white undulations. Sculpted drifts feathered off in intricate patterns.

Travis kicked his reluctant gelding into a trot along the ridge, the rest of the horses following. The air was so still, the land so quiet; the cold seemed to throb with a vibrancy that defied the senses. It bit into the very soul with needle teeth.

"Deep cold, fer sure," Travis murmured, his breath floating off in lacy white. His beard had already frosted and was now icing. "Wal, this coon figgers we'd better find us a hole. How about it, you hosses? Ye ready fer grass?"

He glanced at the distant Big Horn Mountains, etched so clearly against the enamel-blue sky that they made the eyes ache.

Travis let the gelding warm to its own pace as they headed down into the valley of the Tongue. Here and there, they had to buck drifts, but keeping to the high ground they made good time.

By midmorning, he had reached the river. He set up camp beside the main channel, where the current ran free of ice, and unpacked. From the fallen cottonwoods, he cobbled together a makeshift corral and turned the packhorses in.

After collecting wood, laying a fire, and forting up the packs, he stepped into the stirrup and urged his reluctant gelding out of camp.

The big bay whinnied, his cries echoed by the pack string as Travis trotted downstream, cutting for sign. Where the river looped, he encountered what looked to be an Arapaho burial ground. Hunched over the saddle, blowing into his mittens to warm them, Travis counted nearly thirty corpses wedged in the forks of the high branches.

He rode wide, following the river, seeing where snow had blown across the ice in a solid sheet. A mile beyond, he heard the ravens cawing and coyotes yipping.

The scavengers fled at his approach. In the trampled snow he recognized the chewed remains of a frozen horse: Dick's white mare. And just off to the side? That ravaged chunk of meat, just about man-sized? Travis made a face.

The gelding stamped, more than a little spooked by his stable mate's bloody body and the smell of the predators that feasted there.

"Wolf, by God!" Travis identified the carcass. "And not a scrap of hair on it." The ribs had been chewed open, the gut cavity cleaned out. But why would the coyotes have chewed out the ribs like that?

"Bullet hole?" Travis stepped down and started to lead the blowing gelding forward, only to have the animal pitch a fit. "Hyar, now! Don't ye go a-getting spooky with me, damn yer eyes. Whoa, now. What in hell?" Travis checked the footing and nodded at the boggy trap. "Wal, ye've a sight more sense than old Dick's mare had." After tying off the horse, Travis walked out to the wolf carcass.

He pried the frozen wolf loose from the ice. "Sure enough. Look't that. Somebody shot his lights out slick and skinned the hide off."

Travis backed away, patting his trembling horse on the neck. "What do ye think? Like maybe old Dick tracked his hoss down hyar? Ketched that wolf chewing on her and raised him?"

Travis cocked his head, watching his frosted breath rising in the still air. "Wal, I'd make it about ten below, and nigh ter midday. Damnation, Dick, with the snow, I ain't even sure I can find yer carcass, unless the ravens and coyotes raise enough Cain ter signal me."

He slapped his horse and stepped into the saddle. "C'mon, hoss. We'd best get back. If'n by some tarnal luck Dick's alive, maybe so he'll see the fire and come a-running."

With that, Travis reined his gelding around and headed back upriver. With each step, the snow groaned under the gelding's hooves.

It's damn cold. What are the chances he's still alive?

Travis shook his head, heart sinking in his breast.

———

Richard awakened, shivering, momentarily disoriented as he stared around the dark hole. He'd been dreaming about his father. Phillip Hamilton had been sitting at his cherry-wood desk, head in hands. Those old shoulders had convulsed as the old man cried.

Crying for me. I'm not dead, Father.

But the dream had left a hole in Richard's soul. *I*

never understood, Father. We're two of a kind, you and me. Forever frightened of each other.

He sighed and shivered, blinking. Daylight could be seen where the sandstone overhang wasn't covered by snow. Coal, that's what he huddled against, and memory of his horrible ordeal returned.

He'd climbed into the uplands as the darkness closed in. Knowing that if he stopped he'd freeze, he'd continued uphill because camp had to be someplace near the divide between the Tongue and Greasy Grass.

The storm had never relented, and Richard had run out of ridge to climb. Every direction led down...but down toward what?

In desperation, he'd chosen a way with the wind to his back, and finally, after wallowing through drifts, had found this hole and the undercut coal seam.

For three miserable days now he'd hidden here, curled into a ball, wrapped in everything he owned. He sat up, restricted by the hard wolf hide. He'd tied it on with the hair-side in; now it had frozen around him like a knight's cuirass.

His stomach growled its hunger. He'd made a day's supply of jerky last four, and his belly hadn't been fooled.

Damn it, why didn't I take a haunch off that wolf?

Well, no matter, he'd head on south to the Tongue, and Travis would find him. Then he could stuff himself with pemmican and meat. Richard stood, willing circulation into his legs. He picked up his rifle and slung his possibles around his shoulders. Ice clattered from the folds of his clothing.

"By God," he said aloud, shivering. "I'm alive." His toes still wiggled, so his feet weren't frostbitten.

With that, he broke through the cornice of snow, and

bulled his way through the drift that had filled the little drainage channel where he'd taken refuge.

The midmorning brightness of sun on snow blinded him. Shading his eyes with a mittened hand, he squinted around to find the most likely way out of the narrow gully.

The cold began to bite through his hides. Puffing out a breath, he watched it rise, and rise, and rise, then dissipate slowly in the still air. The inside of his nose prickled as if the little hairs were frozen. His beard had iced like a confectioner's Saint Nicholas. "Blessed God, just how cold is it?"

Step by step, he packed a trail and climbed to the top, pulling his way up the last hill by tugging on sagebrush. Snow groaned under his moccasin-wrapped feet as he crested the drifted knoll and looked out in amazement.

In all his life, he'd never seen air so clear. In every direction, the land was sculpted, each fold of the ground outlined in stark white contrast to the crystalline dome of the sky. But such snow! It glowed, as if possessed by an unearthly tint of blue. Against that splendor, the majesty of the Big Horns rose in the west—magnificent slabs of tilted rock laced with woven white and spotted dark green with timber that gave way to an ivory magnificence of high peaks.

God lives here. Richard wiped at his frozen beard, stunned by the sight. Then the bitter cold, and the growling of his stomach, turned his thoughts to other things.

In all the world, the only sound is my stomach gurgling! Now, what, Dr. Hegel, would you make of that?

He studied the route he would take, following the windward side of the ridges downward toward the south. The Tongue had to be there, somewhere.

"Why didn't I just stay there when I had the chance?" he muttered as he started to plod south. "Because I got spooked by a bunch of dead Indians, that's why."

And you thought you were good enough to find camp again.

He snorted, hating to make such an admission, even in the privacy of his own mind.

He'd made barely an hour's progress when he spotted the antelope, perhaps forty of them feeding along a wind-blown ridge.

Make it right, Richard. You'll get one shot, and if you miss... In this cold, you'll be dead before morning if you don't put something in your stomach.

He checked the priming in his rifle and shook his gun to make sure the fire channel was clear. Then he chipped the ice out of the muzzle with his ramrod.

Ever so carefully, he began his sneak, cutting below the ridge to get downwind, first wading, then wallowing, and finally practically swimming through the deep drift in the lee of the ridge.

Heart pounding, he crawled toward the ridge crest, aware that the sun was slanting against him, glaring off the snow. Antelope had unbelievably good vision, and moved at even the slightest show of a head, shoulder, or buttocks.

His elbows for levers, Richard pulled himself over the snow-blocked grass, wincing as prickly pear lanced through the leather of his buffalo coat.

He stopped, judging the amount of time he'd traveled. A full hand's breadth from the slant of the sun.

Now what? Think, Richard. Did they move on? God help me, I can't make a mistake. Not now.

His stomach made a noise like a dying man's groan. Tarnal Hell, even the antelope had to have heard that!

The cold, a palpable presence, leeched his flesh, sucking his strength, devouring the sap of his soul.

If I raise my head, I could ruin everything. But what if they're not here?

Richard fought down a shiver that wasn't nearly as terrifying as the numbness creeping into his feet.

Slowly. Be careful. Don't do anything stupid.

He eased his head up the slightest bit, squinting into the glare, and saw nothing. Just as slowly, he let himself sink down to earth and levered himself forward again. As he moved, the quivering of his arms surprised him. He'd cradled the gun in his elbows as he crawled, and now realized that it too was shivering in time to the rest of his body.

You're tired, Richard. You haven't eaten. If you don't shoot an antelope, it's over.

He swallowed hard, wondering how death would steal over his clay-cold body. When a man froze, did he know the precise moment when the soul left the body? Blasphemous hell, what if he was just as cold in death as in life? He couldn't bear it.

He carefully lifted his head and saw—nothing!

They're gone, Richard. You don't have much time. He pulled himself forward. *This is the last chance.*

Raising his wobbling head, he carefully peeked over the ridge, disappointment rising.

Dear Lord God, they couldn't have winded me and run clear...

The barest flick of an ear caught his attention. The scrubby sagebrush had masked the antelopes' position.

Richard's heart began to pound, blood racing through his stiffening limbs. *There...right there! Don't make a mess of this, Richard.*

He tensed his muscles, trying to make heat to battle

the numbness. Filling his lungs, he carefully pulled himself another elbow length forward.

Careful...careful...

He moved with deliberate slowness, knowing the cold had stolen most of his control.

A doe stepped into full view, her head down as she nibbled the spikes off a sagebrush. Richard barely allowed himself to breathe, afraid she might hear his pounding heart.

She took another step, and Richard could see the frosty breath around her black nose.

At that moment, his stomach growled angrily, and time stood still as the doe raised her head.

Do I rise up? Take the shot?

Another voice cautioned, *For God's sake, no! If you bumble because of the cold, she'll be gone!*

Unsure, he waited, trying not to breathe, but just as suddenly starved for air.

Please, Mother. Just one shot. I need you!

After what seemed an eternity, the doe dropped her head to browse.

Richard eased the rifle into place, sliding his cheek against the ice-cold stock. And, to his horror, couldn't control his wobbling muscles.

In one desperate instant, he tensed his entire body, saw the front sight steady in the buckhorn, and triggered the gun. The pan flashed, eternity hung on an instant, then the rifle boomed fire and smoke.

Richard rolled on his side and sucked in cold air like a drowning man. He could hear the clatter of hooves as the herd raced away. Had he hit?

If I didn't, how am I going to stand it?

On weak limbs, he pulled himself up, used the rifle as a prop, and climbed to his feet. He tottered forward, vaguely aware that the cold had sapped still more of his strength.

He found the place where her feet had torn the snow. A clump of stiff antelope hair lay to one side. Had he just grazed her?

"No. Please! Tell me I hit her."

He staggered on, following the tracks, and, yes, there was a spot of bright red blood in the snow. Then another and another, until the gushing spray of crimson was impossible to miss.

She lay piled up in the deep snow at the bottom of the ridge. Richard dropped to his knees, reaching out with his snow-packed mittens to rub her bristly hair.

"Bless you, Mother. Thank you so much." He swallowed hard, a terrible understanding dawning within him. Throwing his head back, he called out to the setting sun, "*Tam Apo!* Take the soul of this antelope, and grant her eternal peace. This beautiful creature gave her life that I might live. With all my heart, I thank her for the gift she has given me. Please, bless her. I, Richard Hamilton, thank and honor her."

Then, shivering and weak, he slipped his knife from its sheath and cut open the white belly. The hot blood steamed with a sweet musk that fed his soul. Hands aquiver, Richard cut loose the liver and leaned back.

As the sun burned eerily bright in the frozen land, he ate, heedless of the hot red liquid that dribbled down and froze on his beard.

CHAPTER TWENTY

But as long as we remain ignorant of the constitution of natural man, it will be futile for us to attempt to determine what law he received, or what law best suits him. All we can clearly determine in regard to that law is that in order for it to be law, he to whom it obliges must manage to submit to it willfully and knowingly, but also that, for it to be natural, it must speak immediately by the voice of nature.

—Jean-Jacques Rousseau, *Discourse on the Origin and Foundation of Inequality Among Mankind*

Water Deer and Gray Moth arrived at High Wolf's camp two days after the storm. They had braved the deep cold to make the long hike from their band's camp in the foothills to the north.

Both men were tightly bundled, puffing frosty breath, with round snowshoes tied onto their packs, clumps of ice still caught in the thong webbing.

High Wolf greeted them, smoked their tobacco in his tubular steatite pipe, and waited curiously as the formalities for visitors were conducted.

White Alder set food before them. Both men wolfed it down, an indication that they'd eaten little if anything on the journey. Water Deer in turn offered three squirrels, with apologies that their haste, along with the brutal cold, had limited their ability to hunt.

Now Many Elk, White Alder, and Lodgepole huddled around, eager to hear what had brought the men to their camp.

As Willow sat to one side, sewing a pair of moccasins, she, too, studied them. Water Deer was young, lean, with a guileless face. He wore sheephide, tanned to a light brown and painted with red and black circles. His mittens were stained, and his thick moccasins had a scuffed look. Gray Moth, on the other hand, was chubby, dressed in a worn coat from which loose sheep hair filtered like snow, indicating it was nearly worn out on the inside. His mittens had holes, and his moccasins had been wrapped with rabbit fur, the pelts tied on.

While Water Deer glanced enthusiastically at Willow, Gray Moth sat with pursed lips, definitely uneasy as he stared into the tire.

"You see," Water Deer began, as he toasted his hands by the fire and shot another glance at Willow where she sat wrapped in warm furs by the cook fire, "we are great hunters. At our camp, we have meat stacked like firewood. So much we can barely stumble over it. Meat becomes a problem for us, especially since the territory where we dig roots in spring produces in plenty. Isn't that right, Gray Moth? Why, there's times the roots grow so big, and so closely together, they practically pop out of the ground. A woman barely needs to dig them. They almost jump out into her hand. And that's a fact!"

High Wolf now studied the men with new interest. One of his eyebrows had lifted slightly, amusement in the pattern of his crowsfeet.

"But the greatest of our hunters is Gray Moth," Water Deer patted his companion on the back. Gray Moth smiled self-consciously, glancing furtively at High Wolf and Many Elk, who'd taken seats across from them.

"Indeed," Water Deer cried, "there is no one who can sneak like Gray Moth. He is silent as the night breeze. I've seen him ghost up to elk, close enough to touch them. He organizes our spring hunt, and through his skill, we have so much to eat that most of our food is freely given to the coyotes. You know, just to keep it from piling up before Gray Moth brings in more."

"And how is White Rock?" High Wolf asked. "I saw him last summer at the gathering. We talked for quite a while. He was looking healthy."

"Oh, yes." Water Deer waved it away. "As healthy as a bull buffalo. But you know White Rock. I don't think there's another like him among all the People...except maybe you, High Wolf. No one is wiser than White Rock. He knows the ways of the mountains, where the fattest game can be found. Take our camp, for example, always warm, sweet water running from a spring. And I think I told you about the root grounds. Biscuit root the size of a man's head grows there."

High Wolf's lips bent into a crooked smile, and he glanced speculatively at Willow.

Water Deer continued to tell of all the wonderful things at White Rock's camp.

Willow added wood to the fire, then stared out over the canyon. Snow mantled the trees on the far side, contrasting with the cool green of the forest. In the trees, nutcrackers cawed, flitting from branch to branch, while, closer, the chickadees twittered. Sound carried in the deep cold. With her iron needle, she poked another hole in the sole leather and pulled the thread through.

"Things are good indeed," Water Deer continued. "Except for one bit of misfortune."

People shifted, waiting politely.

Willow cocked her head.

Water Deer stared sadly into the fire. "The tragedy is all of ours, of course, but more of Gray Moth's than anyone else's."

"I had heard his wife was ailing," High Wolf stated, as if suddenly remembering.

"We don't know what it was." Water Deer spread his hands. "A pain in her side. Over time, it just seemed to get worse. White Rock sang over her, and we administered the usual cures. She sweated, and followed all the rituals. But..."

High Wolf's expression turned sympathetic. "Ah, we sorrow to hear of your loss, Gray Moth."

The chubby hunter nodded, and cast a nervous glance at Willow. "I've been terribly sad." Then he lowered his eyes.

"Yes," Water Deer continued, "sad indeed. And Gray Moth, with his beautiful children. It was hardest on them. Such bright and wonderful children. Two boys— and a little girl. How lucky we are that the baby has passed beyond suckling. I don't think there are more obedient children in all the world. Just mention that something needs to be done, and they are already running to do it. In all my life, I don't think I've ever seen children so ready and willing to please."

"They must be special children," Many Elk said

neutrally, casting a glance at his own grandchildren clustered under a buffalo robe, kicking and giggling.

"Special," Water Deer agreed. "I couldn't think of a better word to describe them." He glanced cautiously at Willow. "Such children would bring pride to any woman. And Gray Moth could sire many more."

Gray Moth gave the fire a fleeting smile, and rubbed his plump hands anxiously.

"So many gifts. Gray Moth," High Wolf said gently. "But to lose a wife, that is difficult for all. Our hearts are heavy for you."

"It is hard," Gray Moth agreed.

"Well," High Wolf added, "here you may forget your woes for a while. Some of our young men—Rock Hare, Black Marten, and White Hail—have gone to see where the deer are feeding. And, as you can see, we have more than enough to feed you for as long as you would care to stay with us."

"Perhaps you need help bringing in meat?" Water Deer asked. "Gray Moth is a hard worker. Why, there are times we must almost tie him up to keep him from working so hard." Water Deer gave his friend a solicitous glance. "In the White Rock band, we feel honored to have such a one as he. It isn't often that a band can manage to keep a man like Gray Moth—not when so many others offer him and his children a place at their fire."

"White Rock is lucky indeed." High Wolf nodded soberly.

"Enough of us." Water Deer poked at the fire with a stick. "Tell us of your camp, High Wolf. Is all going well?"

"Very well, but perhaps not with the wondrous fortune White Rock seems to enjoy."

Appearing nonchalant, Water Deer said, "We have heard that your daughter has returned."

"Indeed she has, and from a remarkable journey." High Wolf shot Willow a suggestive glance.

Willow set her moccasins aside and crossed to the fire, where she crouched beside Many Elk. "I have recently returned."

"Ah." Water Deer smiled brightly, eyes keen. "We have heard that you, too, have lost loved ones to the Land of the Dead."

"My husband and son," she said. "Last winter."

Water Deer's expression turned appropriately gloomy. "Our hearts are heavy." He paused. "We are all lucky that some *Ku'chendikani* didn't snatch you up with hollow promises of horses and a fine lodge."

"One is here," Willow replied offhandedly, "trying to do exactly that, though he no longer makes such open attempts."

"Indeed?" Water Deer asked, and even Gray Moth looked up, slightly startled.

"Oh, yes," Willow said solemnly. "Now he seeks to impress me by showing what a good hunter he is and how hard he can work. He doesn't make any declarations, but he hints at how good life would be if I went with him. You should hear him. The way he tells it, his camp has more meat than any other."

Water Deer shrugged. "You know how *Ku'chendikani* are. They tell the most outlandish stories."

"They do." Willow used a stick to poke at the fire. "Fortunately, I know him rather well. My husband was his brother, and I lived in his camp, so I know when I hear something that isn't quite right. It would be a little more difficult if I didn't know the people who told me stories."

"It would, wouldn't it?" Water Deer watched her warily. "It's a good thing that here, among the *Dukurika,* we don't tell wild stories."

"A very good thing." Willow frowned at the fire. "A woman who hadn't grown up in these mountains, and didn't know the root grounds, one who hadn't talked much to people from different bands, would be at a disadvantage."

Water Deer reached up under his hat to scratch his head. "How lucky we are to meet up with such a wise woman."

"Some call me wise," Willow agreed. "Others call me trouble. They say I ask too many questions about too many things. That a woman's duty is to her family. I have trouble with that because sometimes Power calls me. When that happens, I must allow my *navuzieip* to do as it must. Some do not always understand that."

"This Power," Water Deer mused, expressionless, "it is unusual in a woman. Some have talked about it and believe it comes to you because High Wolf is such a Powerful *puha-gan.* Some would believe this was a bad thing. White Rock, however, is not one of them, nor are any of the people in his band. We would be honored if a woman with such Power were to come among us. Unlike so many, we do not fear Power and ability, but would value such counsel at our fires."

"Indeed? Then White Rock's band demonstrates a most unusual wisdom." Willow glanced at High Wolf, who sat pensively.

Water Deer rubbed his hands together. "It is said that you have traveled among the White men and brought many fine things to High Wolf's camp. It is said that you have obtained the White man's Power."

Willow briefly met Water Deer's sharp eyes. "Such

talk shows that *Dukurika* are as prone to wild tales as the *Ku'chendikani*. If true stories were told, they would say that I recommend that our people have as little to do as possible with the White men."

"Why would that be?" The slightest of frowns marred Water Deer's straight forehead.

"The White men have a great many wonderful things, Water Deer. But to know them is to discover that they have a great deal in common with Coyote in the beginning times. Like Coyote, they promise many marvelous things, but underneath the promises, they want something entirely different. And just like Coyote, they usually end up tricking themselves and destroying the thing they really want."

"Are they evil sprits, then? Is that what you are trying to tell us?'

"They are not spirits. Not gifted with Power as we know it. They have no concept of *puha*. They are no more evil than Coyote was. No, Water Deer, they are tricksters, very clever, seeking trade to make themselves rich and powerful. But they always end up making a mess of things. And like Coyote, they never learn from their mistakes."

Water Deer sighed, looking muddled. Gray Moth continued to stare at the fire, a terrible weariness in the set of his mouth.

Water Deer collected himself, buoyed by some inner resolution. "High Wolf is lucky indeed to have such a daughter as you, Willow. I can see now, more than ever before, just how wise you really are. I must confess, I had not expected the stories to be true. How lucky Gray Moth and I are that White Rock suggested we come hunting in this direction."

"The trouble with hunting is that you don't always bring home game," Willow remarked.

Water Deer and Gray Moth left the next morning, plodding north up the trail that led out of the canyon. Throughout their visit, Willow was polite and explicit in her descriptions of the White men.

White Hail settled next to her that evening as she kept an eye on the ricegrass cakes and biscuit root cooking on the fire. The children were racing around, playing hide-and-seek in the rocks as they pelted each other with snowballs. White Alder, Good Root, and Red Squirrel played the hand game, their counters resting between two logs. Good Root sang and rocked as she passed the little polished bone back and forth, using sleights to keep its location secret. At. last she stopped and held out her hands.

White Alder chose Good Root's right hand, which to her dismay was empty. Red Squirrel chuckled as a counter was passed to her pile. The fine white coat had changed hands two times since the night Good Root had lost it to Lodgepole. If Red Squirrel's luck held, it would pass to her later in the evening.

Willow glanced at White Hail. The *Pa'kiani* had marked him for life—his once handsome face would be forever off-center because of his crooked jaw. He was a patient man, trying to wear her down with his amiable presence.

The pressure to marry had been subtle. High Wolf had kept his counsel, his face pensive. White Alder had made several comments about women and men, and how *Tam Apo* and *Tam Segobia* each acted as half of a whole.

"Gray Moth and Water Deer, they were only the first," White Hail said neutrally. "I think it will be a busy winter at High Wolf's camp."

Assured that the cakes were browning evenly, Willow took out the ax and the piece of sandstone she'd found to whet it. "Then I suppose High Wolf had better hope his hunters bring in more game than usual. I don't think three squirrels are going to help much."

"You don't look happy, Willow." White Hail pursed his lips for a moment. "Coming home wasn't what you expected, was it?"

The stone rang on the steel as she thought. "I don't know what I expected. In some ways, yes. I've been happy here. In others, no."

"Have you considered why?"

She gestured out to the world beyond the canyon. "My life changed out there. I have a feeling, White Hail: a sense of a coming storm. It's not something you can smell, like snow in the wind, but a different sense, like the one on a golden fall day that tells you that a difficult and bitter winter lies just over the northern horizon. I look around, and see my people basking in the sunshine and warmth, not realizing the leaves are beginning to change color."

"When winter comes, it makes no difference how mild you wish the weather to be. It will be as it will. A person must face it, no matter what."

"And tell me, White Hail, when did sense creep into your soul?"

He chuckled. "When the *Pa'kiani* beat it into me. No matter how I believed in my *puha,* and my skill, they caught me anyway. All the lies I told myself were stripped away like bark from a pine, and only the soft yellow wood underneath was left. From that time, I have known the color of my wood."

"Does that mean that no strength is left in your trunk?"

He watched her hands as she honed the ax. "My branches still reach for the sky, but I understand that a bolt of lightning can splinter even the tallest and strongest of trees."

"Now that is wisdom worthy of your brother."

His laughter was hollow. "Does that mean I might be worthy of my brother's wife?"

"We have had this conversation before."

"Does the White man, Ritshard, still fill your dreams?"

She ground the sandstone harder on the edge.

"Careful," he noted wryly, "if you slip, you'll cut yourself."

If I slip...? Perhaps, White Hail, I already have.

———

Travis scouted for four days' travel in either direction of his camp on the Tongue. Enduring the horrible cold, he rode up to the narrow valley where the river disgorged from the Big Horns, and then down, past the Arapaho burial ground, almost to the Crow village. In that time, he watched carefully for the slightest trace of fire, listened for the distant crack of a rifle shot, and cut for tracks in the snow.

In all that empty whiteness, no trace of Richard could

be found. He stared out over the drifted slopes, stippled with gnarly sage. The broken and rounded land was packed with blue-shadowed banks of wind-deposited white, and the deep cold grew ever more bitter.

He hated this kind of cold; it played hell with the mass of scars crisscrossing his face. The sting worked in around the puckered flesh like little needles prickling him to the bone. His ruined nose took it the worst. He wished for his old wool muffler, but it had been aboard *Maria*—blown to hell along with the boat.

It had been eight days since they'd been separated. In despair, Travis finally rode into his camp, built a fire, and stripped the saddle from his gelding. He'd hung the packs in the trees to keep them intact, away from the doings of coyotes, wolves, and porcupines. He kicked at the hoof-packed snow; the packhorses had eaten their pasture down to dirt.

"It's piss-poor bull, old coon," he told his gelding, running gentle hands down the horse's snow-barked canon bones. "All we've done is run yer fat off, and froze fer nothing." He made a face, patting the horse gently, and muttered, "Damnation, Dick."

The horse flicked a frosted ear in reply, no doubt happy to be corralled with his mates again.

Travis knocked the patchy ice from his clothing and settled himself by the fire. He built a smoke and puffed thoughtfully as he extended his hands to the leaping flames. "Wal, Dick, ye were some, ye was. Made it a sight further than I'd a thought fer a fool-headed Doodle."

He puffed out a weary exhale to watch the delicate patterns of frost rise on the frigid air. How intricately beautiful—yet so deadly. This was killing cold, the kind that snapped trees and crackled ice. An unprotected man would be wolfmeat in an hour, froze solid in two.

So, what now, coon? Give Dick up fer dead?

As he sat, he watched a flock of rosy finches flutter past. How, he wondered, could such little birds stand such bitter air.

Baptiste was no more than six days north, camped with the Crow.

But do I want to go back there? The only thing waiting for me in Two White Elk's lodge is memories of Moonlight. Her soft smile, the light in her eyes.

He grunted disgustedly and extended his chin toward the fire, letting the packed ice in his beard melt.

Face it, coon, all ye got is memories. Too damned many of them.

As the water dripped from his beard, he puffed his pipe empty. Like the cold, heat played tricks with his face, slivers of fire running along the scars. In the corral, the horses stomped, heads down, ice glittering on their backs.

Willow would want to know what had happened to the expedition, and most particularly to Dick. What would her reaction be? The stoic acceptance an Indian showed toward an outsider's death, or the gnashing and wailing for a loved one?

"The first, I'd bet. With a deep sadness." She'd loved Richard, loved him in a way the poor Doodle had never been able to comprehend.

"More's the pity, Dick. Unlike ye, I got ter love a woman with all my heart once. Hell, ye stupid fool, ye done froze ter death, and missed it all."

But then, life was full of that, wasn't it? Getting so close, and missing it all.

I never used to feel that way. What happened, Travis Hartman, that ye stopped traveling just for the going? When did it start being so damned all-fired important to get somewhere?

He made a thick stew, melting snow on the shaved jerky, adding rosehips and slices of pemmican. Then he chopped tobacco from a twist into his pipe.

As the stew boiled, he watched the evening descend in awesome pinks that shaded first into lavender and then into deep blue. The colors reflected off the snow, glowed in an unearthly way in the trees, and left the distant Big Horns luminous.

How silent the land was, but with a kind of clarity that conjured awe instead of loneliness.

Travis snaked his boiling stew from the fire, steam so thick it might have been smoke. Sipping gingerly at the corner of the pot, he savored the taste. An owl finally broke the silence when it hooted in the trees.

Wiping the drops from his mustache, he nodded to himself. "Ferget trying to get someplace, ye ignorant coon. Cast it all loose, and let it float. Green was looking forward, and look what it got him. Me, I'm starting to look backward too much."

He belched, drank the rest of his stew, and cast a glance at the horses standing in the icy gloom. "Reckon tomorrow we'll pack up and go see the Crow. Ye knot-headed hosses would like that. Ye can frisk with their hoss herds, and I won't have ter take care of ye. Then, come spring, I reckon we'll load up and mosey down Willow's way. It won't hurt her any more ter larn about Dick then as now."

The decision made, he pulled his knife and chopped more tobacco. Out in the hills coyotes howled.

———

Richard wallowed through a drift, his antelope-hide pack dragging across the snow behind him. Step by weary step he tramped upward. He was puffing like a steamboat when he finally crested the ridge. On the north side stood a patch of grimly frozen pines. He trudged on, following the ridge to its highest pinnacle.

Gasping and wheezing, he unslung his pack with its frozen meat, and walked out onto the bare rock.

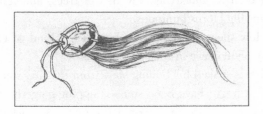

The view was magnificent. To the west, so clear and perfect he might have been able to reach out and touch them, the Big Horns rose in sheer-walled splendor.

He turned slowly, shading his eyes against the glare off the snow. Before him spread a winter-blanched world of ridge and swale, drainages tracing like God's fingers through the rolling hills.

He studied each of the flat valleys and the canted slopes sprinkled with sage and occasional pines. In places, bold lines of rock thrust through the snow to mark tilted slabs of earth. To the southeast, flat-topped buttes stood like wary sentinels in the open basin.

Streams meandered through the gentle valley, the bottoms gray-fuzzed with naked cottonwoods. But which was the Tongue? And where, in all this endless distance, could he expect to find Travis?

He shook his head. "I'd have seen a river, wouldn't I? The Tongue's not just some stream you can leap over. I saw it! In the storm, I saw it!"

He rubbed a frozen mitten over his eyes, squinting against the glare. "I turned, climbed out of the valley."

Unless I crossed the Tongue.

"How?" The river he'd seen was open water.

He slumped then, studying the Big Homs. They were so close now, almost to his right. "I've been walking south for days. Like it or not, I've crossed the Tongue somehow...some way."

He'd slipped on ice—thought it was a frozen pond. Damnation, it could have been the river. He'd been crossing streams every day since, searching out the places where they were frozen across.

He looked back to the north. 'Travis? Are you back there? What do I do now? Backtrack? And if you've given me up for dead, what then? On the horses, you could be halfway back to the Mandan by now."

He was alone.

"Oh, wonderful, Richard. For the first time in your life, you can pick any direction you want—and you don't know where in hell it will take you." Or worse, what—or who—he'd find when he got there. Two White Elk would be one thing; a party of Rees, Pawnee, or Blackfeet something entirely different.

He turned again to the Big Horns, studying the snowy slopes. The south side, Travis had said. Richard studied the slope of the mountains, the way they rose from the south like a humped whale's back. How on earth could he find Willow's village in that maze of steep canyons, unscalable heights, and deep snow?

The faintest of breezes began to prickle on the exposed skin of his face. So far, the air had been still as death. Each night he found enough shelter so that by hovering over a fire, eating, dozing, and exercising, he could keep frostbite at bay.

The wind puffed a little harder, unnoticeable on a

summer's day, but here, with the bone-numbing cold, the air felt like fire.

Off to the south he could see several herds of buffalo —little more than black specks on the snow. Shooting one meant fresh meat, and his outermost moccasins were wearing thin.

"Come on, Richard. You've got to get off this point." The closest shelter was down there, to the south. And if he followed the base of the Big Horns, wood, game, and the other things he needed to survive would be plentiful.

Stepping off the point, he glanced uneasily at the tall mountains. *Willow? Where are you?*

What if he managed to survive, alone, lost, without a horse? Suppose he managed to locate Willow's people. Blessed God, they wouldn't just shoot him dead. Would they?

Aching despair began to chew on his soul again. No matter which direction he chose, it could only end in disaster.

As the afternoon sun dipped toward the southwest, God smiled upon him. He'd been crossing buffalo tracks, and here and there a frozen pile of manure. Nevertheless, it was a surprise when a yearling bull walked out from behind the shoulder of a low ridge. Richard stopped short, carefully lifted his rifle, and eased back the cock.

The animal seemed to gleam in the sunlight, the head and lower body midnight black, the hump and shoulders almost blond. Billows of frosted breath blew out to each side with his puffing exhales.

Nestling the Hawken's butt into his shoulder, Richard set the trigger, aimed for the vital spot just behind the point of the elbow, and shot.

Through the smoke, he saw the bull hunch. Then the animal leaped straight into the air, kicking its back legs with the speed of a rattlesnake. The bull spun, charging away, only to crash to earth in a pall of flying snow.

Richard blinked, swallowing hard. As the snow settled around the thrashing animal, he uncapped his horn, pouring in another charge. When he pulled off his mitten to pluck a bullet from his pouch, the bitter air stung his flesh. Seating the ball on a patch, he rammed the load home, and replaced his mitten before tilting the rifle to prime the pan.

Rifle ready, he approached cautiously, vaguely aware of the blood-spattered snow. The wound in the buffalo's side steamed, blood droplets already freezing on the long black hair. The bull stared vacantly, the eyes glassy in death.

"I'm sorry." Then he raised his face to the heavens and shouted his prayer for the animal's soul. The last of his words disappeared into the crystalline silence. He patted the thick fur. How warm it would be!

Richard glanced up at the slanting sun. Before he finished the tedious job of skinning, it would be dark. He started twisting sagebrush from the frozen soil, and kicked snow aside before laying his fire.

Only when he had a small blaze going did he pull his skinning knife from its belt sheath and begin slitting the thick hide. As the sun dropped into the southwest, Richard peeled back the skin, and steam rose from the fat-mottled flesh. The smell of buffalo filled his lungs, twining with his soul.

Cutting loose choice parts, he propped them over the coals to roast. By full dark, blood-smeared and tired, he had cut the animal apart. Grunting with effort, he tugged the hide to one side. An inch thick through the middle of the cape, it weighed twice what he did.

From the west, the wind continued to rise, wisps of snow like ethereal serpents slithering over the ground.

Richard stopped periodically to eat, kick through the snow, and twist sagebrush free to feed his fire. In the faltering heat of the coals, he dried his blood-saturated mittens.

Now what? He had meat without end, but here, in the open, the wind rising, no shelter presented itself. Turning to the hide, he realized the outside had already frosted. With frantic haste he tugged it out flat, then folded it double, hair-side in. The edges where he'd hacked off the legs were already frozen stiff. Another gust of wind roared out of the darkness, pelting him with snow and searing his face. Richard hurried to crawl inside until the hide lay on him like a heavy blanket.

"Dear Lord God," he whispered, tucking himself deeper into the soft curly hair. He pulled himself into a fetal ball and hugged himself. The pungent and pleasant smell of buffalo closed around him.

The wind had begun to gust, driving the terrible cold until it cut like a saber blade. He couldn't afford a mistake. As he lay shivering inside the hide, his thoughts turned to Boston. Laura's face had a soft glow, her blue eyes twinkling like stars. He imagined reaching up to remove one of her hairpins so that her soft blond hair spilled over his hands like warm gold. In dancing lamplight, he sipped strong ale, and laughed with Will Temple-ton and Professor Ames. Once again he walked the cobblestone streets, greeting every cheery face with a warm salutation.

In the dream, he pictured himself, Jeffry, and Father. Together, they'd sit beside a warm fire. Yes, like a real family should.

That dream of his father crying had touched a fragile

spot in his soul. That could be fixed, couldn't it? That chasm that had grown between them wasn't totally insur- mountable.

Baptiste had once told him, *"White folks think every- body has a pap, just like a right hand."*

"I'll make it right. I swear. All I have to do is make my way home."

Home! He could hear the songs of the shipwrights as they walked up from the harbor. He longed for the seamen, the laborers who lived on Fish Street, the riggers, the caulkers. Once, he'd dismissed them as inconsequential—if he gave them any thought at all. Now, after the river and the *engagés,* he shared a kinship with them.

How fondly he remembered the river now, the warm nights around cheerful fires, Travis's scarred face aglow in flickering yellow light as he smoked his pipe. Richard could hear the songs rising from the throats of the *engagés.* Across the fire, Baptiste's sleek ebony skin had a satin gleam and his straight white teeth flashed in a quick smile. Green stood there, thumbs stuck in his belt, worry battling with his eternal optimism.

But more than any other, Willow stared out at him, that soft, knowing light in her depthless eyes.

If I could just do it all over again. Willow...Willow...I love you so much.

Her lips parted, as if speaking to him, but the words never came. He started awake, listening, expecting to hear her, but only the wind—howling like a thousand lost souls—filled the night.

Before anything else, he had to settle accounts with two people: his father and Willow. And, God willing, he'd make it right with both of them.

He dozed then. It wasn't until he tried to straighten

his legs that he realized something had gone wrong. He kicked out, struggling, only to sag in weary exhaustion.

"Of all the—I'm *trapped* in here!" He tried again, pressing up and out. Over an inch thick in places and full of moisture and blood, the hide had sagged and molded around every contour of his body. Then, in the subzero temperatures, it had frozen solid and clamped him like a vise.

A LOOK AT BOOK FOUR:

Coyote Summer

The thrilling conclusion to the *Saga of the Mountain Sage* series! In 1825, against the backdrop of the majestic Rocky Mountains and amidst a rich tapestry of Indian cultures—Sioux, Mandan, Crow, Shoshoni—*Coyote Summer* tells an unforgettable tale of love and reconciliation.

Heals Like A Willow, a beautiful young Shoshoni medicine woman with ties to the Spirit world, and Richard Hamilton, a Harvard philosophy student new to the frontier, come from vastly different worlds—yet their souls have met and cannot be denied.

But Willow has a responsibility to her people. In visions she has seen the coming White Storm brewing in the East–the endless stream of settlers overrunning her land. She must leave the trading posts and white men behind. Even if it means leaving behind Richard.

Armed only with his philosophy, Richard sets out after her. Facing the harsh reality of the Rockies and an endless expanse of mountains and snow, he realizes that his search for love may bear the ultimate price.

"… it doesn't lack for excitement… Gear succeeds in creating something more than a mere historical novel."
—Roundup Magazine

AVAILABLE JUNE 2023

ABOUT THE AUTHOR

W. Michael Gear is the New York Times and international bestselling author of over fifty-eight novels, many of them co-authored with Kathleen O'Neal Gear.

With seventeen million copies of his work in print he is best known for the "People" series of novels written about North American Archaeology. His work has been translated into at least 29 languages. Michael has a master's degree in Anthropology, specialized in physical anthropology and forensics, and has worked as an archae-ologist for over forty years.

His published work ranges in genre from prehistory, science fiction, mystery, historical, genetic thriller, and western. For twenty-eight years he and Kathleen have raised North American bison at Red Canyon Ranch and won the coveted National Producer of the Year award from the National Bison Association in 2004 and 2009. They have published over 200 articles on bison genetics, management, and history, as well as articles on writing, anthropology, historic preservation, resource utilization, and a host of other topics.

The Gears live in Cody, Wyoming, where W. Michael Gear enjoys large-caliber rifles, long-distance motorcycle touring, and the richest, darkest stout he can find.

Made in the USA
Las Vegas, NV
01 February 2024

85152487R00218